MOTORCYCLE CLUB TERMS

Cut: Usually a leather or denim vest with the club insignia referenced as patches, or colors. It identifies which club you ride with, and show loyalty to.

Sweetbutt: A term used for girls who aren't in a committed relationship of any kind but have been given permission to be in the club and spend time with its members.

Old Lady: A female inside the club that is either married to or in a committed relationship with one of its members, age is not a factor when referencing this term.

Property Patch: An honor amongst clubs as it's a way for women to show which member they're committed to, this is an elevated status that shows you belong with someone from the club, however, this does not mean someone wearing a property patch is a member of the club.

House Mouse: Someone who is given status in the club by doing chores, and cleaning, it can often attach protection and ownership if this service is given by a member.

Church: a meeting place for the highest-ranking club members where decisions are made and private club matters are discussed.

One Percent Patch: 99% of all motorcycle clubs are law-abiding clubs that gather for more of a brotherhood, hobby, or sense of community.

However, one percent of these clubs wear this patch indicating they do not abide by the laws outside of the ones set by their clubs. This may include violent actions for protection, illegal means of earning money, and more.

President: In terms of the motorcycle club this person is the highest-ranking member, making all final calls and decisions.

WHERE WE ENDED

STONE RIDERS MC BOOK 4

ASHLEY MUÑOZ

Cover Design: Wildheart Graphics
Photographer: Regina Wamba
Models: Alexander Denning & Cherie Lorraine
Content Editor: Memos in the Margins
Content Editor: Rebecca Patrick
Editor: Rebecca Fairest Reviews
Proofread: Tiffany Hernandez

❀ Created with Vellum

VIRGINIA 1% RIVAL MOTORCYCLE CLUBS

Stone Riders: President - Killian (The Wolf) Quinn

Chaos Kings: President- Giles King

Death Raiders: President- Silas Silva

Sons of Speed: President- Alec Veda

Mayhem Riot: President-Archer Green

Rose Ridge is a fictional town inspired by Fredericksburg, Virginia.
    All towns mentioned in the book are made up while being inspired by true locations.

CONTENT ADVISORY

This is a Motorcycle Club Romance, however, because it is within the brand of Ashley Muñoz it will focus primarily on the romance vs. the dynamics of the club itself.

This is not considered a dark romance. With that said, there are a few things to watch for while reading:

Parental Neglect

Graphic Depictions of Violence

Kidnapping/ Abduction of an adult.

Adult Female being against their will—Cuffed to another adult (no noncon intercourse exists within this book, however, there is a scene where the FMC is forced to shower, naked with another man against her will. Please read chapter nine with caution.)

Parental Abuse (Referenced not shown)

Alzheimer's Episode

Sudden Death of a Character

Grief

A brief reference to the sexualization of a sixteen-year-old (nothing is done or shown on the page, but the interest from an adult person/villain is referenced on the page.)

For those who stare at the darkness fully aware it's staring back.
Keep looking.
Become the monster you always feared, the one who once controlled you.
Step out of that inky mass as a new creature with teeth and nails and an appetite
for fear.

WHERE WE ENDED

PROLOGUE

DEATH RAIDER TERRITORY TWENTY-ONE YEARS AGO

The flashlight wasn't as bright as it was the last time Mom and I hid inside the big wardrobe. It reminded me of *Narnia*, and sometimes I acted like it was, except there were no coats and no winter. Just guns and leather cuts.

"Read it again, Little Tree." My mom's eyes closed, but I saw her chest rising and falling, like she couldn't catch her breath.

She only forced me inside the wardrobe with her when she was scared, or if someone had hurt her. This time, she was holding her side with a wince. I heard my dad yelling at her…and she always made sure the door was shut whenever he started, so I would never have to see what else he did. It made me sad because we'd just moved to a new club, and he wasn't supposed to follow us here.

But somehow, he found us, and no one ever told him no. Not even when my mom got a new boyfriend.

I watched as she curled into herself while the flashlight lit up the cabinet walls.

I wanted to go find help, but I didn't even know who to ask.

Mom's hand came toward the book, as she pushed it closer to me. "Again."

With one last look at her side, I finally did as she said.

"Om—ombr—" I couldn't say the word, and I knew this would bug Mom, and she'd snap. Not because she was mean, but she snapped when she was in pain. Scanning the next words, I moved past it and kept going.

"Light falls across the pans of my heart, wh—whis--whispering of all the darkness you draw up--on."

My mom smiled, but I saw sweat begin to coat her forehead. "Pans of your heart or panes?"

I checked the word again, feeling frustrated. She'd had me reading this stupid book since I was six, and the words were still hard for me to read, now at seven.

"P—panes."

She smiled again. "Good. Now, keep going and don't stop until this light goes out. Mommy is going to take a little nap, and you're going to keep reading, okay?"

"No, please don't sleep. What if someone finds us?" I begged, worried that she wouldn't wake up.

She gave me a sad grin. "I'll be here. You just keep reading that poetry. Fill your heart with tides and currents, Little Tree, so that one day it'll take you somewhere good and pure."

I wanted to say more, beg her to stay awake, but she kept holding her side and breathing hard, so I just kept reading.

"I have land to build my ho—home upon but my soul has no roots. Apart from you, I'll be forever without a place to dwell."

She said this book was like a train, one that could take me anywhere I wanted to go. But where I wanted to go was somewhere safe, and anywhere my mom didn't have to get hurt, and we didn't have to hide. Sunshine and green grass. Bright skies and seeing my mother happy. It was a dream, something I'd think about day in and day out.

I kept reading, hoping it would somehow make my mom happy again. I wanted it to help her feel better. I read until the flashlight flickered out, and then I curled up next to my mom and closed my eyes. She didn't stir at all, and it made me feel a pinch of fear in my stomach. What if she wasn't okay?

My eyes had mostly adjusted to the dark when the cabinet door slowly cracked open. I jolted up while mom remained asleep.

The person who poked their head inside wasn't a person at all. It was a kid, just like me…a bright one.

"Are you a dream?" I whispered, nearly in awe with how she seemed to glow. She looked like she was made of starlight.

Her eyes slid down in confusion. "I'm a Natty."

"What's a Natty?"

She shrugged and scanned the space next to me. "Are you playing hide and seek?"

I shook my head and glanced at my mom.

Natty looked at her too and she seemed confused, like she wasn't understanding why we were both curled up in here.

"We're hiding."

There was a loud commotion in the room next to ours, so I pulled on Natty's arm until she was sitting next to me in the cabinet, then I shut the door.

"Who do you belong to?" I whispered, feeling her warm arm next to mine.

She whispered back, "Lilly. She told me to go somewhere for a while…she always tells me that when she has people come into her room. I saw this big dresser and wanted to hide inside it."

Boots echoed on the floor right outside our wardrobe and then there was yelling. It was muffled through the cabinet, but Natty let out a small gasp of fear and huddled closer to me. I grabbed the dead flashlight and held it in my hand watching the door. I could use it as a weapon, even if it wouldn't do much, it might do something.

"We just have to stay hidden until they leave, and then my mom will wake up and it will be okay."

Natty's small hand found mine and she squeezed tight.

"I'm scared."

I looked over at her in the dark. "I'll protect you."

"What's your name?"

There was another shout and then it sounded like someone's boots were fading.

I waited until it was quiet again, and all I could hear was our breathing then I whispered,

"Silas."

ONE
NATTY
PRESENT

I<small>T'S FUNNY WHAT YOU THINK ABOUT WHEN YOU'RE WORRIED YOUR LIFE MIGHT</small> be ending.

A favorite memory, a star speckled sky on a humid summer night. That first kiss. That last hug from a loving parent.

My tortured mind tossed up the image of a massive bullfrog, all green and slimy with large, cloudy eyes. The memory was so crisp and clear and agonizing.

So frustratingly annoying.

That frog was supposed to name me victor of the summer frog hunting championships. It had slipped through my fingers at the last second, making me the loser and crowned Silas as the winner.

It was such a stupid memory, but it was stuck there, like a broken record, running on repeat until all I could see were those bulbous eyes staring back at me from under the water. That moment wouldn't have changed a single thing about my life, and yet I remember how badly I wanted to win. I just wanted Silas to see me best him at just one thing. Frogs weren't his specialty, they were mine.

I was better at catching them, drawing them and even taking notes about them.

Which used to drive him crazy because keeping tabs on all the wildlife we'd come across out in the grove was his obsession.

He had to ask me for facts about them, and it used to make me feel a thousand feet tall.

I didn't have a clue why that memory from over sixteen years ago was rotating like a carousel in my head. I was ten and felt like I was the coolest girl on planet earth, all because I felt like I knew more than my foster brother.

Maybe I needed that memory to ground me because if I thought about my current condition, I'd start to lose all hope. It was easier to focus on a competition my ten-year-old brain never got past than the fact that I had been kidnapped and was currently being held hostage.

It helped that I had a theory about this room.

While some might argue that the space didn't really matter, knowing the details of my prison helped me make peace with my fate. It helped me feel in control.

I was nearly positive that I was being kept inside a garage...well at least in some respect. I had walked the length of the walls and knocked on each stud; there were no buttons or switches anywhere along the walls from what I found, but the space was empty and cold. I had found sealed water bottles along the floor, my boot tripping over them as I moved in the dark. Popping the lid, I would sip the water until it wasn't entirely full, and then I'd set it down as a marker against the stud.

My memories on what Silas used to drill into me were rusty and half clips, but I recalled him showing this tactic when he'd returned from one of his trips.

"Hello?"

My voice echoed, bouncing around the empty room, returning to me as though I was an idiot for assuming anyone might answer. The concrete under my feet was cold, which was another reason I had assumed a garage. There was no bay door, or even a slice of light to indicate one was there but tightly closed.

I had no idea how long I had been in here. Except exhaustion hadn't pulled me under yet, nor had I experienced any intense hunger. So maybe a few hours at best.

My mind pulled up the images of what had led up to getting that text from Silas.

There were explosions going off all over the Stone Rider property...I had gotten a text on my phone from Silas, telling me to go outside and head to our meeting spot in the woods. When I arrived, he wasn't there. So I waited, sitting with my back against a tree, all while more and more explosions went off, ripping my home from the ground up. Tears slid down my face as I watched the destruction from the distance. The agony over losing the club was nothing compared to the fear I had over losing my friends.

I should have known then that something was off because leaves crunched from somewhere behind me. Silas would never have been so loud. My reflexes were too slow as a hand came from around the tree, holding something to my mouth. I thrashed, trying to pull at the firm grip over my face, but within seconds everything went dark.

I woke up here.

Fear was a fist around my throat, squeezing until I got to my feet and began to move around the room. It helped me visualize how big the space was, and when I finally felt a corner, and began advancing down that wall, it was a small relief because it seemed very much like I was being held in a residential house.

Just to be sure I was right, I grabbed one of the water bottles and tossed it as hard as I could until it hit the far wall. *Less than a second.*

I did the same thing, but aimed for the ceiling. *Two seconds.*

Drawing up a mental image, I fell into a crouch and pressed my ear against the wall...hoping for some kind of noise. *Nothing.*

I refused to accept that there wasn't something that would trickle through. *A motorcycle engine, pans clanking, men laughing or talking. Anything.*

I stayed there, until I began drifting off. With my arms wrapped around my knees, I waited until I dozed. My eyes were closed, but even when I opened them, nothing changed.

I was starting to feel lethargic, and my stomach began to growl, which had panic swirling in my chest.

Never get to the point where you're desperate.

I could hear Silas in my head, going through drills with me on how to get out of situations like this one. We were only ten when we'd started doing them, but then we stopped.

I'll be back soon, Caelum…I promise.

I pushed the memories away and focused on my hunger. I *was* feeling desperate; I needed to take control. Spinning around, feeling the wall for the bottle I'd used to mark the space earlier as a stud, I moved to the left of it and lowered myself to the floor, until I was flat on my back. I made sure to keep my hand over the bottle, so I knew where not to go, and then I shoved both feet as hard as I could toward the wall. I still had on my boots, so the hit landed with a loud echo around the room.

I didn't wait; I repeated the movement until I felt the wall give.

Drywall caved in around my boots, and I got up, moving to my knees to dig through the hole I'd created. The insulation was going to be a bitch against my skin, but I began tugging it out, until the wall was clear.

Once I was sure it was empty, I felt around and ensured it wasn't brick or anything solid on the other end, but all I felt was cold concrete.

Anxiety began hovering in my chest, that feeling tightening more and more. I was so confident when I'd woken up, so sure this plan would work. *Find the studs, identify the weakest part of the wall. Kick through it. Use whatever you can, there will always be another room you can get into.* Silas' voice was in my head, but I kept coming to a loss for what to do next.

With a shaky breath, I felt the concrete again, now feeling disoriented. The darkness of the room felt like it was closing in around me, so tight I could hardly breathe.

Think, Natty.

Think.

I tried to go through my memories for something more, but all I could manage to focus on was several weeks back when I was out there in the spot, trying to exchange a note with Silas, when I'd been discovered by a random member of a rival club.

He was going to hurt me; he'd told me he was going to hurt me, but I was armed.

Yet, as he advanced, I couldn't seem to make my brain coordinate with my body. My finger was on the trigger, and the man kept gaining ground, but I couldn't do it. Silas had walked up behind me and pulled it for me. He'd saved me from a situation I was perfectly capable of saving myself from, but I'd locked up.

There was no motor function at all when fear was calling the shots. I thought I had controlled this…I stupidly assumed that I was like Silas in that way.

I was just a fraud, a little girl riding the coattails of a boy who wanted to keep her.

My throat burned as I slid against the wall, until my ass hit the cold floor. My fingers trembled as I dusted them off, wiping them on my jeans.

This wasn't going to work.

I wasn't going to get out of here.

I was close to hyperventilating when suddenly there was a sound coming from the left of me. These walls were solid, no doors or handles of any kind, but it sounded like…

Holy shit. A hole in the wall just opened, letting in a slice of sunlight.

I scrambled to my feet, trying to force my eyes to adjust to the way the light cut through the inky black room and the figure emerging through it.

Finally, the man did something on his phone, I could see the illuminated screen in his palm, and suddenly the room filled with light. I winced, holding my arm up to shield my eyes. Once they had adjusted, I realized who had walked in.

Wearing thick brown motorcycle boots, distressed jeans ripped in the knees, and a black t-shirt beneath a faded leather cut. The insignia patch on the front read, SOSMC and I knew that on the back there would be a skeleton atop a motorcycle on fire.

The name sewn above the president patch had a strange sense of hope replacing all the anxiety and fear that had been filling my lungs and chest since waking up here.

Alec Veda.

His dark hair was pushed away from his face, revealing gray eyes that had always looked at me in such a calculating way. My voice came out as a rasp as I took a step closer.

"Alec?"

"Well, if it isn't my little hunter." His voice was smooth and deep as he stopped in front of me, his callused finger found my chin, tipping my head back.

I abandoned the notion that he could have been the one who had taken me or had anything to do with this. Instead, my fear and terror evaporated as familiarity took its place.

"What are you doing here?"

His finger remained under my chin, and my head must have been a little muddled because he wasn't explaining why he was the one who'd walked into the room. Or why he didn't seem surprised to see me here.

All at once it clicked, and that sudden hope burned to poisonous ash.

"Wait..."

His face lowered, that grin revealing his white teeth. I pulled away, but he held me firm.

Hurt slid through my voice. "It was you?"

"It's complicated, Artie." His lips were nearly touching mine, and I tried to yank from his hold again as tears gathered behind my eyes.

"Silas will kill you."

Alec smiled, against my lips. "He's already going to, Artemis. The second we took you; we signed our death certificates."

Alec wouldn't do this...he was the president of a rival club nearby called the Sons of Speed. He would never win a war against Silas. He'd kept his distance all these years; there was no way he was going to try and create a war now, and certainly not by using me.

Dread curled in my stomach like a thundercloud. "Who's we?"

The door cracked again, and a new face emerged. A face hauntingly familiar but one I was positive I'd never actually seen in person.

Alec shifted the smallest bit so he was blocking me. It was how he used to stand when I needed protecting. I tried not to let my memories get tangled in who this man used to be, because it was clear he was not the same person anymore.

The man carried himself like a king, and as he stared down at me, I felt every inch like an impoverished thief. As if I'd stolen something from him, it made something shift in my stomach, like when driving and you hit a dip you weren't expecting.

Alec's throat cleared, as the man stepped closer. If this was who I assumed it was, then he was a different breed of monster.

Different than Silas, and different than Alec...he was truly the blue-print but there was nothing holding him together. No code, no moral fiber...no love.

He was the sort of darkness that corrupted, the kind that corroded and took without mercy.

I stole a step back right as Alec explained, "Natty, this is Fable. My father."

TWO
SILAS
PRESENT

"Tell me again."

I glared at the man across from me, ignoring his hollow cheeks and withered frame. My mother was patched to this man, living with him, in love with him. She'd finally found someone who cherished her, treated her right and protected her. And now he was about to die from the cancer in his gut.

Simon let out a heavy sigh. "I've already told you everything I know."

My eyes flicked over to my mother whose thin lips and clenched fists told me she wasn't appreciative of the fact I had drug the two of them out of bed to answer my questions. The memory of the attack was still a blurred dark mass in my head.

The minute I had called Simon and told him to get down to the Stone Riders clubhouse because they were under attack. I knew he'd go, not for me but because he had been the president of that club for nearly twenty years, until just a few months back.

Now his son-in-law was not only a patched member to the club but married to his daughter Callie, who was pregnant, stuck inside the club while it was being attacked. I knew he'd go, and I remembered the tide had turned once he walked in, but after that I didn't remember anything other than the gravel under my knees and the way my heart felt like it was falling through my stomach when I realized Natty had been taken.

"Silas, of anyone in this room who would have the most information on Fable, you would have more of a lead than us. You studied him for years, you knew his movements, his purchases, his tactics. I haven't talked to him in over twelve years, and Simon likely hasn—"

"Two years…" Simon spoke softly, interrupting my mother. His silver brows crowded his forehead the smallest bit, like he was trying to remember. "I saw him two years ago…he wasn't in Rose Ridge. It was in Richland, so I brushed it off, but I remember seeing him, clear as day at a rally."

That wasn't possible…he'd vacated the country two years ago. There was no way he'd return so soon.

Fable was the president of one of the most destructive and dishonorable clubs in the country. He had left The Destroyers behind to avoid prison two years ago. He'd fled to his homeland in Italy, but if he was amongst his club two years ago then the message I'd sent wasn't quite loud enough.

"Did he see you?" I asked, my gaze snapping up to the retired president.

Simon shook his head. "I don't think so… I just remember Fable's Destroyers were riding with them. So were Sons of Speed."

"Any clue which club he was speaking to?" Simon asked, searching my face for something, not sure what. But I was the one in need of answers, not him. I didn't owe him shit on my family, and while my mother likely knew the answer, she wasn't saying anything either.

Old habits died hard. Or for us, didn't die at all.

Sons of Speed was present when he was seen in town…that was interesting.

I pulled my cell out and checked the time. I was wearing a watch, but I needed something to break up the silence, and the fact that while Simon was an ally and the man protecting my mother, I wouldn't be spilling secrets in his company.

"I have to go." I slid out of the chair and stood.

Simon's expression furrowed as he flicked a quick look to my mother. "That's it?"

"You can't help me. I'm just wasting my time." I walked over to where my mother was sitting and placed a kiss on the top of her head. She squeezed my wrist in that way she always did when she wanted me to be careful. My boots echoed over her floorboards as I walked outside. She followed on my heels, her arms protected her chest as the night hummed with crickets.

"He's baiting you, Silas. You're smarter than this."

Gravel crunched as I neared my bike, my chest tightening at her words.

"You think I don't know that?" I glared at my mother, not wanting to dig into this. Simon had stayed inside, which I was thankful for. There were still too many secrets in our past and too many demons I liked to avoid.

My mother's eyes betrayed nothing, but her lips were turned down, the fists under her cradled arms were clenched tight.

"Then why, Silas? Why are you falling into it?"

I shook my head as I dipped my face to untangle my bucket helmet. I didn't always wear it, but there was a soft voice in my head that wouldn't stop reminding me why it was important that I did.

Silas, your brain is my favorite part of you. My gloomy, dreary prince. Protect it at all costs.

Glancing back up, I let out a small sardonic laugh. "You know exactly why."

She took a step closer, her bare feet hitting the edge of her covered porch. She'd moved out to this little farmhouse on five acres. Lush grass, a huge red barn, fences and pens for all her animals and a house just big enough for her and a dying man to enjoy.

"You have been down this road before, you saved her by letting her go, Son. She knows how to get herself out of this, he won't kill her."

"You don't know that. I did what you asked of me. I found him, I even fought him…I nearly took his club from him."

"But you didn't. You came back," she snapped, stepping off her porch, her bare feet cutting into the gravel.

Her eyes gleamed under the porch light, the desperation that was in her gaze all those years ago still just as demanding now.

"You should have never asked me to leave."

She cut me off, walking even closer, her voice rising. "You had to, and I kept Natty safe. I watched over her." She pointed aggressively toward her chest. "I was the one, Silas. You act like she's not like a daughter to me. Like she wasn't at that kitchen table in my home every single day learning alongside you. You act like I didn't feed her when her whore of a mother abandoned her. You act like I didn't get her clothes and do her hair. You think it didn't break my heart when her own mother offered her up to Dirk? I took her place. I went to hell and back for that girl. I love her Silas. But I also love *you*. I know what demons plague you, Son. You need to think clearly right now."

The memories were as painful as a lash against my back. Killing Dirk all those months back was one of the best moments of my life. I just should have done it years ago.

"It was never your job to protect her."

My mother laughed, tears gleaming in her eyes. "No, it was my job to protect *you*, but you gave so much of yourself to her, Silas, there was nothing left for me to protect. But this is something you won't come back from. You're a threat to him, Son. You always have been. He's been making plans, and we all know none of them ever included Jefferson Quinn or Tuck Holloway. He's got to be planning something with Alec, and now that Dirk is gone, and you're leading the Death Raiders, he's coming for you."

"Then let him come. You can't worry about me, Mom. However, if you are so inclined to panic, then help me find out who is helping him, and where he's staying."

Her face dipped, her dark hair falling over one eye. "It has to be Alec."

"Sons of Speed isn't that big of a club. It has to be someone else."

I stepped closer and pulled my mother into a hug, pressing another kiss to the top of her head. "I will find her and kill him."

"You should have killed Alec a long time ago, Silas."

A tiny flicker of panic swelled in my chest. I wasn't ready to dive into that topic, or even consider that he was involved. Not until I talked to my vice president, Lance, and had him do some digging.

My mother swiped at her face, then laughed again.

"Guess you really will burn the world down for her. You're about two seconds from striking the match...I hope Fable understands the devastation he's about to cause. For all of us."

"Fable has wanted our world to corrode from the start...he has never cared that we burn, Mother. You of all people know that." I straddled my bike and gestured toward her with a nod. She winced, lightly touching her side as if she was remembering all those times we'd curled up inside of a wardrobe, while she nursed her wounds.

I left, not wanting to revisit those memories either. I felt like I was constantly running from one nightmare to the next. All I wanted was Natty in my arms again. I'd waited long enough; Natty belonged to me, and even if this ended in both our lives being forfeited, at least in the end, she'd be buried with me.

Safely cradled in my arms.

THREE
NATTY
PRESENT

A FIRM GRIP ON MY ELBOW WAS THE ONLY THING GROUNDING ME AS I walked through the halls of my prison. This wasn't a motorcycle club; it was a small house. One that had no furniture and no people. Likely a safe house. The ceilings were low, the floors were made of wood and the walls were all covered in forest green wallpaper.

Alec hadn't let me go since Fable arrived, as if he knew his father would take a bite of me, all teeth and nails the second he released me. Fable was nearly as tall as Silas with short gray hair, slicked back, so only small pieces fell across his brow and similar eyes to Alec. Gray thunderclouds swarmed in those irises while his face was sun-kissed and wrinkled, showing his age. His expression was twisted angrily, as if he'd tasted sour milk, and the look of disgust froze over the stern set of his jaw.

We finally stopped walking once we reached the dining room.

"Sit." Fable ordered as Alec gently led me to a chair.

The room was sparse, with just the table, four chairs and a hutch against the far wall. The windows were all covered with white sheets. It was still early enough that it allowed in natural light. The walls were so similar to what was in the Stone Riders clubhouse, it had an ache gaping open in my heart. A pleading prayer coming right after it.

Please let everyone be okay.

Let them be alive.

Fable's stern voice cut into my thoughts. "Tell me your name."

I had a suspicion that he already knew my name, which was why he'd taken me but maybe I was wrong.

A woman pushed through a side door, leading to the kitchen. She had dark hair, green eyes, and a willowy frame. Her gaze quickly scanned the space, inspecting each of us while holding the wooden tray in her hands. She made her way to the table and set a bowl of soup down in front of Fable then let the tray hang by her side.

"Rachel. Please bring bowls for our company."

The woman...Rachel, peered over at me, giving me a blank expression before turning toward the kitchen once more.

Alec took a seat next to me, pulling my chair directly next to his so our knees touched.

I bristled, trying to create space, but he only held firm to the back of my chair.

Fable watched us, taking sips of his soup.

"Your name," he repeated.

I watched him swallow his soup, wondering how I might kill him in that position then sadly recalling I couldn't even kill a man using a gun when he was directly in front of me. For all of Silas's efforts to prepare me for likely this exact moment, I was completely useless.

Alec cleared his throat, his hand on the back of my chair moving to my shoulder.

I tried again to push him off, but he held firm.

"Alec, encourage her to speak."

The man next to me tapped a lazy finger against my shoulder as if his father's command didn't matter. Regardless that I knew it did in fact matter, especially to someone who had become a glorified errand boy for his evil father.

I did what Silas told me and cleared my head, then started counting.

I could take it. Whatever he was about to do to me, whatever punishment, or pain...I could take—

Warm lips pressed against my ear as Alec's hand traveled down to my hip, wrapping around it.

"He'll watch me do unspeakable things to you, Artie. Don't make me do that. Just tell him."

I wanted to rip out of his hold and glare at him. Throw back in his face that he didn't have to do anything his disgusting father wanted. Instead, I leaned forward and leveled Fable with a glare.

"Nomen est Caelum." *My name is Heaven.*

Fable's eyes lit up, his spoon dropping to the bowl with a clank. He waited three seconds before he burst into laughter before replying in Latin.

"Caelum non est verum." *There is no Heaven.*

My smile faltered the smallest bit; regardless, I wasn't surprised in the least he spoke Latin fluently. I was still hoping he didn't. I waited for him to continue. He'd asked for my name, I'd given it, I had nothing left to offer him.

"Your full name."

The smallest flicker of unease slid in through my ribs.

"Natty Langford."

Fable suddenly stood and shoved a hunting knife into the wood table, making me wince.

His eyes were wild, his mouth open as he seethed, "Try again. Last chance."

Alec looked between the two of us.

My mouth parted with an answer then it shut again. There were limits on what I was willing to give. Silas used to warn me not to fold easily, especially not over secrets. *Information is worth more than blood being spilled, or skin being bruised. Details put in the hands of the devil, become weapons.*

Fable pulled his knife free. "Natalia Nikole...." He paused, waiting for me to finish.

I searched his face acting confused.

"Langford."

Fable's gaze narrowed. "You lie almost as well as my son. You're his most guarded secret, and yet I have you. To do with whatever I want."

"What *is* it you want?"

Rachel came back in with two more bowls and a few slices of bread. She was calm as she set each bowl down and arranged the dishware. Her green eyes flicked over to me a few times before bustling back out of the room.

I looked down at the soup and felt my stomach grumble but resisted grabbing the spoon. Alec, however, dove into his meal without looking up.

Fable continued to watch me.

"You think I can't break you?" His eyes narrowed.

I shrugged. "You can't break what's already been broken."

Alec froze next to me while Fable rose from his chair.

"You don't look broken to me, pulchra." *Beautiful.*

My face heated as he drew closer, until his finger caught my chin, tipping my face up.

"Broken, is your mouth dripping with my cum, your veins stuffed with heroin, and your will completely gone. Is that what you want, *Caelum*?"

The way he said my nickname mocked and jostled the stable place inside me that was already starting crumble, the one that had previously boasted with confidence.

He let my chin go. I stared at the bowl of soup in front of me.

"You will help me. You'll either be in my bed tonight, or Alec's. I'll allow you the chance to decide, but you will bend to our will, or we will take it by force. Do you understand?"

Fear gripped me so tightly it was hard to breathe but I managed to nod.

Silas had trained me to deal with many things, dealing with his father wasn't one of them.

My belly was full because I was determined to keep my strength up. Besides, I had no idea if one of Fable's intimidation tactics would include starvation. I didn't do hunger well. Sasha had once mentioned that my mother didn't feed me for a whole week when I was little. Apparently, Sasha put my mom in the hospital when she found out, then made a bed for me in her house, in the same room as Silas. She had to feed me saltines slowly for two days straight while I sipped on water and 7-up, before I could eat real meals again.

Now as an adult, any hint of hunger had my hands shaking and my nerves raw. It was partly why I decided baking would be a fun way to reinvent myself. There would always be a little morsel of food at my fingertips, and I'd never have to go hungry. It also helped to keep my mind busy…like right now, I'd give anything to escape into the kitchen and pull out some flour and sugar.

"This is my room here." Alec gently touched the door near my face, pushing it open.

Without saying anything, I walked inside and kept my arms folded close. A simple queen-sized mattress sat in the middle of the room, decorated with a comforter the shade of cobalt blue. Four fluffed pillows sat against the wall for lack of a headboard. There was a singular dresser to the side, but nothing else.

I inspected the room as Alec shut the door behind me, then locked it.

"Surely there's another room I can sleep in. In fact, I'll even go back to my cell."

I faced him, silently pleading with him to agree.

Alec's ashen eyes avoided me as he moved around the room. His leather cut came off, leaving him in just a t-shirt, and then his boots, revealing a pair of white socks.

"Alec." I tried to get his attention again as he moved to his dresser and clicked on the lamp. The window in his room was only letting in muted colors from the strange opaque glass blocking out my surroundings.

He moved again, this time slipping into the small, attached bathroom. Water flowed from the faucet as Alec brushed his teeth and my eyes roamed to the bedroom door. It was unguarded. I waited for when I heard the faucet turn off and then the toilet seat lift. He began relieving himself, and I hesitated.

Run.

Run, Natty. Just get to the door.

My eyes burned as I stared, my left foot shifted the smallest bit and then as I blinked, I ran for it, pushing myself forward as quick as I could.

My fingers came around the brass handle as a shaky breath left my lungs.

The knob turned the smallest bit right as an arm came around my middle, lifting me off the ground.

Alec shut the door with his foot and began pulling me toward the middle of the room.

"If you step outside of this room, Fable will find you and trust me, Artie, you don't want him to find you."

I pushed against his arm, digging my nails in as hard as I could.

"Ouch. Fuck." He dropped me, inspecting his torn skin.

I spun on him, seething. "Stop calling me Artemis. Stop flirting with me. Just fucking stop. We're not friends, Alec. We are enemies."

He smirked. "I'm not your enemy, and what…only Silas gets to give you nicknames?"

"Yes."

His gaze searched mine before letting out a huff of air and spinning away from me. "You chose the mean one, Natty. Darkness, anger and bullshit. I've known you for just as long, and you're acting like we don't have just as many memories."

We had nothing compared to what I'd built with Silas. He wanted to bait me into conversation, but I wouldn't give him that. Instead, I walked over, grabbed a pillow, pulled the top layer of his blankets off and made myself a bed on the floor.

Alec watched me, then let out a heavy sigh as he slid into his bed, muttering, "Not like we haven't shared a bed before."

I screwed my eyes shut, facing away from him as the hard floor bit into my hips. A very low time in my life had provided me with little options and a gaping hole I needed filled. I had never had sex with Alec, but he did hold me for one very lonely night.

He promised he'd never speak of it, and that was fine because in the end, I had.

"You don't need to remind me. That was the worst night of my life."

The silence in the room was a comfort. Tears burned the backs of my eyes as hope seemed to flatline in my chest. I was supposed to be home by now…if there even was a home left to return to. I wondered how Pen was doing, how baby Connor was…if he got hurt during the blasts. If Silas…

A hot tear leaked through my lashes as I inhaled a shuddery breath.

"Did you tell him…" Alec asked, breaking into the silence, "about that night…does he know that it was me?"

A smirk curled my lips as I turned over on my side and looked up at him in the bed. His arms were tucked behind his head as he stared up at the ceiling.

"Yes, I did."

Alec's face quickly turned toward me. "Yet I'm still alive…explain that."

"It was the only concession he's ever made. He was the reason my heart broke…it was complicated, but he understood the reason I had done it. Besides, he knew I'd never let another man fuck me. If you had, you *wouldn't* be alive."

He laughed while letting his arm fall to the floor, dangerously close to my blanket.

"You assume he *could* kill me. You doubt my skills, Artie. I spent more time with my father than Silas did."

"True but you're forgetting Silas was also raised by Sasha and she's a different breed of monster."

Alec's smirk slowly fell away as his arm returned to the bed, tucking back behind his head.

"That is true…I had no mother worth remembering, but neither did you, so we're similar in that way."

I turned on my back, staring at the ceiling wishing again that this bad dream would end.

"We're not the same, Alec."

The darkness came in and with it, a tiny bit of planning. Once Alec fell asleep, I had a chance to escape.

His chuckle invaded the dark like a nightmare.

"Why aren't we the same, Artie?"

There was a light that shifted near the window, and it made me wonder if someone was keeping post outside. A tiny ping in my gut told me I should try to get close to Alec just to get information, but he was a record played and shattered years prior, and not anything I wanted to start up again.

There was also the vow I made to Silas that terrible night I had confessed what I had done. That I had fallen asleep and was held by his brother. I had never seen Silas broken until that night, and I vowed I would never again do that to him. Not with anyone, no matter how long it took Silas to come back to me, or how isolated I became.

I turned on my side again, wincing at how hard the floor felt under me.

"She became my mother too. While I had them both, you only had the one monster."

The blackness in the room amplified as did the sounds of Alec's breathing until he was softly snoring. The light outside the window made another pass, and I timed it to every twenty-three minutes. Someone was keeping post. Likely several people.

My options were slim, but I felt like I had to fully investigate all of them if I were ever going to get out.

Slipping out of the soft blanket, I cursed Fable for taking my shoes and padded lightly to the door. The lock slid easily to the side and the door opened without a single sound.

Out in the hall was nothing but shadows and darkness, being illuminated by the random flashlight beam through a window. I stepped into the hall and gently closed the door behind me. I veered back toward the direction I had come from earlier. The kitchen would likely be my best bet, as the space would have an exterior door for deliveries.

There were a few doors down the hall, all of which were closed, so I kept to the side of the wall while searching for any movement. I made my way toward the dining room, passing the table and chairs, and placed my hands against the swinging kitchen door right as a hand came over my mouth.

"I'm not going to hurt you, but we have to stay quiet." The voice at my ear was feminine.

I nodded against her hand then felt it fall away. I couldn't see her in the dark, but I felt her hand on my elbow as she pushed ahead of me into the kitchen. We walked until we were tucked away inside a pantry. A click sounded overhead, and Rachel came into view. She wore the same clothes she had on earlier, her hair still braided back and her eyes still alert...and oddly familiar.

"We don't have much time before Fable is done with his women."

I watched as Rachel moved around the small closet, pulling on the lid to a large white bucket. "Here, these are where your boots are being kept. When the time comes, you'll need to know where to go to get your things. I'm leaving a backpack in here too; it will have water and food. You'll be on foot for at least three days."

"Wait, I don't understand." I moved with her, tucking my frizzy hair behind my ears. Hope inflating my chest so much I thought I might die.

Rachel paused for only a second, her green eyes assessing me heavily.

"You're on the outskirts of Rockland, which is a few hours by car from Rose Ridge. There are five scouts outside during the day and only two during the night, which is why you're going to have to wait to make your escape until we can be sure no one is watching."

I turned with her, confused and elated all at the same time. I had so many questions and I felt like she would just disappear the moment I asked one. I wasn't even sure which one to ask first. What was Fable's plan, how come she was with him, what was Alec's part in all this. Why was he doing this now? What was his plan for me?

I settled on, "Why are you helping me?"

Rachel paused, and the way the small light illuminated her eyes nearly had me frozen in place. I knew those eyes. I watched them come alive for the first time when Laura arrived at the club all those months ago. I watched them as they adjusted to becoming president and mourned during Simon's funeral.

"You're..." My mouth opened and paused before realizing I had already asked her a question and she was about to answer.

"I'm who?"

I shook my head. "Why are you helping me?"

Rachel took a step closer. "What were you going to say?"

My voice was nearly a rasp as I glanced behind me at the door, knowing our time was limited, and if I was wrong, she might decide I wasn't worth helping.

"Are you related to Killian Quinn? You have his eyes."

She looked as though I'd slapped her. Her eyes flickered, her mouth gaped, and she backtracked into one of the shelves.

"Do you..." she started, but had to clear her throat. "Do you know him?"

"Very well actually...he's the president of the Stone Riders. He's also my friend."

Tears tracked down her face as she tried to laugh, but it came out as a sob.

"He's good then, like you're good?"

My heart nearly broke in half as I realized this was Killian's mother. His long-lost mother that he had loved so very much.

Stepping closer to her, I gently reached out for her hand and held it tight. "He's very good. He found happiness and love. He's happy."

Rachel sobbed again and pulled me into a tight hug. "That's all I've ever wanted for him. To be good and happy. To find love."

I had no idea why she had decided to leave her son all those years ago. From what Laura had told me, she left him when he was just nine years old. Killian's dad went to prison shortly after, so he was raised by Simon Stone.

There was a buzzing sound coming from her pocket. She pulled back, swiping at her face while inspecting her cell.

"It's Fable. I need to get back. Listen to me, Natty." She pulled me by the shoulders and leveled me with her teary-eyed stare. "You need to wait this out for a few days. Fable doesn't have a plan for you; he just wants to keep you here until he's ready to face off with Silas. He knows it will mess with his head and force Silas to react rashly. He's likely going to take pictures of you with Alec and try to force Silas to act first. So, wait it out, see if you can get Alec to aid you."

I shook my head. "He won't."

"You have to try. Fable is leveraging his hold over the Sons of Speed. If he doesn't have them then he's not strong enough with just the Destroyers. Especially if you say Killian is the president now of the Stone Riders. Silas has the Death Raiders...Fable will be too outnumbered. He has to take the Death Raiders from Silas, it's his biggest play."

"But why?" I shook my head not understanding why he just popped up out of nowhere after all these years and suddenly wanted power.

Rachel's phone buzzed again, and she clicked the light off, plunging us into darkness.

She whispered briskly, "Watch the patrols, lunch will be the safest, or early near six when they trade positions."

"Come with me," I whispered back, but she was already opening the door and slipping out.

I bit my lip, knowing I had to be quiet. Rachel slid out of the kitchen, leaving me behind. I grabbed a few cookies from the pantry and then snuck out behind her. I was nearly to Alec's door when it suddenly swung open, and a pair of angry gray eyes greeted me.

FOUR
NATTY
AGE TEN

RIPPLES IN THE LAKE HAD ME SCANNING THE SURFACE FOR FROGS.

The summer heat soaked into my back as I lay across the worn foot bridge, my face inches away from the water. I told Silas I could catch at least five by dinner, and so far, I'd only caught three. The only rules were the frogs had to be as big as our palms, and not any smaller.

He was watching me from the other side of the lake where he was fishing. Every now and then, his dark hair would shift from the wind, looking like a dash of black feathers. He'd shield his eyes from the sun and stare in my direction.

Patientia, Caelum

Silas was starting to get better at Latin lessons too, and while I still hadn't translated that little bit, he called me Caelum enough that I learned it meant heaven. I wasn't sure why he called me that; he always just blushed when I asked him.

I wondered if he couldn't say my real name in Latin. *Natus* was simple enough, yet he never said it. Silas got off easy because his name was the same in both languages. It was yet another reason why I wanted to win this challenge. He seemed to win at everything else.

Just then the splash of water had my head lifting. Two bulbous eyes stared at me from just above the surface. The frog was massive, and all I had to do was slowly reach forward and wrap my hands around him, then ease him into my bucket.

I started sliding on my belly, slivers from the worn dock slid into the skin of my stomach from where my shirt rode up. I didn't care, this frog was mine.

My hands were nearly in the water when suddenly someone plopped down next to me, their face an inch from mine, hands dangling in the water.

"How many frogs you catch so far?"

The frog swam away, leaving ripples in its wake.

"You scared it!" I shrieked, slapping my hands against the dock.

I slid my hands under me and pushed up right as the person next to me did the same, and I came face to face with a boy my age. My brows caved in as I took in his familiar nose and hair, his jaw shape and even his lanky body. He looked like he could be Silas's twin.

"Who are you?"

His eyes were a different shade of blue. Where Silas's were light, like water found on the moon, this boy had gray ones, like thunder clouds stuffed inside glass.

"I'm Alec." He smirked, then dropped his gaze to my hands. "And you're Artie."

My confusion only worsened. "Artie?"

He ruffled his jet-black hair, which was shorter than Silas's. "Yeah, for Artemis."

"My name isn't Artie or Artemis."

He stared at me like I was clueless, or should have figured it out already. "You're a huntress."

My hands found my hips as I opened my mouth to argue with him giving me such a lame nickname, when Alec was suddenly shoved off the dock. A loud splash followed as Silas stood there on the edge, his chest heaving. His glare was stark as he stared at the water where Alec finally emerged, coughing.

Between breaths, he managed to yell, "What the heck, Silas?"

I glanced between the two, still shocked by their similarities.

"Her name is Natty. Not Artemis, not Artie. Just Natty…and you're not allowed to talk to her."

Rolling my eyes, I let out a sigh and leaned down to help Alec out of the water.

"Silas, I'm not your toy. I'm like your foster sister."

Silas turned quickly, snapping at me. "You're *not* my sister."

It hurt when Silas acted like I wasn't his sister. I'd been living with him since I was seven, sleeping on his floor in a small sleeping bag. I was like his sister, he just never wanted to admit it. I wasn't sure why he was always so overprotective when it came to me.

Alec was nearly to where my outstretched hand was when Silas moved again, but this time he pulled the belt loop of my jeans. I assumed it was so I didn't fall but as soon as Alec got to the ladder, Silas hauled me back so I was behind him and away from Alec.

Sopping wet, Alec climbed out of the water, and swiped at his face. Those gray—blue eyes on fire as he stepped toward Silas. He was taller and had more muscle, but Silas didn't step back. He didn't wince or flinch. He didn't seem afraid at all.

"I don't want your little hunter, Brother. I only wanted to come say hello. Dad's here, he wants you to come back to the club. He's taking you with him for a few months."

I looked between the two, confused and cautious. *Silas had a brother?*

He was leaving again, and this person...his brother, had been going with him each time?

He'd never told me.

Never once mentioned it in all the different times we'd talked after his trips.

Alec shoulder-checked Silas on his way back to land, giving me one last glance.

I stood there with the sun drying the wet spot on my shirt from when Alec went into the water, splashing me. I waited for Silas to explain. When he finally let out a sound, it was to lean down to pick up his discarded fishing pole. I had a million questions, and right as I was about to ask, Silas muttered softly, "Stay away from Alec."

FIVE
SILAS
PRESENT

I HADN'T STOPPED RIDING FOR TWENTY-FOUR HOURS.

My legs were sore, my back ached, and I smelled like shit, but fuck I didn't care.

I knew I needed to sit for one fucking second and think, but if I stopped moving then the rage and fear would consume me as effectively as fire. I couldn't breathe around the ball of fear expanding in my chest with every breath I took.

I needed to do something so this rage wouldn't devour me.

The gravel parking area near the front of the Death Raiders clubhouse was busy with members catering to their bikes while others watched me with a sense of unease.

The doors opened easily under my boot as I kicked them open, which sent a few stoned members skittering. A cloud of smoke rose above the large sectional set up in front of the flatscreen. Heavy metal played quietly in the background while two chicks were fucking on the large flat screen.

That rage reared and all I wanted to do was smash everything in the room until there was nothing left. Better yet, I wanted to burn it all to the ground.

I settled for kicking the coffee table, which had a few bongs on it, and other shit for rolling joints. It all fell to the ground with a crash.

"The fuck, Silas," Geo screamed, getting to his feet, while blowing out a stream of smoke. He was mid-thirties, stocky and high as shit. A waste of space and resources. He had orders and was clearly ignoring them, which was something I wouldn't tolerate.

I gripped Geo by the throat and threw him down on top of the flipped coffee table and broken glass.

He moaned, trying to roll to his feet, but I gripped him by the cut, halting him. "Get these colors off, now."

A few members sitting around the space shuffled back, gaping at the scene unfolding. What I was doing wasn't done in clubs, not typically. There usually needed to be a severe reason for someone to be kicked out of a club, but on the rare occasion it could simply be because they pissed off the president.

"I'm patched, Prez...you can't," Geo sputtered in a weak argument, but I let him drop and then pulled out my knife and began cutting around the letters defining the club he belonged to.

Geo shrieked. "Wait, no...Prez...please."

I didn't do begging. It was a complete waste of my time and only worked to further annoy me. Once I had his patches cut out of his leather cut, I stood and looked around the room.

"Anyone else not understand the fucking orders I gave?"

When no one responded, I tossed the patches down on Geo's chest. "Get the fuck out of my club."

People moved, a few guys flicked an angry glare at me, but didn't say anything. Geo had been in the club for years, but he'd gotten lazy and complacent. Besides that, all my men understood the message I'd given them, which was to be scouting and looking for Natty. Not getting high while watching porn.

"Turn this shit off." I threw a look over at Dozer, one of my captains, and then walked into the back of the club where my room was located. It doubled as my office, which some people in the club didn't approve of, but I didn't give a fuck. It meant I didn't have to see naked bunk bunnies or sweet butts stumbling out of rooms or have to hear them fucking.

I could have moved into the old house my mom lived in, but the memories were too difficult to deal with.

The door to my room was locked as usual, so I pulled out my key and pushed inside. The space was dark because I had picked a room without a window. The small space illuminated when I clicked on the desk lamp.

Nothing had changed. My twin bed was still shoved against the back wall. The oversized wardrobe my mother and I used to hide inside sat against the adjacent wall, which held my clothes and guns. A small bathroom was cut into one of the walls, where a shower, sink and toilet were. Two chairs sat in front of the desk on the other end of the room, along with filing cabinets and a few bulletin boards.

Simple. Dark. Lonely.

Just like me.

I pulled off my boots and shed my clothes, then walked to the bathroom. I let the cool concrete under my feet calm me before stepping under the spray of my shower. The hot water nearly scalded my skin as I scrubbed and tried not to think about the fear tearing at my insides.

Instead flashes of gold would come back to mind. Memories that felt more like snapshots of a different life invaded my skull, making tears burn the backs of my eyes.

Silas, keep the Jeep straight, I'm going to fly.

Natty's closed eyes while she stood on the seats of the Jeep and threw her arms out. The way the wind pulled at her hair, as if the very sky wanted to take her from me. The way I was enraptured by the glow of her love. Something I never once deserved but claimed just the same.

My gut churned as memories assaulted me. An entire life with her, and yet we hadn't even begun living ours.

Not the one owed to us.

I flicked off the shower and quickly dressed, pulling my boots back on over a fresh pair of socks. There was a knock at my door, and I already knew who it was.

"Come in."

I turned from the door, checking my guns to ensure the clips were still full.

"You scared the shit out of them." Lance, my vice president, spoke up from behind me.

I smirked, still turned from him.

"They deserved it."

I heard him hum but then he shifted. "I was out scouting, otherwise I would have been here to keep them in check."

I already knew that, but I finally turned to face my friend to let him know.

"Figured."

Lance nodded, and I realized he looked tired. Standing at nearly six foot four, he was a tall motherfucker. Built like a truck with lean muscle; he was toned from years in the military. He was Black with more tattoos than even me, most of which I was still too chicken shit to ask about. He was a few years older than me, but the fucker seemed to be aging better than me, as you wouldn't know he was older than thirty.

I was about to turn twenty-eight, which made me remember Natty making me a birthday cake last year while working at The Drip. She'd left it in the display case.

Written in white frosting were the words:

Felix natalis mea tenebris silva *Happy Birthday, my Dark Forest*

I'd give anything to see another in that stupid glass case again. This year, I wanted to watch her bake it from the privacy of our own kitchen.

I blinked away the image and faced my vice president.

"Any leads?"

Lance shook his head. "Nothing yet…have you talked to the Stone Riders yet?"

I shook my head, moving over to the desk. He was leaning his ass against it, his long legs stretched out before him with his arms crossed.

"They might have video footage…might be something there as far as making an alliance with them. Especially if they care about her."

Lance knew Natty. He'd started as a prospect in the club back when Natty was still here. Many of my members remember her, but out of respect for me, they never talk about her.

"Want me to head over?" Lance tapped his arm, his only tell when he didn't want to do something. I didn't blame him. He had a history with Killian Quinn, one where Killian had promised to gut my vice president the next time he saw him. Lance could hold his own; I wasn't worried about him, but the focus had to be Natty.

All other bullshit aside.

"I'll go. Just keep things going here, no more of that shit that I walked in on. All members are scouting or visiting their connections in other clubs to see if anyone has heard anything."

Lance nodded, then shoved off the desk.

"You gotta take care of yourself, boss. Just remember that."

I scoffed while we exited the room. "Finding her is the best way I can care for myself."

My second let out a sigh and walked ahead of me. I veered to the exit and walked over to the abandoned house that still stood like a relic on the side of the club.

Stepping inside, I inhaled and immediately wanted to tear my fucking lungs out.

Bad idea.

I turned around and walked right back out, slamming the door as I went.

SIX

SILAS

AGE 15

The strap of my duffle snapped the second I stepped off the bus, which felt like a perfect way to end a really shitty month.

The glass door slid shut, and the air brakes released as I walked to the platform and away from the rest of the people dropped here in Pyle, Virginia. Forever a running joke with my stupid half-brother whenever I was forced to see him.

Look who came in from that Pyle of shit.

Alec was a cocksucker who needed a swift punch to the jaw.

"Silas."

I lifted my head in the direction of the parking lot and saw my mom there, waving at me. I looked down at the broken-up cement along the curb as I made my way over. I hated seeing her this soon after getting back from Fable's. I usually wanted to walk back to the clubhouse, so I had time to shed the slimy invisible film that seemed to coat my skin from all the fucked-up shit he'd had me do.

My mom's dark hair was swept up into a ponytail, dark sunglasses framed her face and…shit. She was wearing a new property patch.

I tossed my bag into the back of the open Jeep. It was July, so the top and sides were all removed. She gave me a tiny smile, the smallest one I'd ever seen, and I hated that each time I got back, and the older I became, it seemed like those smiles became less frequent and significantly smaller.

Her hand came to my hair, brushing it to the side. "You look older."

"It's only been a month."

She removed her hand and let out a sigh. "Still look older."

I moved around the hood of the Jeep and settled into the passenger seat. She let out a sigh and took her place behind the wheel. "Wanna practice your driving?"

Shaking my head, I stared out at the dying weeds in the field next to us. I hated this town. I hated this fucking broken down bus stop and the fact that my mom was still living with the Death Raiders. I wanted her to leave them, to leave everything and take me and Caelum with her. I wanted to get the fuck away from motorcycles clubs...I wanted to get away from death.

Mom started the car and reversed from the spot, heaving a sigh.

"You gonna tell me what happened this time?"

I scoffed, shaking my head. "You gonna tell me who you're patched to now?"

Her being patched to a member was dangerous for me, for Natty... for her. There were no members of the Death Raiders that I trusted with my mother. But she always had someone asking after her, trying to date her, kiss her...fuck her. She knew how to defend herself, so no one ever hurt her, but I wished she'd just stay single.

"Dempsey."

My head swung around. "You're patched to a captain in the club?"

She kept her eyes on the road, didn't even spare me a glance. "Yes, Son. I am."

Fuck.

My anger was simmering, already boiling at the surface, and I just couldn't see her go through this again. Not after everything she had done to get us away from the Destroyers.

I kicked the dash and screamed at her. "Did you learn nothing from being with Fable?"

She pulled the Jeep over, dust flying as she did it.

"Silas Damion Silva," she snapped, pulling her shades off. "Don't you ever speak to me that way!"

"You nearly died, Mom! Several fucking times in case you forgot."

"Don't speak to me about what I went through." She pointed at her chest, her voice shaking. "You saw a fraction of what happened and while you don't like it, this is my life and Dempsey is a safe choice."

Tears burned the backs of my eyes. I hated this. I hated her for allowing it. I just wanted a normal life, one with a mom who didn't have scars on her stomach from when my father held a blow torch to it just to send a message. One who didn't have to teach me a second language that no one used just to be able to have conversations that didn't get us killed.

"I don't want him near Natty." I looked off to the side, clenching my jaw.

Mom was quiet for a second when she finally let out a sigh, turning the engine over.

"Natty doesn't come around the club often; she comes home at night, stays for her morning lessons and then she leaves. She doesn't like being there without you around."

I didn't reply, but something in my stomach felt like it had finally unwound.

Relief.

We drove back in silence. Once we hit the dirt road leading to the clubhouse, my stomach tightened again in dread. I hated this fucking place.

Mom parked outside the small house off to the side. She was able to grow vegetables and keep chickens that cut on food costs for the club, so they gave her, her own little two-bedroom house. It was old and weathered, but at least it wasn't inside the clubhouse and it gave her the chance to have a tiny bit of privacy.

The engine cut off and there was already someone yelling and laughing off to the side of the club with two members drinking while working on their bikes. One of them leveled me with a glare as he sipped on an amber bottle of liquor. The cut over his chest told me this man was going to be a problem I had to solve.

Dempsey.

He stood and tossed the bottle, heading over toward my mother.

I grabbed my duffle, clenching my jaw again as I bit back all the words I wanted to say to him. The threats that he better treat my mother right would all be wasted on any member in this club. They had no code they lived by, no morals; they were just like my father.

Soulless.

I ignored what I heard as he pulled my mother into a hug and started up the porch steps, shoving in through the front door of the house.

The house was old, the floors withered and brittle. They creaked under my boots as I walked, and the doors were barely holding together, the glass knobs loose as I turned mine. A bed barely big enough to hold me sat against the far wall, a simple gray blanket was tucked nicely around the single mattress. No one had touched it since I left a month ago.

My eyes fell to the floor, seeing the small bedroll still laid out, a red sleeping bag over it with a flat pillow at the head. Natty had been sleeping on my floor, but not my bed.

I let the duffle slip from my shoulder and land on the floor then found the loose floorboard near my desk. The board came up easily as I gripped it with my nails and then found the small white note tucked inside.

There was a circle drawn with two t's inside it. Which meant she was in the grove.

Shoving the note in my pocket, I set the floorboard back and then grabbed my notebook.

The clubhouse was surrounded by barren, flat ground with dead grass and tumbleweeds that littered the dirt. The sky was hazy and hot as I trekked down the canyon and stared at the green water filtering through it. Across the bridge and up the other side of the hill, there was a small patch of forest that offered lush green grass, privacy, and shade. It was a nice hiding place for Caelum and me when we wanted to train or just to talk.

The shade from the tall trees hit my neck and face as I entered the grove. The grass was soft and silent under my boots, and the t-shirt against my back almost felt too thick as I pushed in farther. I knew where she liked to go and where I would find her, so I went until I found the small pond we used to visit when we were kids. There on the dock, where she used to catch bullfrogs, she sat with a book in her lap.

Her golden hair blew behind her in the small breeze that wafted over the pond, sending scents of honeysuckle and cedar over my senses. I tried to memorize every flyaway strand of her hair that blew in the breeze, the way her sun-kissed shoulders looked in that dress and walked closer to her.

The thud of my shoes hit the bridge, but Natty didn't turn, and that was something I liked about her. She was so calm and unassuming; she was the last rays of a sunset that kissed the world before dipping into starry oblivion. Since I was about nine years old, I realized I wanted to be the kind of person who could be compared to galaxies, like her. But as I grew up, all I found in my chest was a black mass. A void where nothing could survive.

Finally, lowering myself next to her, letting my feet dangle, she turned her face toward me. Green eyes, glittering and rimmed by thick, black lashes. Her lips spread wide in a smile that made something in my stomach swoop painfully low.

"You're back."

Words wouldn't come so I lifted my finger to grab a piece of gold as it flew around her face. I wrapped it around my finger as I watched her eyes examine it.

"Was it bad this time?" Her whisper cut through my sternum as effectively as a sword.

Bad didn't cover what my father did…what he subjected me to. There was no way to explain the darkness that came for my soul, hungry and always waiting every single time I stepped onto the bus and was forced to see Fable.

The feel of the gun in my hand, the heavy weight of taking another's life when I had no choice in the matter at all. The blood that poured into the dirt under a sunny sky, the green grass now shimmering red. My father patting my shoulder as he turned away.

Now take the tips of his fingers, Silas. Alec, you take the teeth.

Natty pulled my hand free from her hair and tangled our fingers together.

"Tell me, Silas. You always tell me when you come back, and you let me take some of it from your shoulders."

My voice cracked. "Isn't sitting on my shoulders, Caelum."

She watched me, tugging my hand closer and holding on tighter.

"Then from your soul," she murmured, and leaned her head on my shoulder. "Let me take it from there."

"I'm not letting you near this diseased thing." I'd laugh if it wasn't so fucking painful.

The truth was my soul was forfeit, and at fifteen, there was no hope that I wouldn't turn out exactly like my father.

Natty let out a sigh. "Silas, you're not beyond hope. You never will be."

My throat was tight, and it seemed to swell with something uncomfortable. "How do you know?"

"Because you have me, I'll be your hope. I'll be your sun, your moon and anything else good in this world. Give me your dark and I'll hand you all my light."

For the first time since I was first shoved in front of my father and told to kill, I wanted to cry. And fuck, if I did.

A single tear slid free from my lashes, and the warm breeze hit my face. Then another and another. I couldn't keep them back as I let all the rage in my heart break through my walls and I let her have it. I sunk down, until my head was in her lap, and I let her fingers comb through my hair and I cried as the sun bathed the world in a summer glow.

I let Natty take my hurt, my demons, and I trusted that she was bright enough to keep them all at bay.

It was dark by the time I got back home.

Natty had gone into the club to check in with her mother…it was merely for appearance at this point. She slept here, even if it was on the fucking floor. She had clothes here. My mother shopped for her and took her to doctor appointments. She was ours, but her mother was a petty woman who made my mom's life hell if Natty didn't pretend she was related to the woman who couldn't keep her legs closed long enough to avoid getting knocked up by some random club member.

My mother was sitting at our kitchen table, a skillet meal prepped, still warm and three plates set around the space. A tiny pang of guilt pierced through me.

"Sorry, didn't realize the time," I muttered, walking to the sink to wash up.

My eyes burned from crying, and my body felt lethargic from the lack of water I'd taken with me. All I really wanted to do was take a shower and go to sleep, but my mother had cooked. I would never make her feel like I wasn't grateful for the fact that she was a good mom, especially in a club full of shitty ones.

"Natty visiting her mother?"

I nodded, taking a seat next to her. "She'll be back in about thirty minutes…Lilly said she bought Natty some clothes or something."

My mom scoffed, then sipped from her beer.

"Clothes Natty will likely burn if they're anything like what Lilly wears."

That was true. Lilly wore a lot of leather, and Natty wore cotton t-shirts, jean shorts and flowy dresses that twirled around her ankles when she walked around the house.

I nodded my agreement then scooped up a bite of the chicken, broccoli and rice.

"Silas…you're different this time. I need to know what Fable made you do."

I kept my gaze down as I continued to chew.

Mom stared at me, silently sipping. Then lost her patience.

"He's training you to take over The Destroyers…surely you know that."

Shaking my head, I swallowed and replied, "Alec will…"

"Alec will be set up somewhere else. You're his first born. He wants you to take the Destroyers."

"I won't."

Her eyes softened, her beer lightly hanging from her fingers. I didn't know where Dempsey was, but I refused to ask.

"You will, Son. You will do whatever he asks of you…why do you think he's doing all of this to you?" Her left hand gently pulled at the long sleeve I had on, pushing it up. The knife marks were still raw from when I didn't please Fable. Drawing blood was a reminder that there was always more pain to be felt.

At that moment I wished my mother could fight Fable. I wanted her to protect me, to tell him I didn't have to go anymore, and in any normal legal custody exchange I wouldn't have to, but there was nothing normal or legal about my relationship with my father, or hers.

Fable took what he wanted, and half my mother's body was broken and burned from fighting him off when I was little. She held on for as long as she could, but this was always going to be inevitable.

"Then how do I stop it? How do I stop *him*?"

My mother pulled my hand into hers and gently stroked it, like she used to when I was little. "You learn from him, Son. You train, and you tuck away every single piece into your brain, you turn it into a weapon…"

"And then?" My voice came out weak and I hated myself for it.

She gave me a sad smile. "And then you kill him."

SEVEN
NATTY
PRESENT

THE MINIMAL LIGHT FROM THE WINDOW BLED INTO THE ROOM LIKE AN ominous dream I couldn't seem to wake up from. The metal around my wrists pinched as I tried to move my arm away from Alec's head. It made me hiss in pain.

"For fuck's sake, Alec, these are too tight."

The cuff around his wrist, connecting us, was significantly looser and it was currently attached to the hand tossed behind his head. He didn't care that it forced me awkwardly close to him, nor did he seem to mind that I was in pain.

He confirmed as much when he clicked his tongue, staring up at the ceiling. The grayish hue of the room led to a brightened ceiling, and it had me wondering if there were still guards rotating in shifts outside our window. It honestly had me wondering how thick the opaque glass was, and if I could somehow use these metal cuffs to break through it.

"If you didn't want to be locked up then you shouldn't have tried to run."

I thought back to the moment he'd opened that door and found me sneaking in, he was beyond angry, so much so he grabbed me, viciously tossed me on his bed and slowly leaned over my chest, dragging his nose down the length of my neck. My breathing hitched as fear climbed my throat, coating my mouth like ash. I didn't think Alec would touch me, but his hands landed on my hips, where he gripped me, and his knee landed between my thighs.

"Don't," I rasped, unsure of what he was going to do but desperate for him not to do it.

He'd drawn back and stared down at me, then pulled my left wrist up and aggressively slapped the handcuff on. My diminishing freedom hadn't really sunk in until he slammed the other link onto his wrist.

"There, Artemis. You've been chained to your beast, now you can either slay me, or fuck me, but you're not getting away without doing one of those things." His anger twisted with hurt, and I hated how it made me feel. This dance Alec had done around me my whole life, always making me feel horrible for not choosing him. It only worsened after that night together all those years ago.

I stared at the dark green color along his walls, listening as Alec started falling back asleep. It was morning, and I was hungry. The silence in the house was unnerving. We were obviously staying somewhere not many people knew about, if any. While there might be a few members moving around outside, I hadn't heard any of them enter the house. Even after Rachel had mentioned Fable having women over, I had never heard a single moan, shout or scream.

It was complete nothingness and being locked in this room was driving me crazy.

"Won't your club miss you?" I turned my face, inspecting the man chained to me.

His dark hair was skewed messily, all dark strands that matched his dark brows. He had equally dark lashes, and I assumed perhaps he'd gotten those from his mother. Silas didn't have long lashes like that; if he did, they might lessen how beautiful his eyes were.

Alec let out a sigh, bringing his free hand to his chest to scratch. "I have people in place taking care of things while I'm gone."

"So you can be gone for however long this thing will take? What if Silas never shows up?"

I knew that wasn't going to be the case, likely as much as he did, but I wanted more information from him.

"So what if he doesn't...you'll be mine, and Fable still gets what he wants."

I clenched my fingers into a fist where he couldn't see. "Which is what?"

Alec's chest expanded with a sigh, but he just let out a chuckle.

"So close, Artemis. So close, but no, you're not getting his plan from me."

Frustration frayed my nerves.

"So you think he'll come here to this location?" I toyed with a random thread from my shirt, realizing how bad I smelled. As far as I had gathered, it had been two days since I arrived. While Alec had been showering every day, I refused to join him. Instead, I stood awkwardly outside the stall, ignoring the wet spray hitting me, and whatever made him groan and grunt while inside.

"Not here. He won't be able to find us here...we made sure of that. But our men are watching for his club to make a move, we're also monitoring the Stone Riders."

"Why go through all of this work just for a little payback? Aren't you worried about losing your allies, or your club? This sort of ripple could have major ramifications."

Alec laughed. "Baby, the only thing I really care about currently is keeping you."

A sour feeling filled my stomach as reality crashed back into place for me.

"I'm not yours to keep, Alec."

He turned his face, his gray-blue eyes landing hard on mine. This felt intimate, us lying in bed together, creating pillow talk. All I had to do was tug my hand and remember there was nothing romantic about this.

"The way I see it, you're not being kept by anyone, least of all my brother."

I turned away and faced the wall so he wouldn't see how badly my chin began to tremble from the hurt he'd just caused. Because regardless of the past I had with Silas, there was truth in what he'd said...a thread of honesty that was far too painful for me to accept.

EIGHT
SILAS
PRESENT

THE STONE RIDERS HAD THREE GUARDS POSTED AT THEIR FRONT GATE. I assumed I'd have to put up a fight to get in, but when they saw it was me, they let me through without issue. Either they remembered me helping them when they were attacked last, or Killian had put an order out to let me pass if I showed up. I didn't really care which, I just needed to get inside that club and talk to them.

I rode down the gravel path and parked directly in front. This time, I kept my cut and colors on because I just didn't fucking care anymore about politics, or offending anyone.

I walked in through the front doors and saw as several members looked away, or gave me a wide berth.

Killian, Wes and Jameson were at the bar, all watching as I approached. Sipping from mugs, and at least they had the decency not to look chummy or happy. They looked about as exhausted as me.

I didn't even know what time of day it was. They were drinking coffee, so maybe it was morning, but I'd just left my club, and Geo was high…

"Silas." Killian nodded at me.

"What time is it?" was the only response I could give.

Jameson gave me that familiar expression that told me he thought I was a waste of air, and he likely wanted to punch me.

"Two in the afternoon."

"How come you're all drinking coffee?"

They all looked at each other like they weren't sure what was wrong with me.

"We've been looking for Natty. Round the clock shifts."

I must have waited too long to respond because Killian set his mug down and then placed his hand on my shoulder. "Come on, let's head over to my house."

I followed, feeling numb, and humbled. Not even my own club was looking for Natty, and here this club was doing it just because...

Because this had become her family.

Watching my boots as we exited the club and walked down the freshly done walkway, I didn't even realize we'd entered Killian's house until I heard female voices.

"Silas." It was a gasp and then suddenly Penelope, Natty's best friend was in front of me, her baby up on her shoulder as worry creased the spaces next to her eyes and turned her lips into a thin line.

Laura, Killian's ol lady came up next to her, arms crossed but offering me a small half-smile. The fact that she didn't want to stab me was progress, considering I'd once held a gun to her face.

I had nothing to give them. Not a single fucking answer and the reality of it sank in my chest like a boulder hitting water.

I shook my head because words wouldn't come, but then Callie, Simon's daughter and Wes Ryan's wife, burst into the room holding something in her hand. She slapped whatever it was onto the coffee table, which is when I realized that half of Killian's house was missing.

"The fuck happened?" His garage had been removed, along with part of his dining room area. There was a wood frame up with tarps in place; otherwise, half his house was gone entirely.

"The explosion." Killian waved me off, sounding exhausted.

Callie gestured me over, and I realized the thing she'd tossed down was a map.

"Okay, we've been working on this for a few days, and this is what we think." Callie bit off the top of a permanent marker, spitting it to the floor. "Natty was last seen here, but she received a phone call right before the blast from you, Silas."

Her eyes bounced up, landing on me. I took a seat on the edge of the couch and watched as she marked an x over the Stone Riders clubhouse.

"I think she got a text, something that would have pulled her away. Where would she have met you if she thought you were asking her to?"

I leaned forward and pointed to the edge of the property where Natty and I passed notes.

Callie marked it with an x.

"It was Fable, we know that much, but how did he know about your meeting place?" Penelope asked, still burping her baby, Connor.

Jameson pulled on her hips until his wife was standing between his legs. Jealousy scorched my throat and burned all the way down into the dark pit of my soulless stomach.

"Same way he knew where I lived, I suppose."

I had a home on the outskirts of Rose Ridge that no one knew about, not even my mother knew about it and while I didn't go there often, one night I did and found a picture of Natty pinned to the door. It was my father's sick way of telling me he could get to her, or me any time he wanted.

Fucker was keeping tabs, that much was clear, I had just severely underestimated how close he had been watching.

"So have we checked cameras on the roads leading out of that area? What about trail cams, didn't we have some set up?" Wes asked, looking between Killian and me. "After the warning about the Chaos King that had been found out there, the one that you took care of, Silas, we set up trail cams."

Killian pulled out his phone, but Laura hopped up and ran over to a small desk in a spare bedroom and came out with a silver laptop.

She slid it in front of Killian, who handed her his phone, and the two started clicking and swiping away until they were turning the screen around to us, showing us the footage from the day we were attacked by Tuck Holloway and Jefferson Quinn.

I was given better access to view it than anyone else as I leaned in and examined the screen.

It was grainy but I could make out the tree where Natty had sunk behind, staring off at what was probably the clubhouse that was being blown up. My heart lurched forward in my chest as I watched her looking so frail and afraid. She kept checking her phone and I knew she was looking to see if I had contacted her.

She was out there because of me. She trusted me, and whoever had duplicated my contact, convincing her to come…they had done their job in tricking her.

We watched for three minutes until there was suddenly someone walking up behind her. They had dark hair, similar to mine. A gaiter mask covered their face, but I knew that walk. I knew the tattoos along his arms.

He pulled a white rag out of his pocket and then brought his arm around the tree and covered Natty's mouth.

"Fuck," Killian rasped, shaking his head. Laura had tears in her eyes, Penelope was sobbing with little hiccups and Callie looked worried.

My rage was untethered and wild. Like a whip of lightning crashing and clinging to every single place inside me.

"Who was that…do you recognize him?" Jameson asked.

"Alec Veda," Penelope answered and my eyes flew up.

Everyone turned to look at her.

Callie asked, "As in the president of Sons of Speed?"

"How the fuck do you know Alec?" I glared at Natty's friend, not that I was angry, but I was surprised, and I didn't like surprises.

Everyone's gaze coasted over to me, then ping ponged back to Penelope.

She hesitated. "My mom dated a member in the Chaos Kings, Miles… well, he wasn't always faithful to her, so one summer when he'd left without leaving us a dime, she tested the waters with Sons of Speed. She found a guy there who she started seeing a few times…I went with her, and I remember when we stepped into that club and saw their president. Alec Veda is hard to forget."

Jameson's grip tightened on her hips as his eyes narrowed. "Hard how?"

"He's just intense…and then there's that tattoo, you can see it in the video, it's of Artemis, Goddess of the hunt. She's got this golden hair and green eyes. Her bow has all these swirls of darkness and sunlight bursting from it, it's beautiful. I remember staring at it when he crossed his arms over his chest, realizing the arrow in her bow points directly at his heart. I remember it being such an odd thing to have inked for the president of a motorcycle club. Especially when he has all this simmering anger and rage around him like..." She looked up at me. "You actually. He reminds me of you."

Yeah, that's what happened when we shared a fucking gene pool. That tattoo would be the first thing I took from his flesh when I found him.

Penelope's stricken face turned toward me as she asked, "Why would Alec Veda go after Natty? She's never once mentioned him, or Sons of Speed for that matter. There's no way there's a connection there."

Fucking Alec. I wanted to give him the benefit of the doubt. As angry as I still was with him, after all these years, I had a soft spot for him because of our past. Because he was my blood. And for one solitary night, while Natty had needed me, he'd been the one to step up and comfort her. Natty assumed I hated him for it.

It broke me, but I was more grateful than I was angry. With a curt tone, I declared to the room. "There is a connection."

The room waited for me to continue, and fuck...I guess I was about to open this can of bullshit with these people, not because I liked them or needed them but because they'd had a map ready to go with places marked so they could narrow down where Natty was last seen. They cared about her. For that reason and only that reason, did I explain.

"He's my brother."

Killian stood, shaking his head, then loudly cursed. "Fuck. Me... Of course he is."

"That's some important information...you made it seem like you'd barely met Fable...how true is that?" Wes asked, crossing his arms. Callie, his wife, was on the floor still, rubbing a hand over her pregnant belly, lost in thought.

"Fable is Alec's father...and mine. We were raised together...in a way at least. We were both carted over to our father's house once a year, forced to stay for months at a time, sometimes longer. While there, we were exposed to Fable's special brand of parenting, if that's what you want to call it."

Penelope took a seat in Jameson's lap, shifting her baby on her shoulder.

"And Natty knows him?"

My jaw clenched painfully hard as I nodded. "Alec would occasionally be dropped off in Death Raider territory with me."

"You made it seem like a surprise when Fable turned up," Killian said accusingly.

I thought back to our conversation that night, I had confessed to the group that Fable was in town. I had made it sound very vague and as if I barely knew my father.

"Didn't trust you."

He scoffed, shaking his head. "Do you now?"

"Not even a little bit."

Wes laughed; Jameson muttered something about me being an asshole.

"So, Alec took her then, not Fable?" Laura glanced around at the group.

I shook my head. "Alec and Fable are working together."

That news silenced everyone.

"Fable would likely not have any houses set up over here, right?" Penelope seemed to be thinking out loud while stroking her son's back.

I stood, needing to move around. I hated this feeling of being so fucking useless.

"It's hard to tell...he could have had houses set up the whole time he was in hiding, or nothing at all. Just depends on how long he's been planning this."

Penelope seemed lost in thought then pursed her lips. "There was a place...a safe house of theirs. The man my mom started seeing from Sons of Speed...he took us there a few times because he could have it to himself, or not get in trouble for messing around with Chaos Kings property. I left them alone while I ventured to the lake nearby. This was a long time ago, so my information is likely wrong and dated, but I will never forget this because on our way to that house, we passed by a chain of businesses that made me laugh. *Wendy's, Loves, Dicks, Hooters.* They were all lined up one after another, and I would just laugh because it seemed ridiculous."

Did Natty enjoy this complete and utter mundane gibberish from her friends?

Penelope waved her hand. "Anyway, there's a dirt road half a mile or so after Hooters and it goes back quite a ways, there's a house at the end of the road…It could be something."

"What town was this in?" I asked, uneasy about how far they could have taken Natty.

Penelope looked hopeful as she said, "Rockland."

Rockland was hours from Rose Ridge. If I got on my bike now and started, then I could make some decent time. I'd have to do recon, but I could manage. It would be night by the time I really got set up, but it wouldn't matter. I just had to get to her.

I stood, not listening to what everyone else was saying or discussing. I had enough to go on to follow up on the lead, so I didn't need to hear anything more, but suddenly Penelope was in front of me again with her baby.

Her blue eyes searched mine as if I owed her something.

"You can't go right now; you need to make a plan and have back up."

I tried to move past her when she held her son out. "Open your arms."

"Excuse me."

She held her swaddled baby out as if she were about to place him in my arms.

"Palms out, come on."

I peeked at her husband, and he only sipped from a bottle of water with a smirk on his face.

"I'm not going to leave you alone until you open your hands."

I shook my head. "I don't know how to—"

But my palms were open like she'd suggested and suddenly her gaze fixated on a tattoo I had on the inside of my palm, near my ring finger. Her eyes narrowed enough that I began dropping my hands once more, but she cleared her throat and stepped closer.

"Like this." Penelope pushed her son into my arms until he was being cradled against my chest. "Support his head at all times."

My mouth gaped like a fucking fish. Did she really expect me to stand here and hold her—

Penelope dropped her voice, gesturing at my left hand. "Natty has a tattoo just like that, in that same exact spot."

I stared at her son and ignored her curious tone. She remained there, arms crossed and staring as if I were about to open up to her about my ink.

She finally let out a sigh and moved away from me, which allowed me the chance to really inspect this tiny human in my arms. Soft dark hair crowned the top of the baby's head, his soft blue eyes were gentle and his button nose was adorable as fuck.

How did people do this? How did they hold something so precious and perfect and then let it out of their sight to grow up?

I could never do it, never love something so much only to watch it leave me. If I were there when Natty left, there would have been a war. I'd likely have lost my life because there was no world in which I could watch her walk out of mine.

"Who knew that Death itself would actually be good with babies?" Killian joked, passing by while I stood like a statue with Connor in my arms. I knew Jameson was watching me like a hawk from across the room, but for all my faults and as evil as everyone seemed to know I was, hurting children was where I drew the line.

"Pen is right, we need a plan. We can't go half-cocked, Silas. We need intel, and to get the layout, we want her back safely, not shot in the cross-fire, or hurt because we snuck up and didn't know his security measures. Why don't you go back into the clubhouse, stay in Natty's room."

A quick shot of panic shot through me at the notion of waiting. I had to play this right because this club had already been searching for her. They had a map. They were her friends...her family. It wasn't like I could just go and not have them chase me. They could endanger our entire rescue if they showed up without a plan in place.

It was like swallowing nails to agree to stay put, but I knew it was the right thing to do. For Natty.

I didn't trust myself to walk with Connor in my arms, so I gave a pleading look to Jameson who seemed to understand and left his perch to come grab his son.

Once he was safely in his father's arms, I took a step back.

"I will give you one day to organize what you need to…just one, and then I'm going in with or without you."

The eyes around the room remained on me while I turned on my heel and walked out of the house. Within seconds, my phone was up to my ear, my vice president on the line.

"We have a club to visit tonight."

The only man I ever called a friend hummed in reply, "We leaving a message?"

Gravel crunched under my feet as I made my way over to my bike. I gave the club one last glance, wishing I could bury my face in some of Natty's clothes, or sheets, just so I could have her scent wrapped around me.

"We're sending an eviction notice."

There was a pause, which didn't happen often with my second. He was level-headed, unlike me, but he was fair and calculated.

"Which club?"

Going to war with a club wasn't something to take lightly, especially for one as dangerous as ours. Just the same, it had to be done.

I straddled my bike and ignored the blood roaring in my ears as I pictured my brother, and what he might be doing to Natty.

With ice in my tone, I simply replied, "Sons of Speed."

NINE
NATTY
PRESENT

IT WAS STILL DARK IN THE ROOM WHEN A PHONE BEGAN TO RING. I FELT groggy as sleep continued to pull at me, like tiny talons. My arm ached, my eyes burned, and I tried to fall back asleep until the second ring blared through the room. Adrenaline surged forward like a spike in my chest as the realization of what that ringing meant.

A phone meant communication.

Help.

I could find it and call someone.

Sitting up lightning fast, my chest heaved as I looked over at the side table, seeing nothing. The phone rang again, but there was no light, nothing at all indicating where the device might be.

Alec was positioned between me and the end table, and with my arm chained to his, there was no way to get around him. Besides, I didn't want to crawl over him. I had to think through a plan, just as long as whoever was calling stopped and he didn't wake up.

I held my breath as another loud ring resounded through the room.

Alec stirred, but I was too enraptured with the idea of freedom to fall back to my pillows. Instead, I waited and watched as he slowly twisted to the side and pulled the phone out from the drawer. There was no way to charge it in there, so he must have already done so, or had a burner phone.

His thumb slid over the screen as his deep voice replaced the ringing. "What?"

There was a pause, while someone spoke, and then Alec was sitting up, mirroring my position.

"What the fuck did you just say?"

The person on the other line said something else, but I couldn't make anything out. Alec's face was highlighted by the limited light coming through the clouded glass. A floodlight of some kind outside, maybe a porch light or a passing flashlight.

A rogue piece of hair fell over his forehead as worry creased his features.

"Caught on fire how?" he snapped at the person on the phone. "The club is guarded...there's no way..." He trailed off again.

A smile slowly worked its way up my face as I realized what had happened.

Silas.

Alec seethed, working his jaw. "What's left?"

The person on the other line must not have given him very good news because violent cursing filled the room as Alec listened.

"So the entire fucking club burned the fuck down, and all of you just stood there. Or what? What the fuck are you telling me right now?"

His voice continued to elevate as rage fractured each word, giving my heart tiny little wings. I hated that I was becoming the type of person who relished in another's pain, but my life was spiraling out of control and Silas was sending me a message in the loudest way he could.

"No. Fuck." Alec let out a heavy sigh, shaking his head. "I'll call you first thing in the morning. I need to think through this. I can't leave, so this will have to wait. Set up operations in one of the safe houses."

He hung up the phone and the silence in the room felt heavy.

The air left my lungs as I fell back into the pillows and fought a smile.

Finally, Alec looked over at me, and I stared back.

"He knows you have me," I mused, hoping it would continue to piss him off.

A horrible sneer tilted his lips up as he threw the phone against the wall, the pieces shattering as they fell to the floor.

I pulled a pillow over my face to smother my laugh.

"Time to get up, Artemis, your little shower ban is over."

Alec tugged me off the bed. The light pouring into the room meant that I'd been asleep for a good while. But what was more concerning was seeing Alec fully dressed. Which meant he'd disconnected our cuffs at some point and I missed it.

I'd also missed him dealing with the fallout from the fire. His face had no residual anger or tension. He was like a blank sheet of paper, staring at me as if I were simply an unruly prisoner he was sent here to bathe.

Alec hauled me into the bathroom, flicking the light, which illuminated the same forest green walls that he had in his room.

A knock sounded on his bedroom door, which had me frantic. Fearful it was Fable and desperate that perhaps it was someone here to help me. Knowing Silas was trying to send me a message had me wondering if he'd figured out where I was being kept, and if perhaps he'd found me.

Alec cursed as he walked with me back toward the door and opened it.

Rachel was standing there, a pile of sheets and towels in her hands while she briefly glanced over my body, focusing on my hand for the smallest second.

"We need to change these sheets. I'll be just a minute while you go get something to eat."

Alec watched as Rachel moved to the small dresser, where she set down her pile and then began changing the sheets. I could tell her that we hadn't been having sex, but I was too scared that Alec would take it as a challenge and try to fuck me. He would try, and I would go down fighting him with every breath in my lungs.

A frantic desperation in me wanted to beg her to help me again, regardless that I knew she couldn't. It felt like days since I last saw her or had any hope at all that I could get out of here. Alec's expression shifted as he watched me stare at Rachel, and instead of moving out of the room, he extended his free hand.

"I'll take them and change them myself. Then when we're done showering, we'll come out for dinner."

Rachel blinked, nothing on her face changed at all except for the smallest flick in my direction. I wanted to scream. I wanted her to fight him with me and help me out of here, but I wouldn't risk her safety. She had a son to get back to, and I'd do just about anything to make sure she had that reunion.

Once Alec had shut the door, and I felt like a piece of my heart had caved in, we wandered back into the bathroom. I tried to focus on the tiny window above the shower, which let in a degree of light. I took in the white tile on the floor, the basic silver faucets and walk-in shower. Leaning in to turn on the hot water, Alec gave me his back. He had scars littering the exposed skin from where his tank top didn't cover, some from burns others looked like blades. I nearly gasped because I'd seen these before...

He twisted, catching me as I stared.

"Don't fret over my scars, Artie. Your precious Silas got more than me, and on occasion took my share because he's an idiot."

Tears edged in the corners of my eyes because Silas wasn't an idiot; he had a good heart. He was good. Regardless of all the dark that his father poured into him, he remained steadfast in his goodness. I didn't want to talk about him right now, not as I was about to debase myself in front of his brother.

"Remove them." I held up my wrist as if I wasn't bothered by the abuse he'd obviously endured.

Alec's eyes, so much darker than his brothers, seemed to soften as he let out a sigh. Maybe I wore him down, he was likely just as tired of being chained together as I was. I watched as he produced a key from his pocket and my heart soared as he unlocked our wrists. I rubbed the redness around mine, muttering a reluctant thank you as Alec moved around me. "Just get undressed, Artie."

Assuming he'd give me privacy *and* freedom was too much to hope for, so I turned away from him and slid out of my t-shirt and jeans, feeling my fingers shake as I slipped off my bra and panties. I knew Alec was watching me, and I knew, as much as he might care for me, he didn't really give a single fuck that this was making me uncomfortable.

I faced the shower, covering my chest with my arms as I stepped inside, but Alec was right behind me a second later, stripped naked. The sound of metal clicking filled the space as he grabbed my hand and cuffed my wrist once more.

"What..." I looked up as my abductor connected the adjoining metal to his wrist, glaring down at me, while completely naked. His chest was packed with muscle, and he had more hair than Silas did, but any lower than that, I refused to look.

"You need any help washing that gorgeous hair of yours, just ask." He winked, moving under the spray, making his black hair skew to the side.

A dark rage barreled into me, so dark and fierce, I screamed. Shoving my arm up, my wrist was at his throat as I pushed against his windpipe with all my strength.

"Fuck you!"

Tears gathered in my eyes as spit flew against his cheek. I didn't care that I was naked, or that he was.

I had hit my limit.

Alec had kept me from Rachel, or anyone else who might see me, talk to me or help me. He had brought me my meals and uncuffed me long enough to secure me to a lead pipe in the bathroom; otherwise, I didn't leave. Finally Rachel came and he wouldn't even let me out of the room to go to the kitchen. I needed out of this house and away from him.

It seemed to line up with what Rachel had said about Fable just wanting me alive and here to taunt Silas or draw him out. I assumed he'd either give me to his second born son as soon as Silas was dead, or just kill me himself. One or the other, either way, my life was looking dim and so fucking small if I couldn't get free.

Alec's free hand wrapped around my hair, gently tugging until my head was tipped back.

"So fucking gorgeous." His eyes darkened as he suddenly moved us backward, as if my hold on him was nothing but air. My back was against the wall within seconds, and he was standing over me.

"What is it my brother calls you?" His lips moved against my ear, his erection was hard and slick as it slid against my abdomen. "Heaven?"

My eyes pushed close; my lips trembled as the hand holding my hair moved to my hip.

"Should I taste you, and see why he calls you that? Or is it something I could only discover by fucking you?"

He wouldn't rape me.

Deep down, I knew he wouldn't...still, fear gripped me painfully tight as my voice shuddered. "Let me shower in privacy." With one last quick breath, "Please."

Tense eyes assessed me then an odd emotion flitted through them as his gaze dropped to my lips. "I will, Artemis. I promise...Just give me this one thing, don't make me take it from you."

My chest felt tight at the reminder of all he'd taken so far. At the realization that there wasn't much left remaining.

"What?"

I didn't want to give anything more, every piece of myself that I had left, I wanted to hold tight and hide from anyone else who would force it away.

"Kiss me."

That was one thing I wouldn't give him. "No."

My head shifted, trying to move away from his gaze, but he moved with me. "Then tell me why you're still waiting for him...I don't understand it, Natty. He left you...and then you were traded like a fucking baseball card to a different club, and he still never reclaimed you."

I turned my face. "Stop."

His fingers gripped my chin. "Don't you get it yet, Natty? Silas has his priorities, and you aren't one of them. He's been around, watching you, hasn't he...everywhere you go?"

I glared up at Alec and tried to push, but his body covered mine and he wouldn't budge.

"Do you know how pathetic it makes you look that you're willing to play house in another club, pretending to be some baking princess who wouldn't dare hurt a fly, all while you're just waiting for your dark prince to come and tell you it's okay to come home?"

"That's not how it is." I pushed again, my hands sliding against his slick skin and getting nowhere.

He drew closer, his erection had mostly died down thankfully as he pressed close. "You're choosing not to live your life, Natty. You could move on with someone who wants a life with you and yet you're just frozen."

He slapped the tile next to my face. "You will always be the runner-up to revenge and the mistress of vengeance. He wants the darkness more than he will ever crave your light."

Like a soaked piece of paper, Alec had just reduced my life to a limp mass of blurred lines and smeared ink. Fat tears began trailing down my face, and I hated him for bringing his hand up to cradle my trembling jaw.

With his last words, every ounce of fight I had lifted from me like a cloud of steam and in its place was complacency.

"You have others who crave that light. Others who have needed you and all the hope you always saved for *him*. You have those who would also rip the world from its axis just for a chance to belong to you."

Alec continued to stare at me as I cried. His thumb came up, swiping at my tears, only to then smear them along his lips, tasting the salt with his tongue.

My head tipped back as I asked, "does crushing me really bring you so much pleasure?"

"If it's the only way I'd ever get to keep you, then yes." Alec's lips brushed against my jaw.

I stared at the tile, waiting for him to be done with me because the fight had left me years ago when my choices had first started to be stolen from me. Back when Dirk had begun his obsession with me...when I'd become a thing instead of a person. That's what Alec had reduced me to, and he had no idea how deep his betrayal gutted me.

Alec finally registered I wasn't engaging with his ministrations, and he released me, shifting under the warm spray. I moved as well and began washing my hair. I didn't care that Alec was watching me, or that he started washing his own body with a bar of soap, a mere few inches from me. I didn't care that when he cleaned his cock, he stroked it several times and, in the process, the slick tip touched my thigh.

"Did he ever get branded for you?" His whispered words were followed up with a pleading look, as his hand wrapped around his cock. "Did he get a tattoo anywhere on his body that represents you? Because I did, Artie, all of this is for you."

His arm flexed, the one he'd connected to me. As if he wanted me to see it every single day.

I rinsed my hair. "Silas only has one tattoo that matters to me."

Alec only stared at me, stroking himself. "Does he look at you like this? Does he see the way your back dips just enough to leave a dimple right here?" He brushed his finger over my lower spine, making me flinch. "Does he think about sinking his tongue into every hole you have, only to prepare it to be filled with his cock?"

His wrist rotated quicker as my skin began to pebble from the cold air. The hot water was gone.

"When's the last time you were fucked by him?"

I covered myself with my arms. "I'd like to get dressed."

"You can get dressed, but I'm going to finish first and you're going to watch me. You're going to see what you do to me, what you've always done to me, and you're going to remove your arms so I can see those tits while I do it."

My nostrils flared in anger. Hurt whirling inside me like a tornado.

"And if I don't?"

His caresses became more insistent, the head of his cock weeping with clear cum. Eyes hooded, he explained, "If you don't then I'll have to take a step closer and paint your skin, or I could have you lick it from the tiles once I finish all over the shower floor."

I set my chin, glaring at him.

"This is sexual assault, Alec. Are you really stooping so low as to take something from me that I'm not willing to give?"

My heart thrashed as I tried to remain stoic and calm.

I thought I knew him.

All these years, I had assumed there was an understanding between us, a clear line that he'd never cross, no matter what or where we landed in life.

His smile was crooked as he stepped closer, turning off the water as he advanced.

"Seems being the good guy holds no bearing with you. Darkness is what gets you off. It's your kink of choice, so as much as you're saying you don't want it, I know if I were to slip my tongue between those silky soft thighs, I'd be able to taste that you do."

"Don't do this, Alec." My whisper cut through the sound of his slick erection being stroked.

He didn't stop, his hips thrust forward as he fucked his hand, harder and harder until he reached up and roughly placed his hand against the tile near my head.

His groan was like an explosion in my ears, making me slam my eyes shut. I wanted to block him out, the sound, the feel of his sticky cum coating my stomach. All of it.

He shuddered, trying to catch his breath.

"Clean yourself off."

I looked around, but there were no towels in sight. "Turn the water on—"

He shook his head. "Use your fingers, smear it, then lick them clean."

Horror washed through me as I glared. "I'm not—"

"I'll remove your cuffs for the rest of the day," Alec offered, cutting me off in the process.

The temptation was so intense, so achingly sweet that my fingers twitched near the mess against my skin. Alec's hair still dripped, fat water droplets rolling down his face as he watched me with hooded eyes. I knew deep down if I gave him this, he'd take everything from me. There would be no line, no standard at all. He'd see my weakness, and in doing so, he'd use it to control me.

So, I kept my chin raised and I stared.

His left eye twitched. "I said to clean yourself, Artemis."

"And I won't touch any part of you, even if your cum has to dry to my skin."

A moment passed, then another, where he merely stared at me. His erection gone, his scowl in place and finally he let out a low scoff.

"Suit yourself. Let it dry, Artie…stay covered in my cum, it only turns me on."

Alec finally allowed me to leave the shower, still chained to him through the handcuff. I covered my chest with my free arm, and didn't ask for a towel, knowing it would be fruitless. Alec dried off, brushed his teeth and then we finally moved to the bedroom.

"Will I be sleeping naked, or will you be giving me clothes?" My skin was freezing, and the drying semen on my stomach began to feel uncomfortable. Alec didn't answer, just tossed one of his shirts at me. I stared at it, knowing I was going to need him to disconnect the cuffs if I wanted my arm inside the sleeve.

He moved away from me, but I yanked his wrist as hard as I could, making him turn to face me with a grimace.

"The fuck, Artie."

"I need to put my arm through the hole, uncuff me."

He glared, his gaze dropping to my heaving chest, my pebbled nipples and the white stain he'd left against my stomach. I'd been sunbathing with Laura as often as possible before all this, so my stomach was fairly tan.

"Maybe I should keep you naked, Artie. I do enjoy the view."

He pulled the small chain between the cuffs, drawing me closer to him. "That's exactly what will happen to you if you try anything when I unlock these, do you understand?"

Defeat was a soaked thundercloud in my chest. I envisioned fighting him. I had a beautiful delusion that Rachel had left me a knife, or something to defend myself, but I knew she wouldn't risk her place here to offer that. Her kindness to me was attempting to get me out of this room, but it had failed. Just like I had.

With a reluctant nod, I waited as Alec unlocked the cuffs. I slipped the shirt over my head and as soon as I pushed my arm through the hole, he slapped the cuff back on.

He stared at me while I moved with him toward the bed.

"It's dinner time."

It sounded as if Alec were suddenly feeling remorse over what he'd said and done to me. Having more freedom with his proximity, I turned away from him, curling into a ball against the wall. Memories of a past life rushed through me painfully fast as I ignored Alec's commentary. He kept talking, but I wasn't listening anymore.

My mind drifted back to what Alec had said about me being pathetic, and how the love of my life didn't really want me. It wasn't like I hadn't heard it all before. Silas *had* let me go, choosing his plans of vengeance over a life made with me. While most people weren't privy to what had happened, and not even Alec had gotten all the details surrounding it right, it still served as a reminder that The Roman was a slave to his club, and to his darkness.

He was a dark forest, obstructing all the light.

And I was parched earth in need of his shade.

We were impossible, and the idea that we could ever be anything more than two passing ships in the night was laughable.

I closed my eyes, pushing out the tears that kept trying to push forward and I did the one thing I had trained myself not to for these past two years.

I remembered.

Age Sixteen

Silas was gone again.

This time he'd left in the middle of June, right after we'd started our annual frog hunting tradition. It was different this summer though. We'd finished our studies in May, and then we started driving. Neither of us had a car; we just borrowed Sasha's Jeep. She didn't mind as long as we were careful and safe, and promised to never touch any of the shit being channeled through the club. The older we became the more it seemed to bother her that we were both so close to the Death Raiders.

I would never touch drugs regardless. Watching my mother get high and choose drugs over keeping me fed removed any temptation I might ever feel for that shit. Silas too, he was smart...he was the college kind of smart, and everyone knew it. I had overheard his mom talk to him about applying places, but Silas never answered her.

I'd even brought it up once while we were out learning to drive stick together, the Jeep jerking with every push of the clutch and us laughing as the gears ground. We'd barely made it down the road when Silas pulled off and decided we should go swimming instead. Soaking wet, and shimmering with beads of water against our skin, we laid out on the dock watching the minimal clouds float by.

"Will you try to go to college?" I turned toward him, loving the way the blue in his eyes turned almost aqua in this light. He swiped a hand over his thick hair, letting tiny drops of lake water linger on his chest. He gave me that stare that always struck me quiet, because he followed it up with a blinding smile.

One that made my breath hitch.

"Only if you come with me."

A scoff crept up my throat as my heart sank. "And what, sleep on your floor while you get yourself a degree?"

His head dipped but I didn't miss the way his cheeks flushed pink.

"Maybe not...maybe instead you just sleep *in* my bed, and we share the degree."

I sat up, folding my legs under me, ignoring the way his eyes tracked my every move. "We can't share a degree, Silas, that's not how it works."

I'd skip over the sharing the bed thing completely because while I was completely and devastatingly in love with Silas, I knew better than to ever imagine he'd care for me in that way. It was something we'd danced around since we were kids, something neither of us had ever confronted. We were getting older though and I'd catch him looking at me differently.

His eyes would linger on my legs and my lips.

Small touches would land on my back, and he was finding reasons to hold my hand more and more. I only wanted it to mean that he saw me how I viewed him, but he'd yet to make any official move. I noticed it when he'd found an old dirt bike behind the clubhouse and informed me, I needed to learn how to ride. He'd sit behind me with his hands over mine on the throttle, teaching me how to hold it steady. Other times his hands would remain on my hips while we navigated the small lot behind the house. Even when I started getting comfortable with riding and transitioned to bigger bikes, Silas would remain behind me, holding me.

"I don't see why not." His severe glare caught me again, making words die on my tongue. "You're already in here." His palm covered his heart. "Half of you at least...you've got the other half of mine in there." He pointed at my chest. "Not like they'd want me to give half the effort when a simple solution would be to go as one whole."

My heart sank because I knew he was telling the truth and I didn't have the grades or the money to go to college. I didn't have the drive either; as it was, I'd barely graduated high school through the state, and whatever homeschool program Sasha used with us. She had us take state tests at a local school; otherwise, Silas and I did all our educating at her kitchen table.

Being separated from him was a painful knife twisting over and over in my chest. Every day that he wasn't here, every night he was gone...it all felt so wrong. It was how I knew I'd never survive after we were old enough to move away from the club and start our lives. Silas could leave this place, go to college and work on Wall Street if he wanted. He could be someone who helped configure moon landings and space shuttles. He was brilliant, and yet the only aspiration he seemed to have was spending time with me.

With him gone, it left a gap in my life I struggled to fill.

I applied at a few places to work, but the club was miles from anywhere local. I could walk, but Silas had always warned me to be smart, not desperate. One solo walk on the club road at night and I'd be sorry, so working was out unless it was something I found within the club.

Most people knew I belonged to Lilly, the strung-out bunk bunny who sucked club cock, and whatever other depraved things they'd ask for, all for drugs. Not money or food. No, that she'd leave me to beg for and when I was younger, I cared enough about her that I would take her whatever I found. I don't anymore. Now, I keep it all for myself. Because it finally dawned on me that I was alone in this world. At the mercy of Sasha and the strange admiration of Silas; otherwise, I would be homeless with nowhere else to go.

Dempsey, Sasha's man, had offered to move Sasha and Silas into his house off the club property, but that invite didn't include me. With Silas gone, Sasha allowed me to continue sleeping in her son's room and I was fine with staying on the floor, but one night, when missing him became too intense and the loneliness in my chest had nearly tore me open, I crawled into his bed and inhaled what remnants of him that I could find. *Campfire. Our Lake. Summer.*

I didn't like the way my life seemed to stop spinning and existing, unless Silas was at the center of it. I knew it wasn't healthy and, in a way, I was just like my mother, except Silas was my drug, this home our club, membership of just two.

Weeks passed where I busied myself in Sasha's garden, keeping it green and helping as much as I could with her trips to the farmer's market. She'd established a good customer base there, several of whom had shown up just for her week after week. It was nice to help her, and any time she tried to pay me, I'd just slide the money back into her purse. Her teaching me, feeding me and giving me a place to live was more than I could ever pay back.

There were nights I could tell Sasha wanted the house to herself, or to spend time with Dempsey without me around, so I'd go down to the lake and sleep on the dock, staring up at the stars. Occasionally it would be too cold, so I would go inside the club and find the smallest possible corner and use a blanket to hide while I dozed off. I repeated this process enough times that Sasha had noticed, and one night, discovered my little spot while the club was having a huge party. The blanket covering my tiny oasis was ripped from me, while Sasha's face came into view.

I had a pair of headphones on, some I had found in her son's room. I slowly slid them off.

"What are you doing in here?"

The lights from the club made me wince, and the music from the club pounded in my ears.

"I'm sleeping."

Sasha glanced around quickly, seemingly worried with her dark brows drawn in tight.

Her hand shot out and pulled me up. "We have to get you out of here before someone sees you."

I wasn't sure why she was so panicked, considering I had been around this club all my life. Even longer than Sasha and Silas had been. They arrived when I was just six or so and by then, I had already seen a world full of horrors someone as good as Sasha couldn't protect me from.

I stood quickly, grabbing my bag and blanket, trying to follow her through the rear part of the club. We had bypassed a few couples, and one round of pool when my mother suddenly appeared. She had a tray full of shot glasses balanced on her palm, and a sour look stretched across her face. Her blonde hair was curled and lifted into a pretty updo. Her makeup was thick, and her clothes skin tight.

"The fuck you doing in here, Natalia?" she spat.

She may have been speaking to me, but she was glaring at Sasha.

My mouth parted, ready to answer, but Sasha just continued pulling me behind her, eyeing the approaching group headed our way. Sasha tried to divert us, so we'd head in a different direction, but my mother was suddenly there again, stopping me by digging her fingers into my arm.

"No, let him see her, Sasha." She yanked me so hard, I faltered backward, and I saw Sasha's eyes get big as fear stamped out all that usual confidence she carried.

I tried to track what was happening but within seconds, my mother's arms had pushed me hard enough that I wavered forward, and I was running directly into someone's chest.

A gruff laugh escaped the man's chest, his fingers were on my upper arms and then his whiskey breath, laced with weed covered my face.

"Who the fuck do we have here?" He laughed, so did a few men around him, and then my mother smiled, and I realized what had just happened. She'd found a way to secure herself a useful position in the club.

While her looks were fading, her hair thinning and her hips diminishing—She was becoming irrelevant, and I was her ticket to remaining flush with drugs.

"This is my daughter, Natty." She spoke loud and proud as if she were truly a mother. As if she was the one who had helped me when I'd gotten my first period, or who shopped for my first bra. Like she was the one who helped me learn to read, or how to write.

Sasha was fuming behind me, and I knew she was going to fight my mom again. She'd done it before, punching her square between the eyes when she caught her trying to hand me off to someone who wanted to touch me as payment for the drugs she craved so badly.

This was no different except I was bigger, and Sasha had less ability to control what happened to me, and Silas wasn't here.

Pain radiated up my arms as the man holding me squeezed, forcing my eyes up.

I knew who the president of the club was. I had been watching him from afar my entire life, but I had managed to escape his attention for sixteen long years. Now, unfortunately it seemed my mother had effectively ended that as Dirk seemed to stare with vicious intent.

Sasha stepped up next to me, gently pushing me to the side, and I knew in that moment as Dirk's hands left my arms, that Sasha would do anything for me. She would die for me, take a bullet, but I also knew beyond a shadow of a doubt this wasn't about me, it was for her son. She knew Silas was attached to me, in some capacity…I was his favorite thing about life right now and while I knew it would pass, his mother would do anything to keep me from falling to pieces.

I was a glorified teddy bear to her, and merely a golden egg to my mother.

There was no one that wanted me to stay in one piece simply because I was me, and it was the right thing to do, except for maybe Silas.

I didn't hear what Sasha had promised Dirk, or the way she had flirted, nor did I pay attention to the way my mother pinched the back of my arms, hissing threats in my ears.

Within mere minutes, Sasha was walking us into the night air, the stars hanging overhead as if there wasn't a whole house full of sinners just existing right below it. A crater in the dirt, full of raiders who worshiped death.

"What just happened?" I was breathless as fear clung to every syllable I managed to get past my teeth.

Sasha didn't reply until we had crossed the club yard, the garage and a few spare houses. Not until we were pushing through her front door.

"Dirk knows you exist, Natty. That's what just happened."

Sasha kept the lights off, flipping only the one above the microwave on. I cradled my arms to my chest, unsure of what this meant exactly.

"He's known about me…I've been in the club, around here—"

Sasha shook her head and I noticed her hands were shaking. "No, you don't understand. He wants you, Natty."

"You're right, I don't understand…" My voice shook.

"I'll break it down for you. You have big tits, a tiny waist, and golden —silky hair that touches your ass. You're beautiful, Natty. More than that…you're sexy…and Dirk likes to have first dibs on anyone in the club that looks as good as you do."

My eyes burned, fingers trembling. "I'm only sixteen…he wouldn't… he can't."

Sasha glared; her jaw tensed as she let out a heavy sigh.

She didn't have to say anything more. There were angels and demons that danced along a minuscule line in these motorcycle clubs. So far I'd veered toward the safe side of things, for the most part…but Dirk was a bad man. Someone who wanted to hurt me, and now if he knew I was here…

"Will he come for me?" I gripped the back of the chair until my nails sunk into the wood.

Sasha's trembling fingers came up to her hair as she tucked a few pieces behind her ear.

"I'll do everything I can to protect you, Natty…but I need you to promise me you'll stay away from the club. Do not go over there, no matter what. Do you understand?"

I nodded and when I saw Sasha grab a beer and start to leave, I turned toward the hall only to stop mid step and spin back toward her.

"I don't think we should tell Silas about this."

Sasha took a sip, and I might have been mistaken, but tears were gathered in her eyes when she shook her head. "No, I don't think we can. He'll try to murder Dirk and get himself killed in the process."

That was my concern as well. Silas was protective of me in a way that made him forget logic and act first. I gave her one last nod, agreeing that this thing would stay between us and then I turned and slipped back into the only room I had ever felt wanted in.

TEN

SILAS

AGE SEVENTEEN

THE LEATHER CUT WAS TOO BIG ON ME, BUT I KNEW IT WAS POINTLESS TO SAY anything about it. Dirk, the president, was a tall man, built thick as a tree with faded ink all over his body. His glare landed on the patch sewn in under my name.

"That going to be a problem for my club?"

I knew which one he was talking about, but I wasn't sure how to answer him. At only seventeen I should be a prospect, especially considering my lack of involvement with the Death Raiders since living on club property.

I had no desire to join this club, in any capacity, but this past summer took my remaining freedom, soaked it in red and painted a target on my back. A beacon of warning straight from my father, who happened to be proud as hell. The name on my cut wouldn't have any power unless it was on a patch and people started talking about it. I knew my father had plans to force me into his club, the Destroyers.

Tactically it made more sense to hide among the ranks of a lesser evil in the Death Raiders.

I should have known my father would have contacted Dirk and told him about my new moniker.

Dirk's silver brows came together in concern, bringing me back to his question.

"No, sir."

"If I need your services, you'll be at my disposal as long as Fable hasn't requested you."

My stomach bottomed out as I processed what this new name meant for me, and what it meant for those who had more power than me. I refused to be a pawn used to kill at will, but I was running out of options. I gave him a nod and slid my gaze to the side, seeing my mother wearing Dirk's property patch.

Her dark hair was pulled back, so I had a clear view of her back, proudly proclaiming that she was now his property. Natty wouldn't step foot inside the club and now my mother was dating the president. Something had happened, but I couldn't piece together what, especially as neither my mother nor Natty would talk about it, so I searched for Dempsey.

I found him working at a local mechanic shop, still wearing his cut so he was still a part of the Death Raiders but his captain's patch was gone.

He barely looked up from the interior of the hood when I approached him. The sound of tires being rotated and power tools echoed around us, but I made sure my voice was loud enough for him to hear me.

"What happened between you and my mother?"

Dempsey pulled a red rag out from his back pocket and let out a sigh as he moved around the car.

"Thought you hated me."

I moved with him, shrugging. "Got over that after a while. Why is she with Dirk?"

Dempsey was clearly hurt over the situation. I could sense it in the way his shoulders were rigid, his mouth was tense, and his jaw was locked.

"All I know is I came home one day and she told me it was over. She got real emotional, cried a bunch but no matter how much I asked what the problem was, she just sobbed. Never told me. Just said we were over. I fought for her...I went to Dirk, and I fought for her, but..."

He trailed off, but he didn't need to say anything more.

"That's how you lost your captain's patch?"

He nodded, solemn and serious.

"Nearly took my life, but Sasha stepped up, started kissing him, distracted him...I don't know why she's with him, Silas, but I can tell you it's not because she cares for him. Your mother hates that man with every single piece of her soul. I finally had to accept that your mother was always a survivor and this new relationship might just be part of her lasting...she's planning something, or he's a means to an end. Whatever it is, she's doing it willingly."

That didn't fucking help ease my fears or worries even the slightest bit.

I shoved off the car and gave him a nod as I exited the garage.

That was two weeks ago, and with all the demands the club has put on me, I've barely had any time to see my mother or Natty. The former had essentially moved in with Dirk, leaving the house to me...well to us, but I hadn't really been alone with Natty long enough to enjoy it.

I planned to change that tonight.

My initiation to the club was short since a few of us had pledged. The club was loud as the night went on, and I slipped out through the back door, heading home. I could see the fairy lights burning gold through my bedroom window. Natty had bought a shit ton of them over the summer and hung them all over my ceiling, along with green vines. It looked like something from a cheesy movie, but I'd never tell her to take them down, not when each light was a reminder of her.

Soft music played as I used my key to slip in through the back door. I shed my cut, leaving me in just a t-shirt, jeans, and motorcycle boots. Then ran a hand over my hair, wishing I'd showered earlier.

"Natty?"

"In here!" she called from the kitchen.

I found her at the island counter cutting vegetables. Her hair was tossed up into a bun with loose pieces framing her face, which made her blow a puff of air to move it out of her eyes.

A smile crept along my face, unbidden. A piece of sunshine breaking through the storm in my chest.

"Feel like I haven't seen you since I got back." I settled across from her as she chopped celery.

She kept her gaze down. "Been busy."

The sound of the music filled the dead air, the house was stuffy and warm. Sweat rolled down her neck and gathered near her hairline.

Eyeing the kitchen window, which my mother always had open, I was curious at it being closed. In fact, all the windows were closed.

"How come you've shut all the windows?"

She kept chopping, keeping her gaze fixed on her dinner. "Sasha isn't here. You weren't either."

"So?" I wasn't following her logic.

With a sigh, she finally set down the knife, and in a deeper tone than what was natural for her, she mocked my words. "Caelum, first rule of not dying. Don't be a fucking idiot. Don't make it easy for anyone to break in."

Oh.

"Forgot about that." I rubbed my neck, feeling like shit.

"Mom hasn't been sleeping here for a while then? How long have you been living with this heat?" I had been on the road, and in the club… in between jobs, so I hadn't even slept here yet.

"It's fine." She turned away from me and dropped the celery into a large skillet.

It wasn't though. Natty was trying to stay safe, and she seemed more worried than normal.

"Does this have anything to do with why you won't step foot in the club?"

Her back was to me now, so I moved away from my spot and slowly came up behind her. I only hesitated for a single heartbeat before placing my hands on her hips and pulling her into my chest.

"What aren't you telling me?"

I was terrified she'd reject me, but her hand came over mine, warm and solid. I closed my eyes and pinned my forehead to her shoulder, breathing her in. I'd wanted this for so long, to cross this line with her. To move us from platonic friends, and proverbial foster siblings to this, where I could touch her and tell her how she seemed to exist in my bloodstream.

She had been my obsession for as long as I could remember, and this moment of finally being able to hold her without fear of her slipping through my fingers had been something I'd been waiting for.

She let out the smallest sigh and leaned into me. "It's nothing. I'm just trying to be smart, and I've been working, so I'm not here that often. When I am here, I want to be aware of things. You taught me that."

Her finger stroked my hand, and I pulled her closer, hugging her to my chest.

"I missed you."

She turned in my arms, and I reached forward to turn off the burner. Her green eyes were bright and full of something I'd seen a million times before but could never place.

"I missed you too. Are you going to tell me what he did this time?"

This again. She always asked and I always let her take some of my burden, but this time...as the new name began circulating, a deeper shame accompanied the truth I had to share.

"Not this time, Caelum. Please just let me keep it all inside this time," I whispered, pinning my forehead to hers.

Her hands came up, stroking my back. "Maybe we're at the age where you can show me in a different way, not using your words. You can pour that darkness into me, Silas. I can carry it. You can have me... in every way, you always have anyway."

Hope sparked in my chest along with a deep longing that nearly robbed me of breath.

"Are you...are you sure?" My mouth was so close to hers, so close I could smell the cinnamon on her breath, and the way she smelled like new books, sunshine...and gunpowder, "You've been shooting?"

She nodded. "I practice every day, just like you trained me."

My hands disappeared into her hair, towing her closer.

"And yes, Silas." She wet her lips, watching mine. "I am sure."

I pulled her chin up, not letting any more time slip by and pressed my mouth to hers. Her lips were soft, silky and perfect. She moved her mouth with mine, opening for me and twisting her hands up around my neck.

Our first kiss, and I couldn't help smiling into it. She laughed, and then her tongue came out, tracing my bottom lip.

"Give me the rest, Silas. I want all of it."

Her whispered demand went straight to my heart, like a hammer shattering all the rock around it.

I walked with her in my arms back to my room, laying her gently on the bed.

There, we shed our clothes, along with the casings of our souls, until we were completely exposed, openly surrendering to one another. I held her in my arms while I claimed fragments of her heart, fusing them with whatever was in her soul, and I absorbed it all into mine.

"Caelum," I rasped, kissing her deeply, knowing it was a vow just as much as a plea. My lips trailed over her skin, memorizing every taste.

She was mine, and after taking all her firsts and offering her mine, I knew she would be for always.

She asked, hours later, when we were tangled together in the sheets. "Tell me why you call me it."

"Call you what?"

I smiled, knowing what she was talking about but wanting to mess with her.

This truth, one I had realized couldn't be more true if I were to ink it into my very marrow.

She pushed at my shoulder. "You know what."

Caelum.

"You're the closest I'll ever get to heaven, to redemption or being found worthy. I look at you, and I see hope. Isn't that all heaven is? Hope, eternity spent in the one place we can't imagine living without? You're that for me. You're my religion, Natty. My place of worship and devotion. God wants nothing to do with me, but for some reason he still gave me you."

Tears gleamed in her eyes as she stared up at me, the string of lights reflecting her emotions.

"You *are* good, Silas. You think you're covered in all this darkness, but I see past that."

With a scoff, I shook my head. "You're the only one who ever did."

Her warm fingers found my jaw, pulling my face back toward her. "You only need one person, Silas. I live in a world made up of two people who care for me. That's enough. I don't need more than that."

Fuck, it was hard to argue with her when she placed our lives side by side. I was never abandoned the way she was. I had never been handed to a man for payment...thankfully my mom was there and stopped anyone from hurting her. But it still happened. She had no one but us. It made me pull her closer, pressing a kiss to her shoulder.

"I want you to feel safe around here, and even come to the club for certain things."

"Why? We've gone all this time without going...why change it now?"

She wasn't going to like this, but it was too late.

"I patched in..."

She shifted so she could see me better. "As a prospect?"

I shook my head. "Dirk made an exception...I'm an official member, I have a rank."

Natty was silent at that, so I was about to push on when she suddenly sat up. The sheets stayed in place as her golden brows dipped into her forehead.

"I want to see it...your cut..."

Something in me twisted uncomfortably. My head began shaking on instinct, but she shocked me by sliding out of bed, lightning fast, that sheet still wrapped around her.

I tried to move with her, but I fumbled out of bed, the remaining sheet catching around me, right as she walked back into the room with my leather cut.

She held it up with two hands, inspecting it.

"Wow...feels weird seeing it like this. Feeling it."

I watched as she stroked over the patches, and my name...and my gut sank as she began tracing the letters under it.

"What is this one...The Roman?"

My mouth wouldn't open. I couldn't tell her.

I wouldn't tell her.

Her head swiveled, her eyes pinning me down as she implored again, "What does it mean?"

"It's just a nickname. Everyone gets one."

Natty let her arms drop, as she ran her fingers over the patch one more time.

"When my property patch gets made up, I want that one on it. I want to be the property of The Roman."

My heart flipped in my chest; a thousand fireflies released at the sight of that smile.

"What makes you think I'd patch you?" I couldn't stop my smile as she sauntered back toward the bed.

"Novi omnia secreta tua."

A burst of laughter left my chest. "You know all my secrets, huh?"

Her lips pressed into my sternum while she nodded.

"When you wear it, come around the club with me...it will give you protection and let everyone know you belong to me." I pushed pieces of her hair back behind her perfect ears.

I could see she was still unsure, but after a few more lingering kisses, she relented.

"If your name is on my back, I'll go."

"Deal." We fell back into the sheets and began kissing until our bodies tumbled back into a rhythm that was becoming familiar to us, two waves crashing together, creating a riptide.

The club was noisy and completely packed.

I had never really noticed how many patched members there were, but every place I seemed to turn, there was someone new. Natty was next to me, wearing my patch with my name on her back...including my new nickname. The insignia of the reaper in the middle.

Her hair was braided, pulled over her shoulder, so everyone had a clear view of who she belonged to. Music blared, uncomfortably loud as people partied around us. Within the week since talking to Natty about doing this, she seemed to be comfortable with the idea but now that she was here, she seemed tense as if she was worried about someone finding her.

Maybe it was her mother she was concerned about.

I had to focus on our surroundings, so I just pulled her close and draped my arm over her to ensure she was safe. We joked with a few prospects our age, laughing and even playing pool. We ate some food, and Natty drank a diet coke while watching the mayhem unfold around us. She didn't seem bothered by it, or really surprised by anything that happened, yet she was still jumpy anytime someone shouted or came up behind us.

She was tucked into my side when there was suddenly a familiar face in the crowd, his smirk so annoyingly confident that I wanted to punch it right off his mouth.

"Big brother." Alec dipped his head, then his eyes traveled to Natty and his entire body froze. "Wow...so you two are," he stammered, as if he were truly astonished by the fact that we were together.

Natty gripped my hand. "You seem surprised that we are."

Alec's eyes narrowed, but his smile grew. "Not at all...I knew it was only a matter of time. I just assumed that perhaps you'd realize what a fucking psycho my brother is and not want to touch him with a..." He snapped his fingers, as if he couldn't remember.

Addressing me, he asked, "What's that saying again? Wouldn't touch it with a ten-foot cross, was that how it went?"

Natty's gaze slid up to mine, her brows folded in. "Is he drunk?"

Alec moved closer. "I see you're proudly wearing his new nickname on your back, he explain then how he got it?"

Fuck.

"Alec, just leave it—"

"Well, well, well," a new voice boomed from beside us, revealing Dirk and his inner circle. "It's Fable's sons...The Roman and The Wrangler."

Fear spiraled through my chest, reeling so fast that I was afraid I was going to throw up. I wanted to push Natty behind me, shield her from what she was about to learn but something else happened then. Something that didn't seem right. Dirk's eyes tapered, as if he just registered who was in front of him. He stepped closer to Natty, and she quickly stepped back.

They knew each other.

How the fuck did they know each other?

"I see you've patched a fawn." Dirk clicked his tongue, his fingers were out as if he were about to touch Natty's hair. His eyes gleamed with lust, an unnatural hunger reflecting there. Alec stepped to the left, blocking Dirk's view of Natty, as if he sensed it as well.

I spoke softly, keeping my eyes on Dirk. "Natus redi ad domum cum Alec et ibi mane, donec veniam ad te."

Natty, go back to the house with Alec and stay there until I come for you.

She didn't hesitate. She moved behind Alec and tugged his sleeve until he'd caught on to what I'd told her. He gave me one glance from over his shoulder before he followed her.

Dirk was about to say something as he trailed Natty's exit, but my mother suddenly appeared. She handed Dirk a beer, and then whispered something in his ear. His hands came down, grabbing her ass roughly and pulling her closer. I looked away because I refused to watch my mother get treated like that.

Pushing through the crowd, I headed back across the club, veering for an exit. My mother's hand was on my elbow moments later, pulling me into a small alcove.

"What in the hell do you think you're doing?"

I remained silent, watching as her dark eyes sharpened. Her arms came down over her chest, and she took two steps closer.

"Why did you bring Natty in here, and why the fuck did you give her a patch?"

"I joined this fucking club as a way to stay out of my father's."

She shook her head, her jaw moving as she lowered her voice.

"That is not what I'm questioning. I am asking why you gave Natty a patch, and why she was physically in this club?"

Why was she acting like she didn't know how I felt about Natty? She was the one who used to tell me to be careful and not to scare her off. She has always known how the two of us feel for each other.

"You always knew I was going to be with her."

My mother clicked her tongue. "Yes, fine. I knew that, but why did you bring her into the club?"

I was starting to get a headache. With a heavy sigh, I said, "Why don't you cut the shit, and just tell me what the fuck is going on?"

She paused, staring at the spot behind my head as if she was trying to decide the right way to say her peace.

"You can't afford to be distracted, Silas. You know I love Natty. I adore her, but the things Fable is asking you to do...don't make her a target, Son. Just focus on training. Use this club as a means to gain allies, and a wall of sorts to stand behind while you learn."

I didn't want to do this with her right now.

I was happy.

For the first time in such a long fucking time, I was waking up with a smile on my face. Natty's presence, in my bed, next to my heart each day, was like waking up with a clean soul. It was addictive, and something I refused to live without. I wasn't good enough to spare her from becoming a target.

"You need to let this go...for years you've pushed it, but you're pushing too hard." I went to move past her, but she gently grabbed me by the shoulders.

"Son, I love you. But I know your father, and whatever horrors you've seen so far is nothing compared to what he will turn you into. You have to keep your head clear, you only have one more year where he'll continue to take you, if that. Now that you're patched here with his permission, it may be Dirk who pulls the strings."

I scowled, feeling exasperated. "Then it's a good thing I have you pulling Dirk's, isn't it?"

Her face twisted with malice, and I instantly felt like shit. My mother did things with a purpose behind them. The very fact that she was with Dirk meant she likely had an end game; whatever it was, I trusted her with it.

"Dirk will only be distracted for a few months, maybe a year if I'm extra vigilant...he'll move on and he will notice what you're doing or what you aren't doing. Do not bring attention to Natty, and if you can help it, stay in the shadows, stay in the background for as long as you can."

That darkness appeared to seep back in. A web of evil I couldn't seem to outrun.

My mother seemed to know I was done. She moved to the side, keeping her arms folded in tight. I made my way out through the back and moved to the house, coming in through the garden. The first thing that set me on edge was the laughter.

I could hear Natty's sweet giggle from outside the gate, which meant she had the windows open. So, she felt safe with Alec...and confident enough that he'd keep her protected.

My boots padded softly in the dirt, soundlessly so neither of them knew I was near the window. I stopped short when I heard Alec speak up.

"Seriously though, you aren't the least bit curious where his new nickname came from?"

Natty let out an exaggerated sigh. I could see her through the window, balancing on her forearms, while Alec sat on a stool, both of them picking at a pan of French fries between them.

"He'll tell me eventually."

Alec scoffed, dipping his fry in sauce. "I don't think he will."

My gut twisted because he was right. I'd never tell her how I had earned the title, *The Roman.*

Natty paused, toying with the ketchup bottle.

"Do you really think it will make that big of a difference to me?"

My stupid brother leaned closer, touching the leather cut still on her shoulders. "You're wearing his patch, so yeah...figured you were the kind of person who would care about something like this."

"Fine, tell me." Natty gave up, stretching while letting go of the bottle and pushing her hands through her hair.

I could go in and interrupt, stop Alec from telling her, but some dark and twisted part of me wanted him to do the dirty work. I wanted to watch her face when she learned what sort of monster I truly was. I wanted her to face it and test that eternal sunshine that seemed to be setting in her chest.

Alec leaned in, arms folded on the counter.

I held my breath.

"Silas was given the nickname, The Roman, because of how he chose to torture our father's enemies. We were each given a choice...a gun to the back of the head, a hammer to the eye, a carving project with knives..."

Natty went very still, but softly asked, "Which did you choose?"

My brother seemed caught off guard by her question, but he answered just the same.

"Gun to the head. The only form that wasn't torture."

He wasn't explaining the other piece to that...how he'd put that gun to the head of our target's families. It was torture in the worst way imaginable.

"And Silas?" Natty asked, her voice so sweet and light, it felt like an angel was sitting there with a demon, discussing the loss of souls.

Alec's lips twisted to the side. "Silas chose to crucify his victims. He thought that up all on his own, and our father completely loved it."

Hating myself wasn't enough, I knew I didn't deserve Natty but like fuck was I going to share her with anyone else. I left my perch near the window and opened the back door, alerting them both to my presence.

Alec's gaze stayed on Natty as I entered, but hers immediately jumped to me, her gaze prodding and searching me for any damage. I saw relief flitter through her gaze when she realized I was fine.

"Get the fuck out," I said to my brother while slipping out of my boots and cut.

He laughed, shaking his head. "How about, 'thank you, Alec, for watching over my friend.'"

Natty watched the interaction between us, her eyes shrewd and calculating.

Turning toward him, I smiled showing my teeth. "That patch on her back make it seem like she's just my friend? She's mine, and I think you fucking know that. She has been since we were kids, and I won't thank you for doing something I knew you'd enjoy."

His gaze moved to Natty's briefly before he stood from his stool.

"Till next time, Artemis." He gave her a salute and then left through the front door.

"I hate that nickname." She exhaled and then gave me a smile. "You were by the window listening."

I kept my face expressionless as I flicked off the light for the kitchen and we moved into the bedroom. We still had the twin we were both squeezing on, but it was perfect. She was perfect.

She shut the door and slipped out of her clothes, pulling on one of my t-shirts.

"So tell me then."

"Tell you what?" I stretched out, wearing just my boxers, while I stared at the ceiling. The lights were off, so just the fragments of light from outside filtered in. She crawled in next to me, so I began stroking her back. I tried to imagine us in a different life. One where I'd snuck into Natty's window, her loving family asleep but protective of her. Her going to high school like a normal seventeen-year-old. Me following her through the halls, obsessed with her. Her dad warning me off. Her mom loving me, sneaking me dinner before Natty's dad came home from work.

I gave the ceiling a sad smile.

Her fingers brushed over my neck. "Tell me why you chose crucifixion. I know you, Silas. There's a reason you chose it."

"What if I chose it because I'm sick and twisted inside?"

She hummed, caressing my jaw. "Perhaps, but I think there's something else."

It was a waste of our time pretending, so I filled my chest with air and then let it all out, praying she'd still want me once I spilled my truth.

"I didn't want them to die. The gun to the head would have killed them faster, but they'd still die. The knives would have only been allowed if they'd passed from the blood loss. Every option my father presented ended in death. I thought of something, anything that would be so outrageous that my father would leave it alone. I couldn't imagine how badly it would hurt to be nailed to a piece of wood, but in the end, after I came back and let them down, they'd still have their lives. I should have known my father better...after the first few that I'd done, he'd patted me on the back. I walked away, setting a timer on my phone for when I could circle back, but he called me back to finish it."

It was a cruel joke.

A fucking test.

But Fable had been so thrilled, so fucking excited.

"My father loved the new tactic so much, he started giving me more people to target. I began crucifying my father's enemies, and in doing so, I became The Roman."

A tear from Natty's cheek slid against my chest as she whispered, "Tantum tenebris."

So much darkness.

I felt my own eyes begin to burn as the reality of how my life had changed, set in. How I'd been forced to become a murderer. An executioner. Now I had this perfectly pure person next to me, and she was seeing all of it. One day there would be someone better, someone whole, and they would show her that this life we lived was fucked up.

Her body moved closer, her hand wrapping around mine until she was pulling it up to her lips. "You belong to me, Silas Silva. No matter what you do, no matter how he tries to indoctrinate you with his darkness, at your core, you're pure light. I'll be here reminding you of that for as long as you want me."

A tear slipped down the side of my face as I tried to swallow past the lump in my throat.

Eventually I was able to say the only thing I could think of.

"Forever, Caelum. I'll want you for that long, and then longer when the devil demands my soul."

She kissed my chest. "He can't have what belongs to me."

ELEVEN
NATTY
PRESENT

SOMETHING HAD CHANGED.

It was as if the air in the room had suddenly been sucked out...it started with the low rumble outside, which had me quickly sitting up in bed and searching for the source. Alec was asleep next to me, his hand still cuffed to mine.

For what felt like the thousandth time, I tried squeezing out of the metal restraint. My wrist was raw and red from how many times I'd tried to slide it free; it wasn't budging but with him asleep, I had to keep trying. I had to do something...maybe I could try suffocating him, or hit him so hard in the dick, he couldn't breathe.

But it all still left me with the issue of being chained to a man that easily weighed two hundred pounds with his height and all that stacked muscle. There was no universe in which I could drag his dead weight around with me.

The rumble came again, this time there were shouts going off outside. Then gunfire.

Hope soared as I searched the clouded windows for any indication on what might be happening, because opposition could mean a rescue. Alec finally woke up and realized his little hiding place was under attack, so he pulled me off the bed and briskly walked to the door. I trailed him, still in just his shirt, nothing under it, my feet bare and my hair wild.

"What the fuck is happening?" he bellowed as he thundered down the hall. With his bare chest, his boxers and all the ink on his skin, he looked like an angry god. It was early enough that light flooded the halls and the dining room.

The rumble of motorcycles echoed louder than before outside, which had me turning toward the windows but Alec yanked me into the kitchen.

"Fuck, who's attacking us?" Alec murmured under his breath, scanning the counters for something. I saw Rachel huddling down on the ground, near the pantry with a wild look of terror in her eyes. She looked up as we entered, and then slowly stood.

"It started ten minutes ago, but Fable isn't here. I have no idea where he went...he was just gone when I woke up, and now we're being attacked."

Alec slammed another drawer closed, cursing. I was close enough that I could slide a knife free from the drying rack. I had to be slow about it, as to not alert him. I waited until his head was turned and reached, but I must have overestimated his peripheral vision because once he realized what I was doing, he pulled me close, so my free hand was now locked in his.

"We need to get out of here."

I wouldn't slip through the cracks and be held hostage again. I couldn't. Whoever was attacking had to mean my freedom. Somehow, someway.

I tried to push against Alec again. "Let me go!"

He held tighter.

"Rachel, help me. Please, we can take him if we both just..." Tears burned my eyes, and I must have looked wild and unhinged because I began tearing at Alec's skin, scratching and marking as I screamed for him to let me go.

Rachel moved toward me, but with one look from Alec, she closed her eyes and began rubbing at her wrists until her back was against the wall. She obviously had endured some sort of torture or abuse. My heart was a wounded, panicked thing. I knew she was struggling but I needed her help. I was desperate for her to use this one chance to free us both.

A loud scream came from outside the exterior kitchen door, accompanied by a gunshot. I jolted with how close it came, making my footing slip and my back land into Alec's chest. It allowed him to get a more secure hold on my hips, but before I could even try to start fighting him again, the door slammed open.

Brightness flooded the kitchen; I couldn't make out who had stepped in, but I heard their voice, and it was a familiar echo, a soothing, dark caress over my heart.

"Caelum," was rasped and broken, like he'd finally found the one thing on this planet that was precious to him.

You could only fight monsters with bigger monsters; my heart belonged to the worst one I knew of.

I gave a tiny sob as Alec pulled me backward, making my feet slip out from under me, but my eyes had finally adjusted as they landed on Silas. He was tall and so perfectly outlined by all the darkness in his heart that I nearly choked on my tears. He wore his leather cut, his hair a slash of black across his forehead, and his arms were swathed in dusky tattoos, all the way down to his fingers.

Trapped pieces of the moon stared back at me, a flicker of relief glimmering in them. Time seemed to stand still as we stared at each other, and I wondered what he saw as I stood in his brother's arms, wearing his shirt. How I must look with my hair wild, frizzed and my bare legs on display as Alec tugged me farther into the kitchen. From Silas's expression, it wasn't good, and it worsened when his gaze dropped to my hand.

It was as though all the sound and sight had suddenly stilled and bled into one vibrant dark stroke of black. His eyes narrowed, and his jaw clenched so tight I thought it might break. He took a measured step forward, the gun dangling in his right hand, then it was tossed to the counter with a loud echo. Which told me that Silas had a much more violent punishment in mind for Alec than a simple bullet to the head.

"Brother, please do explain to me why the *fuck* you've cuffed yourself to my wife?"

Alec froze behind me.

I heard his small intake of breath and noticed mine had stalled in my chest too. Silas had never claimed me in such a manner, especially not in front of anyone. A fluttering sensation mixed with relief swelled inside me, even as I was being held by a monster. Even as I knew this was dangerous. Silas had swept it all away with one word.

Wife.

"Silas," Alec stammered while we both watched the man known as The Roman procure a meat cleaver that was magnetized against the back wall.

"I'm going to allow you the chance to choose, Alec. I'll either cut high enough so that tattoo of Artemis, which we all know you got for Natty, is removed from your body completely. Or you can lose your hand. Personally, I think you should choose the arm, make a big statement since that's what you originally intended by getting this fucking piece, right?"

There was shuffling from near the back, and Rachel darted out of the room through the open door. I watched her go, wondering if Killian would find her.

Alec was slightly shaking, and I wasn't even sure he noticed that his hold on me had gone slack. I left his arms and moved as far from him as possible, while our hands remained connected by the cuffs. I saw him eye the firearm that had been discarded on the counter, just a few feet from where I was standing.

There were veins protruding from Alec's neck and forehead as he watched his brother slowly move around the counter in our direction. "Silas, let me expl—"

"Choose!" Silas roared his eyes going wide, his lips twisting angrily. "Your hand or the tattoo you had created because of your obsession with my fucking wife!"

"I didn't know you were married," Alec stammered back.

Silas laughed. "You knew she was mine, Alec. She's been mine from the first moment you saw her. Don't pretend you didn't know. Hand or arm?"

"Just fucking wait, let me talk to you about what Dad is doing. I can help you." Alec tried to get Silas's attention, but he was already in front of me, blocking my view, facing his brother. Nowhere for him to go.

"I'm losing my patience and the longer you're cuffed to my wife, the more violent my thoughts are becoming."

"Just wait...Silas, no...Fuckkkkkkkkk."

Alec's words faded into a soul-shattering scream along with a loud thump and the sound of metal clattering to the counter.

There was so much screaming.

I knew Silas had removed Alec's hand, and with there no longer being any resistance when I tried to pull my arm, I covered my chest and took a few steps back. Alec continued to scream obscenities behind me, but I refused to look.

I heard Silas speak over the yelling, "Do not ever touch her again. She does not belong to you; she is not your toy, and she certainly will never be your girl. Next time, I'll take your heart."

Out of the corner of my eye, I saw Alec holding his bleeding stub to his side, seething in anger.

"Fuck you, brother."

I felt numb as I watched, completely detached from the moment. I knew Alec had lost a hand, and that should have bothered me, but all I could think about was leaving this house. I wanted to go home, back to my room in the Stone Riders club. I wanted to wake up, have this all be a dream, and go back to how things were.

Silas tossed something and bent down into a squat in front of Alec. With his finger, he pushed against the tattoo on Alec's arm, making him seethe in pain. "She was never a huntress or a goddess. She was none of those things."

Alec tried to stand; his teeth were clenched so tight, and he was starting to grow pale. His gaze clashed with mine and I wanted to cry. Not for him, or what had been done to him, but because of the friend he used to be to me.

"She is to me."

Silas turned toward me, his focus on where I was watching. I couldn't seem to tear my eyes from Alec or push out what he'd said. I wanted to scream all the pain that was locked in my chest. All the agony and anger, but nothing would come out. Instead, Silas stood and his hand came to my hip, guiding me away from the scene and toward the open door.

Giving one last glance to his brother, he said. "You locked her up, thinking you could make her love you…but you can't force the sun to shine, just like you can't stop it from setting. I hope betraying her trust was worth it, Alec."

A void seemed to catch me on the cusp of his words, and the word betrayal seemed to stick around my heart like a thick stone. Swinging, hitting my sternum with each pass.

Alec had betrayed me. He'd hurt me.

Silas pulled my hand, and I realized we were walking out of the house.

We stepped outside, my bare feet pressed into the dirt right as Silas pulled me into his arms, bridal style. I winced as the light hit my eyes, my days inside making it nearly impossible not to recoil. Instead, I allowed my head to be tucked under Silas's chin as he walked us to safety.

I felt dazed as we hiked, the bright sun making my eyes slide shut, but my heart hadn't stopped hammering in my chest. I had no concept of time, of how long we walked, only the loud pounding in my head that seemed to go on and on and on.

"You need to wear these."

I was set back on my feet, which had my eyes cracking. Suddenly a pair of sunglasses landed on my face, and I saw Silas standing next to his bike, holding his leather jacket out to me. I lifted my hand to accept it and saw the blood-stained manacle dangling from my wrist. My stomach tilted, but I pushed past it so that I could get the hell away from this place.

Slipping into his jacket, there was a comfort that came seeing his name cover my chest. His coat was too big for me, so it covered the oversized t-shirt I was in, and most of my upper thighs. I inspected the bike with a recoil tightening in my chest.

I did not want to get on that. As often as I had hoped for Silas to come for me, now with the bloodied cuff, and not wearing any pants, I just wanted to curl into one of the bushes and sleep until the pain around this entire situation lessened.

Kidnapped.

I'd been abducted by someone I thought cared for me.

Someone I once sought as a refuge.

"We're going to ride like we used to, Caelum...come crawl into my lap." That deep voice was a rope catching around my frayed mind, pulling me back to shore.

He straddled the leather seat of his bike, one hand going to the handle, as the other was held out for me. I approached him, my hands still shaking. My mind going back to bullfrogs and peaceful creeks. I wanted to go back in time and erase.

Erase.

Erase.

Erase.

"He refused to give you clothes?"

My focus went back to those eyes that were foundation stones for me, and nodded. My voice would get caught around the explanation of the dried cum currently coating my stomach.

Silas met my gaze. "You're safe now, that's all that matters."

Was it? I'd been hiding behind the walls of another club for two years, waiting for Silas to come and get me and I still didn't feel safe. I felt hunted.

I felt disposable.

I felt forgotten.

"We have to go." Silas flicked a quick look over my shoulder and I knew he was right. This rescue is what I had been waiting for but my limbs locked up.

He watched, wary and seemingly confused, until finally he reached for me and pulled me over his lap.

I adjusted so my legs went around his waist, my hands tight around his neck. Our faces were inches apart, my hair blew in the wind, acting as a shield as Silas held me to him, his gaze lowering to my lips.

"You called me your wife," I whispered, my voice shaking.

The space next to his eyes crinkled as he pushed a piece of my hair behind my ear. "It's still true, isn't it?"

Was it?

I didn't answer him as I buried my face in his shoulder and closed my eyes.

Silas lifted his other hand and started the bike. The familiar roar soared through me like a set of wings, lifting my hopes as I wrapped my body around his and he sped off, leaving my captors and the cage I was kept in.

We rode for only half an hour or so before Silas pulled off near a gas station. The air was still crisp and the sky still a stark blue overhead, but I remained oblivious to what day or time it actually was.

"We need to get you some clothes. It's three hours back to Rose Ridge."

Silas helped me off his lap, the separation already feeling too cold, too far. Fears that he'd walk away again slithered into my chest, creating a poisonous condition.

"Pyle is closer, just take me there, we'll be protected by your club."

There was a calculated look in his gaze, but there was also fear. Rejection stabbed at my gut, a reminder that two years had divided us and perhaps he had a new life now. Maybe he had a person back there waiting for him.

Silas loved me in his own way, and was protective of me but he'd also stayed away from me for two years. The distance spoke louder to me than any attempts at safe keeping.

I was standing there, next to Silas's bike while his jaw worked back and forth, and I knew what he was thinking. I knew it so well because it was the only thing he had been doing for the past two years.

Running. From me.

My emotions were raw; my body chilled and exhausted. I wouldn't survive his rejection, so I just turned away, clutching the leather of his jacket.

"I can't go in like this." I looked down at my bare feet, wishing I had grabbed the go-bag that Rachel had prepared for me.

"I'm not leaving you alone out here."

A large semi-truck drove by, causing a gust of wind to blow my hair up and ruffle Silas's. We stared at one another, his glowing blue eyes that always felt so unnatural and perfect. He was trying to work something out, that or wait me out.

"Didn't you have people with you when you invaded Fable's safe house?"

Silas raised a dark brow at me in question.

"Your club...or the Stone Riders, did anyone help you?"

His shoulders lifted right as his phone rang.

"You didn't tell whoever it was that you were leaving?" I asked, completely exasperated.

"Didn't realize I had to." He lifted the phone to his ear. He began listing off directions to the gas station we were at and then within the next few minutes, two bikes rumbled down the road, followed by a double cab pick-up.

Wes Ryan and Killian Quinn slowed their bikes until they stopped in front of us. My heart lifted at the sight of them, but it nearly shot through my chest as I registered who was in the truck. Penelope's dark hair was visible through the window, and I launched myself forward as Jameson parked.

Pen opened her door, jumped down and began running at me. Tears streamed down her beautiful face as she hiccupped and pulled me into a tight hug.

"I'm so sorry. It was all my fault," she murmured into my hair.

I held her so tight I worried I might break her. I'd never had any friends outside of Sasha and Silas that cared enough about me that they'd cry over my absence or go with their husband to pick me up during a raid.

"No, it wasn't. Don't put that on yourself, Pen. I got that text and left the club because of it."

We separated, both of us crying as the men began talking to each other behind us.

"You came with Jameson?"

Penelope nodded. She had hair dark as a raven, it was long, nearly brushing her waist. With blue eyes, perpetually pink lips and thick lashes, she was a stunning bombshell. I'd met her when she'd arrived with Jameson King's previous club, the Chaos Kings. She was pregnant when we met, which reminded me.

"Where's Connor?"

Surely, they didn't bring him with them.

Pen smiled. "Staying with Callie and Laura. They wanted to be here, but everyone agreed that it was too dangerous."

"They're right; I can't believe you even came." I flicked a quick gaze over to Silas who was watching me.

Penelope did the same, her gaze landing on her husband. "We didn't know what sort of condition you'd be in. I suggested having a vehicle you could travel back in that didn't put you at the mercy of the weather or being on the back of a bike."

My best friend was a genius.

Her happy countenance fell when she saw the handcuff still connected to my wrist.

"Oh my god, Natty."

Her whisper might as well have been a thunder crack. I wanted to go home. To my bed, my clothes, my safe room, protected by a club I knew. Besides, I already knew Silas wasn't going to take me to Pyle. Fuck, he likely was never planning to come back and claim me in the first place.

"Let's go home. I don't want to be here anymore," I muttered, pulling on Penelope's arm.

She was about to guide me back when suddenly someone scooped me off the ground. I looked up and saw Silas, his expression grim and miserable as he carried me to the truck.

"You aren't walking over all this asphalt and loose gravel without shoes." His voice was all grit, holding just a thread of fear. His arms were so familiar and yet they weren't because he'd opened them and let me go.

"Are you coming back with us?" I didn't want to ask it for fear of his answer, but it would drive me crazy not knowing the whole way back.

Once we got to the truck, he set me in the back seat, letting his hands linger on my waist.

"I'll be right behind you."

With the click of the door, I watched through the glass as he stayed put, watching me. I wanted to scream that I wanted him beside me, not behind me but I was too tired. Emotions cracked and bruised my insides, forcing me into a tiny ball on the seat. I felt Penelope crawl in on the other side and her soothing voice tell me it was okay. My hair was moved from my face, but all I felt were the tears still streaming down my face.

TWELVE
NATTY
AGE NINETEEN

THE WARM AIR BLEW THROUGH THE FARMER'S MARKET, RUSTLING THE SMALL canopy I'd sewn for Sasha's cart. Each week there was a line formed in front of our little spot, customers waiting to buy her fresh produce, eggs, herbs and even honey.

I had finally started accepting a wage from her because she could easily afford it. Every week she'd completely sell out of everything she'd brought that day, and often had to even turn people away. It was a sweltering day in June when we heard the rumble of engines coming down the main road.

With Silas gone again, this time I had no idea what he was doing with his father; he was just gone again and every time he returned to me, he was a little more jaded and shattered. I felt like he was slowly slipping away from me, but I had no idea how to stop it. I'd even asked Sasha if she could talk to him about stopping his visits, or whatever the fuck they were, but she only hummed, listening but never agreeing.

"My son's business is his own. I won't interfere with what he's trying to do." That was the answer she'd give me, and while I completely bristled at her lack of help, I did understand it.

The group of bikers making their way toward us all slowed as they turned into the small park where our cart, along with several others, was set up. People were milling about, but had frozen at the fast approach of at least fifteen Death Raiders.

My stomach clenched tightly as I watched them all park and joke while they slid off their seats. Dirk, the president, was the first bike in line, next to him was his vice president, and then down the line it went with his captains. My back felt exposed in the spaghetti strap dress I wore, without my property patch. Sasha had removed hers as well because of how hot the cart would get.

She quickly dug hers out from under the counter and slipped it on with shaky fingers. I hadn't brought mine with me and felt mortified and naked without it.

"Go into the back, Natty," Sasha ordered harshly, under her breath. Dirk and his men made their way toward the cart, but there was still a line of customers waiting to be helped.

Hesitating, I walked closer and muttered, "I can help. I'll just keep my head down and keep assisting while Dirk talks to you. He's here for you."

Her hard gaze was pure ice as she snapped back, "Get in the back."

I did as she said, scurrying through the curtain that covered our crates and extra inventory and took a seat against the wall. The heat nearly suffocated me, but I just endured it, waiting until Sasha told me it was safe to come out.

There was a crack in the curtain allowing me to watch the front, so I was able to track Dirk as he cut the long line of customers Sasha had, effectively ruining her image and reputation with them. My insides bristled with the need to go out and apologize to them. They'd been waiting in the heat all this time, only to be found at the mercy of the Death Raiders.

Several customers already walked away, giving a long glance at the leather cuts and glancing over at the bikes. Sasha had never once broadcasted her affiliation to the club, but now there was a good chance she'd have no returning customers thanks to it.

"Close up. Want you back at the club, we have some shit going down today."

Sasha smiled up at him, but I could see the lingering tension in her face. The forced smile, the radiating anger. "What stuff? Should I be worried?"

Dirk pulled her forward by the front of her tank and kissed her hard. "No, baby, not worried, but I need my playthings where I can find them. Which reminds me." Dirk looked over Sasha's shoulder as if he were looking for something…or someone.

"Where's that pretty assistant of yours?"

My breathing stopped, my head jerked up, and my fingers shook. Sasha started toying with Dirk's cut, leaning over the counter to kiss him, but he pushed her back.

"You always fuckin' do this. You think I don't know what you're doing? Where the fuck is she?" He pushed hard at Sasha's shoulders until she was falling back a step.

Sasha's fingers trembled as she pushed some of her hair back. "Not here. Bitch left me stranded today."

Shit. Should I run? What if they saw me from the back?

Dirk gave one last glance around the cart, before taking a step back.

"Pack it up, get back to the club. I wanna fuck you before I have to deal with this shit tonight."

Sasha nodded, but didn't let out a breath until Dirk walked away. She hung up her closed sign, which was a fancy piece of wood I had crafted for her and attached twine to. It dangled over the counter, while the few remaining customers groaned in protest. Sasha took a crate, walked out to the line and began handing out what she had left for free to everyone who was still in her line.

Once she was back, and her crates were mostly empty, she began storing what was left.

Sasha's movements were hurried, as panic filtered into every single gesture. It wasn't until the Death Raiders left that I finally emerged to help her.

She spoke low but swift. "I need you to stay out of sight. Especially tonight. I have no idea what he's planning, but I want you safe. Do you have a hiding place, somewhere only Silas knows?"

I shook my head. "Just his room…or the pond, but other people know about the pond; some people have started fishing there."

"When we get in the Jeep, braid your hair back. Put on a hat and wear sunglasses. We need to hide as much of you as we can. I'll pull around the back end of the club. You'll have to walk back to the house, that way no one sees you from the club."

Panic surged forward in my chest. I wanted Silas.

I nodded, packing crates and salvaging the eggs and produce that would wilt from the heat.

There was another rumble of a bike engine that had my hands freezing and Sasha's head snapping up. Another Death Raider was slowly making his way toward our cart, but this time he stopped near the back and when I realized who it was, I dropped what I was holding and sprinted out the back.

Silas lowered his kickstand and unclasped his helmet right as I made it to him. His arms opened and he pulled me into his lap, and then his lips were on mine. His hand moved into my hair, over my ear and then he smiled against my lips.

We broke apart with heaving breaths. "What's wrong?"

I tucked back a loose hair of his and searched his face for any bruises. He always had bruises when he came back.

"Just missed you."

Sasha chose that moment to come out through the back, her arms crossed over her chest.

"That's not it. Dirk is planning something, asked me to close early and get back to the club. She needs to ride back with you, and you need to make sure no one sees her. Then once she's safe in the house, you need to get to the club."

Silas was trying to work it out, I could tell by the way his dark brows dipped and his eyes narrowed on his mother. He wouldn't ask here though; he'd get me on his bike and we'd be off.

"She done here?"

I was about to protest but Sasha nodded. "Yeah, I'm heading out too."

He grabbed his helmet and slid it over my head, clasping it under my chin.

"What about you, you need to protect that beautiful brain of yours. It's my favorite thing about you, my dark and brooding prince."

He smirked, just like he always did, then he adjusted me in his lap, so

I was straddling his hips, my chest molded to his chest, his lips at my ear.

"Anything happens to you, Caelum, and my brain won't matter. Nor my heart, or anything else that allows me to breathe. It's you or it's nothing, my love."

I kissed him, slow and with filthy promises of what was to come later that night, and once we broke apart, I wrapped my arms around his neck while he started his bike. The way we rode was illegal, but nothing Silas did obeyed the laws of this land, so me riding in his lap was nothing. I remained tucked to his chest as we rode down the road. A short distance to the club, but since we were cutting through the back, we had to go slower.

Silas placed his cut over my shoulders and held my hand as we walked back to the house, cutting through the garden. The sun was starting to set, the heat still as thick as ever. Last summer, Silas had found a way to buy air conditioning for the house, so I could keep the windows locked without overheating.

The moment we stepped inside, the cool air hit me, and I sighed with relief while peeling off layers.

"What are you doing?" Silas asked, tracking every move that I made. I wasn't normally this brazen or bold in his mother's house. She'd been here less and less, and I'd gotten used to being alone. My dress fell to the floor in the middle of the living room, leaving me in a bra and thong.

Bending my arms to unclasp my bra, I smirked at him.

"I'm showering. Wanna join?"

He shifted on his feet, glancing at the windows briefly. The shades were open, but none of the members ever walked over here, or bothered with this old house.

He was taking too long to answer, so I let the bra drop and lightly traced a line up my stomach and over my nipples.

"I'm supposed to head over there...I don't want to make anyone come looking for me, which would bring them here."

I stepped forward, until I was directly in front of him, feeling my heart burst with tiny sparks. "Okay. I'll see you later then."

I pulled his hand up and kissed along his knuckles. He'd gotten new ink along a few of them. It seemed each and every time I saw him, he had more and more added to his skin. I loved them, and more than that, each time he got back I'd make a game of tracing the new ones with my mouth.

"Fuck it, if they come looking, I'll remove their ability to see."

The hand I was holding moved into my hair as he pulled me into him, his lips landed on mine, demanding and desperate.

Moving with his mouth, our tongues met, hot and ready as we both moaned. My fingers dug under his shirt, skirting layer after layer of muscle as I moved up his torso. We broke apart only long enough for his shirt to be pulled up over his head and then his mouth was on mine again.

We moved backward as Silas pulled me, his hands on my hips and mine were up around his neck. Our kissing turned urgent as we made our way into the kitchen. He muttered something filthy against my mouth, and then I was being yanked up, my ass roughly settled on the surface of the island.

Silas settled between my spread legs while keeping his mouth secured to mine, until his hands moved to my hips again. He traced the fabric of my thong while smiling against my lips.

"I'd like to ruin this." He snapped the strap at my hip.

I returned the smile, my mouth still desperate for him. Spreading my legs farther, I pulled away and said, "I think you already did…"

His eyes dropped to the apex of my thighs with a feral gleam. I knew he wouldn't be able to resist, so I leaned back on my elbows so he had a better view of my heavy breasts, puckered nipples and thong.

His mouth came down over my belly button, his tongue paving a path down to the top of my mound. He let loose a moan as soon as he encountered the fabric covering me.

"Hold very still, Caelum." He pressed a gentle kiss right over my covered center, which was soaked completely through. His smile and appreciative groan went straight through me.

I couldn't see his hands, or where they'd disappeared to until suddenly a knife was produced. It was more like a hunting knife with a serrated edge, broad tip and the handle was black, with the grim reaper's scythe etched into it.

My mouth parted as the cool metal touched my thigh. Perhaps it'd been just too many weeks without his touch, but seeing the hunger light up his eyes as he stared at my center had me ravenous.

I wanted to move, shift and push into the tip to feel him draw something out of me. I'd always loved the way he fucked me, with ruthless abandon and complete and utter worship, but adding in this element of danger had me craving more.

"You're shaking," he rasped, slowly dragging the tip of the knife along my thigh, until it was gliding right at the edge of my thong. "I know it's not from fear, Caelum…no this is something much worse. You think you want me to push against this perfect skin, draw blood and swipe it up with my tongue?"

A moan erupted from my chest as I dared to lift my hips the smallest bit.

With a hiss, his free hand held my opposite hip in place. "You've missed me."

"More than you fucking realize," I choked out; a gasp caught in my chest as desire writhed low in my belly.

His tongue clicked as the blade cut through the fabric at my hips as easily as warm butter. Silas gently pulled the black fabric away, exposing my slick pussy to the cool air of the room.

"You know I'd rather use this knife to carve out my own heart than mark a single piece of you. So you'll have to stash that little fantasy away because I'll never be able to take the look of blood on your skin. Not while there's a heart beating in my chest and air expanding in my lungs."

Now that I knew he wasn't going to use that knife against my skin, I lifted my hips in a silent plea for him to fuck me.

"I will, however, let you play with my knife." His voice dropped into a husky promise as he flipped the knife, the blade pointing at the ceiling as the butt of his handle was used to gently pry my pussy lips apart.

"Oh my god." My head fell back as Silas used the smooth metal of the handle in the most prolific way.

"I think I might decide to keep this knife after all. It was a gift for you, but seeing it slide against your greedy pussy has me reconsidering."

I lifted my head to watch as he used the tip, bobbing up and down in the air as he adjusted and moved the end along my slit. I was soaked, near combusting, as the harsh edge hit my clit. Warm fingers held the handle firmly in place while Silas hovered above me.

"Show me how desperate you are, beautiful. Can you come from simply fucking this knife?"

Another deep moan left my chest as I began to shake. The sounds in the room were obnoxious as I moved my hips with abandon, fucking the butt end of his knife with recklessness. Wetness seeped down my ass and onto the counter as Silas watched me lose myself to the sensation of this thick object being used to get me off.

My breathing increased, heat crawling up my neck and face, not from shame but exertion.

"Silas," I gasped, locking eyes with him.

He smirked down at the scene, and I knew how crude it must look. The tip of his serrated edge was sticking up in the air while the handle of his lethal knife remained in my cunt. Soaked and slippery from my arousal. I could also feel those firm fingers begin dipping farther into my pussy, while the metal remained against my clit.

It was too much.

"Fuck. Shit." I shuddered as I came against the knife. My entire body felt wired and primed for him to take more, provide more. It was a powerful orgasm, but I'd had better from him. I needed him.

"I need you."

He slowly pulled the knife up, and while maintaining eye contact with me, his pink tongue came out, licking every inch of the handle clean.

"So fucking sweet."

This man would be the end of me. I lie there watching as a familiar jealousy overcame him and he tossed the knife to the side, and then gripped my hips in a vicious hold.

I was lifted, my pussy pulled closer while he descended and began devouring me. My legs were up over his shoulders, my back barely on the counter as he feasted, lapping at all the remaining arousal. He moaned so deep it reverberated against my clit, making me gasp in response.

His tongue divided my puffy lips, sinking deep into my center. It was all-consuming, further soaking me and prepping me for the stretch of his thick cock that would be coming after. I loved it and writhed against him. He'd be greedy enough to wrench another orgasm out of me, and I had a feeling that was his plan as his tongue slowly swirled over my clit.

It felt so good, my heels dug into his shoulders. I was mumbling something incoherent. I didn't want another orgasm unless it was on his cock, so I tried to resist, but it only encouraged him to use that tongue slower, and more languid, drawing out my pleasure until I couldn't hold it in any longer.

I screamed, and then I was being lowered while still moaning my second wave of complete bliss when Silas pushed three fingers deep into me, moving them rapidly.

Wetness suddenly squirted out of me, and Silas groaned his pleasure.

I hadn't done that except for one other time when we were in the shower. He groaned deeply while pulling me off the counter. I must have missed when he lowered his jeans and boxers because he was naked against me as he carried me to one of the kitchen chairs.

He sat down and pulled me into his lap. I was still breathing hard, while he lined himself up with my center. My hands were on his shoulders, and then he was filling me with his fat, deliciously long cock.

"Silas." It was a prayer, as I begged him for more. I'd already come twice, squirted, and now I was a filthy creature, desperate for him to fuck me raw.

His lips found mine as he moved under me, rotating his hips up, but the movement had my head falling back.

"Forgot what it's like for you. Such a tight fucking fit, and all mine," he rasped, his face tucking into my neck as I rolled my hips against him.

The wood of the chair creaked as I began taking control, fucking him as hard and as earnestly as I desired. Our eyes locked, until he picked up one of my breasts, and with slow movements, he licked my nipple.

It had me clenching around him. "More."

He complied with a smile, moving to my other breast. Lapping slowly while I held onto the back of the chair and fucked him as hard as I could. His mother could still come in at any moment; we both knew this, but we were too far gone to care. She usually gave us a wide berth after Silas got back from a trip because we were insatiable for each other.

Still tucked into his small room on that twin bed, not caring at all that we'd once shared the space as kids. Now when we hit the bed, our clothes were shed, our mouths fused, and he was quick to slide his cock inside me.

"I need to fuck you harder," Silas muttered into my neck, while picking me up.

I was deposited on the table, on my back. He liked to fuck me like this because he liked watching my tits bounce.

He slammed home, and I watched as every thick inch somehow made its way back inside me. Slick and veiny, his cock was perfect. I lifted my hips as he pulled out and drove in again, harder this time.

I jolted in place, my tits indeed bouncing as he nearly growled in appreciation. This was what I loved. When he lost himself to his lust, his carnal side, and for all his talk of ensuring I never got hurt, he didn't seem to realize how hard he held me, or how firm he thrust his engorged cock into me. I loved it. Even as the table wobbled under us, and I shuddered with another orgasm. My fucking third in a goddamn row.

I was panting like I hadn't had water in ages while he cursed and lifted my leg to get a deeper angle.

"So fucking deep. You grip me so well."

I loved how he talked when he lost all sense.

He drove harder, which made the table slam against the wall with a thud and then another as he pulled out and filled me once more.

"Want to make you my fucking wife, and do this every day for the rest of my life."

I was still coming down from my high when I processed what he'd said, but it hit like gold infusing my limbs. I couldn't speak, I could barely even breathe as he finally came with a shout and shaking limbs.

Once he finally pulled out, he watched as his release began dripping out of me. He stared transfixed, just like he always did.

Sometimes he'd use it as a way to mark me. Or he'd pull it out and let me lick it from his fingers. Once he just spread my legs and instantly hardened again, shoving himself back into me until he came again.

I didn't care what he did as long as he continued to do it with me, but this time my mind was drawn to what he'd said.

We both needed to catch our breath as we came back down from the high. He helped me off the table and turned to find a rag for the mess I'd made when he'd made me squirt.

I watched as his back shifted with all that muscle, and then I just blurted.

"Did you mean it?"

He stopped mid wipe, slowly standing, still naked and sweaty. His longer hair fell across his forehead and my fingers shifted to push it back.

"Mean what?"

For some reason I was nervous saying it, but I swallowed and said, "Making me your wife."

He stepped forward; his mouth parted right as a hard knock landed against the front door.

Instinctively, I covered my breasts with my arms, but I was in the kitchen, out of sight of anyone who would be on the porch.

Silas narrowed his focus on me, standing close enough to hold my hip.

"Go take your shower, baby. I'll stay until you're out and I know you're safe."

I knew better than to draw this out; he had to get back to the club.

With a dip of my head, I moved toward the hall, but before I'd entered the bathroom, Silas called at my back.

"I've wanted to make you my wife since I was seven years old. Whenever you're ready to carry my last name, you're welcome to have it."

I paused, smiling back at him. The knock came again from the front door and before I could reply, he was turning around to pull on his clothes. I dipped into the bathroom and shut the door while hope blossomed in my chest.

Hours slipped by while I remained huddled in Sasha's closet. It had the wardrobe her and Silas would hide in all those years ago. It was big enough for me to lay down in when I took out all her guns and ammo.

Half an hour after my shower, I heard the first signs that something might be off. More members than normal were pulling in, drinking, yelling and getting worked up. There were too many, and if any of them decided to check out who was in the house, there would be no hope for me. So, I'd taken my phone, my sandwich and two bottles of water with me and pulled the wardrobe doors shut.

Sometime after that it sounded as though the entire sky had fallen on us as the rumble of even more engines rattled the windows and the very foundation of the house. There were shouts and a few gun shots. I had no idea what was going on, but I knew it wasn't good. My fingers trembled as my nerves tangled into a ball of anxiety in the pit of my stomach.

I'd texted Silas, but he hadn't even seen the message. Same with Sasha.

At some point I fell asleep and when I woke, it was still dark outside, but Silas had finally texted me.

Silas: Where are you?

I shot back a text explaining the wardrobe and within minutes he was knocking against the door.

Sliding out from behind the space, I let him pull me into his arms and carry me back to our room. Sasha was sitting at the kitchen table smoking a cigarette, which was something she never did unless she was scared.

"What happened?" I asked Silas quietly, as he shut and locked the door.

He moved to the windows and checked those too, then pulled all the bedding off the mattress and laid it on the floor. I watched him with a quirked brow.

"What's going on?"

His voice was all gravel as worry threaded each word. "We're sleeping down here tonight. Not risking gun fire."

I lay down next to him, curling into his chest as he began stroking my hair.

"Dirk had someone kidnapped tonight. The daughter of Simon Stone."

The word Stone caught my attention. "Stone Riders?"

He hummed a yes, still staring at the ceiling, so I waited for him to continue.

"Her father came to broker a deal for her, but before he showed up, her boyfriend snuck in and rescued her."

It slowly registered then the seriousness of what had actually happened. Dirk had abducted someone…a girl.

"How old is she?" My voice was thick with emotion as fear began forming and taking a new shape in my chest. Of what Dirk was capable of.

"Eighteen, I think…close to our age…Mom and me, we helped get her out but Dirk found out we were involved."

Dread was a solid block of cement in my gut as I began to process what this meant.

"He'll punish her," I mused nearly in shock.

If he wanted to punish Sasha then it meant she no longer stood favorably in his eyes. Which meant she could no longer protect me from him.

"I need to leave tomorrow morning. Dirk sent out a group of men to look for something, but I have a bad feeling he's trying to find *someone* to traffic. I need to stop the raid and make sure no one gets hurt."

Utter defiance and worry warred in my heart as I knew that was the right thing for him to do, but a feral desperation had me begging him to stay.

"Please don't leave, Silas. If your mom might be in trouble then I think you need to stay."

"She knows how to take care of herself. She'll just lie low. If she goes anywhere, you need to go with her. I won't be gone more than a few days."

I sat up, glaring down at him as tremors worked their way into my fingers and hands. I didn't want to tell him about Dirk's interest in me. I knew Sasha would hate me if I did and I owed her too much. She'd sacrificed herself and her own happiness to keep him occupied, so Dirk didn't look at me. I wouldn't betray her by telling her son that I might be in danger.

Glancing away a stubborn tear welled in my eye, falling down the tip of my nose.

Silas wiped it with his thumb and pulled me back down.

"I'll be back before you know it, I promise."

I knew he would, he always came back, but this time I feared what might happen while he was gone and without Sasha there to protect me, what might unfold while he was away.

"Make me your wife before you leave again," I said quickly.

Silas's gaze snapped to mine, narrowing.

"What?"

"Make me your wife...you said you wanted to, if you're leaving tomorrow then make me your wife tonight."

He started shaking his head, but I stood and started looking for a sundress to pull on.

"Natty, it's midnight, how are we supposed to—"

I turned back, my expression firm as I found a pair of boots, "Lance was ordained last summer for his mother's wedding. He can do it."

Silas was up, blocking me from the window. I guess in case there was random gunfire.

"Rings?"

I held up my palm. "Give me a tattoo."

He was shaking his head, his jaw working back and forth, but I was determined. If he was leaving me here, and I knew Dirk would come for me, whatever happened to me would be done as Silas Silva's wife.

"You're only nineteen..."

I shrugged, pulling on a sweater. "You're twenty."

"We're young, baby...we have our whole lives—"

I stepped up and cut him off with a kiss, pulling his hand to my chest, forcing his palm to cover my heart. "I don't know what tomorrow will bring, but whatever it is, I want to face it as your wife."

His lips found mine and he laughed.

"We need a license and to apply for shit...it takes time. I'll marry you, Caelum but let's do it right."

Grabbing his hand, I pulled him out of the room and toward the back door. "Tonight, Silas. Marry me tonight."

Silas followed me into the starry night, and with my hand firmly in his, I knew I could face whatever was coming next simply because I'd face it as his wife.

THIRTEEN
SILAS
PRESENT

He bound her to himself with a pair of metal cuffs.

He fucking trapped her in that house, in his clothes with no help, and no way to run. Natty had no idea what it looked like when I walked into that kitchen. How feral her features had turned when she was clawing at Alec, yanking and pulling to be freed.

I'd never seen her like that before. It took me back to when she'd been traded out of the Death Raiders club, and Simon Stone had taken her. I remember how angry I was, how out of control I felt…and even that didn't seem to compare with the image I walked in on, or what it did to my insides.

Pure shrapnel sat in my chest after seeing her chained to my brother. Her wrist was red and irritated, as if she'd been trying to get free for some time. Her face was pale, her hair frizzed and wild. Her eyes were red and watery, as if she'd been crying and couldn't hold back the emotions.

She was a shell, a husk of what she once was…and that fucking killed me.

Jameson's truck slowed in front of me as we approached the Stone Riders clubhouse. I followed suit as did Killian and Wes. We eased in through their new gates that had been set up after the attack. Once we were inside, we went at a snail's pace down the long drive until we were all parking in front of the newly-restored entrance.

Several members were milling about, their cuts all on, and I noticed quite a few had shotguns in hand. Patrols were set up, and it seemed there wasn't a single person who wasn't on edge.

I parked my bike, indecision warring in me as I saw the back door open to the truck and Penelope climbed out.

I should leave.

Let Natty get back to her life and disappear. This had become her home, and I was just a visitor here. A trespasser that would never be welcome.

"What the fuck, Silas?" Killian yelled, briskly walking up on my left.

I parked my bike, and stood so we were nose to nose. "We waited for you…just like we agreed, you were supposed to call us, not walk in there by yourself."

"Didn't need you endangering your people." I explained, flicking a quick gaze to Jameson's truck. That was half true, the other half was simply that I refused to wait for them to get their shit together. Killian narrowed his eyes and opened his mouth about to say something, but I saw Natty's door open, and she was about to climb down on her own.

I moved, leaving Kilian standing there while I walked toward her. Familiar green eyes met mine, red-rimmed and cautious. The fact that she looked at me like she wasn't sure she could trust me was like a knife in the chest.

"You're not getting down on your own, Caelum." I held my hand out, and she accepted, sliding into my arms from the door. I held her to me as I set her down and let her walk. I'd carry her but her shirt would ride up and her ass would likely be on display. I was already on edge; I didn't need these fuckers seeing her exposed right now.

She kept her head down while we walked, and I found that I was desperate for my bright, shining ray of sunshine to come back to me. I wanted her to reach for me, try to touch me. Do something that reminded me we were husband and wife. That we weren't so far down this road of separation that we couldn't find our way back.

She'd welcomed my touch before the explosion…she'd answered my phone call, had run into my arms when I had called for her that night in Wes Ryan's house. So why was she acting so cold toward me?

"Oh my gosh!" someone called from the side, and I knew it was Callie.

Sure enough, she walked briskly over to us, holding her pregnant belly. Tears gathered in her eyes as she took us in, and Natty opened her arms for a hug. Laura came next, baby Connor in her arms as she walked over to us.

The girls all hugged, and Natty reached for Connor only to stop when the metal cuff came into view. The empty one still had blood smeared all over it. The women all went silent at the sight of it.

"We need to get that off you," I murmured from behind her, gently pushing at the small of her back to get her moving again. It used to be that her hand would find mine when she needed to feel grounded, but she wasn't reaching for me. My stomach twisted with tiny pricks of fear as I reached for her and pulled her hand into mine.

She faltered for only a second when we connected but she recovered quickly, smiling as we passed more Stone Riders.

There were people muttering hellos and gasps as Natty walked back into the club. Laura, Penelope and Callie all trailed closely behind her, giving her all the support I ever hoped she'd have. Emotion swelled in my chest as I saw how the people in the club responded to her. She'd finally found a family here. People who cared for her.

The woman who maintained the kitchen, and as far as I knew was considered the club mother, came forward. They all called her Red from what I remembered.

She had white hair pulled up high, her lips painted red, her lashes long and exaggerated. Her chin wobbled as she saw Natty, then her arms opened wide as she pulled her in for a tight hug. I caught sight of Natty's legs and a spike of irritation went through me again. She needed to find some fucking clothes.

"My gosh, Natty, look at this." Red picked up the cuff, inspecting it then turning toward the crowd. "Anyone have a key?"

I stood behind Natty as Red addressed the club, holding my wife's wrist. "Usually a universal key will work. She needs to get out of these cuffs."

Someone pushed forward holding up a paperclip. "I can try picking it. I've done it quite a few times. I'm pretty good at it."

The man was in his early twenties or so; he gave Natty a shy smile before gently cradling her wrist in his hand. I gripped her hips, leaning over her shoulder to watch him work. I relaxed when she leaned into me.

"Thank you, Rune." Natty smiled at him as the metal cuff unconnected and her wrist was freed.

He gave her one last smile before looking up and catching my gaze. I remembered his name, Killian and Wes used it when they were trying to fuck with me over her being handed over to a club member. I glared and he stumbled once on his way back into the crowd.

I heard Wes laugh distantly behind us.

Taking her hand in mine once more, I turned us toward the stairs and ignored everyone else who wanted to say hello to her. We needed to be alone for one fucking second. I hadn't had her all to myself where I could touch her in over two years.

"Wait." She stopped, pulling on my hand.

I turned with her, worry feathering my brow when she looked behind her at the group.

"I need to talk to Killian; his mother was the woman who ran out of the kitchen. She needs help and we have to—"

Pushing closer, I pressed my thumb against her bottom lip to stop her from spiraling. She needed to focus on herself, not some woman who got herself tangled up in Fable's bullshit.

"I'll tell him, I promise. Just let me get you settled and I promise you I'll tell him."

She hesitated for one more second before giving in, then she followed me up to her room. I produced the key and unlocked her door.

"You have a key to my room?" She asked, sounding surprised.

I looked over my shoulder and smirked. "You think all this time you were in this club I wouldn't have a way in?"

She pushed past me, walking toward her closet.

"Yet, you never used it a single time."

I smiled, securing her door with the lock.

"How do you know I never used it?"

Her eyes rolled, her blonde hair curled in waves down her back. The sun slid into her room through her windows, lighting up the white carpet, the green vines along the ceiling and the different sketches along the walls.

"So you what, snuck in and watched me like Edward watched Bella?"

She moved to the bathroom where she turned on the shower, letting the room fill with steam. My chest felt tight as I watched her hesitate in the middle of her floor, her hands curled into fists. She didn't want to touch the shirt she was in...or maybe she didn't want to see what was under it. *Or did she not want me to see her naked?*

Fuck that. She wasn't pushing me out, I wouldn't stand for it.

I moved, slipping out of my boots and my cut, so I was just in front of her with my t-shirt and jeans.

The steam curled around us as I stared down at her disconnected expression and then I tugged on the hem of the shirt she was hesitating with and slowly pulled it over her head.

She gave a tiny hitch of breath as unbidden tears began trailing down her face. I checked her stomach, her breasts, all of it seemed unscathed, but entirely more perfect than I remembered. Relief swelled for only a second before she grabbed a clean rag from her shelf, stuck it under the hot spray of water, then began scrubbing at her stomach with so much force I worried she'd tear her skin.

She just kept scrubbing as she sobbed.

It ruined me seeing her like this, so I stepped closer, gently reaching for the rag from between her fingers and let it fall to the floor. She continued to cry as I pulled her into my arms and stepped into the shower.

She curled into my chest, her arms going around my neck as I tried to soothe her.

"Tell me what happened, Caelum. Give it to me, like you used to take all my darkness, let me have yours."

I tried to ignore how it felt to have her pressed into me, naked and wet. She'd always been like this for me.

Perfection.

Heaven.

I pressed a kiss to the side of her head as she began to calm.

"Let me take it, Natty. Give me your demons, baby."

Her chin pressed into my bicep as she clung to me while I helped wash her hair. We stood there until she was clean then I reached around her and turned off the water. I watched her slowly step out of the shower as the steam began to dissipate. Her hair frizzed, the ends curling as they touched the top of her ass.

Now that she was done crying, I had a chance to really look at her. Bright green eyes, her narrow nose, and high cheeks, those bow-shaped lips. My heart thundered behind my soaked t-shirt and sopping wet jeans.

It had been too damn long since I'd held her in my arms like this.

"Salve Caelum." *Hello, Heaven.*

I smiled, tucking her hair behind her ears.

She smiled back at me, her voice a light rasp.

"Tenebris." *Darkness.*

Her fingers gently slid under my wet shirt and pushed it up until it was over my head and dropping to the floor. She traced my chest and stroked down along my stomach muscles, one by one until she was trailing the copper button on my jeans.

"He asked me how long it's been since I've been fucked."

Her head tipped back as she tugged the button free and pushed the material down. I continued to stare, feeling desperate and in awe that this was really happening.

"Do you know how long it's been, Silas?"

My throat felt thick as I rasped in reply, "Two years and twenty-three days."

Her gaze snapped up to mine, her eyes tapering.

"And how long has it been since you've been fucked, *husband?*"

Shit, I couldn't think when she called me that.

Her delicate fingers dipped into my boxers, pushing those down next. I inhaled a sharp breath as she slowly slid down my frame until she was on her knees in front of me.

"Answer me."

I shuddered as she lightly gripped my cock in her hand. "Two years, and twenty-three days."

She smiled up at me. "So you were faithful to me?"

"Where else would I go, Caelum? You're my home, my heart…my entire fucking soul."

She let me go with a grin, her hands on my thighs.

"Then lets—"

"We're not doing this right now. You were just kept hostage; you need a second to process that."

I pulled her up but she pushed at my chest and began walking back into the room.

"You've been gone for two years, Silas. I'd assumed you'd be eager to have me."

Grabbing her by the wrist, I pulled her back into me.

"I am eager, but we're not going to start with you on your knees, on a cold bathroom floor while you suck my cock. That's not how this will go. If I have you, it's on my terms."

She tipped her chin back, and her eyes were so full of hurt that it nearly robbed me of breath. I'd hurt her by letting her stay with the Stone Riders, when all I wanted was to keep her safe, I managed to hurt her.

Gently gripping her hips, I pulled her closer and pressed my mouth to hers. Our kiss was like those stories I grew up reading, a memory pressed into pages with ink, old and tattered, nearly forgotten. I moved us to her bed, laying her down, relishing the way her lips tipped up as I hovered over her.

"I remember this," she whispered, stroking a finger down my heart where a tattoo of her name was. I looked down, seeing her new ink of a tree, hating that I had to witness her getting it done through a pane of glass, seething as she chatted with the artist like it was the easiest thing in the world to have our story mark her in such a dark way.

Her dark forest. Her untamable patch of earth, never to be inhabited.

Instead of remarking on it, I pressed a kiss there. "It's what's under the ink, that's ours, Caelum. The blood in our veins, the way our souls curl into each other, finding solace. You're my home."

She held my palm to her mouth, where she pressed a kiss to the tattoo under my ring finger.

"If I'm your home then you've been gone for a very long time, my love."

I stared down at her, lightly brushing a rogue curl from her breast. She'd never stopped being mine, but I knew the two years I was gone would be something we had to work through.

Instead of giving her honesty, I parted her thighs and settled my hips between them.

Her knees came up, until her ankles locked behind my back, my hand slid under her back, pulling her up.

"My beautiful, stunning wife." I smiled into her mouth. "Still so perfect after all this time."

I prodded her slick entrance with the tip of my cock and slowly eased myself inside her.

Imprints of her nails marked my back as she adjusted to my size, her breathing became shallow and her moans became sharper.

"Silas." Her hips rotated, and I rested my hand on her waist, pulling her into me as I pushed mine forward.

Our breaths mingled, fighting for air and words as our mouths parted on silent screams.

Fucking her was a sweet song, a memory buried in every touch of her skin, every kiss and moan she surrendered to me. This was the peace I used to find when the darkness would try and consume me. I'd find myself buried in her, losing myself to the caress of her touch, the way her thighs slid against mine, her eagerness to have me. Fuck it used to be everything to me.

How had I gone this long without her?

I bent my head and sucked one of her nipples into my mouth as I slowed my hips, my cock sliding in and out of her. I teased her with gentle pushes and light laps of my tongue. Her fingers twisted into my hair, pulling as she hissed for me to go harder.

I smiled and indulged her, thrusting hard and firm and making her gasp.

Rising up, I pushed on her stomach as I repeated the movement, pulling out, only to drive inside, harder each time. Her head rolled to the side, her mouth gaped and then she was screaming my name.

Closing my eyes, I tried to hold onto exactly how she looked with my name falling from her lips, my name branding that tongue, that heart soaring with me, dripping from every part of her. I came so hard, I nearly cried. Falling forward, I groaned deeply, spilling inside her.

Our breaths were fast paced, our chests rising. Her fingers returned to my hair as she stroked and soothed the wet pieces. When I finally pulled out, I sat back and watched as my release coated her puffy pussy lips. She had a thin trail of hair down the top of her mound, but her slit was bare, revealing how she'd stretched for me, and would be sore.

It had my mind barreling back to the shower, to her scrubbing.

I gently stroked her slit, the mess smearing it while I asked, "did he…"

She shook her head. "No…he made me shower with him and he watched me…"

Her lip began to tremble as she started and stopped. I watched her carefully and decided to lie next to her, pulling her into my chest. Fuck the mess. We'd deal with it later.

"He stroked himself, while talking about how much better he'd be for me than you. How pathetic I was for waiting for you…he told me he was going to finish on me. When he did…he told me I couldn't clean myself, unless I… He wanted me to…"

She stopped again, her voice hitching. I soothed her hair, kissing the back of her head. All while my heart rioted in my chest. Taking his hand wasn't enough.

He was going to die.

"Why didn't you return to me, Silas?" Her voice was feeble and broken.

My eyes watered at how defeated she sounded. How scared she must have been. If it weren't for me, she never would have been in that house, or in his bed. She never would have been taken by my father.

Clearing my throat, I finally replied, "I did, baby. It was a little late, but I came."

She turned in my arms, those green eyes locked on mine in a tangle of pain and hurt.

"I mean before this…why have you waited this long to come for me? Alec said you would have never claimed me if they hadn't taken me, and part of me feels like you still haven't. Like you're death itself, here to steal the rest of my life and run off to hell with it, leaving me abandoned and alone."

Because you were better off here, without me.

Because all I do is bring death.

Because you deserve to be happy.

Because I love you.

I need you.

I'd die if anything happened to you.

Instead of telling her all of that, I leaned in and kissed her.

She tried to say something else, but I kissed her again and then we were falling back into the sheets, and my hands found her thighs, my cock found her slit, and for the second time in twenty-four hours, I fucked my wife.

FOURTEEN
NATTY
PRESENT

THE SMELL OF FRESHLY BAKED BREAD FILLED MY LUNGS, MAKING MY NERVES settle and a smile stretch on my face. My apron was in its usual spot, even after all the devastation and the explosions, Red had hung it right back where it had always been.

The fabric was black, and soft as I pulled it from the hook and tied it around my waist.

"Figured you would be back in here as soon as you got home," Red said, coming up from behind me. She set a hand on my shoulder and squeezed.

I fought back the urge to cry at how good it felt to have a place that felt like home. People who loved me like family. A place that held something as simple as an apron for me.

"Still baking bread, I see?" I felt a little strange saying it. Only a few days had passed since the explosions, my abduction and yet it felt like everything had changed. Red had been baking loaves of bread for months now, nonstop. No one really knew why, or what was behind it, but the clubhouse constantly smelled like heaven.

Red gave me a small smile, but it didn't reach her eyes.

"I ever tell you about my kids?"

I fell into familiar rhythm as I dusted the surface with flour and then checked the canisters to see if they'd been replaced.

Flour.

White Sugar.

Brown Sugar.

"You have never mentioned your kids to me, Red," I mused while sifting through the smaller spices. I was in the mood to make snicker-doodles.

Red paused, wrapping one of her loaves with cellophane.

It was nearly six in the morning; no one but the two of us were awake. Silas was still asleep in my bed, and while I should have stayed there, curled into his side, there was something itching under my skin to get up and get back to my life. I had no delusions that his sudden appearance for the sake of my rescue meant he'd stick around. The last thing I wanted was to let my guard down.

"That's because I don't have any."

My hands froze around the cream of tartar; my head dipped as I processed what she was trying to say.

With a heavy sigh, Red started working on a new batch of dough, her gaze on the cutting board.

"About six months ago, I woke up in the middle of the night standing outside in my nightgown. I was holding Brooks' leather jacket as if it was a baby, and I was so angry with him that he nearly couldn't calm me down."

I twisted toward her; my throat dry.

A tiny piece of white hair fell from her updo as she worked out the dough, rolling it with her hands.

"I was screaming and crying for a child I never had. I was convinced I was a mother, Natty. To my very bones. I still have nightmares at night over the feelings of loss, as if I'm grieving something I never even had."

I had no idea what that must feel like, but my heart hurt for her.

"What did you do?" I whispered, gently setting the ingredient down, fully engrossed.

"Brooks took me to the doctor; they said it was a sign of onset Alzheimer's. When the doctor told me it would only get worse, some-thing inside me just snapped. I knew my mother's mother had it, and there was a chance I might get it, but to have my brain betray me into thinking I had children...to have kids that I grieved, that, in my mind, I loved. Only to realize it's just my brain playing tricks on me...I felt betrayed in the deepest sense of the term."

I wanted to cry from how broken she sounded. I hated how useless it felt to just stand there and listen to something so devastating. I inspected the floor, unsure of what to say, but Red filled the silence.

"It took a week for me to get out of bed, to wrap my mind around the fact that I was literally going to lose it. Then I decided to start doing something every day, so repetitive that there would be no way to forget."

Oh no. The bread, it finally made sense.

"Red, that's not how—"

She looked up, her gaze on mine. "But it's working...I feel like my mind is stronger, like my memory is going to be okay. Every day I bake bread, and it seems so simple, but it's helping me, Natty. I stopped thinking about the incident, and instead, I have started thinking about how many people we can feed with something as simple as a loaf of bread."

She glanced up at me then returned her focus to the dough. "I don't need pity, honey. I just haven't shared that with anyone, and now that you're back...if something were to happen, or if I have an episode or..." Her voice hitched, and I moved.

Leaving the counter, I wrapped my arms around her in a tight hug.

"I'm here, Red. For anything you need, we've got you."

She silently cried into my shoulder for only a few moments until she sniffed and pulled back. Then it was as if nothing happened. Her smile was back in place, her no nonsense attitude as she bumped my hip.

"You might not be around here much longer now that your man has come for you."

A tiny twist rooted deep in my chest. He'd only came for me because I'd been taken, not because he was finally ready for us to be together.

"I'll be around. I'm not leaving." I returned to my station, trying to hold in the storm of emotions battering my chest.

Red watched me with narrowed eyes.

But she didn't say anything else, and that was one reason I loved working in the kitchen with her. She knew when to drop a subject. We worked next to one another in peace for another hour until we heard the front door of the club open, and then there were thumps on the stairs leading down to the main room.

I watched with apprehension as Silas made his way to the bar. His light eyes found mine immediately. He didn't say anything, but I knew he was wondering why I'd left him in bed without a word. The way his gaze traveled down my apron to where my hands were dusted with flour had my face heating.

Killian and Laura walked up to the bar, then Harris and Brooks. Each of them seemed to give Silas a wide berth, which made me smirk.

He gave me one last once-over before moving around the bar and making his way into the kitchen. Red clicked her tongue, in a warning.

"No one is allowed back here—"

Silas didn't even give her a single glance; he just kept walking until he was directly in front of me.

Whispering in my ear, he said. "Dolemus, sed praecepta tua mihi irrumabo significant cum uxor mea hic adest, hoc modo vultus." *Sorry, but rules mean fuck to me when my wife is in here, looking like this.*

My eyes fluttered shut as his hand came up to my jaw, gripping it firmly as he leaned into my space and pressed his mouth to mine.

He would have just announced to everyone that we were married, if he hadn't whispered it. The memory of when we'd gotten married burned in my chest as more of a warning than a cherished reminder. The reality that he hadn't even asked me. Not technically...it was me who pushed to be bound to him.

Just like always.

I tried to push those memories away as his mouth moved over mine, as his tongue pried my lips open and he claimed me in ways I hadn't been touched in years.

Finally breaking the kiss, his forehead came to mine, his whisper coasting across my lips.

"I was hoping you'd be in bed this morning."

My hands came up, twining through his hair, old places where I'd etched every part of Silas inside my heart ached at the feel of him. "I'm a baker, babe. I'm up before the sun."

He played with the straps of my apron, and whispered. "You are the sun."

Just like that, I felt sixteen again, obsessed and head over heels for my broody foster brother.

A smile lifted my lips, as I thought up something more to say, but Killian interjected by yelling across the kitchen from his spot at the bar.

"We ever going to get to hear what happened with Fable? Can you guys' press pause and clue us in?"

Silas let out a small sigh then whispered in my ear, "Is this what having friends is like?"

I smiled and pulled his hand in mine.

"Yes, baby. This is what having friends is like, now let's go have breakfast with them."

We ate breakfast without anyone throwing a punch or drawing a gun, which, with Silas, I considered that a big win. He didn't have friends, or anyone in the club that was fond of him in any capacity, so I was unsure how everyone was going to receive him, but it went well.

Once we were finished, Killian was talking to Silas about something when Laura pulled my hand, dragging me toward an empty corner of the kitchen.

Her blonde hair was down, curled, and her property patch, indicating she belonged with Killian, was over her hoodie.

"Nat, are you okay?" Her eyes softened and even watered a little.

I flicked a quick glance across the room, seeing Silas watching us with a quizzical look on his face.

"I'm okay…" I said, pushing back the memory of last night's breakdown.

Laura's lips turned down into a frown.

"Killian is going to bring up what happened, and I refuse to let him do that if you're not ready to talk about it. Fuck their plans and what they want to know. They can wait until you're ready."

I watched as her expression became so protective and it just made something in my soul ache. Instead of answering her, I stepped forward and pulled her into a hug.

"I'm not okay yet. But I will be and stopping that asshole will be a step in that direction."

She squeezed me back. "If at any moment you need to stop, just say the word, okay?"

We separated, both of us swiping at our eyes, and then she surprised me by saying, "Pen forced Silas to hold Connor."

My eyes rounded. "Oh my god."

She laughed into her palm. "It was hilarious but so cute."

"Tell me you snuck a picture." I quickly looked over my shoulder to make sure Silas wasn't on his way over.

Laura was watching too as she pulled her phone out. "Of course I did. I planned to show you the second you showed up."

The fact that she had faith that I would show up moved me.

"You guys thought I'd be okay?"

Laura paused, giving me a confused look. "Girl, we had maps, security footage. We found you because of Pen. I guess her mom dated someone from Sons of Speed or something but she remembered one of the locations."

Her phone came up, and on the screen was an image of Laura's living room, Silas standing there in his cut, his dark jeans and black boots, staring down at Connor all bundled up in a deep green muslin blanket.

Seeing Silas holding a baby was like a live wire hitting me in the ovaries.

Holy shit.

I mentally pinned that image to dream board material because suddenly the idea of having kids with my husband wasn't something felt too far out of reach. The image came and went within a single second but still hit me harder than a brick.

A small cottage, the bedroom window open with the curtains shifting from the summer breeze. Silas standing there without any leather, or cut... our son held to his shoulder, while he patted his back and reciting poems and stories that he'd learned as a child in that soothing tone of his.

Laura whispered, "One of these days you're going to have to explain your relationship to me, because if I didn't know better I'd say he acted like you were his—"

"You both ready?" Killian interrupted us with a gentle hand on Laura's shoulder.

We both looked up from the phone, as if we were guilty of something. He looked down at the phone and smirked.

"She tell you about our little search party for you?"

I moved with them toward the main hall. "I heard."

What I didn't say was how it made me feel that they cared enough to arrange it. Or that Pen was the one who located me, or that Laura had known I'd want a photo of Silas with Connor. She had no reason to entertain me or my relationship with the man who had held her at gunpoint and threatened her life. She had done it for me.

Silas was the president of a motorcycle club.

He had people loyal to him, and I'd never begrudge him that, but these were *my* people.

The Stone Riders was my home, and after two years of hiding here, I had finally accepted that this was where I was meant to be.

For as long as I could remember that had always been Silas...wherever he was. I was happy to just tag along, run in his footprints, land where he'd lead. Now, I wanted my own path...even if it meant soldering that hole in my heart that he'd left me with.

I'd been bleeding out for two long years...maybe it was time to bind it, and let it scar.

We were seated in a room I'd never been in before.

The Stone Riders called it Church, their place to meet and discuss... I'd seen them disappear a thousand times into this room, but I'd never been inside it. Silas held me in his lap, his hand protectively over my stomach, almost like he was afraid I'd disappear any second.

Killian glanced at Laura briefly, who gave him a small nod.

I assumed that was their way of discussing my mental preparedness for this conversation.

"Walk us through what you heard, what was told to you."

Killian's voice was calm, but there was a cold edge to it. Wes had arrived with Callie, so had Penelope and Jameson. Harris was next to Pen, holding Connor. Brooks and Rune were on the end. I missed Giles. I was happy that he'd taken over his cousin's club, now the president of the Chaos Kings, but I still missed his smiles and happy demeanor.

I watched everyone's gaze drift over to where I sat, most of their focus actually fell to the man holding me, which helped me find my voice.

I rubbed my hand over the one holding my stomach and cleared my throat.

"Fable and Alec are working together...but Fable is the one with the plan, pulling the strings. Alec is his lap dog, does whatever Fable says."

Wes glared at Killian, then peered over at Jameson as if they were all silently speaking. I ignored it and kept talking.

"From what I gathered, Fable wants Silas distracted. He was hoping my abduction would have him so distracted that he'd be able to take the Death Raiders from him. Or at least that's the story they tried to sell me."

"So he didn't want to hurt you?" Penelope asked, wincing the smallest bit. "I mean that wasn't his purpose for taking you."

I shook my head. "He would have, and threatened it, but he gave me over to Alec..."

Silas's grip tightened around my stomach.

With a shuddery breath, I tried to continue, but Wes asked, "What do you mean by gave you over to Alec, did he separate from Fable? Just trying to figure out if there are multiple locations."

The hand moving along my spine froze and I felt Silas move so he crowded my back.

"Fable wanted me alive, out of the way...he has plans for Silas, that much I know. It's all about him. Alec has...well he had affections for me from when we were younger. He—"

Shit, maybe I couldn't say it.

It was as simple as saying I was handcuffed to another human for four days and was emotionally manipulated, while being sexually assaulted.

But I couldn't seem to say a single word.

"He treated you okay?" Laura asked quietly, tentatively while glancing at Callie and Pen.

Her words were soft, but they felt like road rash, gravel sliding under my skin, burning in a way that made me feel like I'd never be okay again.

The answer was burning in my throat, to explain what he'd done, but with everyone's eyes on me, I couldn't.

"Non hic Caelum." *Not here, Heaven.*

I sunk into Silas's chest and took a deep breath. Everyone in the room must have realized I wasn't ready to talk about it because Killian spoke up.

"Was there anyone else there that you can remember?"

My eyes flew up.

"Yes." I looked over my shoulder, trying to see Silas, but I was sitting too close. "Silas was supposed to tell you."

Killian leaned forward, waiting for me to continue, while glancing back at Silas.

This time I adjusted myself so I could make eye contact. "You said you would tell him."

His hand idly slid up my back, where he toyed with the ends of my hair.

"Said I would once you were settled. You're not settled."

I let out an exasperated sound. "Silas, I can't be—"

"Can you just tell me?" Killian interrupted; an angry edge set to his jaw.

"Yes, sorry. There was a woman named Rachel there…she showed me kindness and didn't seem to be there completely of her own free will. I'd like to go back and look for her."

The president of the Stone Riders stared at me with a bewildered expression until something in his gaze shifted. He glanced quickly over at Laura and then back at me.

"Rachel? Did she…" He paused, as if he was too nervous to continue. "Was she," he tried again, this time his throat working—his Adam's apple moving.

I nodded as my own emotions began to grow thick in my throat. My eyes burned and I wished there weren't so many people in this room right now.

Killian stared, his eyes going wide until he breathed a simple, "how?"

"We didn't get to talk much, but she tried to help me the first night I was there...she made me a little escape bag...but I wasn't given the chance to use it."

Laura placed her hand over Killian's, gripping it firm as tears began welling in his eyes.

It was Wes who spoke up, ordering men around.

"Rune, get a team prepped, we're heading back out immediately."

Rune jumped up, along with the other members around the table, all but Wes, Jameson and Killian, and filed out of the room.

Laura waited until they were gone and cleared her throat and asked me, "Are you sure?"

I could understand her desire to protect the man she loved; she didn't want to get his hopes up.

"I'm positive." I glanced back over at Killian. "She has your eyes, mentioned you...said she only ever wanted you to be happy."

Laura's lip wobbled, her chin quivered and then she was out of her chair and throwing herself into Killian's lap, whispering something in his ear. He buried his face in her neck as he held her to him, and he murmured something back.

It seemed the rest of us wanted to give them a moment of privacy, so we all stood and exited the room. Silas was at my back, his hand guiding me as we walked. Penelope came up next to me and wrapped her arm around mine.

"We need to catch up. Connor needs some more stuffed penises, care to teach me how to create those masterpieces?"

I broke into a laugh as Silas asked from behind me, "You knit stuffed penises?"

"Look what you've done, Pen, you started a rumor!" I joked, swatting her side.

She laughed into my shoulder. "They're supposed to be squids according to her, but they don't look it. Just think one day you two might have kids, and your entire nursery will look very phallic."

I nearly started choking at Silas picturing a nursery full of squished penises, but more than that, us having a kid. We were married; it shouldn't feel that insane to imagine, but it did.

The silence at my back was loud enough to make the swooping in my gut feel like a failed nose dive from a plane.

Silas would never want that...he had his club, and no doubt he'd be after Fable now that he was back, just like he had been all our lives.

Penelope flicked a glance over her shoulder, obviously catching on to the awkwardness of the moment. I didn't look, but whatever she saw had her lips pursing and her grip going slack.

"Well, when you're free, why don't you come over to my house and you can see Connor. We'll go to that pond you love so much in the back."

"Sure, sounds good." I squeezed her hand and she walked ahead of us, exiting the club while Silas led me to the stairs, and we headed back up to my room.

Once we were inside, I walked to the sink and started rooting around for cleaning supplies. It had only been days, but I just felt so weird and out of place...like I needed to reset. Silas walked past me, heading toward my bookshelf, where he picked up one of the small plush squids I had knitted.

I assumed maybe he'd comment on the way it looked like a penis like Pen had, but he cradled it like it was precious and then he gently set it back in place and moved on to one of my framed photos. It was of Penelope, Callie, Laura and me at The Hollow. It was after Laura had sung a full set, taking the entire night for herself. Her fans requested it, and we were all so proud of her.

"I've been in your room several times. I've looked through your things, and I've never noticed these things." He turned toward me, looking lost. "Not with context."

"And what does having context help with?"

"Knowing you."

I laughed, dropping my chin to my chest. "Silas, you know me better than anyone."

He was in front of me when I lifted my gaze again, his eyes softening as he reached forward and tugged one of my curls until it wrapped around his finger.

"I know the old you, Natty. I don't know this version of who you are now. You wake up before anyone else, and bake for fun, you knit tiny creatures that resemble dicks, you have friends that would die for you..."

I stepped closer to him until my forehead pressed into his chin, and his hands came around my waist.

"I still catch frogs...I just do it in Pen's fancy pond. Much to her dismay and annoyance."

He pressed a kiss to the side of my head. "Why does it bother her?"

"Because I force her to catch them with me...guess I don't like doing it alone after growing up with a partner."

He hummed and held me while the day began unfolding outside with vibrant colors of blue and gold. Silas must have opened my shades this morning because the natural light in my room was generous.

"You opened my shades this morning?" My hands came up around his neck.

Silas froze, and in the stiffness of his back and rushed breath that hit my neck, I knew.

I knew he hadn't opened them.

I knew someone had been in my room.

More than anything, I knew Silas would be leaving me again.

We disconnected abruptly, Silas lightly shoving me behind him. His phone was out, dialing someone. Killian and Wes were off locating Rachel, so I wasn't sure who he was reaching out to.

"Get me Garrison," was all he muttered into his phone while walking toward the window that sat over my bed. He pocketed his phone and I stood there feeling foolish for momentarily forgetting that he had an entire club that he was still president of.

I followed closely behind Silas until my knees hit my bed, and I could see through the glass. I wouldn't have noticed it at first, but there, stuck to the pane was a white piece of paper taped with a clear piece of tape.

Silas peeled it off and inspected it, his face growing pale as he did.

"What? What is it?" My hope was that Pen had managed to come in here and left me something sarcastic.

But he turned, face grim, and when he finally looked at me, it was with that same look of despair he had that night we were in Wes and Callie's house. The night he'd shown up, scared for my safety. He'd called me down and I ran to him; it was the first time in two years that he'd called for me. I was in his arms, and I felt his tremors, his fear soaking into every fiber of my being. It was after Fable nailed a picture of me to his door...a door I had no knowledge of. Apparently Silas had a home somewhere, not even I knew of.

I stepped forward and plucked the note from his hand before he could deter me.

The note was written in black pen, and the words were simple but managed to erode my confidence in this thin veil of safety I assumed I had here in the club.

> You took my sons' hearts.
> One lost his hand.
> The other seems to have lost his mind.
> You owe me a legacy...
> I haven't decided if I just want to end you by carving out your heart or fuck you and fill your womb with another heir.
> Either way, you're mine.
> See you soon, daughter.

I dropped the note and took a step back; my lungs felt tight, and I couldn't seem to get in enough air.

"Natty." Silas stepped forward, but I withdrew.

How did I get air?

Silas was speaking again, but I couldn't hear him.

"He was in my room." I was on the floor, my knees up and leaning against something hard. Arms came around me, holding me tight. Lips pressed into my hair.

"I will find him." Silas rocked me, but all I could see was that note, and Fable's eyes when he struck that table with the knife back when he'd taken me and began demanding answers about my name. Of course he had known the whole time. He wanted me to confirm it, and then use it against me.

Silas was still speaking, something soothing, but his words didn't penetrate the panic clawing through my chest cavity. It was so intense, and it burned.

"He's going to find me, Silas. He knows where I sleep. He's been in here."

My space. My safe place.

Where was I supposed to go? What was I supposed to do?

A white cottage with a fenced-in backyard, a patch of green grass.

"I know, baby, but this is still the safest place for you. I'll tell Killian, and he'll reinforce the club. I'll send Death Raiders to fix this. You'll be protected at all times."

Something in my brain was misfiring because his words should be bringing me comfort, but there was a rope untethering, one knot at a time. Wasn't this what people did with panicked animals? They spoke softly, promising a better future, while they removed anything that had once connected them.

"No, it...I don't want that, I want you." My words were rushed, my eyes closed as I continued to breathe.

Silas didn't speak; he just continued to hold me.

"They'll be the best of the best, Caelum. I'll be back...but I have to find him. I have to."

No. Don't leave me. Don't go. Not again.

I wanted to say it, to beg it, but somewhere deep down refused to give him those words. Not when he'd take them and bottle them, only to do what he saw was best in the end. I used to think it was the war always brewing in his blood that kept us apart, but now I saw it for what it was.

A vendetta with his father...and what was the absolute worst part of this, was I didn't even blame him. Not after seeing all the ways Silas had changed throughout the years from Fable's training.

Revenge would always come first, and while I understood this specific time, it had to do with me, it was still the same score to settle from years back.

It burned that Alec was right, and while Silas may see it as protecting me, I wouldn't survive another two years of him trying to keep me safe from a distance. This would be our end, and we'd never even really had a beginning.

"Please don't go," I managed to whisper with my voice cracking.

His hand moved to the side of my face, tilting it back, and right as I opened my mouth to continue pleading, his lips were on mine.

He moved savagely, kissing me like he used to when he'd leave me after we'd turned eighteen. I tried to pull away, but he held me firm.

"I'm not leaving you. I'm here." His hand moved to my chest, over my heaving breasts. "I'm always in here."

His lips returned to mine, sensual, slow and violent all at once. I moved with him, lost in his taste and his familiar touch.

"Silas." A sob finally broke free from my chest. "Don't go."

We stayed like that, rocking back and forth in each other's arms. But eventually it came to an end with a firm knock against my door.

Silas broke away first, holding my face in his palms. "Natty, the man on the other side of that door is named Garrison. I trust him with your life, which you know means I trust him with my own. He is going to sweep your room every time you enter it and go with you wherever you go."

I was already shaking my head, a fresh tear dripping down the tip of my nose.

"I'll come with you. Just take me with you this time."

His stare softened, his dark hair cutting over his forehead, his pale blue eyes searching my gaze for something...I had no idea what.

"I have to find him, and in order to do that I have to hurt a lot of people."

I gripped his arm to stop him from retreating then let out a strained breath.

"I want to be your partner, Silas. I don't need to be kept in a tower while you go fight all our enemies. Let me just stand with you. I'm—"

My voice broke off, as worry and panic edged into my throat.

"I'm tired, Silas. I'm so tired of being alone of being left…just," I squeezed my eyes shut, "please just don't leave."

Silas was quiet, and it gave me hope that he was considering what I'd said.

Minutes passed, our fingers threaded together, each second building my confidence that he'd stay.

"I'm not ripping you from the only home you've ever had to hunt him. If I do then he wins. I will not let him win, Natty."

I released his shoulders and stepped away from him.

Silas stood behind me, regarding me warily.

"I'll be back to see you, I just have—"

"Don't bother." I moved to the window to look outside, desperately trying to hold in a scream.

He stayed behind me, silent and stoic.

I laughed, staring down at the backyard. "How ironic that one of you locked me away, desperate to keep me and the other doesn't seem to want me at all."

"Don't fucking say that. You know it's not like that. I'll go and come back to you."

There was a buzzing happening in my ears as old memories tore at my mind with invisible claws. I was staring at nothing when I heard Silas shout.

"Are you listening, did you hear what I said, Natty?"

I spun around, tears gathering again.

His jaw clenched, "Did you hear what I said? I'll be back, Garrison and Lance will be watching you. You'll be safe. I need to keep you safe."

"Right. Just like you had to let me stay safe after I was traded to this club." I don't know why I said it. The situation was out of his control, and I hadn't told him the devastating truth of what had happened but a part of me was still bitter that I had to take that truth and swallow it as if it were a shard of glass.

Silas glared, as though I were now one of his enemies. He'd never looked at me like that before. "I couldn't simply walk back in here and take you back…it would have started a war."

Another laugh tumbled from my mouth as tears traced a path down my face. "You waged nothing but war over your father all our lives. You were designed to start them, endure them and end them. Regardless of that, if you were waiting to avoid an incident with The Stone Riders and The Death Raiders, you could have when you became president months ago. Once you killed Dirk, you could have made the decision to come for me. You had the manpower and the numbers….but you never did."

Silas moved toward the door, and I felt like something was separating from my body as I watched him go. I couldn't do it again. I wouldn't.

"If you walk out that door, we're over." I whispered loud enough for him to hear me, painfully aware that I was about to break my own heart.

Silas didn't bend to anyone's will, including mine.

The silence in the room grew uncomfortable. My hope had grown long, tattered wings like something from the deep. A dark place made up of broken dreams and loneliness. I held my breath, waiting…

"Tu meus es sol, luna mea. Vitam meam. Revertar ad te." *You are my sun, my moon. My life. I will come back for you.*

With that, the door opened and closed on a whisper.

I spun around, my eyes watering as I stared at the floor. A familiar ache unfurling in my core. I knew Silas had men outside my door, keeping me safe but it didn't erase old trauma.

With a shaky breath, I walked over to my closet and turned on the light. There, under a false floorboard, I stared at my past. Photos of a younger Silas holding a frog bigger than his head. An image of him writing in a journal, testing his ability to write poetry because he'd grown addicted to it. My eyes trailed over the two hand guns, boxes of ammo and letters I'd gathered throughout the span of time I'd been separated from Silas.

My fingers trailed gingerly and ever so carefully over the leather jacket with the Grim Reaper stitched into the back. Printed in white, circular text:

Property of Silas Silva
The Roman

Options were never set before me, they'd always been taken. Removed. I was merely shoved into a corner, a tower, some place to be kept safe. My mouth sealed to prevent a war, while ignoring the battle that raged in my heart.

I broke when I arrived in this club. Repaired only by kindness, friendship, independence, and this great hope that I'd be back with Silas. I was tired.

So tired.

Releasing a pent-up breath, I brought my knees under my chin and sat alone in my room, staring at the floor that held pieces of a life I no longer recognized. Clarity finally came in the form of a plan. A decision.

It was time I took my life back into my own hands.

FIFTEEN
SILAS
PRESENT

I HADN'T HAD A CHANCE TO CHANGE OUT OF MY SULLIED JEANS OR DIRT caked t-shirt before getting an urgent text from my vice president regarding Natty. So I drove into the city, meeting Lance a block away from Natty's little coffee shop job. I was told she'd returned to it as if she'd never been taken in the first place. Garrison was keeping me updated on her as much as he could, but apparently there was an issue that they had decided to take up with my vice president instead of me. Which was why he'd called this meeting.

My best friend sat on his bike, his feet planted in the gravel, while staring at his cell. I wouldn't allow anyone else in the club to be so relaxed when I pulled up, but Lance got a pass because he could still kill me with alarming accuracy while watching cooking videos on his phone.

"What the fuck was so important that they could only tell you instead of me?" I snapped, letting my bike roll to a stop before lowering the kickstand.

Lance kept his face down, but lazily drawled, "Try again, and check that frosty as fuck tone, please."

I'd smirk if I wasn't so upset over having to walk away from Natty again. Leaving her wasn't something I enjoyed doing, at any fucking point in my life, but my whole life revolved around keeping her safe.

This was the right thing to do, and even if it meant she hated me for it, I'd still leave if it meant the threat against her life was being hunted.

"Can you please tell me what the team is concerned about regarding my wife?" I gave him a fake smile, all teeth, then flipped him off once his face lifted.

Concern was there now, and it gutted me.

"Natty keeps leaving. Also why do you smell like lemons, and why the fuck do you have dirt all over your clothes?"

I already knew Natty had started leaving, so I lifted my arms to indicate where we were...and that I was more than aware that she'd gotten back to her routine. As far as the lemons and the dirt...not a chance in hell was I touching that.

Lance shook his head. "She leaves on a bike, Silas...and she's been visiting rival clubs."

What.

No...that wasn't right. She rode around on a little yellow moped.

Lance glared at me as if he was reading the thoughts in my head. "It's a Yamaha Xabre...fast as fuck too. She lost her detail twice while entering Chaos King territory up in Richland."

What the actual fuck was she doing going up to Richland?

"It gets worse."

My eyes narrowed on my friend, all while my breathing became more difficult.

"She slipped her detail during her shift at The Drip...we didn't notice until that night, we thought we could find her, but she didn't come back last night. The reason the guys were too afraid to tell you is because they're fairly positive you're going to kill them."

My head was pounding as time seemed to stop, and the air felt like it had thinned so much that I couldn't breathe in anymore of it.

"You mean to tell me that my wife has been driving into Chaos Kings territory and as of this last little trip, hasn't returned, and is in fact there, right fucking now?"

Lance dipped his chin.

"It's not Garrison's fault...none of us knew she'd have that bike ready to go, or that she seemed to have an agenda, or a person in The Drip that was blonde and would have traded aprons with her. Sometimes they keep their faces down while they work, so it's hard to tell the difference. We've helped watch over her for two years. We knew her routine, her habits…we knew what to look for. She took us by surprise, Silas."

I noticed he was saying "we," which would take the heat off Garrison and his men.

My legs were already moving toward my bike, my hands shaking. I heard Lance trying to warn me, but I didn't fucking care. Natty wasn't doing this. She was not going to get taken again by my father simply because she was pissed at me.

Lance hopped off his bike and advanced toward me until he was standing in front of me.

"Take a second and explain to me what the fuck is going on. You came out of the Stone Riders property a week ago, pissed as hell. You ordered me to stick around the property and watch over Natty…and you've been putting yourself at risk every day since. Just tell me what happened."

He was right, and deep down I knew I had to allow other people in so that I wasn't carrying all this shit by myself…I just wasn't sure how to do that without everything falling around me.

Digging into the pocket of my jacket, I pulled out the scrap of paper that had sent me hunting and handed him the note Fable had pinned to Natty's window, letting him fill in the blanks.

"How the actual fuck did Fable get through all the security the Riders have set up? That place is secured better than most prisons."

I was still trying to piece that one together as well.

"A mole is the only thing I can think of, but it's not my club and the president is currently out looking for his fucking mother, so I can't bring it up."

Lance sharpened his focus; I knew he was trying to work something out.

"So you moved in your own security without Killian's consent?" His dark brow flicked up in silent question.

I nodded.

"Was Natty on board?" Lance tucked his phone into his jacket pocket.

A shaky breath left me as I shook my head. "She's pissed at me. Didn't want me to leave."

"Then maybe you shouldn't have. You forgetting the last time you left her and she got traded without your approval or consent?"

My back molars pinched together as I worked to keep my sanity in check.

"You know better than to bring that up to me, don't be fucking cruel. He got into her room somehow, Lance. I have to find him."

He shook his head, returning the note to me.

"He likely knew this is how you'd react. You are the only person who knows what sort of bullshit he'd use on Natty. If he knows where she's sleeping, then she needs to be moved and quickly. You can't leave her here, even with a team of Raiders to protect her."

My stomach clenched.

"Doesn't seem to matter now anyway, she left and all the protection I promised her wasn't even able to stick with her."

My best friend winced, and I felt slightly shitty about that. It wasn't his fault or the team's...they were right. Two years, Natty had the same routine. The fact that none of us knew she'd even purchased a bike was humbling, even to me.

Lance finally let out a sigh and leveled me with a glare... "You can't leave her, Silas. If something happens to her, you will cease to exist, my friend, and I can't stand by and allow that."

"I can't hunt him and drag her with me. He'll be watching me."

Besides, I couldn't take her from this place. She had friends here. A job she loved, and people who cared about her. *She'd already left though... on her own.*

"I need to go find her," I muttered quietly, still trying to piece together why she went to Richland. The Chaos Kings were an ally of Killian's, so I knew she'd be safe, but what did this have to do with Fable...or anything else for that matter? I couldn't work it out, but I needed to get to her.

Lance nodded, watching me keenly.

"My advice...you need to give Natty a bit more credit. She's more capable than anyone else I can even think of regarding Fable, and Alec.

Stop worrying so much and just accept that she might be able to help you."

"Good thing I didn't ask for your advice."

Lance chuckled, and with a quick buckle of his helmet, he let out a sigh. "You forget that I was the one watching as you two exchanged those vows that night. I was the one who knew no matter what you said would ever compare to the strange connection you formed as kids. She slept on your floor, right under your nose for most of your life, like that was a normal thing or something. You both were so fucking careless, regardless that the rest of us knew how dangerous it was to fall that hard, so young. Still, I watched in awe as she kept loving you. I remember her lighting up like the sun when you'd arrive. Nothing but a dark thunder cloud, and she never gave a single shit."

He laughed, which had me letting out a small chuckle as well, along with an unbidden tear. My memories were the worst form of torture.

Lance sobered and met my gaze. "You've punished yourself for letting her down...you've suffered, Silas. Keep her, love her. Start fresh with her."

Without another word, he dipped his head and shot off on his bike toward Pyle.

Starting my bike up, I headed in the opposite direction toward Richland, letting my best friend's words soak into my heart. Maybe he was right.

Perhaps it was time to just stay...

My mind threw up images of a time I felt the same and had ignored it, knowing something deeper was going on.

Knowing, she was slipping through my fingers but going regardless.

SIXTEEN
SILAS
AGE TWENTY-TWO

THE MEN IN MY FATHER'S CLUB ALL LOOKED AT ME DIFFERENTLY NOW. WHEN I was a kid, they'd sneer at me, even push me around, always trying to toughen me up. Either they didn't know the purpose of Alec and I being there, or they just didn't care.

Their cruelty only pushed me harder. Now as an adult, being here on my own volition, and not simply because a custody agreement said I had to be, they seemed to look at me in a new light. Their glares would linger, and a few would drop down to my hands, but most of them had fear hardening their stares. My reputation as The Roman had spread, even to surrounding clubs, and now when we had opposition, it was a whispered plea that I wasn't the one to dole out punishment.

I was tired of this though.

Exhausted really, but every time I thought I might be getting somewhere with dismantling this club, or my father's role here, something else would happen that would draw it out. Most recently it was the arrival of his brothers, who offered extra protection, and by extension, stepped in to take on new roles within the club, which helped reinforce the various ways I had weakened it.

For years, I had systematically been sabotaging my father's plans, his runs, and different connections. Inventory of new weapons would arrive, and I made sure they were destroyed in a freak accident. When negotiations were supposed to go down for a meet up with members from the cartel, I made sure to tip them off so they were able to steal the product my father planned to leverage.

He had no idea it was me, neither did Alec, but my efforts were working. I just needed to keep at it.

The problem was consistently trying to tear down his club meant I was away from my wife.

Shutting the door to my room in the club, I pulled out my phone and navigated to the text thread with her.

Me: I miss you

A few minutes passed before she saw the message, then the dots bounced around for nearly another minute before she replied.

Natty: I miss you too…a lot actually, anyway you can cut your trip short and come back to me?

I felt her words like a punch to the gut. *Come back to me.*

Me: I will do everything within my power to return to you as soon as I possibly can.

She didn't message me back for a while. I lay down and rested my eyes, thinking of her. My mind constantly threw back the images of her from our wedding.

Lance took us out to the dock in our grove, carrying a lantern and a Bible.

He had hung the lantern with the swinging rope we'd tied to a tree, then, under a sky full of stars he married Natty and me. She had on a white dress with pink roses printed all over in little patterns. Her hair was braided into a crown around her head, and her smile couldn't be rivaled. I'd never seen her so happy.

Originally I'd had plans to ask her when things had settled down a bit, and when we married, I wanted it to be a big affair. But Natty didn't have friends, unless she'd made a few at work…otherwise it was just Mom and me.

So, this was better. We'd driven into town after our vows and had a man named Jackhammer ink two similar tattoos under our ring fingers.

"This will likely fade," he'd warned. Natty and I just smiled and welcomed the challenge.

> Natty: You've been gone for almost four months, Silas. Please come home.

I stared at her text, feeling nervous and worried. That gut feeling that there was something she wasn't telling me surfaced.

> Me: Is everything okay?

She took her time responding again, and it was enough to get me moving. I wasn't sure what the fuck was going on back home, but I knew she needed me. I hated being away from her, and for her to ask me twice…nearly begging me, meant something was off.

I got on my bike and within the span of two hours, I was rolling to a stop in front of the house. My phone still hadn't gone off with a new text since I had asked if everything was okay, and I had no idea where Natty was.

From the side where the Death Raiders club entrance was, I heard a noise and suddenly Dirk was walking out, laughing with a few of his men.

He spotted me and paused.

There was something about his expression, and I would never forget the way he'd looked at Natty when we'd started dating at seventeen. I never had been able to get the way he stared at her out of my system. Was I missing something where he was concerned?

"Silas. You're back early," Dirk muttered, walking closer.

I didn't respond, but I did get off my bike and unclasp my helmet.

"You know where my mother is?" It was safer to ask about her, than bring attention to Natty.

Dirk looked concerned, like he was in deep thought.

"Last I saw, she was doing that farmer market bullshit with that blonde girl."

I dipped my head, ignoring what it did to hear him talk about Natty.

"She's real clumsy by the way…" Dirk said with a chuckle. I froze, the blood roaring under my skin was a violent scream.

"What exactly do you mean?"

One of Dirk's men shifted behind him, smothering a smile. It put me on edge.

"She was at work I guess…don't know, I heard it third hand from Sasha. Apparently, she was trying to carry a tray of drinks or something and ended up breaking a finger. Can you believe that?"

No. I actually couldn't, but I needed to talk to Natty.

Ignoring Dirk and his men, I resumed my position on the bike and headed for the town square where they held the farmer's market.

We were in my mother's Jeep, parked up on a hill where the stars stretched over us like a velvet blanket. The moon was a sliver in the sky, and my wife looked like she belonged up there with them. It took me back to being seven, opening that wardrobe door and seeing her for the first time.

I assumed she was a star.

"Why are we out here?"

Because I didn't believe her when she told me everything was okay.

"Just wanted you to see stars." I opened my door and walked over to hers.

She quirked a delicate brow at how I had phrased that, but she seemingly brushed it aside as we made our way toward the front of the car.

"Here." I held her hips and lifted her to the hood, where she sat with her feet dangling. She was in one of her flowy dresses that covered her knees. Her finger was in a splint, her story about work being the reason still had me on edge.

We settled in, her on the hood, me standing next to her while we tipped our faces back and stared at the sky. Natty let out a sigh and then toyed with my hair.

"What do you want in our future, Silas?"

She wasn't supposed to be the one spearheading questions, but I humored her.

"You."

I couldn't see her, but I knew she was rolling her eyes as she let out a sigh.

"Okay, you have me. What else do you want?"

I knew what I didn't want, but I was too afraid of ruining it by saying something out loud.

"Tell me." She tugged harder on my hair until I was turning to look at her.

I turned and spread her thighs apart, then shoved her dress up until she was just sitting before me in her brown boots, and the tiny scrap of pink fabric covering her pussy.

"I know what I don't want."

Her hands cupped my jaw as I stroked up and down her thighs.

"What's that?" she breathed, nearly on a whisper as my thumbs traveled up to where the edge of her underwear met her thigh.

"I don't want you to lie to me, or tell me things are okay, even when they aren't." Not looking up, I pressed a kiss to her knee as I pulled her waist closer.

"I don't lie to you, Silas." Her whisper cut through me as a rogue breeze swept over us.

She did though, I could feel it. I just didn't know how or why.

"So you promise everything is okay?"

She was spread deliciously wide, her legs cradling my chest as my face hovered low, near her stomach.

Her hands wound through my hair, dragging me closer to where she was likely soaking the fabric.

"I promise. Now are you going to tease me, or do you have plans for me?"

The pad of my thumb brushed over her slit, forcing out a hiss.

I smiled and pushed against her stomach. "Lean back."

Natty complied, which had her hair fanning out over the windshield.

I looked up, piecing every inch of her to memory, and then I leaned in and pulled the fabric covering her pussy to the side and then gently pried her open with my tongue.

She tasted how she always did. *Sweet, intoxicating and completely mine.*

With a guttural groan, I gripped under her legs and pulled her closer until her ass was nearly hanging off the hood. Then I buried my tongue into her heat, sucking and licking until she began writhing against my face.

This was where her and I existed in the most perfect rhythm.

Loving her, tasting her and owning her, it was the only drug I'd ever allow myself to become addicted to.

"Silas," Natty moaned as loud as she wanted, giving her happiness to the stars. Her hips rotated, making a slick sound as my tongue ravished her cunt. I pushed back on her thighs, spreading her wider, and then I stood staring down at her like a crazed man.

The cold air hit her exposed center, her legs pushed up, so all of her was bared to me.

Her head lifted, likely in question, but I gently pushed three fingers into her and groaned.

"Let the stars see you, Caelum. Let the heavens witness how depraved and fucked I am to take you out here, right where all of them can bear witness to my obsession. I'm nothing but darkness, and I'll continue to steal your light for as long as you have air in your lungs and you carry my heart within your chest."

I tugged the button on my jeans, and pushed them down just enough to release my cock.

My wife tried to close her legs, but I held them open.

"You're going to take my cock, Natty. You're going to keep these legs open and let me fuck you so hard that it'll take you a few days to even close them properly."

She wheezed something incoherent, but I didn't wait; I pulled her down against my thickness, engorged to the point of pain and let out a groan.

"More."

I nodded, trying to breathe through not coming already and then I moved, slowly pulling out and sliding back inside my wife's tight heat.

Her back lifted from the hood, her hair swayed in the breeze and her tight pussy clenched around my heavy erection.

"Yes, Silas. Yes." Her nails had found my shoulders, her chest now aligned with mine. We fucked slowly as I rotated my hips, and she ground against me. Her nails scraped against my scalp, and I wondered how we must look to those bright, shining stars above us.

Two people in love, desperate for each other to the point of obsession but torn apart too frequently to ever move forward.

"You asked what I want." I slammed home, while she dug her nails into my skin, rasping for more in my ear. "I want a future, Natty. I want to fuck you when I wake up and kiss you before bed. I want to watch you dance in a home that belongs to only us. I want firelit winter nights and star speckled summers."

Natty tossed her head back and shattered.

I kissed her shoulder and found my release shortly after hers. Our heavy breathing filled the air as I held her to me, her ass just barely touching the hood of the Jeep.

"I want to be a peaceful man, Natty. Someone who helps the earth grow, especially after doing so much to take from it."

Her wild eyes found mine, shining under the stars. Her hand found my jaw and she leaned in to kiss me.

Soft.

Gentle.

"Then build your hope inside of me, Silas Silva. I'll keep it safe and I'll make sure our dreams come true for the both of us."

My chest pricked with the reminder that I didn't deserve her or her holding my dream in her chest.

I let her have it anyway.

SEVENTEEN
NATTY
PRESENT

I WAS BEING IMPULSIVE.

No doubt about it. I really should have thought through this plan a bit further before hopping on the bike I'd been hiding for the past year and jetting off like a bat out of hell toward Richland.

I'd effectively lost the men Silas had put on me, which was good because they wouldn't have made it past the gate. No Death Raider would have been welcomed here, regardless that my very own cut had the grim reaper across the back. The only reason they allowed me passage was because Sadie, Giles's old lady recognized me.

The distant sounds from the club echoed through the large kitchen I was standing in. A woman named Gene was glaring at me as if I'd just stolen something from her. I knew she was carrying a knife behind her back in case I made any sudden moves, but I was holding one too.

"You're saying you know Giles?" She lifted her chin toward me.

Understandably, one of the guards had let me in, but no one knew why. As soon as I was within those metal gates, everyone looked at me like I'd grown a third eye and then they scrambled, trying to grab me.

I said to get Giles, and they put me here to wait. That was last night when I arrived in the middle of the night and was told Giles was on a run. I was given some food and treated like an inconvenient prisoner, where I was watched, monitored and regarded warily for twenty-four hours. Sadie had tried to come visit, but no one let her in. Perhaps because they felt like I was a threat of some kind. More likely though, they would have been in deep shit if they let something happen to their president's woman.

"Giles was vice president of the Stone Riders before he became the president of your club. I've known him for years, so yes. I know him."

Gene's eyes narrowed further. "He has an old lady, so if you're here to create trouble then I'll—"

Oh boy. If only she knew that Sadie was one of my favorite Sweet-butts. We'd often take shots together, and she'd opened up to me about her frustration over Giles not claiming her.

"Natty?" Giles burst into the room, interrupting Gene's little warning.

I turned and smiled at my old friend, then opened my arms as he stalked toward me and pulled me into a hug. Giles was stocky, only slightly taller than me, with dark blond hair and soft brown eyes.

"Hey Prez." We separated, but I caught his blush. Being asked to take over the club for his cousin, Jameson, was a big ask, but there wasn't another person better suited for it than Giles.

He searched my face, confusion warring with his features.

"What are you doing here?"

"I need help…and I sort of went rogue, so I'm calling in favors."

Giles' eyes went wide after I'd mentioned favors, as if he was remembering the fairly large one he currently owed to me.

"Shit. Ya…whatever you need."

I smiled and walked past him, only to stop when he choked on a gasp.

"The fuck, Natty. You aren't serious."

Turning on my heel, my brows dipped as I stared at him in confusion, but his stance had become guarded, and his gaze frozen, as if he'd seen a ghost.

"What?"

Pushing a hand through his hair, he let out a strained breath.

"I always assumed he was just obsessed with you…I had no idea you actually belonged to him. You can't be here. He'll burn my club down."

My property patch.

My feet faltered for a second, nervous about the tone Giles used.

"He won't…I promise you…he only does that when I'm taken against my will."

His brown eyes continued to spear me in place, as if he couldn't be convinced to let me stay.

"Sons of Speed took you?"

I nodded slowly. It was complicated but true enough.

He ran another hand through his hair, taking a step closer.

"Okay, I hope you're right…for the record, he isn't coming in here. He's fucked in the head, Natty. A ghost to the men here. Someone as terrifying as death itself…like a scary bedtime story."

"I'm not worried about Silas, Giles. I just need to call in my favor with you and I'll be on my way. Likely before he even realizes I slipped his little detail."

Giles stopped walking again, letting out an agonized groan. "Fuck, this is going to be bad. I can feel it."

I smirked and followed him out the kitchen doors and down the hall where an office waited.

This was going to work. It had to.

I just had to trust that I was making the right decision.

I was out of the Chaos Kings' gates the following hour, riding back toward Rose Ridge. I was really hoping I wouldn't run into Silas, but I'd been gone for over twenty-four hours, so there was a good chance he was close by.

No fires had been started yet, so I knew he hadn't arrived. He would have absolutely burned the whole thing down if he knew I was inside, especially considering they wouldn't have allowed him in.

It was understandable that they didn't, not after all the shit the club had been through after being hijacked by Tuck and Jefferson...splitting the club, and now having to reunite under new leadership. My hope was that considering the club divided, there were going to be quite a few men still lingering that had connections to the initial defectors. Jefferson Quinn and Tuck Holloway were the ones who had brought Fable into this mess. Apparently, there was a connection between the older members.

Since so many members had been privy to the plan Jefferson had for taking over, I was betting on those members still lurking around Richland. I was putting Giles in an awkward position by requesting what I did, but we needed to find Fable, and I was willing to pull out every resource available.

My bike slowed as I came to a stop sign. My boots hit the dirt right as a familiar bike came into view. Silas wasn't wearing his helmet, but he had on a gaiter mask, and the second his eyes landed on me, they blazed with fury.

Shit.

My stomach flipped with nervous excitement because for two years I had remained in a nice, safe cage where he could always check up on me. This was the first time I'd dared to play the same game that he was playing. He couldn't see my face through my visor because I had opted for a full head helmet and my bike was more of a sports bike compared to his Chopper.

He started for me, but I revved the throttle and put my boot down to steady the frame as I turned to the right and sped away. My husband could chase me if he wanted to scold me about staying put and being watched by his Raiders.

My hair flew behind me as I leaned over the engine of my bike, my focus on the road ahead, while flicking my gaze every so often to the small side mirror. Silas was right behind me, revving his engine to taunt me. He was also very clearly humoring me because while my bike was going nearly seventy miles per hour, he seemed as if this was amusing to him. He sat upright, one hand on the throttle, and the other hanging down by his side.

I knew him well enough that if I continued to push, he'd do something insane, like pull me right from the bike onto his lap and give zero fucks about my bike crashing. I doubted very much that he wanted me riding at all, so to save my precious Yamaha, I pulled off on a side road where tall stalks of corn hid us from view.

His engine roared behind me, then cut off right as I lowered the kick-stand for my bike and slid off the seat.

My heart nearly pushed through my chest as I took in Silas. Seated on his bike with both legs down, steadying the frame, he wore a gaping tank, which revealed all the ink that saturated his skin. He wore no patches, no colors. Nothing that would identify him as a Death Raider. I hadn't seen him without those patches since he was seventeen years old.

He tugged the gaiter mask down so I could see his mouth. His eyes were storming, his lips were flat, his expression practically screamed that he was silently rioting in that beautiful head of his. My helmet was still on, but for the sake of this game that we were playing, I removed it and set it on the seat of my bike.

His glare remained indifferent as he waited there on his bike, looking like the villain who usurped a king.

I walked to him, and he tracked my every step. Once I reached his outstretched leg, I placed my hand on his shoulder and slid in front of him, letting my legs fall to the side. I wore leather pants, motorcycle boots and my leather property patch, which covered my arms. Under it, I had a simple, loose tank and sports bra.

Silas tugged under my ass, pulling my legs over his hips, and then his nose was in my neck where he was inhaling.

I felt like his drug of choice. While he'd never seemed to dabble in anything but nicotine, his lips traveled over my jaw as if every cell of mine was laced in heroin.

"Did you forget yourself, *Wife*?" he rumbled close to my ear.

I smiled, stroking his neck as I whispered back, "Not at all, *Husband*. I've simply remembered myself."

His chuckle was short-lived because his mouth had attached to my throat, sucking and kissing while his hands slid under my jacket, grip-ping my ribs.

"You still under the assumption that we ended somehow?"

He was going to punish me for that, but hopefully he'd wait until I could properly enjoy it.

"Are you still under the assumption that I need to be kept behind in order for you to keep me safe?"

He pushed my jacket off, which allowed the soft breeze to brush against my skin. His lips were ravenous as he moved them down my chest and then my shirt was lifted and I was in front of him in just my sports bra and leather pants.

"Me wanting to keep you safe shouldn't mean we end." He pressed a kiss to my stomach then unzipped my bra and let my breasts spill free. His mouth was on them in an instant, kissing, and sucking on my peaked nipples. The breeze slid over them each time Silas relented, and then he stared in fascination as he dipped his head once more to slowly lick the pink buds.

He knew this sort of slow torture worked me up, but it did the same to him if the thickness pressing against my core was any indication.

My back was stretched out awkwardly across his bike frame, my head between his handlebars, and I trusted Silas to keep us steady. We'd fucked on the back of his bike plenty of times before; he always knew how to keep us safe, but he was also not thinking super clearly right now.

"It shouldn't mean we press pause either, Silas. Which is exactly what we did all those years while you left me for Fable."

"So it's one or the other?" His tongue traveled down the center path between my breasts, which left me shuddering. My hands went to his hair, tugging and pulling him closer. My hips lifted, desperate for friction.

His head lifted, revealing a devilish smirk. "You bought yourself a bike."

He hadn't just noticed...he brought it up for some other purpose, that was how Silas worked. I was trying to discern what it would be when suddenly Silas was lifting me. My legs went around his hips as he cleared the bike.

Green stalks of corn blotted out the sky, standing tall, and offered enough protection that no one was going to see us from the road. Which was good because my husband deposited me in front of my

Yamaha. He picked up my helmet that was sitting on the seat and hung it on the handlebar, then stared at me with a hunger I hadn't yet witnessed. With his hands on my hips, he turned me and then gently nudged his leg between mine, which forced my palms to land on the seat of the bike.

"You seem proud of this method of freedom. Escaping the detail I set for you, not having anyone watch over you while Fable is out hunting you. It's cute, Caelum. But now you're going to take my cock while I bend you over the back of this little bike you seem to be so proud of."

"My bike will fall over…I'm not—"

His hand came over my mouth, his lips at my ear. "You should know me better than that, Caelum. I'd never let anything happen to you, and by extension, your little bike."

I did know that. Silas was a lot of things but careless and cruel wasn't one of them.

Letting out an uneven breath, I looked at the stalks of corn, my hands pressed into the seat of my bike and then bit my lip when my his hands gently pulled down the leather at my hips. My thong went with it, until my ass was on display, the chilled breeze gliding over the exposed skin.

I heard him spit, which meant he was coating his cock, readying it for me. He'd done it dry before when I wasn't ready, and it wasn't a pleasant experience. He was too massive, and honestly even with him lubricated, it usually took a few strokes for me to get acclimated.

"Bend over."

I did as he said, leaning over the seat, trusting that he would hold us both up. My eyes fluttered shut as I released the fear of what I'd been through, and what might come, and just enjoyed the feel of Silas taking me in the middle of a cornfield.

I felt younger, freer. I loved the Stone Riders and all that they had done for me, but having Silas back felt like I was ten again, sitting on a warm dock with no other care in the world but frog hunting.

The head of his cock pressed against my center, and with a groan, he gently nudged it inside me, inch by inch. My nails pushed into the seat painfully hard as I held my position, relishing how full I felt.

"Goddamn, you're perfect." Silas breathed against my ear, holding my shoulder as he adjusted himself. My legs were spread, my boots slightly dragging in the dirt as my chest was planted more firmly over the seat.

My bra was still unzipped so my tits were mashed against the cushion. A moan escaped me as Silas slid out and then sheathed himself once more, the slickness from my arousal coating him as he moved back into place. Once he set a rhythm, it felt so good that I began to lose myself. The rocking of the bike was a distant thought, my boots dragging, Silas gripping my chest and pulling me up so that he had a better angle.

He was ruthless with how he handled me, like I was merely a ragdoll he had stuffed full with his cock, and was now fucking me senseless.

"You may be free to do what you want, Caelum, but you're still mine. Which means..." He tilted his hips and thrust into me, making me gasp. "If you go to a rival club, I will follow. And if I can't tear them apart for taking you in, then I'll fuck you so hard, you'll never forget."

I was suddenly pulled off the bike and spun around. My legs went around his him as he carried us into the thick cornstalks. My lips went to his, our mouths resuming the fucking that his cock had started. His tongue swept in, claiming me in delicious ways.

We moved to the ground, the soft earth under us as Silas held me in his lap. My knees went to either side of him, pressing into the dirt as our mouths stayed fused together. I didn't even notice when he'd notched his erection at my wet slit.

He lifted me so that he had enough leverage that it allowed me to slide down onto him and then we were fucking again, ruthless, fast and hungry.

My hips moved with urgency, taking him as deep as I could, and allowing him to hit that place inside that needed him so badly. His hands kneaded my ass, pulling me impossibly closer, and I was lost.

Falling and flying.

My mouth parted on a scream and I barely registered tattooed fingers sliding over my tongue. I sucked on his fingers, as his other hand squeezed my ass, and then he was groaning his own release, freezing in place with one last hard thrust as he filled me with hot, sticky cum.

"My fucking god, Silas." I tried to catch my breath, kissing the hand that fell away from my mouth. He peppered my jaw with gentle kisses as we both worked to catch our breath.

He muttered something that sounded like, "my fucking wife," but I couldn't quite make it out. I didn't need to. I knew what he was thinking, and that was the problem with us.

We knew each other's souls, inside and out, and we both knew how this would end.

I'd push, he'd cave because he only wanted to exist if it meant I was safe. I didn't want to take advantage of him, but I also refused to live without him any longer.

Pressing a kiss to the side of his eye, I curled into his chest. Knowing my thighs would be sticky, and his erection would soon be softening. I didn't care. I wanted to stay exactly where I was.

"I'm a stain on your soul, Caelum. There is no removing me."

No truer statement had ever been made.

"I don't want to remove you, Silas. I want to exist with you...and the only way to do that is to hunt the same monsters you are."

He let out a sigh and tucked a few strands of hair behind my ear.

"I've seen the dark side of Fable, Natty. I know what depraved things he has done. I will not risk you being with me when I find him."

He seemed to forget that I was held captive by the same man. I may not have had to witness all the same horrors he did growing up, but I felt the tendrils of fear attached to the atmosphere he created. I felt the terror.

"Then we're at a stalemate, Husband. I won't stop."

Silas cradled my face; my knees were still pressed into the earth and the stalks of corn swayed above us from the gentle breeze in the air.

We could hear cars on the road we'd turned off of a ways back.

"If anything happens to you, I'll burn it down."

I tilted my head. "Burn what down?"

His unsettling light eyes arrested me, holding the very air in my lungs hostage as he said with all seriousness that I knew was within him. "Every last thing that makes up this world. The clubs, the people. The towns. I don't care. I'll take it. There's a dragon somewhere curled in this heart of mine, and it's greedy for you, Natty. Obsessed, insane and absolutely feral to keep you safe."

The severity of my choices began sinking in.

Silas wouldn't stop or settle until I was back behind the gilded doors of the Stone Riders. We'd stay out here, in this cornfield, fucking and fighting until I agreed to go back because he was that serious about my safety.

With a heavy sigh, I pressed my forehead to his.

"Escort me back."

I felt him physically relax at my resignation, but deep down, he'd have to know me better than that. I may be willing to return, but it certainly didn't mean I'd stay.

EIGHTEEN
SILAS
PRESENT

Natty didn't expect me to remain in the Stone Riders clubhouse with her.

I could tell when I walked her up to her room, and then dropped my duffle bag to the floor. Her green eyes narrowed on it, her pink lips fell into a thin line and then she toyed with the ends of her hair. It was what she did when she had to rethink a scenario.

She used to do it a ton when we were younger and used to have competitions. Spelling, board games, or frog hunting. There were always things we were trying to best each other at. But this wasn't a game. It was her life, and I needed her to realize that I wasn't playing around.

I needed her to stay here and be safe. If she needed me here for a few days to drill that home, then I'd stay.

Her little attempt at freedom did not go over well with me and the fissures still radiating in my chest were a reminder that every single day this woman could and likely would ruin me.

I had no idea what she did with the Chaos Kings, or why she was there. I knew she had a link to Giles from when he'd lived here in the Stone Riders club. I assumed there was a connection to her showing up there a week after I had left her, but I wasn't worried enough to ask just yet. Currently I was focused on the fact that we had to move Natty out of this room.

As much as I hated the idea, and I knew she would as well, it had to be done. Fable had been in here, and there was no way she'd ever relax enough to be comfortable here again. She proved as much when I lifted her dress up over her hip and began tracing a finger over the silk covering her cunt.

She had gently shoved me away with a shudder while casting a glance up at the window. Even under the blankets, she had whispered that she felt like he was watching or listening to her.

As the early shades of dawn crept into the room, she woke like an eager sunflower awaiting the first drop of sunlight. She smiled at me with that grin that said she was still trying to find a way to undermine me being here. Still she kissed me then quickly dressed in a sundress. On her feet, she wore a pair of boots, and her hair, she pulled back into a braid.

Like a fucking puppy, I followed her downstairs where she pulled on a black apron over her dress, it was blank, but I stared at it wondering if I could somehow add a property patch there too.

Property of The Roman would look really fucking good stretched across her breast.

"You going to help me?" She gave me a coy smile while pulling out different canisters and spices.

I'd never baked a day in my life. I'd watched her bake a thousand times while she worked at The Drip, but I had never been this close to her while she did it.

"Wouldn't know where to begin."

She held her hand out. "For starters, you just stand next to me...and if you don't want flour all over your somber black clothes, then find an apron over there."

I turned away from her, finding the spot she'd indicated. The Stone Riders kitchen was well-lit with long counters stretching along the sides and a massive butcher block counter in the middle. A myriad of smaller stainless-steel tables were holding wrapped loaves of bread, all piled as if they were ready for delivery.

Tying the apron off, I walked back over to Natty and stood next to her.

"What's with all the bread?"

Natty peered over my shoulder and a sad smile slid along her mouth. "Long story...but Red should be in here baking right now...I'm curious where she is."

I didn't care enough to ask any follow-up questions. This life she had in the Stone Riders club was important to her, so I tried to make it important to me, but honestly, I just didn't give a fuck about this place or anyone in it. I felt like I had to share my wife with them, and for that alone, I detested this place.

"What do I do first?"

Natty set a bowl in front of me and a canister of flour. "Sift this for me."

She showed me how to hold the metal sifter and the mechanics of pouring in the flour. Once I had it down, I did as she'd instructed and watched as she worked. It was quiet and serene while she moved, and when it was time for me to move onto mixing wet ingredients, I did so without question, all while I remained transfixed by her.

There came a time she had to open a new bag of flour, and instead of reaching for a knife from the butcher block, she slid her hand under the bar and produced a familiar knife that I had once gifted to her. The sight of it had my eyes narrowing.

"Is that..."

She slid the blade through the bag, the black handle with the grim reaper engraved on the butt gleamed under the lights.

With a breathy voice, she muttered, "the knife you fucked me with when we were nineteen?"

That was the night she became my wife...it wasn't something I could easily forget.

I watched her, not confirming or denying.

With a smirk, she flipped the blade around, showing me the thickness of the handle. I remembered how it had fit around her puffy, gleaming pussy as she bucked her hips against it. The handle was large enough that it got her off, and I knew she'd kept it but fuck...to have it here, in this kitchen and something she touched nearly every day.

I took the blade from her and stuck the tip into the butcher block.

"Yes, that one. Do you use it often?"

Her hips turned, making her face me. Her left hand trailed up my chest as she leaned closer to me. "I use it in the kitchen, but every now and then, when I get lonely, I'll take it upstairs, wrap the sharp tip with a towel and use the butt the same way you did."

Adrenaline surged through me at her sultry, playful tone.

Gripping her jaw, I pulled her in close enough that my lips were at her ear. "Do you think of me when you do it?"

She nodded while letting out an airy gasp. "Always."

That was the last straw for me. Slipping out of the apron I'd put on, I shifted, holding her hips so they kissed the counter. Her hands came down, gripping the edge as a white plume of flour dusted the front of her apron.

"Silas." She breathed a warning, as I gently pushed on her back and forced her chest to rest against the counter, the bowl of wet ingredients tipped to the side, and a few eggs rolled out of the way, falling to the floor and cracking as I held her there.

My hand slid under her dress, lifting it so I could see her ass. She wore a pink thong, which slid up right through the center of her crack, leaving the skin of her toned, surprisingly tan ass on display.

"You outside sunbathing where men can see you, Caelum?"

Her hands shifted, making a few more eggs fall near my boots.

"What?"

I pressed my thumb into the shape outlined against her skin. "You have a tiny white heart on your ass, Natty. Like you placed a little marker there to see how dark you're getting."

She swatted my hand away and turned to get a look at what I was seeing.

Her green eyes slid up, leveling me with a glare. "Pen has a great private terrace that gets a lot of sun. Laura joined us one time and brought these cute little cut outs to use."

My mind was going crazy with images of Killian and Jameson seeing Natty in a bathing suit...based off her tan line, a very revealing one that shows most of her ass.

"We're always alone when we sunbathe…no one sees us, don't worry."

That helped settle a dangerous monster brimming under my skin.

"You're going to stay perfectly still, just like this while I kneel behind you and taste you. Do you understand, Caelum?"

"Silas, what if someone…"

I pulled her hair back, arching her neck, while pushing my leg in-between hers. She let out a breathy moan as I pressed my knee there.

"I don't care who walks in here, or if they see me fucking you, but I'll be a gentleman and kneel, so no one sees me. I'll use your dress as a cover if needed."

"Now, you'll have to be quiet, so I'm going to have you bite down on the butt of that handle you like to fuck occasionally. Can you do that for me?"

She gave a swift nod, and I pulled the knife up and gently placed the butt of the handle between her teeth until she bit down.

"Good girl."

Stroking a hand down the expanse of her ass, I slowly dropped to one knee while I worshiped her. I spread her cheeks wide, forcing her thong to the side as I settled my tongue against the tight space I'd been thinking about since I first flipped up her dress.

She let out a low whine as I began pushing my tongue around the tight hole while my fingers began rubbing slow circles into her clit. Her pussy already soaked my digits as I brushed along her silky slit. While I was ravenous to taste her, there was something so perfect about having her just like this, with her ass spread wide for me and my tongue teasing her.

Another moan slipped through her clenched teeth as something shifted and dropped from the counter. She was adjusting her grip while rocking back into my face.

I moved so my thumb remained in position over her hole and then my mouth lowered to her pussy. It was me that let loose a groan as my tongue traced a long line up her soaking lips, all that wetness now in my mouth as I closed around her clit and sucked.

She was shaking above me as I worked her messily and loudly. Her ass was still spread, my hands going to either side, so I had a clear view of her. She was gleaming with surrender, and I lapped up every fucking drop.

She made a squeaking sound as she squirmed, her hips moving, as if they were desperate for purchase, so I added my open palm to cover her pussy while I licked along the expanse of her crack.

She fucked my hand while I licked and rotated my fingers against her.

My cock swelled in my jeans, precum leaked, making me uncomfortable and wet. I needed to fuck her.

I quickly stood, hovering over her back as I began unbuttoning my jeans, and whispered near her ear.

"You going to suck my cock, and let me finish down that pretty throat of yours, or are you going to let me fill your cunt up?"

Her hands shifted, pushing more things away from her space as she spit out the handle of the knife.

"Fuck me. Fuck me now, Silas."

I shoved the fingers I'd fucked her with between her lips, covering her mouth while I gripped my cock and slid home, filling her core to the brim with my thickness.

She froze as I pulled out, watching as every gleaming inch left the apex of her thighs and then I relished how tight she felt as I pushed forward again. Her hips rocked against the counter, and a moan left her chest as she shook under me.

We were both barely hanging on by a thread, and I knew the Stone Riders could all be waking, any of them coming in at any moment. But fucking in a motorcycle club wasn't a foreign concept in these places; most people just lowered their gaze and kept moving.

I pulled Natty's hair, lifting her chest while I began thrusting my hips forward. She was moaning and screaming against my hand as I moved faster and pushed in harder. The entire counter shook as we fucked. The way her ass looked with my engorged cock sliding in and out of her pussy as I took her was enough to send me over the edge.

She bit down on my fingers right as I came, gripping her hips in a vise. Her inner walls tightened around me, and right as she came, screaming my name, I removed my hand so everyone could hear her.

She was panting, and I was smirking while I pulled out of her, and slowly slid her thong back into place.

"Keep baking, Caelum. Make me something sweet while my cum slides between your thighs and makes them sticky. When I eat this delicious treat, I want to think about how you've carried me with you, feeling it with every move you've made. I want to look at you and know you're remembering how good my cock felt inside you, and how devastating my tongue felt."

"Fuck, Silas." She breathed, trying to adjust her apron, and wipe it clean.

"Next time you wear that apron, it'll have my patch on it, and you'll be naked under it, riding my cock."

Her smile was slow, warm and completely mine.

"Then you better make sure we're in our very own house."

Killian and Wes had left their club in the hands of Jameson King, who was not my biggest fan and liked to remind me of that fact as often as he could. It had been a few days since I returned with Natty, and he'd been glaring at me like he was sucking on a fucking lemon ever since.

I approached the porch he was perched on, while he was drinking a cup of coffee, looking tired as fuck.

"You even fit to babysit this club?" I pushed past him with a slight shove to his shoulder.

He let out a sigh as he followed me back into the club.

"My wife is currently talking to your…" He paused, scrunching his brows together. "What is Natty to you again? Your girlfriend, victim… you never have clarified."

"Just mine, don't need to clarify shit for you. Where are they?"

Jameson looked up, indicating Natty's room. "They have Connor up there with them."

That was his way of warning me not to go up.

Ignoring him, I stalked toward the stairs, but Jameson called at my back. "You can't leave Death Raiders in the club like that. We can move

Natty to the cabin, but it's going to be a problem for them to stay in here. Killian won't allow it."

I turned back toward him, resisting the urge to punch him in the face.

"Then Killian can tell me that. I'm not listening to your babysitter bullshit; you've got no authority here."

"It's too many fucking Death Raiders, Silas."

I took a step closer. "Fable made his way into your club, Jameson. Through your guards and your walls. Don't talk to me about having my men in here."

I took another step toward the club while Jameson looked as though he was grinding glass.

"I'm not doing anything because of my respect for Natty, but don't test me, Silas. Roman or not, I'll go toe to toe with you."

Natty chose that moment to exit the club, her brows raised in surprise as she took both of us in.

I muttered to the former Chaos King, "My men stay."

Jameson peered over my shoulder to where his wife and son were now exiting, and then leaned closer, lowering his voice.

"She's my wife's best friend. I don't want her to go, but surely you can see that this won't work. You're not a Stone Rider. You never will be."

I tipped my chin toward her. "No I'm not, but she is."

Natty and Penelope weren't close enough to hear us, but they'd begun whispering together.

Jameson's glare cut through me and landed on Natty. "Yes, she is, so trust us to keep her safe. We protect our own."

I returned his glacial expression, not worrying about lowering my voice as Natty drew closer.

"Yet Fable still got into her room."

Jameson's eyes tapered. "Then you might need to make a decision. Because we can't coexist."

This was all bullshit I already knew and felt, but my options were limited. However, I wouldn't be leaving Natty unprotected any time soon.

I could try and explain it to Jameson. How there was a hole in my heart from the last time I did that.

Would I leave her to keep her safe, or would I stay and force her to lose the only place she ever called home?

While there wasn't a way that I'd ever let her go, there was a tiny piece of my heart that had already accepted that I needed to make up for what she'd been put through. Her having a happy and fulfilling place to call home with a family is all she's ever deserved.

If it meant she'd have to see me go in order to have that, I'd give it to her in a heartbeat.

I didn't get a chance to respond because when I went to open my mouth, there was a loud rumbling of engines that began echoing down the long drive.

We all turned in unison to see that Killian and Wes had returned, their men were with them and on the back of Wes Ryan's bike was a familiar looking woman. But it was the man wearing the full-face helmet on the back of one of the other members' bikes that caught my eye.

I saw his tattoos first, the ones I hadn't removed yet. Then I noticed his missing hand that was slung to the side of his body in a sling. Why the fuck had they brought my brother here?

I caught Natty's confused expression as she watched them approach. I was about to walk over to her and take her hand, when she lunged from the porch and ran toward the group.

NINETEEN
NATTY
AGE TWENTY-THREE

WINTER NO LONGER GUARANTEED THAT SILAS WOULD BE HOME.

His required time with his father had come and gone, and for some reason he continued to return to the viper's nest.

Being his wife didn't guarantee that I'd see him either or have any of his time. I was subject to waiting around for him just like his best friend, Lance, and his mother Sasha. We all danced around the subject, as if the mere mention of Silas Silva was the equivalent of saying a curse or talking about the boogie man.

The Roman was being tossed around more often than his real name anyway. This notorious tale of a man with a heart as dark as night: black and hate-filled as he tortured his victims, working as the executioner for The Destroyers. It was all just talk between drunk bikers, looking to one up each other with stories.

But at night, I'd hold his pillow to my chest and let my lungs expand with the hope that all those stories were false. Just far-fetched tales made up and exaggerated. Because my husband couldn't withstand any more darkness in that heart of his.

Which was why I didn't understand this need of his to return to his father...

"You look sad, Artie. It's almost Christmas."

I glanced up at the man who'd just crowded the space next to me at the bar. Alec's dark hair was slicked back, revealing his blue eyes and long lashes. He sipped from a dark bottle of beer as he assessed every inch of my face. My eyes, lips, and ears.

It was as though he was looking for what might be different about me since the last time he'd laid that confusing glare on me.

In another life, I'd toss my left hand out and boast about being married to his brother. I'd gush over being his family now and laugh about how we would spend the holidays together. In this life, no one knew I was married to Silas because he was worried it would put too big of a target on my back. One larger than the property patch he put there.

I had no ring on my finger, and no proof at all that Silas and I had actually said those vows to one another that humid summer night, nearly four years ago.

"I'm not sad, just tired." I finally quipped back at Alec, curious why he was at this bar of all places.

I wasn't in Pyle, which, if Silas were here, he'd likely have a melt-down over…but he was gone, again, and Christmas was in two days.

I'd begged him to stay, and he begged me to understand why he had to leave. There was also the small issue of Dirk watching my every move, and when he was able to get me alone…it wasn't pleasant.

Alec pushed in closer, so I could hear him over the noise. "You're not wearing your property patch."

No, I wasn't. But not for the reasons he assumed.

"This isn't a biker bar…and this town isn't Death Raider territory. I'm not trying to cause any waves by being here."

Alec seemed to understand, which was probably why he wasn't wearing his cut either. He'd recently pledged with the Sons of Speed, a club a few hours west of Pyle. I hadn't seen him in a few years…but Lance had mentioned it once in front of me, which was the only way I knew anything about Alec's life.

"Why are you here?" I volleyed back, curious now why he was so far east.

His lips quirked up while he took a long pull of his beer. "Thought I'd spend the holidays with family…my mom lives in Rose Ridge now."

"She does?" That surprised me...mostly because I knew nothing about his mother, or him.

He laughed, dipping his head.

"Yeah, she died last winter from an overdose. They tossed her in a grave down at the Rose Ridge cemetery, flat stone the size of a brick over the top of her grave. Might as well have kept it unmarked; it wasn't like anyone would care enough to visit her."

I sipped my soda water and focused on the way his eyes turned contemplative.

"Not even you?"

His face lifted. "No...not even me...thought maybe I could find someone to fuck out there, right on top of her grave as a nice Merry Christmas and fuck you to her."

Damn.

"So, not a good relationship with her then?"

With another scoff, he shook his head while looking around.

"No, nothing like the precious Hallmark movie that Silas and his mother Sasha are living out."

I bristled at his mocking tone. They were the two most important people in my life, and regardless of Alec's shitty upbringing, he wasn't about to talk shit about them in front of me.

Sliding off the stool, I set my glass down, about to leave, until Alec moved to block my path.

"Sorry...I know your team Silas...I didn't mean anything by it."

"Don't talk about them in front of me. Not ever," I warned, glaring up at him.

He gave me a solemn nod, pulling my stool out once more. The sound of billiard balls knocking together echoed from a pool table, off to the side, where there were a few guys laughing and joking together. The bar was calm for the most part, and not very busy. I liked the easy atmosphere.

"So...tell me why you're here, all alone in rival territory, just two days before Christmas."

I was slightly buzzed from the cranberry vodka I'd had just fifteen minutes earlier. I had to be, that was the only reason I felt compelled to tell him why I was all alone in this small town at this bar that was playing Mariah Carey Christmas ballads, on repeat.

"Silas left again. I asked him not to, because I wanted him here for Christmas…but he—"

I stopped myself because this was Alec, his brother that had been nice to me, but overtly flirtatious.

"I'm just looking for a change of scenery is all, and I like that Rose Ridge does the big starlight parade, with the lighting of the tree. The whole town gets in on it, and it's like a scene from that Dr. Suess movie."

Alec scrunched his nose. "The one with the Grinch?"

I nodded as a smile lifted my lips.

"There was snow here last year, and the whole town looked like a Christmas card."

"So you're going to pout here, all alone, because my brother is an idiot and is off doing our father's bidding?"

A tiny string unfurled in my brain, like a strand of curiosity, one that would surely kill me if I tried to follow it. Just the same, I dug into it with both hands because I was starved for details.

"You know what he's doing?"

Alec's eyes nearly sparkled under the low lighting of the bar. He gave one slow look to the left, then leaned closer. "Other than letting you slip through his fingers?"

We were close enough that it looked like we were sharing a secret or might be lovers. I drew back while clearing my throat.

"I'm not slipping through his fingers."

Alec's lips twisted into a sneer. "If you were mine, you wouldn't be here."

"You'd tell me where I could go and couldn't go?" I raised my brow in question.

Alec laughed into his beer. "Damn straight. You go where I know you'll be safe."

Silas wasn't any different. Except he never made me feel like I couldn't go somewhere, or that he'd be angry if I did. He just appeared like a wraith and reclaimed me, as if I was, in fact, slipping through his fingers.

"He'll be back by Christmas. We have a tradition where every Christmas we exchange—"

Someone laughed from behind us and started singing along with the Christmas tune that had just started playing. The bartender checked on us, seeing if we needed refills, and then Alec's face dipped closer. "You exchange…"

"It's stupid to anyone who hasn't been us for the past seven years."

His whistle echoed over the loud music and bustling bodies, making me laugh.

"Stop."

"Seven years, damn…have you ever even been with anyone else?"

I shifted on my stool, so I was facing away from him, cradling my glass. "I've never needed or wanted anyone else."

"Okay, I won't argue with you about the semantics of only being with one person. Tell me what you exchange with him."

"Love letters we've found in poetry, books, music…things that have inspired us. Each year, it's a gift to see what the other found because it's always something that reminds us of the other person. Last year, Silas found this beautiful poem written by someone who had observed the love Edgar Allen Poe had for his wife. The extreme lengths he'd gone to in order to have her, protect her and love her. Even in her death, you know he kept her bones under his bed for a time."

Alec's face soured. "That's fucking gross."

I shrugged, feeling a blush heat my face. "I mean it's all gross when you think about it. He married his cousin, but in a different time, a different space where those things weren't viewed through the same lens we're looking through…it was considered beautiful."

"I can see now why you and my brother are such a great match." Alec's gaze moved, watching a group of guys who had gotten closer, one of them had been watching me from across the room, and was now sitting beside me.

Ignoring the man at my back, I sipped my drink hoping he wouldn't—

"Excuse me." There was warm breath against my neck and a hand on my shoulder.

Shit.

Alec leaned past me, invading my space. "Fuck off."

The man behind me leaned over my shoulder, getting closer to Alec and I was just caught in the middle. Not an ideal place to be.

"Are you her boyfriend?" the guy asked, and I let out a sigh. If Silas were here that guy wouldn't have ever walked up to me in the first place.

"Don't have to be. I'm here talking to her, and you need to go somewhere else."

I slid off the stool and faced the man, giving him a flat smile.

"I'm not with him, but I do have a boyfriend. I'm not interested." It burned me not to say husband. I had a fucking husband, not a boyfriend.

I was a married woman. But I was also all alone…in a city that I didn't belong in.

The reminder that I was being kept from Silas by this invisible line drawn by his father threaded through my breast, tugging and poking like an aimless needle.

My feet carried me out of the bar, back into the cold, and when the door closed a second time, I knew Alec had followed.

"What are you going to do if he doesn't show up in time?"

I turned, taking in the gray sky, the clouds pregnant with snow. The ground was frozen, and our breaths clouded in front of us. Alec's features looked crisp and sharp under the December sky.

"What do you mean?"

He stepped closer and tentatively pushed a lock of my hair off my shoulder. "If Silas doesn't show up in time for Christmas, will you spend it alone?"

The mere notion made me feel physically sick. I hated being alone.

My mother had left the Death Raiders a year ago. No note. No goodbye. Just gone.

Sasha was my family in theory, but it was like living with a cactus. She was prickly and protective. Her only priority was Silas, and she made that clear every chance she got. If I didn't have Silas, I had no one.

I must have waited too long to respond because Alec took a step closer until his chin was nearly at my forehead.

"Don't spend Christmas alone, Artie. Promise me you won't." His whisper landed as a hot breath against my skin.

My voice cracked as I asked, "Where else would I go?"

"Find me...I'll be here. I joked about my mom's grave, but truthfully, it's the only place I want to be through the holidays. A cold grave, celebrating with the only family I ever had. She was shitty to me on her best days, and deplorable on her worst, but she was my mom. She still bought me gifts on Christmas...still decorated and managed to wrangle a tree inside. It wasn't perfect, but it was ours...and I miss it."

He swallowed thickly. "I miss her."

I had no idea how that felt, other than missing Silas. I'd never missed my mother...not once. I never missed my father because I never knew him.

I had missed Sasha when I was little...even now, there was a part of me that longed for her to love me the way she loved her son, but I knew she just wasn't capable.

"If he doesn't show, Alec, then I'll come spend it with you. Honestly, I wish you two could spend it together, even if he does show up. You're brothers."

Alec's smile was sad, and as he tucked a strand of hair behind my ear, my heart seemed to break in half.

"Cain killed Abel because he was jealous of his offering."

I didn't know much about the Bible, but Sasha had taught us a few of the basics. I knew about Adam and Eve...the Ark, and a few other bullet points. Hateful brothers didn't register.

"So?"

His fingers were still tangled in my hair. "So, I'd do more than murder my brother for what he has."

It was murmured low and as soon as he said it, he took a few steps back then picked up my hand.

"Call me if you need me, Artie." He wrote down his number with a black pen against my palm. Then stared down at me for a long moment before walking back to his bike.

I stared after him, confused.

What did Silas have that would make Alec feel so violent toward him?

Me: It's Christmas Eve...where are you?

Silas: Ran into a complication.

Me: Will you be back tonight?

Silas:...

Me: ?? Silas...will you be back tonight?

Silas: I love you. I will call you in the morning.

Me: You promised this trip wouldn't interfere with Christmas. You swore it to me, Silas.

Silas: I know. If I could leave, I would. I'm sorry.

I stared at my phone feeling numb.

If I understood what Silas was doing, maybe it would make me feel better, but I didn't.

His father was a monster, and as far as I understood, he didn't need to be working with him, or around him, or have anything to do with him.

Bitterness crept into my heart, choking out all sense. The small tree in Sasha's living room was decorated with a string of popcorn, a few recovered bulbs from a bag at Goodwill, and a string of half working lights. There were no gifts under it.

No other decorations were around the house, and I hadn't seen or heard from Sasha in a week. When I'd driven back to Pyle two days ago, Dirk had arrived as well. So far, I had been lucky that he hadn't walked over and demanded to see me. Usually he found a way to torture me, especially if Sasha was gone.

I wasn't eager to run into him again, and the longer Silas was gone, the higher the chance was that I would.

The loneliness and fear dug at my core. The silence in the house crept into that void in my soul, and I couldn't stand it. I jumped up, grabbed my coat and left the house.

Rose Ridge was only a twenty-minute drive, and the entire ride over, I justified my actions with the idea that I was spending time with my husband's family.

Once I had parked in the asphalt lot of the grocery store, I pulled up my phone and called Alec.

He answered on the third ring.

"Hello?"

"Alec...it's me, Natty."

He paused, then let out a small chuckle. "You coming to see me for Christmas, Artie?"

I hated that fucking nickname.

"You offered, didn't you?" I snapped, feeling torn and annoyed with myself. Why couldn't I just be strong and spend tonight alone. I could hide from Dirk. But the idea of hiding in the wardrobe on Christmas wasn't appealing.

"Just texted you the address."

I hung up, took a shuddery breath and began navigating toward the house. It was a simple cabin on the river, with smoke coming out of a brick chimney. The sky was white, flakes of snow blew against my face as I slammed the car door shut and trudged up the rickety steps.

The door opened before I could knock, and Alec stepped aside, welcoming me in.

The house was warm, so I shed my jacket and shoes. The foyer was miniscule and quickly led to where a round table sat with two chairs. Off to the side was an L-shaped kitchen, with linoleum along the floors and Formica counters. The living room had green shag carpeting and two armchairs that faced a large hearth with a roaring fire inside.

Alec wore white socks, threadbare jeans and a simple white shirt. His hair was wet from a recent shower, and his face was freshly shaven. His smile was familiar and stretched along his firm jawline. I hated how noticeable the changes in his face and body definition were from the last time I'd seen him those few years ago. The other day, with his hoodie on, his muscular form was hidden and I had flat out ignored his jawline.

Now, under the fire light, and the pain radiating from my thatched heart, I noticed.

And it made me sick because I wasn't attracted to Alec, but I was aware of how he looked at me. I didn't want to lead him on, and I didn't want this to look or feel like something was happening here that wasn't actually happening.

Alec pulled out a bottle of whiskey, two tumblers and a deck of cards. "Poker?"

I took the filled glass and sipped. "War."

It began to snow in fat, chunky flakes. The fire crackled from behind me, and the tumbler of whiskey was cold under my hand. It made me want to toss the entire fucking thing in the fire just to watch it burn.

Silas hadn't called me or texted.

I watched with fear as the clock wound down, leaving no room for Silas to redeem himself. Christmas had arrived and a sob worked itself up my chest, ugly and full of hurt.

Full of anger and confusion over why I was losing the man I loved to a monster that had ruined his childhood. I had been there for Silas. I had been the one to help him, to love him. To stand by him, and yet I was being pushed away.

It was Christmas, and I was alone.

Alec's arms came around me, and as he pulled me tight into his chest, my fingers clung to his forearms. I realized too late, and after I was far too exhausted that we had moved to the bed. But the broken part of me didn't care. I hoped Silas would somehow walk in and be hurt by what he saw. It was as far as I was willing to go. I would never kiss another man, or have sex with them…but being held by one. To Silas, it would be the same as anything else.

My sobs echoed through the room until I finally fell asleep in the arms of my husband's brother…and quite possibly his greatest enemy.

TWENTY
NATTY
PRESENT

I saw Killian riding first. He had Laura behind him, and the bike next to them had Wes Ryan, and on the back of his bike was a familiar dark-haired woman...

Rachel.

Dust kicked up from the tires, as the remaining members rolled to a stop in front of the club. Wes parked, and Rachel let his waist go as she tipped her head back and took in the Stone Riders clubhouse.

Killian helped Laura from their seat first, then swung his leg over until they'd took a few steps from the bike. Laura moved first, to assist Rachel off Wesley's bike.

I jogged over to Killian who gave me a look of relief which had my heart warming.

"You're back!" I said, catching the gaze of the group.

Rachel stepped forward, tentative at first, but as soon as I caught her eye, she rushed me.

"Are you okay?"

I opened my arms and pulled her into a hug as she inspected me.

"I'm okay. Are you...how did you get away?"

Her green eyes were bright out in the sun, her hair was frizzed and a little tangled, and other than a little dirt smudge on her chin, she looked perfectly fine.

"I took that pack meant for you and I just walked until I saw a group of bikers riding around the area as if they were looking for someone. I spotted the Stone Rider patch, and when I remembered what you'd told me about Killian, I stepped out where they'd be able to see me."

"You've been gone for days…was everything okay?" I directed my question at Killian as he drew closer.

He glanced up at Wes then over at someone behind me, which I assumed was Silas or Jameson. "She was dehydrated…we stayed until we knew she felt okay enough to ride back."

"No issues with Fable?" I knew they didn't owe me answers, and the way these clubs worked, they likely wouldn't give them to me because I wasn't a member, but I couldn't help but try.

Killian dipped his face, and Wes stepped off to the side pulling his phone up to his ear. He was likely checking on his pregnant wife who was at home.

"We ran into a messenger."

Rachel's hand wrapped around mine and squeezed tight as I waited for Killian to continue. Silas stepped closer until he was crowding my back, and it was as if the ground beneath me fell out from under me as Killian lifted his chin toward Hamish, who was riding behind him.

That's when I saw him.

Being pulled off the bike by two other members, Alec stood in front of us, gagged with a white piece of fabric across his mouth. He wore a sling for his amputated hand. The breath seemed to stall in my lungs the second his eyes landed on me and froze.

I wasn't sure what to feel other than shock.

He'd kidnapped me.

Held me captive. Literally cuffed me to him for days on end.

Sexually harassed me.

My throat felt tight as I took all those memories and mentally placed them next to the ones where Alec had been my friend. My refuge in some situations.

A safe person once upon a time. Now I didn't know how to even look at him without wanting to hurt him.

"You don't want to hear this message, Natty," Rachel whispered near my ear.

I glanced at her, my brows furrowed in confusion and then stepped away from her before Silas could hide whatever was in that bag. He was avoiding looking at Alec, which was a tactical move, so I followed suit.

He didn't open it wide enough but it didn't matter, Silas pulled the severed hand out where all could see and inspected the note nailed through the palm.

I read from over his shoulder and felt those invisible spiders crawling down my back, along my scalp and even inside my head. It was as if Fable had invaded my very bloodstream, and I didn't know how to escape him.

My Dearest Son,

Looks like you left something behind when you came to collect your whore.

I was going to give your precious Caelum to Alec as a gift, he has, after all, been pining for years for her. I was inclined to entertain his desires because she'd be out of your way and more importantly, out of the picture.

But now, I think I might want to keep her for myself.

She's taken your good sense, and now cost Alec a hand...and honestly his remaining worth.

So I'll trade you. Here is your brother, now give me your wife.

Leave her with the Stone Riders, walk away from her forever...or she becomes my plaything. Mine to torture and fill, and who knows, maybe she'll give you a little sister after I fuck her enough times.

You know as well as that cunt of a mother that this girl was never supposed to be a part of the plan. - Fable

Silas didn't show any signs that the letter had impacted him at all. He scanned the words, and then shoved the note in his back pocket, while tossing the hand at Alec's feet.

Alec glared daggers at Silas, then shifted his glare to me, but his expression softened the smallest bit.

I ignored him and focused on Silas, turning away from the crowd so we had a small amount of privacy.

"What plan is he talking about, Silas?" My voice sounded strange... as if I'd found an empty well and started screaming into the darkness, my words all returning void.

Silas glanced down at me, his jaw tense and his eyes glacial.

I felt like fear had stepped out of that letter and took shape as a pair of shears, clipping my invisible wings. The ones I stupidly thought I grew after falling in love with Silas Silva.

Dirk had been my personal monster, but Silas had another...one much darker and more depraved. While I assumed I knew how to manage nightmares, it seemed there was another layer of deceit I had been oblivious to.

"Silas, what plan?"

His hand found mine, and suddenly he was pulling us away from the group. I heard Killian curse, and Wes start his bike. My brain connected the dots, aligning them into similar spaces they'd always fell into. I was merely a visitor in this place. I had no one that belonged to me...no one except Pen. I searched for her dark hair, that tiny piece of perfection she kept pressed to her chest as she soothed Connor. I looked for her husband, but they weren't out here.

My gaze dropped to the ground as the gravel turned to grass.

I felt untethered, like I was fourteen again, waiting on a sun-soaked dock for Silas to come back to me. Just so my life would make sense again.

Suddenly a shadow fell over us as Silas pushed my back up against the side wall of the clubhouse, where no one could see us.

His hand planted next to my face, and his nose nearly touched mine.

"He always had plans for me to take over. That was the idea…Alec would be set up with his own club, but he wanted the Destroyers to be mine. My mother knew that was his plan…"

"If that was the plan then why join The Death Raiders as seventeen?" I searched his face, so clueless as to how I had missed so much when we were growing up. I blindly followed everything Silas said and did, too enraptured to ever question any of it.

He dipped, his head, his face solemn.

"Mom thought it would help put a barrier up between me taking over The Destroyers. We knew Dirk just had to die and I had a good chance of stepping in…it was my primary focus and why I went back so often. I needed to learn as much as I could about him."

My arms came over my chest as if I could guard the pathetically weak organ that had absorbed all of Silas, taking in all his darkness and filtering it for the both of us. I was his beam of sunshine all doe eyed and in love, too naïve to ask questions or to demand to be included. I assumed he wanted to be there, doing his father's bidding. I had assumed he was undercutting Fable, or working against him, but Sasha and him…they'd had actual plans in place. A goal to work toward. Something, all this time I could have partnered with them on. Perhaps if I'd been included, I could have told Silas about Dirk. Maybe if I was helping him take down Fable, I could have gone with him, or stayed somewhere else while he worked. Instead, I was just left behind.

His pretty piece of sunshine that stayed put in his room, there to absorb his darkness when he needed me.

Bitterness was a tangled root around my emotions.

"Did your mother ever tell you what happened with the trade?"

The gray hue of his eyes turned violent as he clenched his jaw. "No one has ever fucking told me what really happened, Natty. I came back and you were gone. I was given some bullshit reason, but no. I never got the full story. You sure as hell never told me."

I hated how heavy that statement felt, and how even years later, the fear over his reaction and him self-destructing was too overwhelming for me to just open my mouth and explain it. But he'd never come back for me. "I've never had a chance to tell you, Silas. You were suddenly gone from my life, and I was here...and you acted like I was in a different world, unreachable."

A breath escaped him as he hung his head.

"You *were* in a different world. If I had come knocking on Simon Stone's door, demanding you back, it would have started a war. Especially because Dirk was still alive, and he was the one that Simon made the deal with."

"How nice of you to choose when and how you choose to follow club politics." I pushed the hair away from my face. I knew I wasn't being entirely fair, but I also hated that there was a whole group of people that seemed to know what Silas had been planning with his father, and it didn't include me.

"Why are you upset about this? We're going to find him, and we won't—"

I pushed at his chest so I could get some air. He sidestepped, allowing me to pass, so I began pacing.

"I'm upset because I feel like I keep getting fragments of you, Silas. Tiny pieces that get stolen from me the moment they land in front of me."

His steady gaze moved with me as I continued to pace.

"Caelum."

I shook my head, a tear sliding free. "Don't call me that. Just call me Natty. You've made me think that one day we'd have this amazing life, Silas. This beautiful love story. Yet I've been here waiting for you to come and get me, and you never have. You never did. I was taken from you. That is the only reason you came for me. I am a tiny speck of dust on your map of domination and plans."

"Will you stop it?" Silas moved in again, his hands going to my hips, and his chest covering mine. "Stop saying this shit. You don't even understand what I've done to be with you, to be free...to have the Death Raiders just so I have an army to fight him with. If I go from you, it's only to ensure you're safe. I'm never far, and it's never for long. You're acting like I want to be away from you."

It felt like he did, but I knew those were my own insecurities.

Closing my eyes, I inhaled a sharp breath.

"I know you want to, but I also know that you have some over-reaching plan for Fable. I always thought you were going to leave him behind back then...but you kept returning. We nearly ended because of it, Silas."

The silence between us grew and Silas pushed a hand through his unruly hair.

"We don't end, Caelum. We just keep going, we're like the roots that hold the crust of this fucking earth together. Bound to one another."

Until an earthquake or something came along and shook the crust apart.

"It doesn't matter, Silas. We can be in love and want to be together, but Fable is still coming for me. He wants you to leave me here."

"Honestly, it's difficult not to leave you here, Natty. You have a family, people who love you and care about you. A better life than what I could give you."

My stomach clenched with nerves at the confirmation that he did plan to leave me.

I focused on the ground as his words made a home inside me, and when he walked closer to tip my chin back, I glared at his stoic features.

"Would you leave your Raiders for me?"

Silas paused with his hand resting on my neck, his jaw tensing. "I need them to fight him...once he's gone, I would. In a heartbeat."

"Who will the Destroyers go to? Aren't you worried about someone just taking his place?"

A sad laugh escaped his lips as he tipped his head back.

"No, Caelum. I'm worried about someone taking my place here, with you. You're the only thing that's ever mattered to me. I know you think that's not true because of how I lost you, but it is. I want the best thing for you. I want you to have everything, all the happiness you possibly could withstand in a singular lifetime."

This felt like goodbye, and I refused to accept it.

Stepping forward, I relished the way the wind picked up and brushed against my face.

"You're it."

His eyes narrowed as my hand went over his heart. "I'm what?"

"All the happiness I could possibly withstand in a singular lifetime. You're all of that. Let's leave, just forget the Raiders, the Destroyers, all of it. Run with me, and let's start over."

"What about Penelope and Connor, or your job at The Drip? What about your baking with Red, and your kitchen here?" His voice dropped in challenge, his eyes hardening with that obstinate glare he always used with me.

"Why do I have to live without those things in order to be with you?"

"Because all I bring is death, Natty, and I want you to live. I think you want to live too, and that's good. You deserve to." He pulled me in and kissed the top of my head.

I still felt like he was trying to say goodbye, but I couldn't work out exactly how he was going to say it. If he would just leave me in the middle of the night, or what he'd do, but my chest already ached with the memory of how the last time he'd left ruined me so thoroughly and how, to this day, he still did not know what had actually happened.

Maybe it was finally time he did.

TWENTY-ONE
NATTY
AGE TWENTY-FIVE

It was late when I made my way back to the house. Later than I ever dared previously, but Sasha had texted me Dirk was gone, along with his captains and inner circle of Raiders. So I had opted in to do a later shift at the diner.

Most of the other women in the club worked at Strings, the local strip club, but Silas would burn it down before he allowed anyone to see me dance there. I understood it, but damn they made good tips. Much better than I made down at the Steakhouse.

Being able to work a little later than usual helped, which meant I finally had enough saved up for a new place in Rose Ridge. I knew Sasha and Silas would hate this idea, but *I* hated Pyle, and Rose Ridge was the next closest town that would allow us to stay close enough for Silas to attend club required events.

That was assuming he'd want to come with me.

The wound from two years ago when I'd told him where I spent my Christmas, and with who, was still a strain between us. I had never seen Silas so hurt when I explained through sobs that I'd spent the night in his brother's arms.

Words burned my tongue to explain that it was more than just being lonely. I wanted to tell him about Dirk, and how afraid I'd grown of the leader. How I felt like my every move was being stalked and hunted. If I told him, he'd kill Dirk or try to, and then he'd be killed.

So Silas had slipped back into traveling, being gone. When he came back, he'd hold me, fuck me and we'd fall back into the same roles we always had before, but I could feel the tension between us.

I'd broken him when I'd gone to his brother for support, and while it had been two years, it seemed like he couldn't fully move past it. Regardless that he said he forgave me, and he must have because he never went after Alec.

I hadn't spoken to the man since that night….except for one solitary time. The following morning, I had spent Christmas with my husband's brother, and then I drove back to Pyle. Silas came home a day later, and I confessed what I'd done. After that, things were dust and ash between us. There and tangible but decaying.

Now, he was slowly breaking me by not returning to me like he once did. Silas had been gone now for three months, and I was dying to know where he was, and what he was doing. Sasha wasn't much help.

So it left me with little options but to dream of a fresh start. Away from this place, and these walls that had been both my home and prison since I was a child.

My plan was to make Silas dinner, assuming he came home within the next few weeks, and explain how he could live in Rose Ridge despite the fact that it was rival territory. I didn't know anything about the Stone Riders, but after hearing about Simon Stone offering up so much to save his daughter, it made me feel as though the city would be a safe option.

There was the cutest little white cottage on the outskirts of town, by the old highway that I had been looking at. If we moved there, we wouldn't even be within city limits technically. It had these overextended windows that popped out, with window seats built in. There wasn't a yard that I could see, just all dead grass, and no trees. But maybe I could plant, and help a few things grow.

I had images from the real estate website folded and tucked into my wallet. On my lunch breaks, I'd take it out and stare at it, drawing ideas of where I would put things. The rental agreement already came through, and with the last of my tips tonight, I had six months of rent saved up. If I could get Silas on board with moving with me then I was sure he had funds he'd be happy to pitch in. He was always leaving me wads of cash when he went on runs.

He didn't know that I'd been saving it all for my little cottage fund.

"Sasha?" I called out, shutting the door with my foot and flipping the lock.

I had no idea if she was home, but if Dirk was gone then I assumed she would be as well. Any respite she ever had from that man; she would take. Regardless that he now favored torturing me when he tired of Sasha or any of his other women.

The lights were still off, but my hands were full of the two bags of groceries I'd purchased on the way home. Setting them down on the counter, I assumed Sasha wasn't home since she hadn't answered, but as soon as I turned, I heard the click of a lighter.

The very blood in my veins froze as the voice in the dark echoed through the room.

"Just me, little Fawn."

Terror had an interesting way of arresting me and engaging my flight or fight instincts. When Dirk came for me, I immobilized completely. I didn't consider what weapons were near me, or where the exits were.

I just froze.

I tried to swallow around the lump in my throat, but the knot began to swell. If Dirk was in the house, it meant he was here for me. It didn't matter that I wore the property patch for Silas. Dirk didn't care. I was a toy to him, and he dangled and played with me as he saw fit. Always terrorizing me, just enough so I was still intact when Silas returned.

"Thought I was out of town, didn't you?" Dirk smirked around his cigarette. His tall stature was folded into one of Sasha's armchairs, his wide, barrel chest was covered with a white t-shirt, revealing sleeves of tattoos down his exposed arms. It was the ones along the side of his face that were truly gruesome.

My fingers trembled as I kept my back to the groceries that were going to spoil now.

Dirk slowly stood from the chair, stretching as he went, and exhaling a breath of smoke.

"You did, didn't you? That's why you worked later and drove in past dark. You never come in this late, little Fawn."

He took a few long strides in my direction, making me step to the side, so I had an exit.

Tilting his head to the side, he paused with a smirk.

"You know better than to hide from me. Come here, let me see you."

My heart felt like a thundercloud was roaring behind it. My body trembled and inside I was silently screaming for Silas to come back for me.

"You know the deal, Fawn...come to me, let me see you. Give me your arms."

I took another step back on instinct. We'd done this dance before; the first few months Dirk had started paying attention to me, I'd tried to fight, which resulted in me gaining a broken femur and then a broken finger. Silas showed up at my job, assuming someone there was responsible. He'd stayed home longer than he usually did, which was the only good thing to come of Dirk's attention on me.

Now, years in, I knew better than to run or to fight. Dirk was stronger and a broken nose might be enough to prove to Silas that something was going on. If Silas found out what Dirk was doing, he'd kill him, and then all of Dirk's loyal men would kill Silas and probably Sasha.

"I said come here, Fawn."

A sob caught in my throat as I held my arm out, old burns were scarred into them already but if I wore long sleeves, no one noticed.

His tongue clicked. "This time, I want you to strip for me. I want to watch your flesh burn in a more creative place tonight."

If he was willing to burn me somewhere that would cause Silas to be suspicious, then he was getting more assertive.

"I don't have all night, and if you drag it out any longer, I might just decide to let go of my gracious attitude and fuck you instead."

Flicking a quick gaze to the door, I grabbed the hem of my shirt and pulled it up over my head. Dirk's dark eyes looked nearly black as he stared at my cleavage, and the lacy black bra holding up my breasts.

"Your skirt next."

A tear slid down the length of my lash as my fingers wrapped around the copper button. I flicked it open and pushed my skirt down, leaving me in a pair of black bikini underwear.

Dirk stepped closer, exhaling a plume of smoke against my chest.

"Perfect." He stroked a finger down my left breast. "Soon enough, you'll belong to me, Fawn. All this flawless skin will be mine to ruin. Mine to taste."

I was shaking as another tear slipped down my face, dripping from my chin.

"Take off your underwear, Fawn. You shouldn't have such a fuckable ass…it's too tempting to ignore. I need to see a pink little burn disrupting the perfect smooth skin."

Turning toward the counter, I clung to the edge after pulling my underwear down. Dirk didn't touch me except to extinguish the butt of his cigarette in the globe of my ass. The burn felt the same as always, and yet the shock of pain never seemed to get any easier to stomach. My fingers clenched the edge of the counter so hard my nails chipped.

Dirk hissed, and then groaned as if this was deeply enjoyable to him.

The second he stepped back, I pulled my underwear up, heaving as sobs trapped the air in my lungs.

"If you're worried about The Roman seeing it there, I suggest getting ink to cover it."

I continued pulling on clothing while he made his way to the exit. Before he opened the door, he called out, "If you're so worried about coming home after dark, then wear my patch, Fawn. No one will touch you if you belong to me."

The door slammed behind him as he left, and I ran to the bathroom. I vomited the small remnants of my lunch into the toilet and then I started the shower.

I didn't even wait for it to warm up, the heat would hurt the burn anyway. I just needed to scrub the feeling of him off my skin. The washcloth and bar of soap left my skin raw and red as tears streamed down my face, my braids remained, the loose strands sticking to my face.

I was still crying when the bathroom door opened, and Sasha appeared. Her eyes were wide, watery and red.

"I watched…I couldn't…he would have…" she stammered as fresh tears streamed unbidden down her face.

I nodded, stumbling out of the shower, pulling my towel around me. "I know."

She couldn't fight him anymore than I could, and she'd endured his abuse longer than I had.

"I have to get you out of here, Natty. Things are progressing…which means he's getting more comfortable with claiming you. He offered you his patch…that's not good."

I swiped at my face as I tried to clear my throat. "Where am I supposed to go where he won't be able to follow?"

I had my cottage plans, but Rose Ridge wasn't far enough, and if Silas was going to remain with the Death Raiders, then Dirk would still have access to me.

Sasha looked frantic as she searched my face, her own eyes welling with tears.

"We've held him off as long as we can, honey. I fear the next time he comes, he'll consume you whole. Wherever you go, it needs to be somewhere Dirk won't be able to follow. Somewhere you're protected…"

"But Silas will protect me…he's always protected me, if I just tell him then he—"

A flicker of unease sharpened her focus as she stepped back into the hall. It was a clear answer to my naïve notion and illusion of safety. Silas was her son, and I was merely the foster daughter she'd taken in and helped raise. She loved me in her own way and keeping me safe fell within that column, but it would never be at the sake of keeping her own son safe.

"Silas can't know, can he?" I followed her into the darkened house. The lingering fear in the room still clung to the shadows, creeping up along my spine. The burn on my ass ached, and the smear of darkness on my soul felt permanent. I couldn't keep doing this…I would break entirely and inevitably; Silas would find out and that war would come.

Sasha gave me a pleading look, her eyes welling with tears. "He will die, Natty. Silas loves you with a consuming sort of love…the kind that would burn and burn and burn until nothing but ash was left. Even if it meant he himself perished."

I nodded while a lump continued to form and burn in my throat.

"Get dressed, I have a phone call to make…" Sasha gave my arm a gentle squeeze before turning to leave.

My feet carried me to the room I'd shared with Silas since we were kids. The dark walls holding in years of secrets and a love story that spanned along the expanse of the sky. The string of fairy lights I had hung so many years ago were dim as I flicked the switch. Our modest, queen-sized mattress now filling the floor space I once had as a bed. The soles of my feet touched the rug I'd found on a swap site for cheap; it was soft and looked new.

I remember when Silas had unrolled it, and how he'd looked up at me that day all smiles and happiness.

"When we get our own place, we'll take this with us."

I had beamed with excitement, so much so that it was the first time I had considered looking for a new place for us. It's what had led me to my cottage.

Sorrow burrowed into my sternum, but I pushed past it by getting dressed. I found the old duffle Silas had used when going to his father's house all those years and began stuffing it with my clothes.

I didn't know when he'd be back. I didn't want him to think I was leaving him.

God, he had to know I'd never leave him.

As quickly as I could, I began to write to him explaining what I could without creating a mess for Sasha, who would remain with the Death Raiders.

"Natty, come with me. We're going to stay in a hotel for a few days while he gets the deal set up."

I bustled out of the room, my heart in my throat as I followed Sasha. I gave our room one last glance and trailed her out of the house.

"Your car will have to stay here."

I wanted to tell her about my plan to rent the cottage, and see if that would be possible, but Sasha kept darting her eyes around as if she were worried.

"Duck down in the back, Natty. Dirk can't know that you're leaving."

I did as she said and continued to do as she said for the following two days, hiding out in a shitty motel in a town I wasn't familiar with.

Finally, she told me what was happening, and I had no choice but to accept my new fate.

"Simon Stone agreed to trade a shipment of weapons he just received for your safe passage to his club. He's not the sort of man that would hurt you, Natty. You'll be in the club, your own room, protected…and most importantly, away from Dirk."

"Why would Simon trade such a large shipment for me?"

It was the only thing I could even think to ask because my mind was whirling, pieces of information felt like fragments of shrapnel missing and hitting all at once. I couldn't grasp what was happening, or how I'd lost control of my own life.

Sasha's gaze softened as she moved a piece of my hair to the side. "Other than because I asked him to. He has a daughter, honey. One that's your age. Their club has a code about women and how they're treated. You'll be safe there."

I believed her. I vaguely remembered when Simon Stone had shown up to reclaim his daughter from when Dirk had kidnapped her. I had never seen him myself, but he was a good man.

"Does Simon know I'm technically patched to Silas, which breaks a few codes between clubs. It could be cause for a war…"

Sasha winced the smallest bit, then gave me a sad smile.

"Once you enter the doors of that club, it's better if no one knows who you belong to. Don't speak of him being anything to you." Her gaze flicked down to my ring finger and I had the urge to curl my fist.

"And what about Silas, he won't just accept this."

Sasha let out a sigh then gave me a flat look. "Leave that to me. I'll talk to him…in the end, he'll understand."

But I knew Silas in a different way, and I doubted very much that he would understand.

Sasha began walking, and as I followed, I felt like I was walking the edge of a plank.

The dreams in my chest felt like ash fluttering around with still burning edges, images of a life I dreamed up still visible.

"Sasha, I'm scared." It came out as a whisper right as the rumble of motorcycles reverberated down the street. We were in Rose Ridge; I could see that now. The motel, the only one in the city, and from where we stood, I could see the road into town from Pyle. A group of leather clad riders headed toward us.

"You're going to ride back with a man named Killian. He's the vice president of the club. He's a good man from what I understand, but from there, a woman named Red will take over and help get you settled."

My hands were shaking, and I noticed that my head was as well.

"Wait…I…what about Silas. I have to tell him."

Sasha kept her focus on the oncoming group.

"You have to give him space, Natty. You need to let him go for a time. He's doing something bigger right now than you or him. I'm asking you not to let him come for you. You will have to be the one that creates the distance. You'll need to leave your cell behind, because if Silas thinks he can get to you then he will and right now, in order to avoid a very ugly war, he can't."

She was asking me to give him up. My chest strained; my very soul felt like it was silently screaming for someone to hit pause on all of this. It was all happening too fast.

While I knew it wasn't permanent, I could still feel seven-year-old me seeing that head of dark hair for the very first time when he'd pulled me into that wardrobe with him. When he'd first held my hand and told me he'd protect me. There was a wrongness to this…something that shouldn't be but was too far out of my control to stop it.

"They don't know at all about Silas?"

The group of riders drew closer, until they were stopping directly in front of us.

Sasha gave me one last look. "No, they only know that you're escaping Dirk."

Simon Stone let his thick boots fall to the asphalt, his bike slowing to a stop at the front of the group. His patch said he was the president…he had long dark hair that was starting to gray. It was pulled back into a low ponytail, which somehow left his handsome face exposed, and a very rigid jawline. His tattoos were vibrant along his arms and hands, but his hazel eyes seemed kind. The man next to him was much younger, a few years older than me…maybe by five or six years. He had ink as well but not as much as his leader.

His cut had a patch with a wolf's head on it, and under his name and rank said that was a nickname for him. Another man pulled up next to the VP, and I remember Silas mentioning his name years ago.

Wes Ryan.

His ranking didn't clearly put him anywhere in the club other than an official member. I wondered if he was still dating Simon's daughter...or if maybe she was in the club, and we'd become friends.

Sasha stepped forward until she was standing close to Simon's leg. It almost seemed intimate how close she was. "Dirk accepted?"

Simon nodded, flicking a quick gaze to me. "Yep. She's ours now, under our protection at least...but you need to know we'll never force her to stay there. She'll be welcome to walk out the second she gets there if she wants to, but for as long as she wants our protection, we'll offer it."

Sasha turned back to me, and then pulled me into a hug. It was a gesture she'd made a thousand times. "Dirk will come for her if she leaves."

I looked over at her, confused.

"How would he know if I were to just leave...if the deal is struck then wouldn't he just assume I'm here?"

Simon's face held pity. Wesley Ryan's held nothing at all, and Killian looked at me like I was a naïve girl who needed a life lesson.

"Natty, right?" Simon asked, nodding toward me.

I nodded, shifting on my feet. My butt still hurt from the cigarette burn, and while I'd added some ointment to it, it hurt to feel anything rub against it.

Simon glanced at Sasha before replying. "The trade we made wasn't easily done...Dirk is very possessive over you...the goods we traded cost us nearly one million in an arms' deal we could have made. Now, I'm happy to do it because I'm a father myself and I would have done this for my own daughter. You're like a daughter to Sasha...so our protection extends to you, but make no mistake. Dirk will be watching to see if you leave. I'm not trying to scare you, but he's a ruthless son of a bitch. Whatever plans you made, you may need to place on hold until we can get his attention somewhere else."

Hope evaded me as I nodded in understanding. I'd caught the attention of a disgusting madman. This was my chance at freedom.

"You'll ride with Killian." Simon gestured toward the man at his side.

Sasha reached for my hand and squeezed it. There was a silent conversation she was having with me, one full of soothing words and promises that it would be okay, but my chest felt like the war we were trying to avoid arrived regardless. It was tearing through me with bullets and bombs, creating a mess of gory devastation in my heart.

With numb legs, I walked to the bike where Killian sat and climbed on the back. My arms went around Killian's waist, and then the wind was tearing at my hair as the bikes started back up and the group left the motel behind. The group looped, which meant we passed the motel, and Sasha. I watched her as she stood there, tears visibly streaming down her face as she waved goodbye.

I closed my eyes and tried to pretend my entire life didn't just implode.

ONE WEEK LATER

SILAS

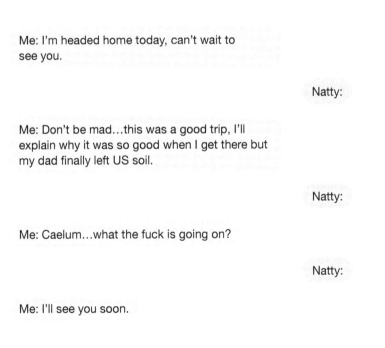

Me: I'm headed home today, can't wait to see you.

Natty:

Me: Don't be mad...this was a good trip, I'll explain why it was so good when I get there but my dad finally left US soil.

Natty:

Me: Caelum...what the fuck is going on?

Natty:

Me: I'll see you soon.

I felt like a weight had lifted as I rode back to Pyle, and it disappeared entirely when the gates to the clubhouse opened and I eased inside.

I'd been gone for way too fucking long, but the outcome was worth it. I'd been slowly building the confidence of my father, that I was his willing soldier, there to do his bidding. For years I had built this image, did the most deplorable things, all so I could gain access to his plans.

I wanted to know where his extra homes were. His women. Where he kept his money.

The ability to exploit him was information too tempting to give up. At first it was difficult to keep up the pretense, and the urge to stop everything just so I could be with my wife was right on the surface...and then Christmas arrived, two years ago and my world seemed to unravel.

I knew Natty was upset.

Fuck, it tore me open to leave her alone. I knew it hurt but that year I'd surprised her by not just finding a love story for her but tattooing it to my skin. I wanted her to read what she meant to me and know that there wasn't a moment when I was gone that I didn't carry her with me.

But when I arrived, she'd been broken. Sobbing and crying and some part of me knew something had happened. I understood this type of carnage was from regret.

She hadn't cheated, even I was sane enough to understand what she'd done was innocent enough, but fuck it ripped me open just the same. She even admitted if I had done the same to her, she wasn't sure she could get past it because an emotional connection with someone ran so much deeper than a physical one.

I knew Alec cared for Natty. He always had, it was why when I first saw him flirting with her, I pushed him off the dock.

He took advantage of her, during a time of weakness, and instead of letting her cry alone in that bed, the motherfucker held her all night.

After that, I threw myself into finishing this with my father. I flipped on him and burned his shit to the ground as quickly as I could. Even that still took two years, but he was finally gone. He'd left the country and I could finally have some peace...maybe find a place to live with my wife, and actually enjoy a sunset or two with her.

I stopped and parked my bike in front of my mother's house, seeing her car parked there.

My legs were sore, my back ached and all I wanted was to see Natty.

Right as I climbed the steps and pushed inside, my mother was there with a solemn expression.

I glanced from her, around the room, confused why she was acting like someone had died.

"What's wrong?"

"I need you to come sit down," she said calmly, like I was an animal she was trying to pull from the corner.

I dropped my gear, pushed a hand through my hair and sat down at her kitchen table.

"Where's Natty?"

My mother's eyes that were darker than mine searched my face. Her hand was on mine, and the affection had my stomach plummeting.

"Tell me."

"She's safe." My mom cradled my hand, but I pulled it away. "I want to tell you everything, Son, but if I do then it could be dangerous for all of us."

My chest felt like someone had stuffed it with cotton, and my organs were starting to fail.

I stood and kicked the chair backward.

My voice carried, with it cracking on the tail end. "Where is my wife?"

Mom winced at the volume.

I leaned closer, growling my ire. "Where?"

"She was traded to the Stone Riders one week ago. She's living with them now."

"What—" My chest heaved…too fast I realized belatedly as I bumped into the counter. "I don't understand."

Tears burned the backs of my eyes and my mother…fuck she was lying to me.

"Caelum!" I stormed down the hall, pushing our bedroom door open. The bed was the same, but our dresser was all messed up, half the drawers were open. *Her* drawers were open…and empty.

A small note on the bed caught my attention.

Silas,

I love you.

I'm yours, I will forever be yours.
-Caelum

"What the fuck is this?!" I roared angrily, storming back toward the kitchen.

Lance, my best friend had arrived and was now leaning against the counter, watching me. My mother had moved as well, glancing at me, then him.

"Just calm down, Silas," Lance suggested coolly.

I narrowed my gaze at my mother. "Fuck that. Tell me why she was traded."

"I can't, Son. If I tell you why she was traded, then you'll start a war. That war will start and end with Natty. The Stone Riders will more than happily sacrifice her if it means avoiding a war."

"She is mine! She's patched to me, she's my fucking wife!"

By the way my mother was wincing, I knew this was the angriest she'd ever seen me. I felt a pressure in my head as tears gathered in my eyes.

They had Natty, which meant if I tried to go and remove her from their club, it would start a war and with the club loyal to Dirk, I had no one that would back me.

I glanced at my best friend who shook his head, as if he was working out what I was trying to.

"Tell me why she was traded. She was spoken for, no one had the right to do that except for me."

My mother placed her hands on either side of my face.

"You must trust me, Son. I did the only thing that would have kept her safe."

It all connected suddenly. "He did something to her, didn't he?"

I was going to fucking kill Dirk. I moved, heading to the door when Lance tackled me to the ground.

"Get the fuck off me!"

"No, Brother. I'm sorry, but you can't go after him. You don't have the numbers yet. You have to be patient and kill him when the time is right, when the club will follow you. You have a new mission now."

I tried to shove him off, but he had me in some fancy martial arts head lock.

"Did he touch her?" My voice was raw from screaming.

How come she never told me. How long had it been going on? Why would the Stone Riders agree to take her?

"I can't tell you any more than that, Son. You will kill him in time, but if you know the full scope, you'll black out and try now. And you'll kill yourself in the process. You need to live; you need to focus on taking him down, so she can come back to you. Until then, you must leave her be."

This must be why she wasn't answering my texts.

"What did you tell her?" I knew my mother had to have told her something. Fuck, I needed to know if she was okay.

"She knows you need space and time. Which is true. She accepted this trade willingly, Silas."

Fuck Simon Stone.

Regardless of what was happening here, he didn't have the right to accept a deal or broker one on her behalf. She wasn't just my property patch; she was my wife. She belonged to me, not the club or anyone else.

"She's been instructed not to mention your connection to her. The Roman is circulating right now; it could put her in danger."

Shit, I knew that was true, but I couldn't seem to wrap my head around the idea of losing her. No, I refused to lose her.

"You need to think this through, Silas. She needs time to adjust to the Stone Riders, they're safe…they have a code they live by."

I pushed up, throwing Lance off my back and began stalking toward my mother. I'd never hurt her, but I needed to understand what the fuck she had done.

"Simon promised me. I've gotten to know him, Silas, and I trust him. You know what he did for his own daughter."

I tossed a chair out of our way. It crashed against the counter, shattering a few glasses. "That was for his flesh and blood, Natty isn't his. No one will protect her the way I will protect her."

"Silas, I protected her," my mother argued, yelling just as loud. "I trust Simon, and you know I would never let Natty walk into danger. Not on my life, Son."

I did know that. My mother loved Natty. While she often tried to show her a firmer hand, I knew how deep her adoration ran for my wife.

"She's mine to keep safe, not yours."

My mother's face fell flat, her eyes narrowing in a hard edge. "While that may be true, you left her unprotected, Son...and while I'm the one who advised you to do it, it doesn't change the facts. There were situations that put her in danger, and after enough time, it was too careless to allow her to stay here."

My mind whirled, viciously tossing images at me of what might have been done to my wife.

"Did Dirk do..." I couldn't even bring myself to ask as my voice broke. Lance was at the entry of the kitchen now, rubbing his jaw where my elbow must have landed.

My mother shook her head. "I know you well enough that if I begin to give you specifics, you'll do something without thinking. I won't risk that. Just know this was the best course of action to keep her from danger."

"Stop. Fuck." My chest felt like it was caving in. "You're talking about her like she's a number on a chart. Or a statistic."

I couldn't breathe. She was gone.

If I were to go right now, the Stone Riders would kill me. I knew that much, and then what.

Tears began welling in my mother's gaze as she watched me fall apart.

My mother crossed her arms, staring down at the floor. "I understand that you're upset, but you need to focus on claiming this club from Dirk when the time is right."

My lips trembled as I seethed, "I don't fucking want this club."

"But you will need it, and the power it offers you. Please understand why I did this. I did everything to keep her safe, Son. Everything."

"How do I—" I needed to breathe, but my chest felt too tight. "I need to fix this."

My mother was suddenly next to me, her face close to mine.

"The best thing you can do for her is let her live her life, honey. She is safe there. Simon is giving me updates nearly every day. She has her own room in the club with a kitchen and bathroom. She keeps to herself, but she's safe. The men have been advised to stay away from her."

"Her cell phone?"

Lance shifted behind me, and my mother watched his movement. She cleared her throat and pulled something from her pocket, and then Natty's phone was in front of me. The red rubber case with yellow baby chicks printed all over nearly made me sob.

"So I have no way of reaching my wife?"

My mother's hand soothed my back as a tear slid free.

"No honey. This is for the best. You'll see, I promise."

TWENTY-TWO
NATTY
PRESENT DAY

THE QUIET IN THE CLUB WAS PEACEFUL.

Silas was outside, doing something with his bike, which was nice because I needed a small reprieve from him. I wasn't mad, but I felt confused.

A little lost, and if I was being honest, afraid.

I had given Silas an out. To run away...and while I knew he wanted me to have this life, and my friends, it still felt like he was trying to find a reason to keep his club and fight this battle with Fable. He didn't realize that I was terrified of Fable, and even if we could run for a time, we could always come back. I would return to Pen, and Red, and the Stone Riders. I just wanted to take a breather from all of this and to finally have a chance to be with him.

"Hey, this seat taken?" Rachel asked, holding her mug of coffee.

Killian had settled her in with him and Laura, in their guest room. It had been a few hours since I last saw her, and since then, she'd showered and changed into a fresh pair of clothes.

I smiled up at her and moved the throw pillow that was on the seat. "No, of course not."

"How are you holding up?" Her dark green eyes were so clear and full of hope.

It made something in my heart thrash like a soft wave, lapping at the shore.

"Me? I'm fine, I was worried about you."

She waved me off. "I was fine. I knew what I was doing."

"Still, a lot could have gone wrong."

She sipped her drink and stared off across the room. "My son—" She choked on a sudden sob, forcing her hand to come up to her mouth. "I thought maybe he would hate me."

I shook my head, already knowing that could never be true.

"He pulled me into his arms and he just—" Tears slipped down her face and she quickly brushed them away. "He hugged me so tight…it took me back to that day I left him when he was nine. I remember seeing that look in his eyes…like he wasn't sure why I was going."

More sobs wracked her chest and I pulled her hand into mine.

"I know he wants to know why I left…and I've rehearsed my response a thousand times, imagining what I would say to him. But now that I'm here, I don't know how to begin."

Squeezing her hand, I cleared my throat.

"Practice. With me, I mean. Try to tell me what you need to say."

She swallowed, swiping at her face with her free hand and then adjusted the pillow in her lap.

"I knew my choices were limited…I was twenty-eight, married to an abuser. A murderer. I knew Simon would protect Killian, but I was positive that my husband was going to kill me. So I had started seeing this guy from another club. My hope was that he could protect me from Jefferson, but I had merely traded one evil for another. I knew Jefferson was going to get caught for what he did, but there was no way to get rid of the man I'd convinced to love me. He was just as bad as my husband, if not worse. So my only option was to spare Killian. Disappear from his life and protect him from that vile man. I had seen what he'd done to his sons, and I never wanted that near Killian."

Awareness slid in slow and steady like the beat of a drum.

"You've been with Fable this entire time?"

Her chin wobbled; she gave me a sad smile. "Not all of us have someone like Silas in our lives, Natty. Some of us remain in the prison because the idea of what the monster will do is too terrible. There is no escaping Fable. Once he has you, he will keep you, and he will use you however he sees fit."

I watched as she silently cried and a fresh, deep resolve settled in my core that hadn't ever been there before. I had always disliked Silas's father for what he did to his son. I feared him for what he did to me. But I hated him for what he'd done to Rachel.

I was going to kill him.

If it was the last thing I did, I would murder him.

"Something you should know, Natty. Something that no one knows about him."

I perked up, feeling her hand tug more firmly on mine. My head was turned toward her as she swiped at her face and regained her composure.

"Fable has no army. His Destroyers no longer exist. When he left the country, he lost all of it. He's here, hoping Silas and Alec will join with him and bring their clubs. But he has no one backing him at all."

No army.

A smile slid along my lips as I realized what this meant.

We had a chance.

"You're cooking me dinner?" Silas asked from where he perched on the edge of the couch.

My back was to him, and while we'd fallen back into whatever routine we always did with each other, there was something strained between us. I felt it like a heavy breeze warning of a storm.

"I'm cooking myself dinner, but you're welcome to have some." I smirked at him from over my shoulder.

I loved how relaxed he looked with his plain white t-shirt, his loose-fitting jeans, and bare feet. His eyes gleamed, and I nearly melted at how they felt on me. We had no agenda at the moment, nowhere to be other than processing that Alec was being held here, as a prisoner in one of the garages. Then there was the little fact that Fable had sworn to take me away from both men and use me for breeding purposes.

"Shoot." I pulled open my cupboards and double checked the rack. Frustration burned under my skin as I set the skillet to the side and began hunting for red pepper flakes.

"What's wrong?"

Did I put it in my fridge for some reason? Sometimes I did that when I was cooking. "I can't find the red pepper flakes, which is a huge part of the flavoring in this meal."

Heaving a sigh, I stepped over to the door. "Let me go check down in the club kitchen."

"I'll go." Silas pushed off the couch. I shook my head, already opening my door.

"It's fine, you can stay here."

He was already behind me as we moved down the hallway. His finger trailed over the skin at my back where my shirt raised, and then it hooked around my belt loop, keeping us connected as I scaled the stairs and veered toward the kitchen.

I paused when I noticed the back door wide open, which was slightly odd. I had started cooking at ten…we were eating late, and while the club usually could be packed and crazy, these last few nights they'd been quiet and nearly empty.

I knew Rachel had already gone back over to Killian's house, and Red would be in her apartment, which sat over the side garage with Brooks, but maybe she'd snuck over here too for something.

"Everything okay?" Silas asked at my back.

I caught sight of Red's white hair through the door and started for her.

"Yeah, would you mind looking in the spice rack for the red pepper flakes? I'm going to go check on Red."

Why was she outside? Was she having an episode?

Fear urged me forward, unaware if Silas was behind me or not. My palms landed against the metal of the exterior door and the dark sky nearly covered Red completely. It was her white hair that made her stand out, but the man she was talking to was hidden.

She laughed with whoever it was, tossing her head back and then she waved the man forward.

"Come inside, Brooks. We need to go feed the kids."

Oh no.

My heart was nearly in my throat as I registered she was having an episode, and the man with her was not Brooks.

"Red," I whispered, but my voice wouldn't come out any higher than a rasp.

Fable was there, smirking like the devil, wearing a leather jacket with Stone Riders patches all over it.

The name sewn into the front said *Brooks*.

No.

Did Fable hurt him?

No. This wasn't happening…not them. Not him.

Not her.

Fable looked right at me, and from where I was, I could see the tilt of his lips as he followed Red. This was all wrong, like a dream I couldn't wake from. They were moving too fast, and I wasn't moving at all.

Like I was in quicksand.

"Red!" I screamed and finally my limbs seemed to work, so I started to run toward her, but my feet stumbled, my knees found the grass as my eyes remained on her beautiful smile. In her mind, she was talking about her kids with the love of her life. I'd never seen her so happy.

"Reddddddddddd!" My throat burned, and suddenly there were arms around me, and a hand covering my mouth right as the gunshot went off.

Red's eyes went wide as she locked them onto me, as if suddenly she were in her right mind and realized what had happened.

My breath caught and tangled with the sob trapped in my chest. I didn't care that we now understood how Fable had gotten in. I didn't care that there were men flooding out of the club house, running after him.

I registered vaguely that I was on the ground, being held, and they were whispering something in my ear, but my eyes wouldn't leave Red's. I was thankful for the darkness because it would cover the blood. All I saw was her beautiful white hair, and those pretty blue eyes, staring.

Staring and staring.

Why couldn't I seem to get any air into my chest? I tasted salt, so much salt. My tears...and my head hurt. It pounded and ached.

"Shhhhh, baby." Silas soothed my hair down and that's when I realized how badly my throat hurt.

I'd been screaming for her. My face was wet, and there was a terrible lump caught in my chest as if I couldn't quite fit all the pain that would be needed to fully feel her death.

Laura was running toward me from her back fence. She was wearing a t-shirt, pajama shorts, and glasses. Her hair was down, flying behind her as she came to kneel next to me. Killian was right behind her, his gun drawn while he was searching the area.

Tears coated her lashes as she stared at me.

"Where is Brooks? Go find Brooks. He has to be here. He has to know...Fable took his cut and...he tricked Red. He's probably in bed, he sometimes falls asleep in front of the tv at seven. He puts up a big game about being a hard motorcycle member, but he loves his hunting shows, and he loves falling asleep in that chair. Check the chair. He's probably asleep right now. He doesn't know that Red...that she—"

Laura stroked carefully down my arm, then my face. Her chin wobbled as she glanced up at Silas. She needed to go find Brooks. He had to come here; his heart would break...he'd be devastated, but he had to be here. "He's gone, Natty. They just found him—" Her lips twisted as another sob seemed to wrap around her voice.

"Found him where?"

"Behind the cabin. He's dead, Natty."

A stupid memory surfaced of Brooks telling me that he only liked classic soda with real sugar, the ones that came in glass bottles. This memory was of him telling me it helped him to not drink as much beer because Red worried about him.

I started hunting them down for him, so he'd have a fresh bottle every time I went to the store. But I'd forgotten the last few times. I'd been so preoccupied...I should have remembered him. I should have been over there, checking on them. They never had kids. They never...

Silas picked me up and took me inside and I closed my eyes, pushing out the image of her getting shot.

Eventually I fell asleep, but all I did was remember, which was somehow worse than sitting awake with this reality.

TWENTY-THREE
TWO YEARS AGO
ONE MONTH LIVING WITH THE STONE RIDERS

Natty

My room was bigger than anything I'd ever had in my life. It was a suite that had a small kitchen, enough space for a couch, bed and full-sized bathroom. It was slightly dizzying to be in a space that wouldn't be shared for the first time ever.

Not to mention, my room was all the way at the end of the hall, away from where any other members stayed. Across the hall from me was a laundry room, and the door next to it was a bathroom. It created a barrier between me and the rest of the club, which was hugely helpful.

I was still shy whenever I did venture downstairs, but a month into staying here, I had finally braved stepping foot in the massive kitchen, but the only reason I wanted to was to see if I could use a phone to call Sasha.

This situation wasn't going to work if it meant I was completely shut off from everyone I ever knew. I needed to see Silas.

There was a woman bustling around the space, humming to herself. Her white hair was piled on top of her head, and the curls were pinned back in place with a black bandana. It matched her property patch that boasted of her belonging to someone named Brooks.

"Umm, excuse me." I cleared my throat, tugging on the ends of my sleeve.

The woman turned toward me with a blinding smile. "There you are! I was wondering when you'd come down here. I'm Red, in charge of pretty much everything, so if you need something, just come to me."

I pressed farther into the kitchen, loving all the natural light that poured in through the windows. There were butcher block counters along the wall, an industrial-sized sink, and professional ovens; it felt like a professional kitchen, but the only person I'd seen so far in this space was this woman, Red.

"A phone?" I asked, hoping her offer for help was genuine.

She glanced back at the pot in front of her where she continued to stir.

"You don't have a cell?"

No. But how was I supposed to explain that? I must have waited too long to answer because Red stopped and left her spot at the stove.

"Come on in here, we have extras." She walked ahead of me into an office that sat just outside the kitchen. The office had a simple metal desk inside and two basic chairs in front of it. There was a pretty window on the far wall letting in a ton of light. For some reason I felt the tension swirling around my chest begin to ease. The Death Raiders club never felt this way. It never felt like it could be a home.

Red opened a drawer and pulled out a package made of plastic.

"Do you have any funds to add minutes to it?" She handed me the package that had a prepaid cell phone inside.

I nodded, feeling excited that I could call Silas. "How much do I owe you?"

She waved me off. "Maybe come down and keep me company in the kitchen from time to time."

She moved out of the office first, not even worried that I might not be trustworthy to stay behind among their club secrets. I trailed closely behind her.

"I can clean, and I'm fairly decent at baking, but if you give me a few pointers, I could probably get better."

Red's expression softened toward me as she returned to her pot of soup.

"I'd be happy to teach you, sweetheart. Do you want some dinner to take up to your room? There's only so many boxes of crackers you can eat before you need to see a doctor."

I was getting sick of being in my room, and the boxes of Ritz I had.

With a laugh, I ducked my head. "How did you know they were crackers?"

"You aren't the first girl adjusting to a new club, sweetheart. From what Simon told me, you've had a rough go of it over there with The Death Raiders."

Just hearing their name made me want to break into hives.

I didn't respond and started toying with the plastic package.

Red placed a bowl of soup in my hands and gave me a warm smile. I looked up and felt like her smile was an invisible piece of thread worming its way through my heart, knitting and fixing the gaping hole torn open by losing Silas and Sasha.

"Can I eat down here…um at the bar?" I glanced over at the space, seeing a few members there but an open spot on the end.

Red walked me over to the bar with her arm around my shoulder, stopping in front of an older member, the name Brooks was stitched into his leather cut.

"This here is my man, Brooks—if you ever feel like one of these Stone Riders pushes you around or makes you feel uncomfortable, just tell him. He'll keep you safe."

The man turned toward me, giving me the widest smile I'd ever seen. He had silver hair braided down his back and a leather strap covering the crown. "Anyone my girl says is safe, will have my utmost protection."

His adoring gaze on Red made me feel relaxed. So I slid onto the stool next to him and began eating my soup, and for the first time in an entire month, I stopped thinking about how badly I missed my husband.

SIX MONTHS LIVING WITH THE STONE RIDERS

Tears streamed down my face from how hard I was laughing. It was so bad; I could hardly breathe. Red kept swatting my arm to make me stop, but I couldn't.

"Why are you two laughin' at me?" Brooks only made things worse by putting his hand to his hip.

We were in their small apartment that sat off to the side and on top of one of the club garages. It was nestled back, so out of the way that I had to be shown where the steps were. The small house looked like something you'd find crowding the shoreline in a beach town. It was painted blue, with wooden decorations, hanging from a rope that clinked together when the wind swirled through them.

Their door was even worn as if it had seen several storms over the years, but their home was cozy and every single faded piece of siding along their apartment seemed to boast of love and happiness. Inside their home, a tiny, two-seater couch faced a large flat screen television. A tattered rocker was angled to the side, with a side table next to it. An ashtray was there that looked like something a child would make in a pottery class during school.

When I asked where it came from, Red smiled and said it was Callie who had made it for them. There were all sorts of tiny treasures around their home that spoke of their deep fondness of this girl I still hadn't met. She was Simon's daughter but had moved away and hadn't returned in several years. I could tell it was difficult for Red to talk about, so I moved the conversation along.

But I saw photos of a young Killian too, and those made me laugh and smile. The vice president of the club had been nice to me in the months since I arrived. Always checking to make sure I was okay, but distant enough not to seem like he was flirting. He gave off brotherly vibes, which made me relax around him.

So as I touched photo frame after photo frame and little mementos of the beautiful history this club had lived, I would smile. Simon Stone was a frequent person in their photos, along with his daughter when she was young. She and Killian looked more like siblings growing up, as they stood there, dirty clothes, tangled hair and glares at the camera.

Brooks and Red had invited me into their home, nearly twice a week for dinner. It opened up our relationship in such a way that they quickly became like pseudo parents I never had. Even as special as Sasha was to me, she never treated me the way these two did. Brooks would teach me how to work on bikes in the garage and ask me to be his helper. He showed me his old Harley that had been in an accident a few years prior; he was working to restore it every time he had a chance.

It allowed me to get to know Hamish, and a man named Harris, and Pops. Killian would stop in and check on us. Wes too. Wes seemed empty inside. Like his eyes were there but not, his soul vacant and searching for something that once belonged there but had left. It made me wonder about Simon's daughter. I noticed he was gone quite a bit too, often on road trips that no one seemed to talk about, so I didn't ask. Although, I once heard Killian joking about how he needed to stop going to DC.

I wondered if that was where the missing Stone daughter had gone.

Mostly, I stuck to myself. Fostering my new life and trying to thrive in the new place I'd been forced to grow.

I tried to ignore the ache in my chest where Silas had always been.

Being with Brooks and Red helped. Especially when we did game night, and Brooks wanted to try his hand at charades, which is what had Red and me laughing so hard that we couldn't breathe.

He'd attempted impersonating a tree, but the way he'd stood there and waved his arms around, while making the sound of the wind, was just enough to push us over the edge.

"You two aren't any fun to play with, you always laugh at me." Brooks huffed, stalking off toward the kitchen.

I was still giggling when Red let out a sigh.

"You seem happier than you were a few months back, and I'm glad for it. You've brought sunshine into our lives, sweetheart."

My gaze slid up to hers and found her watching me with affection. The reminder of sunshine made something prickle in my chest. An ache. I pushed it down while getting up and walking to the kitchen.

"Well, you two make me happy."

Brooks came back out, spearing a piece of pie with his fork. "Well, we certainly should, we're the happiest people you'll ever meet."

Red came up behind him and swatted his arm. But he was right.

They were the happiest people I'd ever met, and I felt, for the first time in my life, that feeling happy could extend further to just being with Silas.

TWENTY-FOUR
SILAS
PRESENT DAY

It was two in the morning before Natty stopped moving every time I tried to slip my arm out from under her. She had a shattered heart, and all I wanted to do was stay here and help hold her together. But the Stone Riders who went after Fable didn't catch him, and now that I knew how he had gotten inside, I needed to find him.

The only person who I had at my disposal that I could interrogate was Alec, which meant I needed to leave Natty in bed. I ensured my men were still watching over her as I exited the room. They were on high alert because of Fable slipping through, although Killian had patrols monitoring the entire property now. I still wanted a man below her window, at the back door, the front and outside her door.

It was dark as I slipped through the halls and outside. The stars weren't out, leaving the sky dark and the breeze cold as I swiftly made my way to the outlier garage where they were keeping my brother.

I entered through the side door, seeing there were three Stone Riders watching over him. This club had a less obvious location for holding prisoners, near the border of their property. I knew this because I'd used it to interrogate Luke Holloway when he started this bullshit war with my father, his dad, and Jefferson Quinn. I assumed they weren't using it currently, simply because of Rachel returning, and then what happened tonight with Red and Brooks.

Alec was cuffed to a lead pipe that connected under a few rows of concrete. He was slumped against the wall, his ass resting against the floor while his leg was kicked out in front of him.

The guards saw me and paused.

"Not asking you to leave him unguarded but give us some space to talk."

They glanced at each other and wandered over to the corner of the garage where they lit up two cigarettes and turned on a game, illuminating that darker corner with the light from the television screen.

Alec's gaze tracked my movements as I pulled up a chair and sat in front of him, leaning forward with my forearms on my knees.

"What's your angle with this?"

Alec's lip curled as he pulled his leg back, bending his knee.

"Angle?"

"Fable sends you with a message to me, right as we rescue Rachel, then he shows up the same night, and kills two of their members... What's the angle?"

My brother chuckled, shaking his head. His hair was greasy, slicked back, and his t-shirt seemed to have stains all over it. I noticed his cut was missing.

"After you cut my fucking hand off, I had to find a way to staunch the bleeding on my own...one fucking handed. Then I took one of the trucks left by the guards and drove myself to a nearby club doctor. He did a shit job of patching me up in case you want to look at the gruesome scar I now have. I look like something Frankenstein botched."

I inspected my nail, growing tired of his sob story. "You seem fine to me."

"Yeah, well, it took me a few days to recover. Once I did, I returned to what was left of my club. We'd scattered to a few safe houses, and Dad found me there."

Fuck, how was he always able to locate where we'd been?

"Fable informed me that he was coming for Natty. I tried to fight him, but I was still too weak from the loss of blood. He knocked me out.

When I woke up, he'd left me with the message and my severed hand. I panicked and made my way here; they found me on the way."

Right. I stood, pacing in front of him. "So you were worried about Natty...and decided to just come for her...and the timing of it all just happened—"

"I don't give a fuck what you think, Silas. It's the truth. I messed up with her...I didn't think—" Alec turned his face, regret and remorse warring it out through his features.

"You didn't think." I kicked his boot to encourage him to continue.

His gaze swung back in my direction. "I didn't think she'd hate me... I thought maybe she'd eventually fall for me. Close proximity and shit."

The top part of his cheeks flushed the smallest bit, and I had to hold back a laugh.

"You assumed my wife might fall for you if you chained her to you and masturbated in front of her, then forced her to stand there while you ejaculated against her skin?"

The flush on his skin worsened.

"I know, I fucked up. I owe her an apology...I owe her more than that, but I'd like to start by trying to fix this. And for the last time, I didn't know you were married."

"Even if we weren't, she wouldn't have fallen for the proximity routine. Natty can't be forced into doing anything. I think at one point she was fond of you, Brother. She had a soft spot at least, especially after that Christmas." I hung my head hating the memory of how she'd turned to him. "But she would have never fallen for you."

Alec's eyes narrowed on me as he tried to adjust how he was seated on the floor. His boot slid against the concrete as his voice sharpened.

"And what of your failures, Silas? She forgave you so easily for over-looking the abuse she endured at Dirk's hand?"

My stomach flipped then strained.

"What do you know about that?"

Flashbacks of conversations, gut feelings and assumptions all slammed into me, but nothing had ever been confirmed. By anyone.

The look in Alec's eyes was like he'd just won a bet. He was going to enjoy ruining me, this I was certain of.

"I take it you were never told?"

"Why would you assume that?" I pushed my hands into my pockets, hating how vulnerable this made me.

Alec's face tilted. "For one, Dirk would have died two years ago, not six months ago. Two, you would have burned the entire fucking club to the ground…as you did with mine."

That panicked feeling rushed back. The unknown creating a frenzy under my sternum. The only choice I had was to remain silent because I had no clue what he was talking about.

My brother leaned closer, which tugged at his good hand, making the metal clank.

"Natty ever mysteriously break a bone, or have a scar that showed up…maybe a burn?"

She'd said it was work. Tripping. The grove when she's tried to climb over a fence.

Dirk even said…

"He knew he couldn't get away with much because you would return home, but every time you left, he played with your wife. He toyed with her, broke her. Hurt her. Burned her."

No.

My feet faltered as my gaze snapped to his. Why did the floor feel like it was falling out from under me?

"Natty would beg you, right? She'd beg you not to leave…anything else feel rushed or like she was panicked about it?"

I fell to the chair, and nearly missed as memory after memory flashed through my mind.

Our wedding, she'd been practically desperate to marry me, and it had to be that night…because I left the following day.

He had been hurting her.

Christmas…she had begged me and seemed frantic that I return.

"Did he…" My voice cracked as I looked down at my hands. "She came to you that December…"

Alec's chin dipped. "I found out later…but yes. She'd gone back home, and Dirk was there. Your mom was gone, and you weren't coming back…she was terrified, so she came to me."

Fuck, my chest was cracking open; there was no other explanation for this pain.

Alec continued, his own voice going hoarse. "One of the Raiders would brag about what Dirk did to Natty, which meant he must have occasionally done things where people saw. I guess one time, he had her lower her bra cup so he could extinguish a cigarette against her tit."

The burn looked as though it was a curling iron incident...she'd covered up what he'd done to her, so it looked like she had done it to herself.

She'd covered for Dirk for years. Fucking years she was abused by him...until—

"Things escalated, obviously which is why she was traded. Sasha saw what Dirk did to Natty one night...it was enough to scare her into calling Simon Stone and beg him to get Natty away from the Raiders."

Simon didn't take her...*he had rescued her.*

My mind was in free fall. Failure and loss warring for first place in my head, my heart, my lungs, my fucking blood stream.

I'd let her down so profusely...how had she never told me any of this?

My voice was more of a rasp when I asked, "How did you find out?"

Alec's glare could cut stone, but his next words essentially did, and I knew I'd never be the same after.

"Raiders talking shit mostly, but Natty confirmed the rest."

I glared at him feeling more hatred for my brother than I ever thought possible. I never assumed my wife would really betray me with her relationship with him. I knew she loved me; I knew she wanted me.

But this...she had never once told me.

Even when I had suspicions and concerns...she had lied to me. Covered for him. Allowed me to leave and put her in danger.

My brother knew her deepest, darkest pain...and still, reunited, she didn't want to share it with me? I'd always shared my pain with her.

Always...I had never held it back.

How could she keep this from me?

I needed to talk to my mother...she'd been the one here, and the one telling me to go. I needed to get her perspective on this.

I stood, ignored what Alec said at my back and navigated my way back to my bike.

My mother was asleep when I arrived on her doorstep and was understandably upset when I continued to rap my knuckles against her door.

I understood it was the middle of the night, but I also wasn't fully in control of my body…I felt like I was in a nightmare, watching myself walk and maneuver through the dark as if I'd already lost Natty and there was no reclaiming her.

The porch light came on, and my mother's door swung open, revealing a very pissed off and angry Simon Stone.

"The fuck are you doing here at nearly three in the morning?"

"I need to speak to my mother."

His jaw flexed, the muscle in it jumping as if he were deliberating on kicking my ass. I wouldn't put it past him. He might be fighting cancer but the fucker was hard as nails and ruthless.

"She's asleep, Silas. Come back tomorrow when she's awake."

He was about to close the door but I stopped it with my hand against the wood. "It's important."

"Silas?" My mother's groggy voice came from inside the house. She came into view a second later, tying the sash of her robe and wincing at the porch light.

"I need to speak with you."

She let out a sigh but gave a small nod.

Simon reluctantly moved and secured the door behind me while I sat down on my mother's couch.

She took the seat across from me in an armchair while Simon walked back to the room, muttering a few curses as he went.

"This is the second time you've woken us up, Son."

I wasn't in the mood to be the dutiful son, or the one who grew up loving and cherishing my mother for her sacrifices. I felt betrayed by the two women who had loved me unconditionally and my gut told me the core of that deceit started with the woman in front of me.

"You never told me what Dirk did to Natty."

My mother's blue eyes went from sleepy to alert in a single second.

She didn't respond, so I continued.

"When she was traded, you alluded to it being for the sake of her staying safe and told me I couldn't do anything because it would start a war."

Her dark hair dipped as she agreed. "It would have."

"You failed to mention that it's a war I would have gladly fought. One I would have endured, sacrificed, and readily ended from." My voice shook with rage and hurt. They wound together like a knot at the base of my throat.

"Silas, at the time, you needed The Death Raiders. You were working on taking your father down. You did the right thing by allowing her to stay with the Stone Riders."

My gaze was frozen, so ice cold that I don't think I imagined it when my mother flinched. "Fuck the right thing. Fuck The Death Raiders and fuck my father. This is the only warning you'll receive from me that I'm leaving. Don't try and find me. Good luck with the rest of your fucking life."

I stood, ready to leave when she bolted after me, grabbing hold of my shirt.

"Silas...wait. You can't just show up and lay this entire thing on me. I was doing the best thing—"

I spun on her, my voice rising. "You removed me from the equation. You didn't give me a choice. You encouraged my wife to lie to me for years, Mother! Fucking years. She endured abuse...do you have any—"

My voice broke, tears welled and my heart broke.

"Do you have any idea what it was like to discover from someone other than her, or even you that she had to turn to other people for protection? While you may be right that you were trying to do the right thing, you were also pushing me to leave. You consistently told me to sabotage Fable, and what good did it do for any of us? He's back and now he's after my wife. I lost her for two motherfucking years, Mother." I was shaking from how angry I'd become and when she only pursed her lips in defiance, I screamed, "TWO YEARS!"

Simon slammed a door from inside the house and began walking toward us with a shotgun.

"Get the fuck out."

My mother's eyes watered as she put a hand on his chest but the gun was leveled at me.

"Fable killed two members tonight. Red and Brooks. Just so you're aware." I said to Simon, then glared at my mother.

"We're through here."

It was nearly dawn when I stopped outside the doors of my club. No one was up, and that was good because I wasn't in the mood to see anyone.

Exhaustion tugged at me, but so did heartache and hurt. Unfortunately, they won over me heading into my room and falling asleep.

I parked my bike, then took off toward the garage where the gasoline was kept. Distantly, I was aware that this was insane, but I'd never felt this broken before. Not after having to crucify people. Not after having to kill, maim and torture for my father. Not enduring burns and scars from him.

Nothing had ever cut my heart the way realizing I'd let her down did.

Carrying two large gas cans back to my old house, I didn't even stop at the door, I kicked it in. Memories of sitting at the kitchen table with Natty while we learned Latin flittered through my mind. I remembered watching her mouth the words, so focused she never noticed how often I'd look at her.

If I was a masochist I'd walk into our old room and I'd allow those memories to build and overwhelm me like one of those rogue, sneaker waves.

Instead, I started pouring.

He'd hurt her in this house. Fuck if I knew how often. He'd terrorized her in the place she lived. The memory of when she'd been too hot because she was too afraid to open the windows came back. It was because of him.

Fuck. Fuck. Fuck.

I doused it all.

Every room was lathered in gasoline and as I turned my back, I grabbed my zippo and clicked it, then tossed it inside.

It caught fire instantly. I took my cut off, and the leather jacket I'd had with me and tossed them both inside.

Lance ran out of the club, coming toward me, frantic.

He should know that frantic didn't work around me.

"Get any original members that rode with Dirk out here," I mused, walking back into the garage.

I had a bag buried in the concrete that I used to use when I was with my father. I pulled it free and slowly unzipped it.

I could almost feel the contents inside whisper a *"welcome home."* This deranged darkness always flirted with my consciousness. Natty would always bring me back, but how would I ever go back to her knowing I'd let her down like that?

While she was bearing all my burdens, she was being consumed by her own.

Buried.

Then I punished her for leaving me. I assumed she wanted to be free of me, that it was just Christmas all over again, where she found solace somewhere else. Angry that I was always gone and needing a different change, but knowing I'd never let her go.

Fuck, how badly I'd ruined her.

Madness crept inside the fringes of my mind and for once I welcomed it.

"There's about fifteen original members." Lance said from behind me.

I took the bag and began rummaging for wood.

"Good, they can help build the crosses."

I turned to inspect my friend, who had his hand on his gun. Smart move.

"Crosses?"

With the duffle dangling in one hand, I had a few boards gripped in my other while walking back toward the yard.

The flames from my house were growing, licking at the sky while members started screaming and scrambling.

"Now might be a good time for everyone else to evacuate the club."

Lance glanced at the burning house and then let his gaze settle back on me.

"I'll have it done. What are the crosses for, Silas?"

A group of terrified men were on their knees being kept in place by a few of my loyal men. Guns trained on them. Most of them were in their boxers, pajamas and underwear.

A few bunk bunnies and Sweetbutts came outside, half-naked.

"Get them out of here."

I let my bag drop and then pulled out the first iron stake that would be driven through one of these motherfucker's hands.

"Silas..." Lance got my attention. "The crosses?"

"We're crucifying them. Every last person who knew what Dirk was doing to my wife."

TWENTY-FIVE
NATTY
PRESENT

MY EYES WERE RED AND ITCHY WHEN I FINALLY WOKE UP.

The sun came in unhindered through my window. Silas wasn't with me, which had me pressing my fingers into his side of the bed.

Where had he gone, and why would he leave me after such an emotional night?

Maybe he'd told me where he was going and I just missed it…there was so much that I had pushed out last night, not allowing it to touch my already fractured heart. I had ignored what people were telling me left and right, and then Silas was holding me and I passed out.

Standing, I stretched and on instinct inspected the window to ensure no more nefarious notes were left behind. Then started moving around to get dressed.

My cell was plugged in, but when I pulled it free, there was no message from Silas, or any sort of phone call or update.

Which was weird…but I shook it off.

Facing the downstairs kitchen was going to be too much at the moment, so I opted to eat in my room while putting on the news.

Sad. Depressing. Horrific. Nothing good ever came from turning on the television unless it was navigating to my favorite tv show.

I pressed play on something familiar but zoned out, too confused and hurt to focus. My toast was gone, but I couldn't stomach anything more. I was slowly curling into a ball onto one of the cushions when someone knocked on my door.

I felt like I was moving through molasses as I walked to open it. Laura, Callie and Penelope were on the other side, all teary eyed and wearing pajamas. We all were quiet, just staring at each other as grief swelled among us like a summer thunder cloud.

Callie came into my arms first, a sob stuck in her throat, and I held her so tight that I started shaking. She'd known Red her entire life; she was like a mother to her. Pen and Laura were around us moments later and we all just fell to the floor in one big support hug.

My friend's pregnant belly was getting bigger now, so we were all careful of her. We all cried for Red, and for Brooks, and for the attacks the club seemed to keep taking. It felt like an hour before we detangled and dug into the donuts Laura had picked up from The Drip. I had just barely checked in with them, returning for a few shifts before swapping with Allison, having her wear my apron when I wanted to lose the detail Silas had put on me.

"You seemed really upset with Silas yesterday, Natty," Laura said, glancing back at my empty bed. I was so tired that my head drifted to the side, inspecting the still unmade bed, empty and cold. Once I focused on the group again, everyone's gaze was on me.

Callie swiped at her face and then brought a cream filled donut up to her mouth and took a generous bite. "What's this I heard about Fable calling you Silas's wife?"

Penelope's gaze swung over to me, and Laura was nodding.

"Yeah, I was curious about that too."

Guess it was time to start explaining this entire thing with Silas. The one thing I'd been tight-lipped about all these years. Bitterness twisted in my chest as I took a bite of a maple bar and began explaining to my friends how I had married Silas at nineteen and for the first time since meeting these women, telling my story.

About thirty minutes and an entire box of tissues later, my best friends were all crying.

"Oh my god, Natty." Pen wiped her eyes. "These postpartum hormones are bad enough but girl, you've been the fuck through it."

"It sort of puts into perspective when he showed up, demanding you go with him after the attack," Laura added.

I glanced back and forth among my friends.

"What are you talking about?"

Callie got up and headed to my kitchen for some water. "I wasn't there, but I heard about it from those two." Her voice echoed from the fridge.

My head snapped back in place, staring at Penelope and Laura.

"He showed up that night we were putting everything back together...before we realized he wasn't with you," Pen started, but Laura butted in by leaning toward me.

"He walked in like some god of death...it was slightly terrifying and also absolutely so fucking cool all at the same time, and when Killian went to thank him for helping, he brushed it off like it was nothing and just said he was there to collect you. That he'd promised he would be back for you at some point, and that day had come."

Pen's eyes softened as if she were going back in time. "When we all realized you were gone, he sort of broke...he walked outside and sunk to the ground."

Callie returned with four water bottles gathered at her chest.

"So to hear that you guys are married...gawwwd, I'm swooning, Natty."

My friends continued to chat about it, but my mind was racing.

He'd come for me.

He came for me before he even knew I was missing.

My heart lifted with hope and soothing out all my assumptions and fears. I needed to see him, but I had no idea where he'd gone or when he'd be back. He wouldn't leave me though.

Not after me losing Red...not after realizing he'd come for me.

It was dusk and Silas still hadn't appeared or responded to me. My arms were folded over my chest as I stood at my window, watching the backyard and seeing the way the clouds looked like a bottle of orange and purple powder had been spilled.

My phone was clutched in my fist, where I prayed and hoped it would buzz with something from him. Any sort of answer or indication that he was alive and okay.

I had yet to go downstairs, still too nervous about seeing the kitchen without Red standing inside it, sassing everyone around.

My heart felt too heavy for my chest.

The sky continued to darken, which meant I finally closed my shades. The light from below peeked up at me, indicating the guard that was stationed below my window. I hadn't noticed him all day but now that it was dark, his light revealed that he was changing shifts with someone.

The guards.

I quickly walked across the floor and pulled my door open. Garrison was there, standing against the wall, staring at his phone. He lazily glanced up at me.

"Do you know where he went?"

Garrison's brow furrowed.

"Silas, I mean…I'm sure he had to have told you where he went, right?"

Garrison gripped the neckline of his cut and glanced down the hall.

"He left around two in the morning, and I think he was headed down to see Alec. Hasn't been up since and I haven't heard anything from him…but."

I was about to go down the hall when his last word stopped me.

"But…"

Garrison looked physically uncomfortable as he shifted on his feet.

"I got a text earlier from one of my friends in the club…Silas showed up and…"

He was starting to annoy me with how he kept cutting off his sentences. His eyes were on me, his face looked solemn as he hesitated.

"What did he do?"

"Could just be a rumor but every single person who rode with Dirk, who was part of that era…he crucified them after burning down his old house."

He…*oh my god.*

My hand came to my mouth as I tried to breathe through the shock of what had happened.

"How many would that be?" My voice was a rasp as my mind swirled.

"If I had to guess...I'd say it would be around a dozen or so...and from what I understand, he placed them upside down on the crosses."

I was going to be sick.

Why would he...

Suddenly, it hit...he'd talked to Alec and then he burned down our old house, the group of men with Dirk.

He knew.

I walked past Garrison and ran down the hall, scaled the stairs and pushed through the front door.

The garage where they kept Alec was lit up enough that I was able to see him sitting on the floor, chained to a pipe. There seemed to be a shift in guard because he wasn't currently being watched by any Stone Riders.

My flip flops slapped against the concrete as I covered the vast garage. There was a slight breeze coming in through open bay doors, ruffling Alec's unruly hair.

His turbulent gaze landed on me the second I entered and remained on me as I drew closer.

"You look worried," were the first words Alec said to me.

I dropped my hands and stretched my fingers out as a way to help funnel my fear.

"Did Silas come and talk to you last night?"

Alec's gaze narrowed. "He came down here last night..." He trailed off, blinking and wetting his lips, like he was struggling to remember. He seemed lethargic.

I crossed my arms. "And?"

His eyes came back up like he'd forgotten I was there. "He wanted to know what my angle was with all this."

"So you guys talked about *you?*"

His head hung, like he was too tired to keep it up.

"Have they given you any food, water?"

"Don't worry about me, Artie." His face came up, and then his sling moved, like he was trying to move his amputated hand.

"I'm not worried about you, Alec. But I need you awake enough that you can answer a few fucking questions."

Across the garage they had a fridge they kept stocked with water and food. I walked over, briskly, agitated that I had to help him at all. Once I had a few water bottles in my hand and someone's sub sandwich, I returned to Alec's place on the floor. I only hesitated for a second before twisting the cap on the bottle and handing it over to him.

His eyes remained on me as he downed the entire thing as if he hadn't had a single thing to drink all day. Then he began unwrapping the sandwich.

I was sitting on the floor, my legs folded, close enough that Alec could kick me if he wanted to.

I gave him a second before trying to get more answers from him, but he beat me to it.

"We talked about you...I got angry with him for making me feel like shit. I told him I fucked up with you and needed to apologize. Silas reminded me that even if I did, you'd never forgive me. So I lashed out and made sure he was reminded of his failures with you, except he never knew about them."

Fuck.

A fissure of panic settled in my chest.

"You told him about Dirk?"

Alec nodded, taking another bite.

I looked down, tugging at a loose pebble in the groove of the floor. After Christmas, I made it my mission to avoid Alec. Which wasn't too difficult but then during one of the times Silas was gone, he'd been there, with The Death Raiders, partying and found his way to my back door.

I didn't let him in, but I took out two beers and sat in the garden under a star-speckled sky. I cried while explaining that I was trapped in a house with memories that haunted me every single day. I had confessed a few things about Dirk, and my fear of him. Not a ton, but a few details had slipped through the later it became. Alec hadn't said much, and when I was ready to call it a night, he merely waved at me and watched me go inside.

"How did he take it?"

"Not well." Alec snorted, shaking his head. "I think he short circuited…he left the garage, got on his bike and flew out of here like a bat out of hell."

"I wish you hadn't told him." My voice was feeble, but I still said it. I knew I owed Silas the truth, but I'd rather he'd never known than ever blame himself for it.

Alec stared at me, grabbing for another water bottle.

"I wish you had a long time ago…maybe you guys would have broken up. Maybe, selfishly, I imagine a scenario in which you tell him, he blames himself so much he can't be with you. In that scenario, you fall for me. You love me and instead of sadness in your life, all you have is sunshine."

"What, then you'd never have had to kidnap me?" I glowered at him. "Besides, I don't want a life full of sunshine. I create my own and crave a cool place to retreat when my world is too big and too bright. Silas and I would have continued even through me telling him, just like we will now. I know he's hurt, but we'll get past it."

My brother-in-law focused on me, as if he was calculating what to say next. His mouth parted with something else he wanted to say, but he shut it just as fast while focusing on the floor.

"I'm sorry, Natty. I'm so fucking sorry for what I did to you. I…" He started, then stopped, as if he were rethinking what he was going to say. A tiny kernel of pity must have been stored up in my chest because it came out, unfurling like a pod in spring. I gently kicked his boot, which had him looking up.

"I was coming for you…to protect you from Fable. I know you have no reason to trust me, but I wanted to help you. If you need help finding him, then use me. I'll do whatever I can to keep you safe."

Right as he said that my phone pinged with a text.

> Giles: I have one…you gotta come tonight though. He's connected to too many people.

I put the phone down and inspected Alec.

"What?"

"How are you with interrogations?"

That contemplative expression swept over his features again. "I'm pretty damn good, about as good as Silas."

That's exactly what I needed.

Since I had no way of finding Silas and this window was about to close, my only option was to trust Alec. For some reason I believed him when he said he wanted me safe from Fable. His father had raised the stakes, and if that meant he'd help me locate his father, then that's exactly what I'd use him for.

TWENTY-SIX
NATTY
PRESENT

GILES ONCE USED CLUB FUNDS FROM A RAID TO NOT ONLY RENT A CABIN FOR a random weekend, but he invited a shit ton of members out and threw a massive party. The cops were called, and Giles ended up getting arrested. One of the fundamental rules about being in a motorcycle club, especially a one-percent club, is there's absolutely no drawing needless attention from the police while wearing the colors of the club. Especially those outside the territory your club is in. It would be different if everyone was together on a raid, or a club sanctioned event that broke a few laws, but individually, it was practically forbidden.

Giles would have gotten his ass chewed by Simon, possibly even demoted, or put back on prospect duties until he could redeem himself. Giles was too nervous to call Killian, knowing he would have been forced to include Simon, so he had the bright idea to text me, asking if I had the money to bail him out. I did, and when I helped him cover up the whole thing, so Simon and Killian never found out, Giles vowed to repay the favor someday.

That day was today.

No guards ever came to check on Alec while I was there talking to him. When I went snooping for the key to his handcuffs, they happened to leave the key on the table along the opposite end of the room. I uncuffed him and then for the sake of speed, and lack of options, had him ride bitch as I rode my Yamaha to Richland.

First, I grabbed my jacket, boots and riding leathers out from one of the smaller lockers in the garage I'd been using as of late, then dressed in a bathroom.

Getting past the detail Silas left for me was the most difficult part of our escape, but I knew nearly every entry point, and weak point in the fence line, from years of sneaking out to leave Silas notes. I found a place to walk the bike, sneak through the fence, and cut away from the men Silas put on my trail.

Once we arrived at the location Giles provided, it was dark, the night crisp and clear. We were walking with the moon blotted out by tall trees, which cast a shadow over the dirt path in front of us.

"You know this Giles guy well?" Alec asked, stepping closer to me, nearly in front of me.

I nodded. "I do. He's trustworthy."

Our steps were quiet as we neared what looked like an old shed. It was roughly the size of a garden shed with dilapidated panels and a thatched roof. Giles appeared instantly from inside.

Pointing a finger behind him, he let out a sigh. "You have an hour, that's all I can give you. We have a story prepped and enough drugs to pump him with to make it stick, so do whatever you need to do to get your info."

Alec gave me one last glance and then pushed past us and entered the shack.

I hung back, not wanting to watch the interrogation.

Giles raised his brow at me, questioningly. "No Silas?"

Gesturing with my chin, I muttered, "His brother."

My friend's face went slack as he looked back where Alec had disappeared.

"There's two of them?"

"Yes, let's hope this guy will lead us to their father."

While we stood waiting in the dark, my mind went back to Silas and the pain he must be enduring. Crucifying a dozen people. All that rage and hurt.

If our roles were reversed, I'd feel horrible. Torn and tattered in ways that weren't redeemable. But he had to be redeemed. He had to come out of this for the sake of our future. Pulling up my cell once more, I checked my messages and saw there was still nothing from him.

I hated how familiar of a feeling that was.

TWENTY-SEVEN
SILAS
ONE YEAR AGO

I checked the box where Natty had started dropping me notes and found that there was nothing new inside it. The familiar disappointment burned under my skin, but I shook it off. She'd only started leaving them a few months ago after she realized I followed her everywhere she went.

She'd tried to call me with a burner phone and I selfishly relished the voicemails she'd left me in Latin. The texts she'd left me were the same, but it was still dangerous. Dirk had started acting more and more deranged around the club. Doing harder drugs, being more aggressive. Which included starting more turf wars.

We'd gone toe to toe with Mayhem Riot, which made no sense at fucking all considering they were in New York, but Dirk rode up, we all went with him, and he wanted to fight.

There was a club from Chicago he was trying to start shit with called The Brass. No clue about their affiliations, but they were a big fucking club. Someone needed to stop him, but until he could be managed, I had to make sure Natty remained safe.

So I watched over her.

Every chance that I got. Waking hours, nights I should be sleeping. I watched, and I waited.

I couldn't go inside the Stone Riders club unless I was clever and slipped on one of their cuts. They didn't know any different as long as I hid any ink that I carried, identifying myself as a Death Raider. I'd done it once, gotten close enough to sit at the bar in their clubhouse and watch her.

She stuck to the shadows, smiling and laughing with the white-haired woman in the kitchen. No one seemed to talk to her or bother her, which put my concerns to rest. She seemed safe...and more than that, she seemed happy.

She liked going to the library when she managed to get a ride into town. She'd do a loop, library, coffee shop, and then the fountain in the town square. The woman she liked to cook with didn't always drive a truck, occasionally she rode on the back of her man's bike, leaving Natty without a ride.

The next day I bought her a yellow moped with a note attached:

Galeam gere tuum cerebrum meum est tertium ventus de te mea res clara, sponsa pulchra. *Wear a helmet - your brain is my third favorite thing about you my bright, beautiful bride.*

I watched as she traced each word, smiling so bright that my chest nearly burst. That was when she looked up, and her eyes landed on me from across the road. I stood, wearing my cut, a t-shirt that exposed me to the remaining chill in the air and way too many eyes on my ink, but I merely allowed her to see me while I was able to see her.

She smiled at me, and I smiled back. It felt like time stopped, and we were frozen, unable to move forward or back. Just stuck there in this divide.

The next night I had a text on my phone with a drawing that was eerily familiar. A circle with an arrow...the symbol for the grove that we used as kids. Then she dropped coordinates.

I'd gone that next day and found a wooden box with a lid attached with a simple nail. Inside was a note.

Quod primum de me amas?

What is the first thing you love about me?

I smiled, then looked around just to see if she was near, but there was no one. We were a ways outside of her club, past the boundary line. She must have found an easy way to get back and forth, but the notion that it was unguarded didn't sit well with me.

I wrote her back and set the note inside, knowing this was dangerous for my heart but also knowing it was only a matter of time before she was in my arms again.

Animam tuam, Caelum. Anima mea ventus est de te.

Your soul, Caelum. Your soul is my favorite thing about you.

Natty rode her moped with pride, and in turn, it made me proud. She finally applied for a job in town, which I liked because it made her less reliant on the club. They paid her for things, but I knew it was tight, and she didn't do enough work to really bring in enough of an income, especially when she was getting her food and living costs taken care of.

This job was at a coffee shop—a bakery where she was in the kitchen, out of sight from the public, making baked goods. It seemed to make her happy.

That's what I had to settle for, I realized.

Watching her from afar as pieces of her hair fell to the page of the book she had started reading in the library. Being enthralled by the way the sun would cut through the windows and catch in her hair as if she was merely an extension of it.

I watched as she grocery shopped for herself but always took back a bottle of classic Coke for that guy Brooks that she liked. He seemed like a good guy from what I had observed.

The Stone Riders went to a picnic at a local lake, and while my own club was raiding somewhere, I was there, on a river rock, watching as Natty sunk her feet into the water, closed her eyes and tipped her face up to the sky.

I'd never seen her so free or so happy, at least not since we were kids.

Tears came when she crouched down, inspecting a frog hopping from stone to stone. She laughed, and it reminded me of a poem. If her laugh could create constellations, then at least ten would have been birthed. Joy was a good look on my wife, and I realized it was an addiction to allow her to keep it.

Time went on where I became her shadow, a dark wraith obsessed with her light.

She knew I was there. Always aware of me, but never able to talk to me.

She'd ask in her letters if I would come for her, and how long I was going to wait.

Each time she did, I'd take the note and leave no response because my mind would go back to her standing in that lake, smiling at the sun. She was safe. She was happy, and she was free.

I knew deep down I loved her enough to let her stay that way.

TWENTY-EIGHT
NATTY
PRESENT DAY

I HAD TEXTED PEN WHAT I WAS DOING SO SHE COULD FILL IN JAMESON AND Killian. It wasn't really their fight now that I was recovered, and Killian's mother was safe. I wanted them to stay out of this, knowing Fable was only coming for me.

Alec and Silas could handle things from here on out, but I still wanted someone to know what I was doing and considering Giles was Jameson's cousin, it was a good idea to make sure he was aware since it was technically considered his territory.

I was pacing around the front of the shed, trying to keep warm when Alec finally shoved the metal door open and started toward me. He used a rag to wipe off his face and sling. He had dark smudges all along his shirt and jeans that I had to turn away from him.

"The old mill in Gundry."

Hope soared as Alec walked to the bike and Giles began heading inside the shack. I waved goodbye to him as he yelled back at me, "We're square, Natty!"

I jogged to catch up with Alec's long stride.

"We have to go back to the Stone Riders and get them, my club and The Death Raiders all ready to ride over there; it's the only way to ensure we can defeat his Destroyers."

I thought back to what Rachel had said and shook my head. "We go now before he has a chance to realize he's been compromised."

Alec paused, inspecting me with his lips turned down. "His army will—"

"Not be a problem." I grabbed my helmet and pulled it on. Alec's hand was at my waist as he gently pulled me toward him.

"Natty, I know you're worried and even nervous but we're going to catch him. We will, I promise you, but we have to do it right."

I pulled away from him so he wasn't holding my hip, then flipped my visor up.

"We go now."

He let out a sigh, clenching his teeth. I continued to stare at him while he crawled on the back, leaving his hand on the side of the seat, as if he were ready for me to sit between his thighs again.

"What about Silas?" he whispered in my ear after I straddled the bike and placed my hands over the gears. His hand continued to cup my hip while we sat there.

My chest tightened while guilt prodded around for entry. I didn't want him behind me, touching me, and I didn't want to do this without Silas...but I wanted my life back. I wanted my future back, so I would go with my husband's brother and make this work.

"We're going to handle this without him," I said over my shoulder, then started the bike.

Alec's arm came around me, engulfing my stomach and holding me tight to his chest. I inhaled a shaky breath and silently hoped Silas would forgive me for this and all my other failures later when we finally had a chance at starting over.

It took us forty-five minutes to get to the old mill and nearly a mile out, I shut off the engine and parked the bike out of sight, so we wouldn't alert anyone to our approach. There was nothing but corn fields around for miles, which made me think back to not very long ago when Silas fucked me in one.

I missed him.

I needed him, but I'd already ruined him by omitting the biggest secret of my life; I had to let him process that.

I wore my property patch, in the form of my leather jacket that fit snugly over my shoulders, and concealed the handgun I had strapped to my ribs. There were many things I wasn't very good at, but shooting and accuracy was actually something I excelled at…when I didn't freeze.

"We need to get off the gravel path," Alec murmured close to my ear, gently pulling my hip off to the side. My boots sank into soft soil but removed the loud echoing sound of gravel crunching. Carefully and quietly, we moved through the corn toward the large silo and lumber yard. There were no lights, no cars or bikes that I could see, and my stomach began to twist with worry over this being a trap. Fable always seemed to be one step ahead of us…and I was hoping that just once we'd be able to have the drop on him.

Alec took my hand in his, keeping me close behind him, and I knew it wasn't the time to fight him.

The cicadas sang and a few distant frogs bellowed as the stars began to appear and then the silo was directly in front of us, looming to blot out any light.

We snuck through the grounds, which were eerily silent and deserted. The reality that Fable was really alone gave me some hope, especially as we snuck in through a side door to the main part of the mill and there wasn't a single person in sight.

There was sawdust on the floor as we walked in and suddenly a large overhead light flicked on, making us both freeze.

Tied to a metal chair in the middle of the floor, with his head hanging lifelessly, was Silas. I immediately started running for him, but Alec pulled me back.

"Wait…this is a trap."

I didn't care. That was my fucking husband tied to a chair. Was he unconscious?

"Silas!"

Alec continued to pull me behind him.

Silas's dark hair, soft as feathers, didn't shift even the slightest. His head just hung there. Fable suddenly walked out from the side, where a wall had concealed him. His silver hair nearly matched Alec's in texture, and his eyes were so similar to the man in front of me. But tonight, he held that similar ghost-like glare that I'd witnessed so many times in his oldest son's gaze. That gaze landed on me, severely, as he made his way to the center of the room, clapping his hands in a slow, menacing way.

"Thank you, Natty, for being so zealous about locating me. This was exhilarating for me. It really was. Getting to watch how close you got, and when you thought you'd found me on your own. You don't think I planted that information in those men, knowing you'd go out of your way to dig this little hole you're in? And my sons, the puppy dogs obsessed with protecting you and ensuring you're safe. I taught them better than this."

My hands shook as I watched him walk to Silas and grab his hair, lifting his face. Blood poured from his nose and lip, but otherwise, he seemed to be okay.

"You've reduced them to this, Natty."

I saw Silas open his eyes, and then it felt like two blue moons inspected every inch of me, then ever so slowly they moved to his brother and froze.

"It was you all those years that kept Silas from truly focusing on the vision I had. You that had come between the brothers, and why Alec refused to join the Death Raiders when I asked him to take Silas' spot. You have single handedly ruined everything." Fable yelled.

My stomach dropped like I'd fallen off a rollercoaster, barreling out of the car and plunging to my death.

Alec pushed me again, until I was completely behind him.

"Oh what Alec, you don't want me to play with the toy you're hoping to get to keep?"

Alec didn't reply, which was probably best because Fable was just provoking us.

But I couldn't stop my mouth from opening and questions spilling out. "What do you want?" I wasn't even sure why I asked it. I knew what he wanted. He wanted me and to punish his sons.

He pointed at me, smiling as if I were a student who just asked the right question.

"You. I want my sons to watch as you breathe your last breath, cry your last tear and say your last words. Will you save them for Silas or Alec?"

Alec shifted the smallest bit on his feet, as if he were preparing to fight. I tried to focus on that instead of the fear braiding itself around my limbs, freezing me in place.

Silas started laughing and the eerie way it slid through my rib cage had me moving again. Even shifting back to avoid whatever was coming next. I'd never heard this sort of laugh come out of him.

Fable glared at his son, then swung his gaze back to me.

"You think this is funny, Silas? Is it hilarious to think that I'm about to murder your wife?"

Alec scowled over at his brother, the two of them seemed to speak without using words.

Fable still held onto Silas's hair, bending at the waist to scream in his face.

Silas just continued to laugh, manically so, as if this was all so funny. But I knew...deep down, I knew this was the madness that his father had sewn into him, stitch by stitch all those years he forced Silas to do his dark bidding.

"You touch her and you die," Alec warned, reaching for my hand but coming empty because I'd folded them across my chest.

Fable let Silas's head go, and I saw the thick column of his throat, covered in black ink, glisten under the lights.

"Don't start acting like you're her savior, Alec. It wasn't long ago you had her cuffed to you, sleeping in your bed. You coveted your brother's wife, and now you assume if you step in and play hero, she'll want you?"

Alec's jaw flexed, but that's when Silas stopped laughing and the air in the room seemed to shift. "Never assume your enemy's weakness."

Fable's focus swung over right as Silas stood from the chair, as if no rope had bound him there to begin with. It forced Fable to stumble back a few steps, being caught off guard while Silas advanced with a murderous expression on his face.

"Never take your surroundings for granted," Silas yelled, dipping down to grab something from the ground. It was a metal rod.

Fable's eyes grew wide, and while he was so focused on his son, I slipped my hand into my jacket and pulled out my gun. Alec noticed and shook his head.

I ignored him and aimed at Fable.

Silas continued to move toward his father, now flipping the metal object around in his hand, as if he'd wielded it a thousand times before.

"Never show mercy."

Fable tripped and was now on the ground. Silas was only a few feet from his father, and while I knew he needed to be the one to kill Fable, I couldn't bring myself to lower the gun. And that's when everything seemed to shatter, like a piece of glass under too much pressure. Silas lunged forward and shoved the rod into Fable's chest, muttering a few incoherent things that Alec and I couldn't hear.

I lowered my gun, realizing Fable was no longer a threat. Silas stood, and when he turned toward me, my gaze dropped back to his father. His hand came up, slow and measured as if time had slowed, just for this moment. My eyes must have grown because Silas stopped mid step. Fable had a gun in his hand, and it was aimed right at me.

I closed my eyes and pictured our pond. I saw Silas when he was ten, fishing without a care in the world and me, watching him while I sat on that brittle dock, soaking in the summer sun.

Silas screamed.

It was a horrible sound, so guttural like his heart was being pulled through his chest.

There was a fevered rush of breath against my mouth, and a confession. "I love you."

My eyes opened as tears rushed forward, and then there was so much screaming, it made a buzzing begin to fill my head. Alec was staring down at me, holding me with his good hand...pain twisted his features as his eyes lowered to my lips.

Why was he in front of me?

My hand went to his jaw, confused, right as we started sinking to the ground together.

That's when I felt the sticky blood begin to coat my chest, but it was coming from Alec's.

"I'm so sorry, Artie. You have to forgive me...I messed up so bad. I just didn't know how else to get your attention. It was like that first time we met." Blood coated his lips as he began coughing and choking.

"Alec," I whispered, so shocked and confused that I held his head in my lap, still trying to figure out what had happened. He'd spun in front of me.

He'd moved so that the bullet hit him instead of me.

Understanding finally dawned, creating panic.

"Alec!"

Silas was back in front of Fable, this time hammering something into his lifeless body. There was blood, so much blood… I couldn't look.

"Artie, you have to forgive me."

My hands were in Alec's hair as he continued to rasp his broken-hearted confession, and I was shaking. My head, my hands, my entire body trembled as I slowly processed that Alec was about to die. Silas ran over, coming to an abrupt stop next us, and dropped to his knees, helping me hold Alec up. I didn't look to see if he was covered in blood. I focused on the gray thunderclouds that were starting to dim in Alec's gaze.

"I saw you on that dock, hunting frogs, and I thought you were the prettiest thing I'd ever seen. Then I looked up and saw Silas glaring at me, and I knew right then and there you'd always be between us. You took my heart just as you took his, but you only gave yours to him. But I think at Christmas, you gave me some pieces too. I have to believe that I found my way in there, Artie, before I leave this earth. Please tell me I did."

I stroked his hair, then traced his nose and eyebrow. "Alec, stop…just save your breath."

He smiled as more blood spurted out.

Silas touched his brother's chest affectionately. "Let him say it, Natty. Whatever's in his heart, let him say it."

"Because I'm about to die." Alec had tears sliding down his face, and my heart cracked in half. How could I take another loss this close to the others? I wasn't built for grief. I was sunshine, and the only darkness I could ever withstand was from Silas. This pain was too much.

Please don't take him. Let him live.

Alec coughed, forcing more blood to come up.

"It was always his, Alec."

He laughed, and then coughed. "Well then, at least I'll take a chunk with me into the grave. I can see the way you're trying to hold me here, while death is hovering above me. I'll die, knowing I've claimed some part of that heart."

I couldn't speak, so I just continued to stroke his hair.

"Seeing you felt like finding a pair of wings. But there was only one of us who could fly, and I'm glad it's Silas. Just promise me that you'll love each other after this. Whatever happened, push it behind you and finally be together. Start a family." He was wheezing now, and I was sobbing.

"She'd be the most beautiful mother, Silas. Have you pictured it…her pregnant, smiling down at her swollen belly. Her laughing and creating more sunshine."

I looked up at my husband and saw he had tears sticking to his lashes, as he answered, "Yes, I've pictured it, Alec."

"Good. That's good. Artie, bury me in the same cemetery as my mom, okay? Promise me that I'll be next to her…and maybe one day I'll be near you and my brother."

Silas picked up Alec's good hand and held it tight. "I promise we'll be together, Alec. I promise you."

"Good because I was a shit brother to you, Silas, but you were the best big brother. I love you. I may have wanted to kill you just so I could have Artie, but I loved you. I'll always love you. I need you to know that."

Silas leaned down and pressed a kiss to Alec's forehead.

"I know it, Alec. I love you too."

Alec's eyes suddenly froze, staring up at the ceiling. For some reason, I kept waiting for him to say something else and my mind couldn't seem to accept that he was gone.

"I promise, Alec." I bent down and kissed his forehead, sorrow bleeding from my raw voice. I was sobbing, tears and snot were all over my face, but Silas pulled me into his arms anyway.

"We need to get out of here, Caelum."

I looked over his shoulder and saw Fable with a metal stake jutting from his brain, and a hole cut into his chest. There was so much blood.

Silas tipped my chin, so I wasn't looking anymore.

"I have no way of knowing if anyone is going to show up. We have to go."

"What about Alec?"

Silas began pulling me away. "I'll call his club and have them come for him, but I'm not risking you out here."

"Promise, Silas. Promise that we'll do right by him." I tugged on my husband's hand until he cradled my jaw and ducked to look me in the eye. "I promise you."

I went with him, leaving my bike behind, and for the first time in my life, wishing I'd hear that stupid nickname just one more time.

Artemis would be buried with Alec and that meant part of me would too.

TWENTY-NINE
NATTY
PRESENT DAY

Silas didn't drive us to the Stone Riders property, or to The Death Raiders. We drove back to Rose Ridge, but instead of pushing through the town, we ended up on the outskirts, near the water treatment plant. We drove a ways out until we entered a vast orchard that I had always assumed belonged to one of the wealthier families in Rose Ridge. The space stretched along the ridgeline of the top of the canyon, where the sun hit the hill the most.

I'd never walked among the trees, but I heard the owner of the bakery mention the varying fruit that grew here, and how delicious it all was. We maneuvered path after path, trees at every turn, making it almost dizzying, until Silas took a slight turn, almost imperceptible in the dark. I perked up because it felt very private, like we were suddenly traveling down someone's personal drive that would soon lead to a house.

Nerves gnawed at my stomach as I waited to see a glow, or something that indicated where we were headed. Silas slowed his bike as the moon guided our approach to a small, brick house. There were no lights, so it was hard to make out all the details, but with the pitched roof, it gave the appearance of a cottage.

The bike stopped, and Silas pushed down his kickstand. The quiet of the night seemed to stretch around us like a bubble, holding in all the horrors we'd just seen…and done.

Silas twisted the smallest bit as he turned to help me off the bike. Once we were standing, his hand in mine, he led me toward the entrance. The single-story house was hidden within the orchard, like we'd finally found our version of the wardrobe we once hid inside. Our own little *Narnia*.

The porch was wide and enclosed as we maneuvered the steps, and gently entered through the screen door. It shut with a whisper behind me as Silas produced a key and my heart seemed to kickstart. Without even a glance over his shoulder, he pulled me inside.

The house smelled like lemon, the sweet kind, and when Silas clicked on a lamp, I realized why.

He had glass bowls of lemons scattered around the house.

His hand remained over mine as we walked along pine floors, and I inspected the white walls, trimmed with the same wood that ran below our feet. My eyes soaked up the small circular table off to the right with four chairs around it. To the left was a generously sized bookshelf that held all familiar books I remembered being stuffed inside a baby blue dresser. Silas had used his closet for his minimal wardrobe, but his dresser was saved for his prized collection.

I stepped closer, seeing on the shelves framed photos of me scattered between groups of books. Me, bent over a butcher block counter, rolling out dough while working at The Drip. Me, smiling at the sky while standing in a lake. Me, laughing at something while the sun caught in my hair, outside the library.

He'd taken all these images of me when I didn't even know he was watching…and then he'd framed them and put them in his house. My throat felt tight as I slipped my fingers over another image of me in a red dress, making a funny face while pointing at Laura. It was outside The Hollow, after one of her shows.

God, how many moments had he stolen and bottled up here, like these random lemons scattered along the shelves in glass jars and vases. I traced a rock that we'd found in the grove one time that we both said had fallen from space. My eyes watered as I touched the leather reading chair and ottoman perched in front of it. The closer I got to the chair, the more I could smell my husband's scent of leather, campfire and spice.

"You live in a cottage." My voice was barely audible as we passed under a rounded arch that led to the kitchen, and a larger living room. He had a television, soft accent rugs, a large hearth, and a comfortable looking couch.

Silas trailed his hand down the length of my arm, which had me moving toward the back of the house. He flicked on another lamp and a bedroom materialized. A king-sized bed with dove gray bedding and white throw pillows, a beautiful rustic headboard, and two side tables that matched with bedside lamps.

I stepped inside a bit farther and then Silas clicked another light, but the space above me began to glow, which had me tipping my head back. Green vines ran along the length of the ceiling, intermixed with glowing lights, which made it look like something from a movie. It was vastly more elaborate than anything I'd ever put up myself. The vines were beautifully braided into cohesive columns, with white flowers woven into each strand, and the shimmering lights were more expensive than any that I had ever used.

"Silas." The air rushed out of my chest as I began to inspect the full scope of what he'd created.

A masterpiece.

"When you were traded to the Stone Riders, I nearly killed Simon Stone," Silas muttered quietly while tossing his phone and keys on the small bedside table. I turned and watched him as he removed his shoes and set them inside a generously sized closet.

When he glanced at my feet, I realized I should do the same.

I was still wearing my jacket, and other riding leathers, so I started to strip.

"My mother didn't tell me why you went. It was elusive and confusing. All I was told was that it was for the best and to keep you safe, but I had no idea why. I just had to accept a new life without you inside it."

Guilt prodded for a place inside my heart, threatening to ruin this moment, but I pushed it out. We couldn't change the past, and it wouldn't do me any good to try and go back in time.

"I was mad at you…it hurt that you felt safer with them…it hurt me that you started finding this new life and this new freedom over there. But then, as I watched you, I realized I had started falling in love with you all over again. Your excitement over the smallest things…your smile. Your love for life."

I was naked, standing in his bedroom as he gently took my hand and led me to the attached bathroom. A clawfoot tub sat in the corner on top of subway tile. A shower with the same tile was off to the side, and a long counter with two brass sinks.

Silas perched on the edge of the tub and started the hot water, adding in expensive looking bubble bath. Once it was full enough, Silas helped me into the tub, but I gestured toward his bloodied clothes.

"You should get in too. To clean up."

He glanced down at his shirt and jeans and winced. I relaxed against the porcelain, watching as Silas shed his clothes, revealing dusky tattoos that made up his toned arms, long fingers and tapered waist. Even down his strong thighs, there were designs carved in intricate detail over his skin. He was a story dipped in ink, his soul a sonnet, constantly bleeding new lines of poetry each and every time his heart broke.

With his focus on me, he advanced toward the tub and as I made room for him, he slid in behind me until I was cradled between his thighs. His arms came around me as his lips came to my ear. "I have a thousand regrets, Natty. Most of them are from before you were ever even traded. I should have let the obsession with Fable go. I should have stayed home with you and found a way to leave. We should have left the club, all of it, and ran. We could have had this years ago."

My hand was soapy as I pulled his hand into mine. My heart ached as grief throbbed there at my core, threatening to push through my emotions and ruin this moment. I knew it was important to Silas. That he needed to say these words, and I clung to him, hoping they'd help heal me as he said them. But all I felt was a sorrow that seemed to sink bone deep.

Red.

Brooks.

Alec.

"You asked me to run with you…recently and I just—" He blew out a breath. "Part of it was that I couldn't relax until I knew he was gone. I needed to keep you safe, but the other part was the assumption that you'd be happier there, with them."

Gone.

Forever.

I realized it wasn't just grief that was keeping my mind at bay, as if an invisible barrier was between what Silas was saying and what I was absorbing. It was that I didn't want to go back.

Not to those nights when terror would crawl under my skin like a disease and fester. Dirk had me too afraid to sleep most nights that Silas was gone. He'd become a demon, hunting my dreams, my waking hours. Fear was the very air I breathed, and right now...in the tub with him, I didn't want to go back.

But this was a piece of parched land I'd never given him access to. For all the light he always claimed to love of mine, he'd yet to see the deserts, the valleys and places inside me that had been scorched by all that forced sunshine. So I let him continue.

And I remembered there was a cage around my soul now made of titanium. It would not break so easily again.

It would hold.

Silas stroked up my stomach and over my breasts. "After hearing what happened to you..." His voice dipped as though he had to work to control his emotions. "That you were being hurt by him...that you covered it up just so that I wouldn't get hurt..." If I were looking at him, I had no doubt his eyes would be full to the brim with pain and an agony that I wished to my bones I could remove.

"I'd die a thousand times over if it meant I could keep you safe. My life is not worth living without you in it, Caelum. You've been my forever since my life started. If you were to end, then I would too. The fact that you didn't realize that...it kills me."

His voice cracked, and I finally turned, making the bubbles shift and move. I got to my knees, letting the water drip, my slick breasts exposed and sopping wet. My hands went to his jaw, and I leveled him with a stare of my own.

"What of my love for you, Silas? Can I not also want to move the sky and crack the earth just to protect you? Loving you has been the greatest joy of my life, and if it meant that I lost a few pieces of myself along the way then it was worth it. Your mom did what she felt was best to keep us both safe."

His hand covered mine over his jaw as he ground his molars together. I felt the muscle shift under my palm.

"She nearly ruined us."

I shook my head. "She knew our love was made of the very same substance that makes the stars stay in the sky, and the currents that spread throughout the rivers. We're an ocean wave: violent, turbulent and steadfast. No time apart would ever diminish that."

A tear slipped down his cheek.

"How do I accept what was done to you?"

His hands came to my hips, stabilizing me against him. I stroked his dark, furrowed brow.

"The same way I accepted what was done to you. I offered you my light. You might need to extend some of your own. You have some in there, my darling husband. I know you do. It's brilliant and beautiful and perhaps it was just waiting for a season of peace to come out."

He laughed as more tears fell from his lashes. Then I stood, stepped out of the tub and wrapped myself in a white fluffy towel. Silas did the same, tying it around his waist. I was about to walk past him, but he put his hand out, gently tipping my chin up.

"I'm sorry you lost him, Caelum. I know you cared for him."

That sorrow felt like a plucked string on an instrument, ready to play to the tune of grief.

"I did care for him; he was annoying and I hate what he did to me. Parts of me will never forgive what he did to me in that house. But there are other parts of me that remember him as a kid, a gangly teen…a friend who was just as much a shield to me as you always were."

Silas pressed a kiss to my mouth, soft and gentle. I followed him into the room where he handed me one of his t-shirts. I slipped the soft fabric over my head and then slid under the covers, watching as Silas did the same.

"How long have you had this cottage?"

Silas pulled me into his arms, making me feel found in ways I hadn't even realized I'd been lost. "I discovered this place by accident about a year and a half ago. I was up here, trying to clear my head after you were traded, not wanting to be too far from you. There was an older couple who would also be up here, so I started helping them. Every day I would pick lemons, help load them, and carry them back to their house. I got so used to being here that I started sleeping on the ground, under the trees. They found me, and the next day, the old man led me here. Said it used to be for their groundskeeper. I bought it off them before they retired and moved back to Texas."

I hummed, feeling tired, sad and happy all at once. The grief over Red, Alec and Brooks was a knife prick against my sternum, refusing to let up or go away but seeing this place, and how settled Silas was, I'd only ever hoped he'd find a place like this.

Silas hesitated, pushing some of my hair back. "Do you like it?"

My eyes slid shut, as a smile slipped free.

"It's better than anything I ever hoped for...would you..." I stopped, suddenly feeling nervous. "Could I stay here with you?"

His soft chuckle was firelight against my exposed neck. "Yes, Caelum. This is yours. All I am is yours, including this cottage."

"So you've been up here, on top of my town, just watching over me like a dark shadow?"

Slow strokes started against my stomach as he kissed my ear.

"Two years, I've never been more than five miles from you."

Pain radiated like a webbed piece of glass, forcing my eyes shut and sleep to claim me.

The next morning was gray and full of clouds that snuffed out the sun. It felt fitting for my mood. Silas had brought me coffee in bed, and I realized I didn't have the energy to leave it. I was sad.

So sad that tears trailed my face, leaving a cold sting behind.

I sipped the coffee, then closed my eyes and fell back asleep.

Silas would wake me for meals. But I wouldn't eat them.

I wasn't trying to be difficult; I just didn't have an appetite. When I slept, I saw Alec's gray eyes right before he stopped living. The way he talked about me one day living a life he'd never be a part of, one where he didn't get to meet his niece or nephew, one where he didn't get to fall out of love with me, and just be the friend he'd always been to me.

I'd see Red's face as we laughed about playing charades. Her hands moving as she rolled out dough. Brooks grease-stained fingers as he helped me tune up my secret bike that no one was supposed to know about.

I'd see things that had knit invisible pieces of hope inside my heart, creating a snapshot for when their presence evaded this world. All that would be left would be those pieces of hope, stuck in our heart like chunks of forever.

Silas stroked my hair as I drifted off again, and I realized it was dark and an entire day had passed. I closed my eyes and let it drift away.

The following day began without Silas checking on me. Eventually my bladder had me leaving the bed. Once I relieved myself, I shuffled out of the room. Still in the shirt Silas gave me, my hair a wreck as I searched the cottage for my husband.

A note was left behind for me, indicating he was working the orchard.

A fluttering sensation started in my stomach. He'd become a peaceful man…a farmer, and I had yet to see him in action.

I turned around, located my clothes that Silas must have washed for me, and dressed.

Then I went in search of the orchard.

Sunshine soaked the world, doting on all the trees. I covered my eyes with my hand as I walked past the enclosed yard, and back down the path Silas had initially driven up. There were white buckets abandoned every few yards or so. I grabbed one and began walking with it, still no idea where Silas was until I saw yellow and remembered lemons.

I found my husband wearing a white, gaping Henley with the sleeves shoved up to his forearms, brown gloves were on his hands. Thick canvas jeans covered his legs, and work boots replaced the motorcycle boots I'd always seen him in. There was also a black ball cap on his head, covering his hair and helping protect his eyes from the sun.

The sight of him...it was like a searing piece of metal plunged into my gut and swiped around. Was this what he meant when he said he'd begun to fall in love with me all over again? Because it was starting to feel that way as I watched him gently pulling a lemon free and tossing it down to a bucket; I felt like I was seeing him for the first time and completely in love already.

"Hi," he said, looking down at me.

I realized I was just staring at him.

"Hi."

"Lunch?"

How late was it?

"I guess."

He smirked then scaled the ladder he was perched on. "Penelope, Laura and Callie would like to send a message along to you that roughly states if you don't contact them by today, they will begin tearing the town apart in search of you, which will include calling in the aid of any and all motorcycle club allies."

I snorted, imagining who drafted that little text. I did need to check in with them...they had to be so worried about me. I just disappeared.

Silas was down, walking along the trees with me, while carrying that bucket, so I turned to join him.

"Would that include yours? We going to talk about what you did, or how Fable was able to get to you, or better question, how you got out of the chair?"

His hand found mine as the quiet in the trees seemed to settle around us. It was so tranquil and perfect.

Finally, Silas took a deep breath and explained, "I gave them up. Lance is the new president."

I stopped and faced him.

"You gave them up?"

Silas pushed a piece of hair out of my face.

"I lost my mind after I discovered you were hurt. I got rid of every single person who was ever a part of Dirk's circle, or had ridden with him. I had to get rid of that house…and somewhere in that blood lust, I wasn't paying attention or watching. Lance was trying to deal with the bodies because I'd created such a mess. I took off toward the grove, but Fable had already been watching me."

I held his hand in mine, stroking along his wrist.

"So he took you?"

"He knocked me out but didn't check me for weapons. I had a slim fragment of iron from the stakes…" He trailed off and that's how I knew he was still good inside. Because even though those men deserved it, he still struggled to even talk about it.

His eyes drifted to some place behind me. "I had a small piece still in my back pocket. I was able to use it to cut through the rope."

"He was toying with us…" I drifted off, but Silas pulled my chin back.

"Doesn't matter. We won. Now let's go see your friends before they find us and murder me."

THIRTY
SILAS
PRESENT DAY

"WHAT IS THIS?" NATTY'S MOUTH GAPED AS I TOOK HER INSIDE THE GARAGE that sat off the side of the cottage.

I smiled, feeling a blush crawling up my neck. "This is my truck."

Her face lit up. "Because you're a farmer now."

"Just get in." I shook my head as she began laughing at me.

We had several flat boxes in the back, ready to be assembled, so we could move her out of the clubhouse today. We were also planning to help pack up Red and Brooks's apartment, regardless that I didn't think she was ready for it. Her grief was getting better, but pieces of pain still lingered around her eyes and mouth when she didn't think I was watching.

As soon as we pulled in through the gates of the Stone Riders club and parked, Laura, Penelope and Callie were there to greet Natty with open arms and offered to help take up a few boxes. I was about to follow her when Killian arrived next to my door.

"Can I help you?"

He smiled, using the expression he often did with his enemies. "Yes, actually. Can you get the fuck inside and have a little chat with us?"

I wasn't in the mood to make waves. I just wanted to move Caelum out and go back home. So I followed Killian inside, into their church, where Wes Ryan and Jameson King were already waiting for us.

"Were you ever planning to tell us that you're no longer the president of The Death Raiders?" Killian tipped his chin up, taking a seat at the head of the table.

I dug my nail into my jeans and tried to withhold the rage simmering under my skin. Still took practice not to react first; those dark things woven within me still had wings, ready to take flight.

"Why would I have to tell you that?"

Wes scoffed and sat forward. "Forgive us for assuming you were one of our allies."

It really was a stupid assumption. This club lived by a code that made them soft as fuck.

"Because it was our guys who had to go and clean up the two dead bodies left behind."

I narrowed my gaze on Killian and flicked an annoyed glance at Wes.

"Why the fuck were you called at all?"

Jameson was leaning back but sat forward to address me. "Because Natty called my cousin to have someone from the original defectors found, gagged and interrogated by Alec Veda."

Still fucking hated that she'd done that, but I didn't blame her. I knew she wasn't able to get through to me at the time and she was desperate to find Fable.

"I called Matt, from Sons of Speed, and told him to come."

"We got there first and cleaned the scene, which meant we delivered a body to Sons of Speed, and now they think Stone Riders killed him." Killian's tone turned icy.

Well, that was a problem wasn't it?

"How the fuck is that my problem then? You should have left it."

Wes sat forward, glancing at Killian. "It was Giles's territory, and that mill is located near product he can't have the police know about. Searching the area was out of the question. So we showed up to help him. Not you, or Sons of Speed. So, yes you will still fix this. Who's taking over for you?"

"Lance Hurst."

Killian muttered a curse.

"He hates Killian," Wes said distractedly.

Killian stood and pushed the chair. "So we gained an enemy by you stepping down, and now Sons of Speed thinks we killed their president?"

"It's not really my concern what happens to your club. I can make a call and fix it with Sons of Speed, but I'm out."

"No, you'll fix all of it by swearing to ride with us under our patch if we need you."

Wes tossed a leather cut on the table.

"You fucking serious?" I glared at all three men. Jameson was smirking, covering his mouth as if he was smothering a laugh.

Killian slid the cut closer. "We're dead serious. You won't even be an official member. You don't have to come to meetings or church. But if we need you to ride with us for any reason, you'll be there."

I glared up at him, then reached for the leather and stopped when I realized what it was.

"The actual fuck."

I stood, holding up the cut.

The Stone Riders name and acronym was on the front but on the back...

Property of Caelum

"You gave me a property patch?"

Jameson burst out laughing; Wes chuckled too and even Killian smirked.

"She gets an actual member's cut because we know that if we need Natty, she'll be there for us in a heartbeat. She'll always be one of us no matter what happens."

A smile crept up my face, actually enjoying their antics. Stupid fuckers were actually pretty funny.

"Fine. I'll ride with you when you need me."

Jameson pointed. "And be sure to wear your property patch when you do."

I walked out of the room, giving all three men the finger.

It was agonizing sitting on the floor, experiencing the grief of the people in this room while they put Brooks and Red's things into boxes.

"Callie, do you remember this?" Killian asked, holding up some piece of pottery that had clearly been done by a child.

Callie started laughing while also crying. She did both, frequently.

"They were the victims of so many of our school projects."

Killian smiled again. "I gave them an entire diorama I made once."

"Do you think they ever cared that we just kept bringing them stuff?"

Simon Stone piped up from the corner. "They loved every second of it. You were the kids they never got to have."

That made my chest feel tight. It took a lot to make me emotional, but suddenly I was on the verge of tears. Maybe because my mother was here with them as they sorted through Red's things, or perhaps it was because my wife was silently crying as she packed the kitchen. But, fuck, the mood was somber.

I left them all in the living room where I'd been packing boxes and pulled Natty's hips until her back was nestled against my chest. She set the dishes down, and abruptly turned, flinging her arms around my neck, burying her face into my shirt.

Sobs escaped her as she shook in my arms, and I just held her. The murmurs in the living room grew quiet as Natty continued to break.

"She hated these dishes." She pulled away, pointing at the offending items. Her face was blotchy and wet.

Laura appeared in the archway, pursing her lips while she watched us.

"What would Red do if she were here, knowing she had to pack something we hated?"

Natty sniffed, swiping at her face, then let out a sweet laugh.

"She'd smash 'em."

"She wouldn't keep any of this stuff...I mean, she loved the minimal lifestyle. She saved her money for her makeup, her leather riding gear, and their road trips. They'd want all of it spread out, given away or used in a bonfire." Natty looked around, folding an old tattered dish towel.

Simon appeared in the doorway. "Then that's what we'll do. We'll say goodbye properly before we bury them. And we'll say goodbye to you too, Natty."

I marveled at the way Natty beamed, as if having Simon offer to say goodbye to her, or give her a send off from The Stone Riders meant something to her. It still warmed some dead place inside of me when I realized how settled she'd become here.

We continued to work, but it all felt a little lighter, now that we knew we would be burning their stuff and smashing a shit ton of dishes. The night fell quicker than any of us anticipated. Natty started drinking with Laura, and the two seemed to have the most fun out of any of us as they danced under the starry sky, raising their bottles of bourbon while loud music roared from the speakers, and Stone Riders remembered two of their most revered members.

I sat on the edge of an abandoned car that had made its way into the back; apparently, it had been caught on fire at some point. But it made for a good place to observe this community that had adopted my wife and helped her discover who she wanted to be. That gave her people to love, to grieve, and to miss. Friends who cried with her, drank with her and held her while she was sad. Raw, unfamiliar joy spread through me like all that sunshine I was always craving from Caelum.

A fresh feeling of hope burst in that organ that had felt dead for so long.

This was our home, our future...these would become our friends. The people we'd spend our holidays with, and I'd have to call to help plan her birthdays. Because while I'd been raised as a Destroyer, accepted becoming a Death Raider, it looked like, through love, I'd reluctantly and permanently become a Stone Rider.

THIRTY-ONE
NATTY
PRESENT DAY

IT WAS LATE WHEN I WOKE, HEARING SILAS READING.

It had been three days since he carried me to his truck, tucked me into the passenger seat and drove us home. I was drunk, completely hammered, but had fallen asleep the second we arrived home.

The next day, I unpacked all my things and managed to fall in love with Silas in completely new ways. Like seeing him build me a new shelf. Hearing him talk to the deer that would walk into our yard, watching him grow into this profession that he now held, and seemed to love. I had always assumed Silas would miss the war brewing in his blood, but peace seemed to suit him better than battle.

I loved him for standing with me in the kitchen while I baked. Silas would eventually move further into the room, and stand next to me, while he helped me cook. I loved the walks we took together in the evenings.

Tonight was such a quiet one, that I'd fallen asleep early.

That deep, soothing timbre that pulled me from sleep, started again, making me look over at what he was reading. He had a notebook open, his handwriting staining the white sheets of paper.

This was something he used to do with me, back when he'd return home to me. We'd talk, cry, fight and then we'd cuddle, and in the middle of the night, he'd read his poetry to me. It was the only poetry I could ever listen to and be at total peace. I knew he grew up reading various poems, some were long and beautiful, others short and powerful like the point of a sword. Sasha had him reading anything and everything, but when he was ten, he had started writing them himself. As he grew, they seemed to grow talons and feathers.

Each word could pierce and make me feel like I was flying, all at once. As his mouth moved, I lowered my lashes, so he didn't stop reading.

"Once upon a time the sun was the brightest it had ever been. It looked down through the sky, and on the land below, searching for something of its equal. The ocean had depths and darkness to it that even the sun's rays could not reach. The desert sands loved to bask in the sun's glow, greedy and boastful of its heat. The trees would die from too much exposure. Everywhere the sun tried, she was either too much or not enough. She began to cry, sending solar storms to the land below and disrupting all the peace she'd previously found. The ocean roiled, the trees burned, and the deserts turned to glass. Nothing could soothe the sun, not until from under the surface of the vast land rose a great darkness. A vast shadow that was not deterred by the raging or the turmoil, and bravely asked the sun what was wrong. The sun stopped crying, its tears of fire holding off long enough that the land below eventually healed itself, for as curious as the shadow was, it did not anticipate the feeling of utter completion when it finally rose and found the sun. For the darkness had craved the light and warmth, and likewise, the sun had finally found a place that could absorb her shine. So the darkness fell in love with the sun, and for as long as the two held each other, sharing the sky, the land was prosperous."

I listened, feeling my chest begin to expand with a new sensation of pride and love. He was so talented, and I had no clue if he was even remotely aware.

"But someone else was watching too. The first man to ever walk the earth."

Silas turned a page while playing with a rogue curl of mine.

"He emerged from the distress the sun's tears put on the land. He came up through the crevices of darkness; pieces of glass and the deepest, inky blue of the ocean made up his heart. Verdant trees became his home, the vast galaxy of stars, his canopy and his great love was the sun. He watched as the darkness lived in the sky, surrounding their great land together in harmony. In complete surrender to one another. The man became jealous."

The story stretched long enough to span an entire book. Man finds a way to capture the darkness and subdue it long enough to steal the sun right from the sky and lock her in a cage. All in the name of love. The darkness wakes hundreds of years later and realizes his love is still in chains, so he slays every star from the sky and blankets all of space in complete blackness. So dark, nothing on land below survives, and when the man realizes he too will not survive, he finally releases the sun.

I realized Silas stopped reading, so I brushed my hand over his abdomen.

"Don't stop."

He turned his head, lowering the notebook.

"I didn't mean to wake you."

My hand drifted lower. "You never do. I love it though, getting to wake up to some epic love story."

Dark brows furrowed as my husband frowned and stared off at the wall. "It's our story, Caelum...but I'm not...I shouldn't have dug into it this soon to everything..."

"Then live out a different part of it." My hand slid under the band of his boxers and passed over his soft length, jutting to the side of his leg, stretching the fabric. He was ridiculous if he was stretching the material while soft. He'd probably burst through it hulk style if he got hard while it tried to contain him.

"Why are you giggling?" he asked with a slight smirk.

My hand squeezed around him, making him hiss.

"Because you're massive."

His hand wound through my hair as my lips found his ribs and I moved closer to his waist.

"You think I'm big? Better show me what you're talking about."

I licked along his muscles and six pack, pushing the covers down as I released him from the confines of his underwear.

"Definitely too big," he mused. "I bet you can't even fit it inside your mouth."

I scoffed. "You know that I can."

"Better prove it then."

Rising up on my elbows, I spit on the head of his erection and began rubbing my hand up and down his veiny shaft. My eyes flicked up to take in my husband's expression, and let out a tiny moan as he lifted his hips. He was already weeping at the tip, and when I ran my tongue over it, his hands found their way into my hair, pulling tight.

Lowering my mouth, I slipped his length inside my mouth, letting the bulbous tip slide over my tongue. I continued moving down until it hit the back of my throat and I started to gag around the thickness filling my mouth.

"Oh fuck." Silas gasped.

I hollowed my cheeks and sucked before releasing him. Once he was out of my mouth, I licked down the side, while cupping his balls. Giving them a gentle squeeze, I wrapped my hand around the base of him, gently pulling him, so my tongue was out, and his cock was being bounced against it.

"I'm going to fuck your throat, Natty. Stop playing unless you're prepared to whisper all day tomorrow."

Arousal pulsed deep in my belly, making me rub my thighs together as I took him deeper this time, sucking and licking until I choked. When I let up again, spit clung to my chin and lips as I took him again and again, and he began rocking his hips, pushing his cock down my throat.

Silas moved, so he was on his knees, and I dropped so my palms were on the bed. My eyes locked on his as he gathered my hair in his hand and then let loose.

"Keep that jaw wide, beautiful, bout to fucking ruin your throat."

This was what I had missed. This feral, unhinged version of him that didn't look at me like a broken, lost piece of himself, but someone he desired and loved.

I opened wider for him, sticking my tongue out, while taking his cock and allowing him to bury himself into my warm mouth. He hit the back of my throat over and over, my hair hard within his grasp, and then he froze.

"Shit. Fuck. Motherfucking shit." He rocked ruthlessly into me as he lost himself and then warmth hit my throat as he found his release.

"Swallow what you do to me. Take every last fucking drop." His hand was on my jaw; the root of him remained visible because there was no way I could take in all of him. The tip of his cock remained lodged in my throat as he emptied himself and shuddered through his release.

He pulled himself free while trying to catch his breath.

I rose up on my knees, dragging my finger up from my navel to my breasts and circling my nipples.

My husband grabbed my jaw and pulled me into a scorching kiss.

His tongue slipped into my mouth, surely tasting the remnants of his pleasure.

"I forgot how addictive it was to fill your belly with my cum. I think you need a little more, Wife."

With one last lick along my throat, he lowered his grip to my hips and shifted me so my face was shoved into the blankets. His arm came around my hips, lifting me so my ass was up and his tongue was slowly prying my pussy open, tasting what he'd done to me.

"You taste like you need to come."

I moaned my response while reaching back to hold my ass cheeks wide for him to access my pussy easier.

I knew him well enough that he'd go for my asshole as well.

Sure enough, he groaned happily while lapping at the tight bundle of nerves there at the apex of my butt, then slowly licked along the seam of my crack until he was plunging into my cunt.

His arms were around my thighs, holding me so that I wouldn't fall forward while he fucked me with his mouth.

"Silas," I moaned, nearly crying from how good it felt to have his tongue slide along my clit, back and forth while pulling it into his mouth in a firm sucking motion. He was slow, methodical, and it was making me insane.

My hips rocked against his face, my pussy soaked, dripping down my thighs as he held me firm and continued to lap at my wetness, murmuring filthy things about how good it was. How I tasted perfect and how badly he wanted to fuck me.

Finally, he released his hold on me, which had me falling forward.

His mouth was gone, and he was hovering above me, over my back as the head of his cock slid against my soaked slit.

"Ready to fill you. You ready?" he rasped, pressing a kiss to my spine.

I needed friction, desperately.

"Yes."

He shoved forward, pushing his granite erection inside me with one push. I let out a cry of pleasure as he hit my G-spot in one go, then he retracted, pulling out to play with me.

"Silas!"

He thrust back inside me, and this time, he set a pace that allowed me to feel everything as he moved. My hips were pulled back, my arm was too, my hand pinned to my hip as he took me deeper.

Our mingling gasps and grunts filled the room right alongside the soundtrack of our slapping skin. He fucked me until I was coming so hard, he muttered there was a ring of cream around his cock. Still, he continued to fuck me. I was sweaty, but I felt so good it was difficult to comprehend ever stopping at all until he was spilling deep inside me once again with a deep, guttural groan.

We were both sweaty, breathing hard and collapsing to the bed, but as he pulled me into his arms again, I had a feeling this was going to be a long night that sleep wouldn't dare interrupt.

For the next week, I fell into a familiar rhythm where Silas and I would wake up together and eat breakfast. All the windows in the cottage were open, so the smell from the orchards flowed through our home, and it settled that tiny ball of nerves that liked to tighten up on occasion, that doubted this was real.

I baked every morning, but this particular morning, I found my black apron modified.

There across the chest, were the words, "Property of The Roman."

My gaze snapped up, seeing my husband standing in the doorway, smirking at me.

"Did you think that name would be retired, just because I am?"

"Sorta." I laughed, smoothing my hands over the stitched words, loving how it made me feel to wear it. With Silas no longer in a motorcycle club, I had no reason to wear my patch anymore. This was a nice memento he'd created for me that I secretly loved.

He shoved off the wall and made his way toward me.

"Do you remember what I said I'd do to you when I made it?"

Excitement fluttered in my chest, working its way down my body.

"You promised to fuck me in it."

His dark brow rose. "No you promised to fuck me in it."

My head was shaking as his hands gripped my hips, and he lifted.

"Yeah, the moment you put it on, you made a nonverbal commitment to lift that dress, and slide that pussy over my cock."

Heat pooled between my legs as Silas marked my neck with open-mouthed kisses, and while he moved me to the counter, and then we made our way to the floor, I couldn't stop smiling. A new way I'd fallen in love with my husband was seeing all the different ways he craved me while we existed together. Doing the very thing we always dreamed we'd do.

Hiking my dress up, I straddled his hips, seeing he had already pushed the band of his boxers down. His erection was gripped in his fist while he stroked up and down, waiting for me to slide down. This position was still a process to adjust to him, so I let out a tiny breath as I lined myself up. Letting the tip of him carefully press through my slick entrance, he shifted his hips up, so that I took more of him.

My mouth parted as he filled me, and then his ghost-like gaze was on the words covering my chest. He reached up, slipped the straps of my dress down, so that under the apron, the tops of my breasts pushed against the black material.

"Fuck me, Caelum," he rasped, gripping my hips.

I smiled down at him and rocked forward while pushing my hands to my hair, lifting the heavy weight off my shoulders while Silas set the rhythm of how we moved.

Sunlight poured in over the counters and soaked up the floorboards. Tiny dust motes danced in the air, as I rocked over my husband's cock. I took him, letting him lift me, and slam me down against him, all while I absorbed the moment of peace and the sense of joy that had finally found a place inside my soul.

There on the floor of the cottage I always dreamed of living in, I fucked my husband while wearing the remnants of his property patch. Relishing that from now on, the only person who had his loyalty was me, and the home he'd ever return to again would be ours.

THIRTY-TWO
SILAS
PRESENT DAY

Fable was buried in an unmarked grave.

Killian's mom was standing over the fresh soil we'd poured over the six foot deep hole. I watched as she stood there, crossing her arms tight over her chest. Her face twisted into a sneer as she spit on the grave.

He'd go on without being remembered, and years, even decades, would go by with no one to visit him or know who was there.

Alec's grave, however, had a white headstone, standing nearly three feet tall. I'd never tell Natty that I was the one to pay for it. Because as far as I was concerned, the asshole hurt her and there was no reason to honor him. But my wife was good, and she had forgiven him.

So, it was for her that I made sure he had a nice gravesite.

She'd even gone with me to explain to the Sons of Speed that it was Fable who had killed Alec. When I explained that I was his brother, it eased tension as well.

The entire club my brother was the president of was gathered around his grave as a preacher began going over scriptures about heaven and hell. Men had their heads bowed, and their cuts on. Several had patches made in memory of him. It touched some dead place in my chest with pride that so many people loved him.

It was a testament that he was a good man.

Caelum was wearing black, her hair down in curls of gold as she cried over my brother's grave. She muttered things while pressing flowers into the fresh dirt. I stood, watching as my wife silently loved my brother, desperately trying to accept that while he may have wanted to win her heart entirely, winning even a fraction was too much for me.

In the end, he won her affection, and that was quite the honor.

Once the preacher was finished, everyone began shifting, tossing roses and leaving bottles of whiskey on his gravestone. Then they slowly began to disperse.

Penelope was off to the side, waiting for Natty. She gave me a quick glance and a smile, then left the cemetery with her friend. They were headed to Penelope's house to eat and plan Red's funeral, which would be the next thing we had to endure.

I waited until every person had left and then I sank down to my ass in front of my brother's headstone, kicked up my leg and opened one of the bottles of whiskey.

"When we were younger, you would always tease me that I was soft on the inside. That I was made up of clouds. Do you remember that?" I took a sip, hating how I was suddenly feeling grief over a brother I had grown to hate.

"But whenever Fable would threaten to cut me open and check, you'd stick up for me. It's why I took your share of the beatings. You were my little brother, and while we had different women raise us, we had the same sick fuck who tortured us. Natty helped me keep those demons at bay, but you were the only person alive who truly understood them."

A rogue tear slid down my face.

"I never thanked you for Christmas…while I hate that you got to hold my wife all night. I appreciate you not fucking her or hurting her. I appreciate that you gave her a safe place to go…" More emotion rose, nearly choking me as I tried to continue. "You saved her…she was nearly taken from me, and you stepped in front of that bullet. I know you loved her, Alec. Deep down, you did, and I'm sorry that you had to live a life without knowing she loved you back. In her own way, she did."

Using my wrist to swipe at my face, I let out a laugh and poured the whiskey out on the grave.

"I hope you find a huntress in the afterlife to love just as much, and one that loves you the way you deserve. Watch over us from time to time, okay."

I got to my feet and tucked my hands into my pockets as I found my way back to my bike.

Under his name on the headstone, I had paid extra for his beloved tattoo of Artemis to be replicated on the stone. So, for all of time, his love for my wife would be remembered.

THIRTY-THREE
NATTY
PRESENT DAY

THE DAY WE BURIED RED AND BROOKS WAS A SOMBER EVENT.

Simon Stone had arrived with Sasha on his arm, wearing his cut, nice dark jeans and his motorcycle boots. He was the first to place his hand on the casket with a wobbly chin and a tear-stained face.

I gripped Red's black bandana in my hand and squeezed it as hard as I could while my husband gripped my other hand. Silas was a shield for me as grief stabbed at my chest, poking holes of vulnerability and instability.

Callie was quietly sobbing into Wes Ryan's chest, her belly larger than ever. She wore a black dress, while Wes wore his cut over a black t-shirt. It was going to be weird for me not to see Silas in one anymore.

But I was also excited about that part of our life starting.

He was a farmer now, who catered to lemon trees and picked cherries and apples.

Our little cottage surrounded by trees and vegetation with bunnies, foxes and deer that frequented our little piece of paradise had me feeling strangely like the moniker Alec had always given me.

Artemis.

I tipped my head back as a breeze covered the crowd, and I focused on the singular casket over the oversized grave. When planning their funeral, we knew there was no alternative option. The two loved one another in life, and in death, their bones would hold each another until this earth ceased to be any longer. Their shared casket sat wider than the average coffin, but Red would have wanted that. They were buried wearing their patches and colors. Red wore her property patch, showing she belonged to Brooks, and Brooks wore his, showing he was eternally loyal to the Stone Riders.

Their joint headstones boasted of love, life and loyalty and etched into the beautiful stone was the sigil for the Stone Riders club.

We walked closer, and through all the ceremony, I hadn't really listened, but now that I was closer, I heard the preacher reading something vaguely familiar. Something that had my head snapping up.

"Ombre light falls across the panes of my heart, whispering of all the darkness you draw upon. I have land to build my home upon but my soul has no roots. Apart from you, I'll be forever without a place to dwell."

My face swung over to Silas as memories came back of him reading that very poem to me the night we met, after I'd snuck into the cabinet with him and Sasha. We had to pass the time, so he found his mother's phone, and used her flashlight to see the book of poetry.

"You, my darling light are a whisper on the wind. Here to love me, and gone with my last breath. I vow to carry you with me into the depths of death, wherever it may take me. I will carry your heart with me and it will allow me to live once more."

Tears burned my eyes, a sob caught in my throat and I hiccupped.

These poems weren't all from the book. Some of them were from Silas…these were his poems.

"I see flowers and think of your heart. Soft, resilient and beautiful, and I pray that no wind will come through and uproot you from my life. Yet I know, even in separation in this life, or death itself will not keep me from chasing you. Because the wind may try to take you, but I am vaster than the sky. So I will chain the swells of storms, I will blind the sun and bind the ocean if it means I get to keep you. I will ruin this very earth if it means you'll be mine."

Silas had pieces of this poem tattooed on his chest.

More tears flowed as I smiled up at my husband. He brought my hand to his mouth and pressed a kiss there.

"I had a feeling Red might like these as much as you do."

He was everything I had ever hoped he'd be. Standing next to me, wearing black slacks and a nice button-down shirt. He looked like a civilian, not a motorcycle club president, or The Roman. I had to remember that before he was all of those things, he was mine.

"This is where it ends, Caelum," Silas whispered in my ear, and I knew he was referencing the path we'd walked that led to their grave. But I heard something else.

I set Red's bandana against the sea of crimson roses littering her casket and smiled.

"No, baby. This is where we begin."

THIRTY-FOUR
NATTY
THREE MONTHS LATER

"You made a baby-sized cut," Callie cried as I held up the little piece of leather. The front said Ford Ryan in white, and the back had a picture of the Stone Riders insignia on a much smaller scale.

Simon chuckled. "Aww that's perfect."

He was thin and frail, using a walker now to get around. The doctors said he didn't have much time left. Which was why he was here, in the hospital, waiting all thirty-six hours of Callie's labor to ensure he was able to meet his grandson.

Wes held little Ford in his arms, gently rocking him as he walked over to Simon.

Silas held my hand as we stood there in the room, offering our congrats to our friends, and dropping our gifts. The hospital had asked us to spread out how many people come at once, so Pen and Laura hadn't been able to come in with us.

Callie was still swiping at her face as she sipped on her ice water.

"That was so sweet, Nat. I can't thank you enough."

I waved her off, watching as Simon and Sasha smiled down at Ford. My husband cleared his throat as he watched.

We both were feeling sentimental about Sasha losing Simon. She'd endured such terrible relationships her whole life, only to find Simon at the end of his. Silas still wasn't speaking to her from their fallout after he found out what happened with me and Dirk.

I had told him that I held no ill will toward her, and she did what she needed to, but there was no budging him. Even now, he stared at his mother and then clenched his jaw, so that muscle jumped aggressively.

I pulled his hand, so he was lowering his head.

"You have to get past this, Silas. We're going to have kids one day and she's going to be their grandma."

Silas only stared at me, then glanced over at his mother.

Sasha was watching us with tears in her eyes.

"If we ever get pregnant, then I'll make it right. Until then, I have nothing to say to her."

I pinched him, but thankfully he didn't say it loud enough for anyone to hear.

"Ford, the fact that you're here is a miracle. I hope you know that," Simon said, holding his grandson closer.

Wes was sitting closer to Callie, stroking her hair as she began crying. I couldn't imagine what she must be feeling, knowing her dad was on borrowed time.

We all just listened to him speak, painfully aware these may be his last words.

"I nearly messed things up to the point where your mommy didn't come back. But thankfully, your dad, he was a smart one, and never moved on. Not for seven years, can you believe that? He waited for her...and then when I faked my death, she was forced to come back. So really, it's me you'll have to thank for this beautiful life you have. And, Ford, it is beautiful. You have so many people who love you, and you'll be the oldest out of all these kids that will be born. You'll be the leader, so be sure you lead with honor, grace and grit. Never be afraid to do the hard things. Never be afraid to be firm. And never be afraid to help someone in need." Simon's gaze slid up, clashing with mine.

The gravity of what this man did for me slammed into me all at once.

The way he sacrificed a trade full of weapons that would have made him money, only to ensure I had room and board, even a job that paid. He surely received the raw end of the deal, and yet he'd only ever made me feel welcome.

Suddenly I was feeling just as emotional as Callie was, considering this amazing man was at the end of his life, and it wasn't fair because we deserved more time with him.

"The Stone Riders may go to you someday, Ford. If they do, lead with your mother's heart and your father's determination and will...and always remember that you're surrounded by people who will be in your corner in a single heartbeat."

Simon leaned down and pressed a kiss to baby Ford's forehead and then handed him back to Sasha who did the same thing. I watched as my mother-in-law rocked the little guy and I knew that she was going to be an amazing grandma to Callie's son, and to mine. What Silas didn't know was, we had about seven months until he had to have that conversation with his mother. Because while we'd been living our favorite version of life in the cottage and while my husband wore coveralls, and worked the orchards, and tended to the chicken, and even the few goats we got, he was also consistently and vigorously fucking me.

Even after I told him I had to take a break in birth control due to an issue with a reaction I was having.

He just continued to fuck me without any consideration at all to the fact that I wasn't against having kids, so I welcomed him inside me, bareback any chance he got. But the idiot knocked me up.

I hadn't found a way to tell him yet, but after our little visit to see Ford, I knew it had to be soon. With the way Sasha stared at her son, I hoped for their sakes, that conversation would go well.

It had to.

This was where it would all begin...this big beautiful life I always dreamed of. We were going to have it, and that meant Silas would need to forgive his mother and be willing to start fresh.

It meant I had to be willing to as well.

A fresh start, a new beginning...a future we always hoped for.

EPILOGUE

Killian

THERE WAS A STRANGE PEACE THAT HAD SETTLED INTO MY LIFE, AFTER finding my mother.

I wasn't sure what to expect when Natty had said the name of the other woman in the club with her, that had been trapped there. To be honest, my mind hadn't really processed that she was real. That there was a universe in which my mother was actually alive, and within arms reach.

Laura's hand still found a way over my chest some mornings, where she'd stroke over the daisy inked there. The one I'd gotten after after my mother left me, and I was old enough to mark myself with a memory of her. Those mornings, she seemed to understand that I needed to lay in silence while I stared at the ceiling. I'd hold her hand there, over my heart and we'd just breathe.

Emotion would clog my throat, and I'd find a way to thank whatever powers at be allowed my mother to find her way back into my life. Laura's easy smiles and friendly demeanor towards my mom was also something I marveled at. I knew deep down parts of her resented my mom for leaving, just like some pieces of me still did. Even if she'd explained why…it didn't change the outcome.

That I was left all alone, with no one but Simon, and the Stone Riders to raise me.

"Let's give it some time," Laura would remind me.

She would follow the same advice with her own mother, who she was still trying to patch up old wounds with.

"We need a bigger house."

Glancing up from my phone, I stared at Laura. She was in the middle of jotting down something in one of her lyric books. She kept them all over the house, in the truck, her new car, and even one in my saddle bag, on the bike.

"What?"

She looked up, meeting my gaze, still leaning over her book, elbows propped on the counter. "Well, your mom is in the guest room for the foreseeable future. My mom asks to visit all the time now. We need a bigger house."

I set my phone down and moved so I was behind her, pulling her hips into mine. I had the ring I planned to give her in my closet, buried in one of the closet drawers I kept ammo in, so she wouldn't find it.

"And what about us…would we need a bigger house for just our little family?"

Her hands came over mine, where they gathered at her waist. Without seeing her face, I knew she had a smile spread across it.

"Are you asking if you can knock me up?"

A laugh bubbled up my chest, "I'm asking if you picture that at all?"

We hadn't been together long, but I knew I wanted to marry her. I knew I wanted a life with her. There wouldn't ever be another for me.

"I like the name Royce."

I kissed her cheek and spun her around. "For a boy's name?"

Her hands came up around my neck right as my mother walked into the living room. Her dark hair wet, braided down her back.

Laura giggled, but didn't move. "For a girl's name actually."

Royce Quinn.

I pictured a little girl with blonde hair and blue eyes, one that liked to sing like her momma. One that had the heart of a wolf inside of her, just like her dad.

"I love that name," my mom said, smiling at us both.

Laura moved out of my arms and walked over to the table. "Thank you, Rachel."

I hated that my mom still looked nervous around us. Like she was imposing.

"When you need the extra room, I can find a different place to—"

Laura's hand shot out to my mom's arm, her eyes narrowed. "When we are ready to have children, there will be plenty of room for them, you and my mom. You are welcome here long past all the seasons we're about to endure, Rachel. You are his home, just as much as I am."

Laura was talking about me, and my heart flipped in my chest. Was it possible to love her more than I already did?

My mom flicked a hesitant gaze my way, and I knew she wouldn't believe what Laura said unless I told her.

"Mom, want to go get some lunch with me?"

Laura already knew I wanted to talk to my mom alone. She'd explained herself to me, and I listened without interrupting, trying to understand what she was telling me. I saw Silas, and knew he was a fucked up man and if his father was responsible for that mess, then I knew what she had done for me was a gift.

I had to slowly start building our relationship up. It had been almost twenty three years since she'd seen me, been around me, or involved in my life in any capacity. That was an entire lifetime. We couldn't simply just pretend our way into this thing, we had to build it.

My mom smiled, moving toward her purse.

"Sure."

We walked outside, both of us wincing at the bright sun. It felt like a new era for the Stone Riders. The immediate threats were put to rest, but there were still lingering ones that I could feel brewing. Concerns that I didn't want to think about until I had no other choice to.

"I like her, Killian. Not that my opinion holds any weight at all but I couldn't have pictured a better person for you. Laura is your match."

That burning sensation in my chest that I got when I considered that very thing about Laura, flared to life. Red had said almost those exact words to me. Grief tangled with the pride I had over being with Laura. Over her choosing me and wanting this life.

"I'm going to ask her to marry me."

Gravel crunched as we walked, until we stopped at my truck. I was about to open the door for my mom when I saw a tear fall down her face.

"I used to wonder if I'd miss all this…these moments of yours. When you'd find the one, fall in love and start having children. I would be stuck in one of Fable's houses, doing some mundane chore, and I would imagine what you'd smile like. How you'd laugh, or blush. I'd think of what you must look like standing at the altar, waiting for her." More tears fell from her lashes.

"For whatever reason, you've found me worthy enough to be here, and witness this. I just want you to know I'm grateful. I'm so honored to be here, with you son. To get a chance to maybe meet my grandchildren, if you and Laura are so blessed with that. To get to see you happy like this, it's been the greatest joy of my life."

My heart split open, my mind going back to that day when I was nine years old. The very last time I saw her. The grief I carried over losing her, and I pulled her into my chest, hugging her as tightly as I could.

"I love you. I used to look at the stars and I'd pray you'd somehow come back to me." My throat began to grow tight as my own tears began flowing.

She hiccupped into my chest, until we had both stood there for a long while, just crying and existing. Once we pulled away, she swiped at her face.

"Fable once talked about how his son had gotten lost, and fallen in love with a star. I thought he was drunk, but it's odd that she was the reason I was able to come back to you. It's as if the stars listened to you, Killian and delivered me home."

I gave her one last hug before helping her into the truck, and then glanced up at the sky.

Whatever the reason was, I wouldn't take it for granted.

Bloggers Against Bikers:
Motorcycle Mayhem Hits Rose Ridge Once Again

Article by ENdVi0lence56:

It should be no surprise to any of you that I'm writing yet another piece regarding the biker gangs of Virginia. It seems our letters to the senate, and even the president have gone ignored. We've even gone as far as taking things into our own hands to rid our cities of this plague of bikers, and yet they continue to thrive.

Here is yet another reason we need to come together and ban their clubs from gathering.

As you can see in the photo pictured below, the small town of Rose Ridge was flooded this weekend with hundreds, if not thousands of bikers. The streets were packed with the headache-inducing sounds of their loud exhausts, and when so many of them are together, it caused windows to rattle, and small children to stay indoors.

Many people reported an inability to access roads. Routes to the grocery store, gas stations and even the hospital were blocked because of how many bikers were traveling together. While we're somewhat used to seeing the local Stone Riders traveling in groups from time to time, this instance was concerning because various clubs from around Virginia were seen.

Mayhem Riot from New York *was seen with at least a few hundred riders.* ***The Death Raiders***, *being led by someone new, from what we'd last gathered. We will have to look into that in our next article because it seems several of these clubs are under new governance.* ***Sons of Speed*** *was also seen in attendance, a new president leading their group as they entered city limits. Lastly,* ***The Chaos Kings*** *from Richland were seen with well over four hundred members traveling through town. Their arrival created a traffic jam that lasted nearly an hour for locals.*

We try to avoid these bikers at all costs because as you know, they each wear what's called a one percenter patch, meaning they live outside the law of our land, and use their own governing rules to live by. It creates violence, and other disorder that isn't needed or respected in small towns like ours. However, for the sake of the story, we did grab one person for a direct quote on why the mass gathering.

*According to a **Harris Kline, of the Stone Riders**, he said, "when a great man dies, it creates a ripple so strong in the community, that there's only one choice but to show up and pay tribute. Especially when he dies twice."*

We aren't sure who exactly has passed away, or what he's referring to that would give us any indication as to how long these bikers will be in town, but I urge everyone to be on high alert.

- *We can end this biker era together if we stay strong and continue to fight.*

Callie

This felt like deja vu but in the most sickening way possible.

I was standing in the same cemetery, nearly the same clothes, and staring at almost the same exact scene. Except this time, I was front and center, not on the fringes of the crowd.

My father passed away exactly two months and one day after my son came into this world. We had the most beautiful eight weeks together, where I got to watch him hold my son, sing over him, and smile down at his little cherub face. He'd hold him in his arms while he sat on his bike, even if it wasn't turned on, he'd sit there and talk to him about riding.

He talked about how to lead.

How to protect and how to love.

Wes gave my hand a gentle squeeze as the preacher started a new prayer for everyone to join in on. This time, the preacher wasn't a dig at my dad, whereas during his last funeral I'd done it just because I wanted to. This time, it was at Sasha's request because my father had found God during his last few months on earth.

I was happy for him.

So, the preacher said prayers, and certain words that didn't register much for me, but it felt like peace. My mind threw back the image of the last time I'd been here, burying my father, when I'd seen Wes standing at the grave...how my heart had felt like it had turned inside out at the mere sight of him.

A smile snuck along my mouth as people from the club began pouring dirt, leaving roses and whiskey on my father's casket.

I went back to the last time I watched a member do this.

My father had faked his death to bring me home, and in turn, I'd found a way back into the arms of Wes Ryan, and managed to claim a few extra months with my father before death took him from me for good. What my father did for me...for us, it went beyond just being a good dad. He gave me a second chance at life with the only boy I ever loved, and he did that by risking everything.

No one was even supposed to know he was still alive, after he'd acted all this out...but then when he'd heard about the attack from the Chaos Kings all those months ago, he'd shown up. I learned later that he'd done that because Silas told him I was inside.

He was the best dad in the whole world, and now he was gone.

Wes held my hand as we moved forward in line. Sasha was holding Ford, as tears slipped down her face. She'd asked as a favor if she could hold my son because she said Ford had become my father's favorite thing about living, and she wanted to hold him as close to her heart while she allowed it to break.

Laura, Killian and Rachel were behind us. I hadn't really looked up from my spot in front of the casket to see who else had attended, but as I stepped to the side, my gaze widened, and my feet faltered.

Wes caught me, helping to steady me. "River." His whisper slid in through my heart, just like it always did. He knew why I'd nearly tripped, and why tears flooded my eyes. He knew that my heart would be pounding against my chest, as if it needed an exit point from my body.

"They all..." my sentence stopped, as emotion clogged my throat.

Wes pressed a kiss to my ear, then stroked my rib. "Yes, River. All of them. They all came to pay tribute to your dad."

The entire cemetery was surrounded by black leather and denim.

Giles walked through a group of bikers, with Brick next to him, both of them wearing their cuts and shades. I saw a few other members doing the same. Two members from Sons of Speed, and the new president of The Death Raiders. Mayhem Riot was in route as well, all the leaders moving toward my father's casket. The multitude of members that rode with them surrounded the service, shoulder to shoulder, rival clubs all standing in unison as they paid tribute to my father.

Silas stepped out of the line, which trailed behind Killian to embrace the new leader of The Death Raiders. I remember seeing him before, his patch read: Lance. He hugged Silas like the two were brothers, but Silas no longer wore the colors from their club. Lance's gaze clashed with Killian's and tension seemed to fill the sticky air.

"Ryan," Lance finally broke his stare with Killian and tipped his head to my husband then smiled at me, "Callie."

I waved but Killian's glare had me hesitating.

"We're all here to pay tribute." Giles said, probably sensing the tension. He probably knew whatever bad blood was brewing between those two from how long he'd been with The Stone Riders.

A tall, thin man wearing the president patch for Sons of Speed stepped near our circle and gave me a soft nod. "And offer a truce...for a time, not forever."

The leader of Mayhem Riot, Archer Green stepped closer, and cast a glare at my husband. Archer was close to Killian's age, but probably older than his early thirties like my pseudo brother. His blond hair was longer, wild and mostly tied back with an elastic. He wore a crisp white shirt under his cut, and a long silver necklace with a cross hanging around his neck. Something passed between Wes and the president before Archer looked at me. "Sorry to hear about your dad, he was a good man. He spoke of you often."

I tipped my chin to catch Wesley's gaze, because I had no idea why my dad would have been talking to Archer Green, especially about me. Mayhem Riot was located in New York, which wasn't far from Virginia, but there wouldn't have been any reason for my dad to go there.

Wes pulled me back into his chest as Killian took over the conversation with the members and we got lost amongst everyone else there to grieve and remember my father. It wasn't until we were the only ones left at my dad's headstone, Ford tucked into my arm when Wes finally let out a sigh, and slipped out of his cut. He'd started doing that more when it was just us. He wanted to remind me that we were more than the club, and while I settled for him being a part of it, he was also amazing about being able to be separate from it.

"Your dad used to pay Archer to send some of his men to watch over you when you traveled to New York for tattoo expos."

What. I lifted my head, searching his expression.

"You watched over me through those years…are you saying my dad did too?"

Wes pulled my hand into his while our son remained cradled in my arms. "Your dad was never aware of my stalking tendencies, River. He missed you, watched out for you and even had his own ways of getting updates on you that never came through me."

My heart felt strangely full and broken all at once. Seven years I was away from my dad, and while I had my reasons, they all felt so insignificant now that he was gone.

"I never knew he kept tabs on me. I never knew you did either…I just assumed—"

Wes kissed the palm of my hand, giving me that easy smile that reminded me of the nine year old boy who used to tell me stories of Peter Pan and Wendy in his tree house.

"You assumed you could leave our world and we'd forget you? Remember what I told you when we were fifteen? You wanted to use a fishing metaphor because you assumed that one day I'd want a fancy, trad wife with a membership at a country club and to attend bible studies on the weekends or something."

His laugh made my smile stretch. I was so convinced at fifteen that he would never want to keep me because of the dysfunctional life I lived, the biker princess with no money and no hope to ever leave this place.

Wes continued, "You said you'd be just like one of the fish I hooked and released back into the sea. I told you that if you wanted to use a fishing metaphor then you'd be the river, not the fish. Same always went for your dad…he loved you, Callie. While this club was his world, you were at the center."

Resting my head against Wesley's shoulder, I stared at the lettering across my father's headstone and instead of a fresh wave of tears, I smiled feeling fresh hope fill my chest.

Simon Earl Stone
Beloved President of The Stone Riders
Eternity may have claimed me, but I forever lay my claim on you:
Callie ~Wes ~Ford
& my Chosen Old Lady, Sasha
When you feel the wind, look up. I'm there.

TWO YEARS LATER
SILAS

My wife really was incorrigible.

She had left me a note with the symbol of our grove on it, and while I knew what it meant, I had no idea what it actually meant.

Our grove was something we hadn't gone back to in years. So why would I randomly assume that's what she meant?

Still, after a hard day's work with the lemons, and the crop across the way with apples, I was tired. All I wanted to do was shower, eat something and then play with my son outside. Just like I did every night.

But every now and then our lives interconnected with those Natty deemed as necessary friends. We'd go to Penelope's house, or Laura's, and sometimes for big dinner parties, Callie's, but rarely did we go off book to some random location.

I assumed she had our son with her, which made me even more nervous. So, pushing away all my reservations, I got into the car and I traveled the half hour to the outskirts of Pyle and parked along the upper bank.

Walking through the trees, I heard laughter and splashing. Then as I cleared the grove and found my way to the pond, I saw her, sitting there on the dock.

Her golden hair was pulled to one side. She wore her one-piece bathing suit, which left her back bare, so I could see her tattoo. She'd gotten the sun being swallowed by darkness with a few lines of script from one of my poems.

She wanted me to publish them, and while I didn't mind it, I also didn't give a fuck.

It was just poetry, all of it inspired by our love story.

My boots hit the dock, and a memory of doing this when I was just fifteen surfaced, making my breath hitch. I'd loved her my entire life, and there was no sign of it getting lesser, or waning in any capacity.

Our two-year-old son was in her lap with goggles on and a pair of water wings.

"Caelum."

My wife turned her face, a smile already beaming on her beautiful face.

"Yay, just in time."

"Time for what?" I took Rook from her, loving how he giggled when he saw me.

"Daddy!"

He had a shock of black hair, eyes that matched mine and his mother's features.

"We're going to teach our son how to properly frog hunt. I hope you're ready, Silas, because a lot of this rests on you."

I let out a laugh as I smiled at the pond below us.

"What rests on me?"

"How quiet you can be."

This was ridiculous. "I'm so much better at this than you are, I don't need to—"

Natty placed her palm over my mouth as a loud croak emanated from below the dock.

"He's down there. You need to get in the pond and swim below the dock."

I shook my head as Rook pulled my lips up and laughed when he finally saw my teeth.

"I'm not swimming down there."

Natty's mouth dropped open. "You have to."

"Why me?"

I hated the pond water. Especially this time of year, there was way too much algae.

My wife scoffed, while crossing her arms, which pushed up her cleavage.

"You can—" She glanced at Rook and then covered his ears. "Fuck me in a cornfield, but not swim in this pond?"

She removed her hands, but Rook started reaching for her again.

"How else are we supposed to teach him how to properly hunt for frogs?"

"Maybe we can make a pond on a much smaller scale at home, like in a kiddie pool."

Natty looked away for a second, listening most likely to another bullfrog when suddenly Rook ran out of my arms, darting behind us.

We both turned, and I jumped up, but Rook was crouched down next to a little frog. His little hands reached down, pulling it up, and both Natty and I were so excited when all the sudden he tossed the frog as hard as he could into the pond.

"Rook Alec Silva," Natty yelled, coming over to scoop him up.

I tossed my head laughing and feeling a tightness in my chest at the reminder of my brother. Funny enough, tossing a frog into a lake was something he'd do.

I watched as my wife picked up our son, and she soothingly talked to him about being gentle with the frogs, and my heart felt like it shifted. I'd been removed from the darkness my life seemed to carry for so long, for two long years. I was a peaceful farmer now, with a wife and son at home.

Our evenings consisted of taking walks through the orchard. Reading poetry by the fire. Knitting squids that still resembled penises, and baking while listening to loud music. Our home was full of laughter, happiness and joy.

It was more joy than I could have ever imagined.

I thought back to what Natty had said to me when I asked what I could do to help get past the idea of her being hurt by Dirk all those years. Natty had told me to dig for my own sunshine and to let it come through. I took that seriously and have worked every day since on making sure my wife sees that brightness in me.

I felt like perhaps I had finally buried my demons, since there was no longer any reason for me to live in that fear that had outlined so much of my life.

"Okay, I give up. This was a terrible idea. I keep panicking about him jumping in and landing on a log that's underwater. I'll just teach him in Pen's pond where it's much less natural."

I picked up my son, who had two rocks he was clicking together, and started walking back through the grove.

"We have to get back anyway and prep for dinner with your mom. She's coming over before she leaves for Alaska."

My mother and I had come to an elusive understanding. Some part of me would never completely forgive her for keeping me from Natty for two years and for not telling me about Dirk, but she was still my mom, so I made sure she was welcomed in our lives.

She was an amazing grandma to Rook, and to Ford, Callie's little guy. After Simon passed, she remained planted in all our lives, as if he hadn't. We all saw the grief she processed and worked through, but Dempsey found his way back into her life, and Natty and I both couldn't be happier for her.

He informed her he was heading to Alaska on a road trip and offered her a spot on the back of his bike. She had plans to leave in a few days, and while I knew there were unspoken things between us, I was relieved that she'd found another good man to care for her. Another second chance at love within this lifetime. I knew Simon would be the great love of her life, but perhaps Dempsey would be someone that kept her company. He seemed to know her, and respect what lengths she had to go to in order to survive. She needed someone like that in her life as this next season of her story started.

"You were baking a shit ton of food, are we having more than just my mom?"

"Oh yeah...forgot about that."

"About what?" I shifted Rook in my arms, so I was a bit more comfortable.

Natty smiled up at me.

"I sort of invited the club."

"The entire club...as in the Stone Riders?"

She laughed and tugged on my hand.

"Sadly no, they wouldn't all fit in our little cottage, babe. I invited our friends."

I stared at her as if I had no idea what she was talking about.

She swatted my stomach. "Killian, Laura, Jamie, Pen...Wes and Callie...."

"Ohhhh right...yeah them." We still weren't friends.

Her eyes narrowed on me like she had read my thoughts.

"And be sure to wear your property patch, so everyone knows exactly who you belong to."

She never tired of cracking a joke about that. I sat Rook in his car seat and let my wife think she got away with it then once he was secure, I gripped Natty by the throat and pulled her closer to me.

"You'll pay for that comment tonight."

She let out a breathy moan.

"Promise?"

I chuckled and kissed her, hard.

"I fuckin' swear it."

If you haven't read the whole series you can binge all four books in Kindle Unlimited or audio.
Start with Wes & Callie's story here with book one.

Bonus content is available on my website
www.ashleymunozbooks.com >>Bonus Content

Finished this series and want to know what to read next?
If your mood is for more smutty smalltown: Start with Resisting the Grump (Unrequited Love Meets Grumpy Sunshine)
If your mood is for more twisty plot, suspense with feral, protective men: Start with Wild Card in the Rake Forge Series (mostly so you can get to King of Hearts where you meet Juan Hernandez)

ACKNOWLEDGMENTS

This one is going to hurt.

I know I only have myself to blame, but it doesn't change the fact that I'm sitting here, wondering how we're already at the end of this series.

I'm thinking back to how nervous I was to even try this sort of thing...a small-town series about active motorcycle clubs wearing the 1% patch.

While most of you know this series was prompted by a real-life encounter and situation from here where I live, I never in my life imagined this series would blow up the way it did. Sometimes, because I'm petty, I'll get inspired by events that make me angry and then I'll craft a story out of it and that's exactly what happened with this series.

Anyway...I just deleted an entire message to the woman who is responsible for this inspiration. Let's move on.

Every day I see posts of people finding this series and falling in love with it, and while I have no idea how Silas and Natty will be received, I'm so grateful to all my readers for sticking with me and for loving this series as much as I do.

Please understand how much you've changed my life with your love and messages regarding this series. I'm honored to have you read my work and to continue to recommend my books.

To everyone who helped me configure this series, put it together and push it forward, I will never be able to thank you enough:

Amanda Anderson, for branding and all the consulting you've done. I appreciate you more than I can ever say.

Tiffany Hernandez, when I think of my team, I see your face and I know you've got my back. I appreciate you and am so honored to have you here.

My husband, Jose, the patches, the journals, and all the package details that went into the PR boxes. No one works as hard as you. No one. Your drive and vision are a pillar in our home, and I'm so grateful to have you in my life.

Gel, thank you so much for all the graphics that you've always provided me with and for always making sure my branding is on point.

Becky Barney, Savanah Greenwell, Melissa Mcgovern, Rebecca Patrick, Echo Grayce, and Regina Wamba—thank you all so much for your support, your dedication and your patience as we get this series exactly where it needs to be. I can't thank you enough for all your commitment to me and to this series.

Amy, Kelley thank you for your continued support with beta reading for me.

To the Dreamscape team, and all the incredible narrators I've had the honor of working with. Thank you for bringing this series to life and for making it incredible.

Here's the first place in print that I'm manifesting a movie or television show. Imagine Sons of Anarchy meets Hart of Dixie. I. Would. Die.

I'm just here, dreaming.

Until our next adventure,

Ashley

ALSO BY ASHLEY MUÑOZ

Stone Riders

Where We Started

Where We Belong

Where We Promise

Where We Ended

Mount Macon Series

Resisting the Grump

Tempting the Neighbor

Saving the Single Dad

Standalone

Only Once

The Rest of Me

Tennessee Truths

Rake Forge University Series

Wild Card

King of Hearts

The Joker

Finding Home Series

Glimmer

Fade

Anthology & Co Writes

What Are the Chances

Vicious Vet

ABOUT THE AUTHOR

Ashley is an Amazon Top 50 bestselling romance author who is best known for her small-town, second-chance romances. She resides in the Pacific Northwest, where she lives with her four children and her husband. She loves coffee, reading fantasy, and writing about people who kiss and cuss.

Follow her at www.ashleymunozbooks.com

Milton Keynes UK
Ingram Content Group UK Ltd.
UKHW022215040824
446478UK00004B/328